HANS ANDERSEN'S
FAIRY TALES

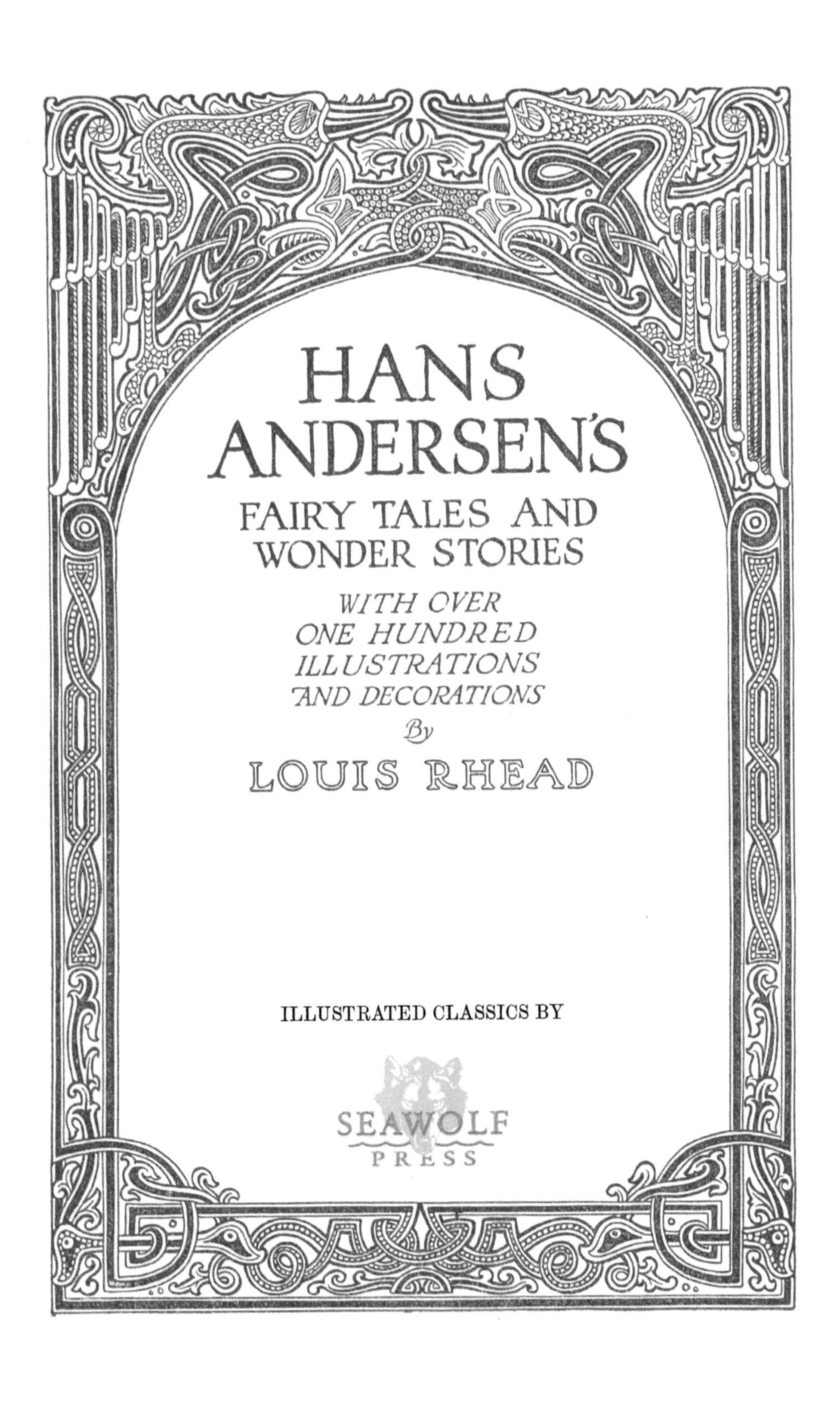

HANS ANDERSEN'S

FAIRY TALES AND WONDER STORIES

WITH OVER ONE HUNDRED ILLUSTRATIONS AND DECORATIONS

By

LOUIS RHEAD

ILLUSTRATED CLASSICS BY

SEAWOLF PRESS

PUBLISHED BY SEAWOLF PRESS

Printed in the U.S.A. on acid-free paper.

FIRST EDITION INFORMATION
The illustrations and cover are taken from the Harper Brothers 1914 edition. The tales are the tales covered in that edition.

SeaWolf Press
P.O. Box 961
Orinda, CA 94563
Email: support@seawolfpress.com
Web: http://www.SeaWolfPress.com

TABLE OF CONTENTS

Table of Contents

I

THE UGLY DUCKLING

IT was so glorious out in the country; it was summer; the cornfields were yellow, the oats were green, the hay had been put up in stacks in the green meadows, and the stork went about on his long red legs, and chattered Egyptian, for this was the language he had learned from his good mother. All around the fields and meadows were great forests, and in the midst of these forests lay deep lakes. Yes, it was right glorious out in the country. In the midst of the sunshine there lay an old farm, with deep canals about it, and from the wall down to the water grew great burdocks, so high that little children could stand upright under the loftiest of them. It was just as wild there as in the deepest wood, and here sat a Duck upon her nest; she had to hatch her ducklings; but she was almost tired out before the little ones came; and then she so seldom had visitors. The other ducks liked better to swim about in the canals than to run up to sit down under a burdock, and cackle with her.

At last one egg-shell after another burst open. "Piep! Piep!" it cried, and in all the eggs there were little creatures that stuck out their heads.

"Quack! quack!" they said; and they all came quacking out as fast as they could, looking all around them under the green leaves; and the mother let them look as much as they chose, for green is good for the eye.

"How wide the world is!" said all the young ones, for they certainly had much more room now than when they were in the eggs.

"D'ye think this is all the world?" said the mother. "That stretches far across the other side of the garden, quite into the parson's field; but I have never been there yet. I hope you are all together," and she stood up. "No, I have not all. The largest egg still lies there. How long is that to last? I am really tired of it." And she sat down again.

"Well, how goes it?" asked an old Duck who had come to pay her a visit.

"It lasts a long time with that one egg," said the Duck who sat there. "It will not burst. Now, only look at the others; are they not the prettiest little ducks one could possibly see? They are all like their father: the rogue, he never comes to see me."

"Let me see the egg which will not burst," said the old visitor. "You may be sure it is a turkey's egg. I was once cheated in that way, and had much anxiety and trouble with the young ones, for they are afraid of the water. Must I say it to you, I could not get them to venture in. I quacked and I clacked, but it was no use. Let me see the egg. Yes, that's a turkey's egg. Let it lie there, and teach the other children to swim."

"I think I will sit on it a little longer," said the Duck. "I've sat so long now that I can sit a few days more."

"Just as you please," said the old Duck; and she went away.

At last the great egg burst. "Piep! piep!" said the little one, and crept forth. It was very large and very ugly. The Duck looked at it.

"It's a very large duckling," said she; "none of the others look like that: can it really be a turkey chick? Well, we shall soon find out. It must go into the water, even if I have to thrust it in myself."

The next day, it was bright, beautiful weather; the sun shone on all the green trees. The Mother-Duck went down to the canal with all her family. Splash! she jumped into the water. "Quack! quack!" she said, and one duckling after another plunged in. The water closed over their heads, but they came up in an instant, and swam capitally; their legs went of themselves, and they were all in the water. The ugly gray Duckling swam with them.

"No, it's not a turkey," said she; "look how well it can use its legs, and how straight it holds itself. It is my own child! On the whole it's quite pretty, if one looks at it rightly. Quack! quack! come with me, and I'll lead you out into the great world, and present you in the duck-yard; but keep close to me, so that no one may tread on you, and take care of the cats!"

And so they came into the duck-yard. There was a terrible riot going on in there, for two families were quarreling about an eel's head, and the cat got it after all.

"See, that's how it goes in the world!" said the Mother-Duck; and she whetted her beak, for she too wanted the eel's head. "Only use your legs," she said. "See that you can bustle about, and bow your heads before the old Duck yonder. She's the grandest of all here; she's of Spanish blood—that's why she's so fat; and d'ye see? she has a red rag round her leg; that's something particularly fine, and the greatest distinction a duck can enjoy: it signifies that one does not want to lose her, and that she's to be known by the animals and by men too. Shake yourselves—don't turn in your toes; a well-brought-up duck turns its toes quite out, just like father and mother,—so! Now bend your necks and say 'Quack!'"

And they did so: but the other ducks round about looked at them, and said quite boldly,—

"Look there! now we're to have these hanging on, as if there were not enough of us already! And—fie!—how that Duckling yonder looks; we won't stand that!" And one duck flew up at it, and bit it in the neck.

"Let it alone," said the mother; "it does no harm to any one."

"Yes, but it's too large and peculiar," said the Duck who had bitten it; "and therefore it must be put down."

"Those are pretty children that the mother has there," said the old Duck with the rag round her leg. "They're all pretty but that one; that was rather unlucky. I wish she could bear it over again."

"That cannot be done, my lady," replied the Mother-Duck. "It is not pretty, but it has a really good disposition, and swims as well as any other; yes, I may even say it, swims better. I think it will grow up pretty, and become smaller in time; it has lain too long in the egg, and therefore is not properly shaped." And then she pinched it in the neck, and smoothed its feathers. "Moreover it is a drake," she said, "and therefore it is not of so much consequence. I think he will be very strong: he makes his way already."

"The other ducklings are graceful enough," said the old Duck. "Make yourself at home; and if you find an eel's head, you may bring it to me."

And now they were at home. But the poor Duckling which had crept last out of the egg, and looked so ugly, was bitten and pushed and jeered, as much by the ducks as by the chickens.

"It is too big!" they all said. And the turkey-cock, who had been born with the spurs, and therefore thought himself an emperor, blew himself up like a ship in full sail, and bore straight down upon it; then he gobbled and grew quite red in the face. The poor Duckling did not know where it should stand or walk; it was quite melancholy because it looked ugly, and was the butt of the whole duck-yard.

So it went on the first day; and afterwards it became worse and worse. The poor Duckling was hunted about by every one; even its brothers and sisters were quite angry with it, and said, "If the cat would only catch you, you ugly creature!" And the mother said, "If you were only far away!" And the ducks bit it, and the chickens beat it, and the girl who had to feed the poultry kicked at it with her foot.

Then it ran and flew over the fence, and the little birds in the bushes flew up in fear.

"That is because I am so ugly!" thought the Duckling; and it shut its eyes, but flew on further; and so it came out into the great

BLEW HIMSELF UP LIKE A SHIP IN FULL SAIL

moor, where the wild ducks lived. Here it lay the whole night long; and it was weary and downcast.

Towards morning the wild ducks flew up, and looked at their new companion.

"What sort of a one are you?" they asked; and the Duckling turned in every direction, and bowed as well as it could. "You are remarkably ugly!" said the Wild Ducks. "But that is nothing to us, so long as you do not marry into our family."

Poor thing! it certainly did not think of marrying, and only hoped to obtain leave to lie among the reeds and drink some of the swamp water.

Thus it lay two whole days; then came thither two wild geese, or, properly speaking, two wild ganders. It was not long since each had crept out of an egg, and that's why they were so saucy.

"Listen, comrade," said one of them. "You're so ugly that I like you. Will you go with us, and become a bird of passage? Near here, in another moor, there are a few sweet lovely wild geese, all unmarried, and all able to say 'Rap?' You've a chance of making your fortune, ugly as you are."

"Piff! Paff!" resounded through the air; and the two ganders fell down dead in the swamp, and the water became blood red. "Piff! Paff!" is sounded again, and the whole flock of wild geese rose up from the reeds. And then there was another report. A great hunt was going on. The sportsmen were lying in wait all round the moor, and some were even sitting up in the branches of the trees, which spread far over the reeds. The blue smoke rose up like clouds among the dark trees, and was wafted far away across the water; and the hunting dogs came—splash, splash!—into the swamp, and the rushes and the reeds bent down on every side. That was a fright for the poor Duckling! It turned its head, and put it under its wing; but at that moment a frightful great dog stood close by the Duckling. His tongue hung far out of his mouth, and his eyes gleamed horrible and ugly; he thrust out his nose close against the Duckling, showed his sharp teeth, and—splash, splash!—on he went, without seizing it.

"O, Heaven be thanked!" sighed the Duckling. "I am so ugly, that even the dog does not like to bite me!"

And so it lay quite quiet, while the shots rattled through the reeds and gun after gun was fired. At last, late in the day, all was still; but the poor Duckling did not dare to rise up; it waited several hours before it looked round, and then hastened away out of the moor as fast as it could. It ran on over field and meadow; there was such a storm raging that it was difficult to get from one place to another.

Towards evening the Duck came to a little miserable peasant's hut. This hut was so dilapidated that it did not itself know on which side it should fall; and that's why it remained standing. The storm whistled round the Duckling in such a way that the poor creature was obliged to sit down, to stand against it; and the wind blew worse and worse. Then the Duckling noticed that one of the hinges of the door had given way, and the door hung so slanting that the Duckling could slip through the crack into the room; and that is what it did.

Here lived a woman, with her Cat and her Hen. And the Cat, whom she called Sonnie, could arch his back and purr, he could even give out sparks; but for that one had to stroke his fur the wrong way. The Hen had quite little short legs, and therefore she was called Chickabiddy Shortshanks; she laid good eggs, and the woman loved her as her own child.

In the morning the strange Duckling was at once noticed, and the Cat began to purr and the Hen to cluck.

"What's this?" said the woman, and looked all round; but she could not see well, and therefore she thought the Duckling was a fat duck that had strayed. "This is a rare prize!" she said. "Now I shall have duck's eggs. I hope it is not a drake. We must try that."

And so the Duckling was admitted on trial for three weeks; but no eggs came. And the Cat was master of the house, and the Hen was the lady, and always said "We and the world!" for she thought they were half the world, and by far the better half. The Duckling thought one might have a different opinion, but the Hen would not allow it.

"Can you lay eggs?" she asked,

"No."

"Then will you hold your tongue!"

And the Cat said, "Can you curve your back, and purr, and give out sparks?"

"No."

"Then you will please have no opinion of your own when sensible folks are speaking."

And the Duckling sat in a corner and was melancholy; then the fresh air and the sunshine streamed in; and it was seized with such a strange longing to swim on the water, that it could not help telling the Hen of it.

"What are you thinking of?" cried the Hen. "You have nothing to do, that's why you have these fancies. Lay eggs, or purr, and they will pass over."

"But it is so charming to swim on the water!" said the Duckling, "so refreshing to let it close above one's head, and to dive down to the bottom."

"Yes, that must be a mighty pleasure, truly," quoth the Hen. "I fancy you must have gone crazy. Ask the Cat about it,—he's the cleverest animal I know,—ask him if he likes to swim on the water, or to dive down: I won't speak about myself. Ask our mistress, the old woman; no one in the world is cleverer than she. Do you think she has any desire to swim, and to let the water close above her head?"

"You don't understand me," said the Duckling.

"We don't understand you? Then pray who is to understand you? You surely don't pretend to be cleverer than the Cat and the woman—I won't say anything of myself. Don't be conceited, child, and thank your Maker for all the kindness you have received. Did you not get into a warm room, and have you not fallen into company from which you may learn something? But you are a chatterer, and it is not pleasant to associate with you. You may believe me, I speak for your good. I tell you disagreeable things, and by that one may always know one's true friends! Only take care that you learn to lay eggs, or to purr, and give out sparks!"

"I think I will go out into the wide world," said the Duckling.

"Yes, do go," replied the Hen.

And so the Duckling went away. It swam on the water, and dived, but it was slighted by every creature because of its ugliness.

Now came the autumn. The leaves in the forest turned yellow and brown; the wind caught them so that they danced about, and up in the air it was very cold. The clouds hung low, heavy with hail and snow-flakes, and on the fence stood the raven, crying, "Croak! croak!" for mere cold; yes, it was enough to make one feel cold to

IN THE MORNING THE STRANGE DUCKLING
WAS AT ONCE NOTICED

think of this. The poor little Duckling certainly had not a good time. One evening—the sun was just setting in his beauty—there came a whole flock of great, handsome birds out of the bushes; they were dazzlingly white, with long, flexible necks; they were swans. They uttered a very peculiar cry, spread forth their glorious great wings, and flew away from that cold region to warmer lands, to fair open lakes. They mounted so high, so high! and the ugly Duckling felt quite strangely as it watched them. It turned round and round in the water like a wheel, stretched out its neck towards them, and uttered such a strange, loud cry as frightened itself. O! it could not forget those beautiful, happy birds; and so soon as it could see them no longer, it dived down to the very bottom, and when it came up again, it was quite beside itself. It knew not the name of those birds, and knew not whither they were flying; but it loved them more than it had ever loved any one. It was not at all envious of them. How could it think of wishing to possess such loveliness as they had? It would have been glad if only the ducks would have endured its company—the poor, ugly creature!

And the winter grew cold, very cold! The Duckling was forced to swim about in the water, to prevent the surface from freezing entirely; but every night the hole in which it swam about became smaller and smaller. It froze so hard that the icy covering crackled again; and the Duckling was obliged to use its legs continually to prevent the hole from freezing up. At last it became exhausted, and lay quite still, and thus froze fast into the ice.

Early in the morning a peasant came by, and when he saw what had happened, he took his wooden shoe, broke the ice-crust to pieces, and carried the Duckling home to his wife. Then it came to itself again. The children wanted to play with it; but the Duckling thought they wanted to hurt it, and in its terror fluttered up into the milk-pan, so that the milk spurted down into the room. The woman clasped her hands, at which the Duckling flew down into the butter-tub, and then into the meal barrel and out again. How it looked then! The woman screamed, and struck at it with the fire-tongs; the children tumbled over one another in their efforts to catch the Duckling; and they laughed and they screamed!—well it was that the door stood open, and the poor creature was able to slip out between the shrubs into the newly-fallen snow—there it lay quite exhausted.

But it would be too melancholy if I were to tell all the misery and care which the Duckling had to endure in the hard winter. It lay out on the moor among the reeds, when the sun began to shine again and the larks to sing: it was a beautiful spring.

Then all at once the Duckling could flap its wings: they beat the air more strongly than before, and bore it strongly away; and before it well knew how all this happened, it found itself in a great garden, where the elder—trees smelt sweet, and bent their long green branches down to the canal that wound through the region. O, here it was so beautiful, such a gladness of spring! and from the thicket came three glorious white swans; they rustled their wings, and swam lightly on the water. The Duckling knew the splendid creatures, and felt oppressed by a peculiar sadness.

"I will fly away to them, to the royal birds; and they will beat me, because I, that am so ugly, dare to come near them. But it is all the same. Better be killed by them than to be pursued by ducks, and beaten by fowls, and pushed about by the girl who takes care of the poultry yard, and to suffer hunger in winter!" And it flew out into the water, and swam towards the beautiful swans: these looked at it, and came sailing down upon it with outspread wings. "Kill me!" said the poor creature, and bent its head down upon the water, expecting nothing but death. But what was this that it saw in the clear water? It beheld its own image; and, lo! it was no longer clumsy dark-gray bird, ugly and hateful to look at, but a—swan!

It matters nothing if one is born in a duck-yard, if one has only lain in a swan's egg.

It felt quite glad at all the need and misfortune it had suffered, now it realized its happiness in all the splendor that surrounded it. And the great swans swam round it, and stroked it with their beaks.

Into the garden came little children, who threw bread and corn into the water; and the youngest cried, "There is a new one!" and the other children shouted joyously, "Yes, a new one has arrived!" And they clapped their hands and danced about, and ran to their father and mother; and bread and cake were thrown into the water; and they all said, "The new one is the most beautiful of all! so young and handsome!" and the old swans bowed their heads before him.

Then he felt quite ashamed, and hid his head under his wings, for he did not know what to do; he was so happy, and yet not at all proud. He thought how he had been persecuted and despised; and now he heard them saying that he was the most beautiful of all birds. Even the elder-tree bent its branches straight down into the water before him, and the sun shone warm and mild. Then his wings rustled, he lifted his slender neck, and cried rejoicingly from the depths of his heart,—

"I never dreamed of so much happiness when I was the Ugly Duckling!"

II

THE SWINEHERD

There was once a poor Prince, who had a kingdom. His kingdom was very small, but still quite large enough to marry upon; and he wished to marry.

It was certainly rather cool of him to say to the Emperor's daughter, "Will you have me?" But so he did; for his name was renowned far and wide; and there were a hundred princesses who would have answered, "Yes!" and "Thank you kindly." We shall see what this princess said.

Listen!

It happened that where the Prince's father lay buried, there grew a rose tree—a most beautiful rose tree, which blossomed only once in every five years, and even then bore only one flower, but that was a rose! It smelt so sweet that all cares and sorrows were forgotten by him who inhaled its fragrance.

And furthermore, the Prince had a nightingale, who could sing in such a manner that it seemed as though all sweet melodies dwelt in her little throat. So the Princess was to have the rose, and the nightingale; and they were accordingly put into large silver caskets, and sent to her.

LOUIS RHEAD

The Emperor had them brought into a large hall, where the Princess was playing at "Visiting," with the ladies of the court; and when she saw the caskets with the presents, she clapped her hands for joy.

"Ah, if it were but a little pussy-cat!" said she; but the rose tree, with its beautiful rose came to view.

"Oh, how prettily it is made!" said all the court ladies.

"It is more than pretty," said the Emperor, "it is charming!"

But the Princess touched it, and was almost ready to cry.

"Fie, papa!" said she. "It is not made at all, it is natural!"

"Let us see what is in the other casket, before we get into a bad humor," said the Emperor. So the nightingale came forth and sang so delightfully that at first no one could say anything ill-humored of her.

"Superbe! Charmant!" exclaimed the ladies; for they all used to chatter French, each one worse than her neighbor.

"How much the bird reminds me of the musical box that belonged to our blessed Empress," said an old knight. "Oh yes! These are the same tones, the same execution."

"Yes! yes!" said the Emperor, and he wept like a child at the remembrance.

"I will still hope that it is not a real bird," said the Princess.

"Yes, it is a real bird," said those who had brought it. "Well then let the bird fly," said the Princess; and she positively refused to see the Prince.

However, he was not to be discouraged; he daubed his face over brown and black; pulled his cap over his ears, and knocked at the door.

"Good day to my lord, the Emperor!" said he. "Can I have employment at the palace?"

"Why, yes," said the Emperor. "I want some one to take care of the pigs, for we have a great many of them."

So the Prince was appointed "Imperial Swineherd." He had a dirty little room close by the pigsty; and there he sat the whole day, and worked. By the evening he had made a pretty little kitchen-pot. Little bells were hung all round it; and when the pot was boiling, these bells tinkled in the most charming manner, and played the old melody,

"Ah! thou dearest Augustine!
All is gone, gone, gone!"

But what was still more curious, whoever held his finger in the smoke of the kitchen-pot, immediately smelt all the dishes that were cooking on every hearth in the city—this, you see, was something quite different from the rose.

Now the Princess happened to walk that way; and when she heard the tune, she stood quite still, and seemed pleased; for she could play "Lieber Augustine"; it was the only piece she knew; and she played it with one finger.

"Why there is my piece," said the Princess. "That swineherd must certainly have been well educated! Go in and ask him the price of the instrument."

So one of the court-ladies must run in; however, she drew on wooden slippers first.

"What will you take for the kitchen-pot?" said the lady.

"I will have ten kisses from the Princess," said the swineherd.

"Yes, indeed!" said the lady.

"I cannot sell it for less," rejoined the swineherd.

"He is an impudent fellow!" said the Princess, and she walked on; but when she had gone a little way, the bells tinkled so prettilyL

Ah! thou dearest Augustine!
All is gone, gone, gone!

"Stay," said the Princess. "Ask him if he will have ten kisses from the ladies of my court."

"No, thank you!" said the swineherd. "Ten kisses from the Princess, or I keep the kitchen-pot myself."-

"That must not be, either!" said the Princess. "But do you all stand before me that no one may see us."

And the court-ladies placed themselves in front of her, and spread out their dresses—the swineherd got ten kisses, and the Princess—the kitchen-pot.

That was delightful! The pot was boiling the whole evening, and the whole of the following day. They knew perfectly well what was cooking at every fire throughout the city, from the chamberlain's to the cobbler's; the court-ladies danced and clapped their hands.

"We know who has soup, and who has pancakes for dinner to-day, who has cutlets, and who has eggs. How interesting!"

"Yes, but keep my secret, for I am an Emperor's daughter."

The swineherd—that is to say—the Prince, for no one knew that he was other than an ill-favored swineherd, let not a day pass without working at something; he at last constructed a rattle, which, when it was swung round, played all the waltzes and jig tunes, which have ever been heard since the creation of the world.

"Ah, that is superbe!" said the Princess when she passed by. "I have never heard prettier compositions! Go in and ask him the price of the instrument; but mind, he shall have no more kisses!"

"He will have a hundred kisses from the Princess!" said the lady who had been to ask.

"I think he is not in his right senses!" said the Princess, and walked on, but when she had gone a little way, she stopped again. "One must encourage art," said she, "I am the Emperor's daughter. Tell him he shall, as on yesterday, have ten kisses from me, and may take the rest from the ladies of the court."

"Oh—but we should not like that at all!" said they. "What are you muttering?" asked the Princess. "If I can kiss him, surely you can. Remember that you owe everything to me." So the ladies were obliged to go to him again.

"A hundred kisses from the Princess," said he, "or else let every-one keep his own!"

"Stand round!" said she; and all the ladies stood round her whilst the kissing was going on.

"What can be the reason for such a crowd close by the pigsty?" said the Emperor, who happened just then to step out on the balcony; he rubbed his eyes, and put on his spectacles. "They are the ladies of the court; I must go down and see what they are about!" So he pulled up his slippers at the heel, for he had trodden them down.

As soon as he had got into the court-yard, he moved very softly, and the ladies were so much engrossed with counting the kisses, that all might go on fairly, that they did not perceive the Emperor. He rose on his tiptoes.

"What is all this?" said he, when he saw what was going on, and he boxed the Princess's ears with his slipper, just as the swineherd was taking the eighty-sixth kiss.

"March out!" said the Emperor, for he was very angry; and both Princess and swineherd were thrust out of the city.

The Princess now stood and wept, the swineherd scolded, and the rain poured down.

"Alas! Unhappy creature that I am!" said the Princess. "If I had but married the handsome young Prince! Ah! how unfortunate I am!"

And the swineherd went behind a tree, washed the black and brown color from his face, threw off his dirty clothes, and stepped forth in his princely robes; he looked so noble that the Princess could not help bowing before him.

"I am come to despise thee," said he. "Thou would'st not have an honorable Prince! Thou could'st not prize the rose and the nightingale, but thou wast ready to kiss the swineherd for the sake of a trumpery plaything. Thou art rightly served."

He then went back to his own little kingdom, and shut the door of his palace in her face. Now she might well sing,

> "Ah! thou dearest Augustine!
> All is gone, gone, gone!"

III

THE SNOW QUEEN

FIRST STORY.

Which Treats of a Mirror and of the Splinters

Now then, let us begin. When we are at the end of the story, we shall know more than we know now: but to begin.

Once upon a time there was a wicked sprite, indeed he was the most mischievous of all sprites. One day he was in a very good humor, for he had made a mirror with the power of causing all that was good and beautiful when it was reflected therein, to look poor and mean; but that which was good-for-nothing and looked ugly was shown magnified and increased in ugliness. In this mirror the most beautiful landscapes looked like boiled spinach, and the best persons were turned into frights, or appeared to stand on their heads; their faces were so distorted that they were not to be recognised; and if anyone had a mole, you might be sure that it would be magnified and spread over both nose and mouth.

"That's glorious fun!" said the sprite. If a good thought passed through a man's mind, then a grin was seen in the mirror, and the sprite laughed heartily at his clever discovery. All the little sprites who went to his school—for he kept a sprite school—told each other that a miracle had happened; and that now only, as they thought, it would be possible to see how the world really looked. They ran about with the mirror; and at last there was not a land or a person who was not represented distorted in the mirror. So then they thought they would fly up to the sky, and have a joke there. The higher they flew with the mirror, the more terribly it grinned: they could hardly hold it fast. Higher and higher still they flew, nearer and nearer to the stars, when suddenly the mirror shook so terribly with grinning, that it flew out of their hands and fell to the earth, where it was dashed in a hundred million and more pieces. And now it worked much more evil than before; for some of these pieces were hardly so large as a grain of sand, and they flew about in the wide world, and when they got into people's eyes, there they stayed; and then people saw everything perverted, or only had an eye for that which was evil. This happened because the very smallest bit had the same power which the whole mirror had possessed. Some persons even got a splinter in their heart, and then it made one shudder, for their heart became like a lump of ice. Some of the broken pieces were so large that they were used for windowpanes, through which one could not see one's friends. Other pieces were put in spectacles; and that was a sad affair when people put on their glasses to see well and rightly. Then the wicked sprite laughed till he almost choked, for all this tickled his fancy. The fine splinters still flew about in the air: and now we shall hear what happened next.

SECOND STORY.

A Little Boy and a Little Girl

IN a large town, where there are so many houses, and so many people, that there is no roof left for everybody to have a little garden; and where, on this account, most persons are obliged to content themselves with flowers in pots; there lived two little children, who had a garden somewhat larger than a flower-pot. They were not brother and sister; but they cared for each other as much as if they were. Their parents lived exactly opposite. They inhabited two garrets; and where the roof of the one house joined that of the other, and the gutter ran along the extreme end of it, there was to each house a small window: one needed only to step over the gutter to get from one window to the other.

The children's parents had large wooden boxes there, in which vegetables for the kitchen were planted, and little rosetrees besides: there was a rose in each box, and they grew splendidly. They now thought of placing the boxes across the gutter, so that they nearly reached from one window to the other, and looked just like two walls of flowers. The tendrils of the peas hung down over the boxes; and the rose-trees shot up long branches, twined round the windows, and then bent towards each other: it was almost like a triumphant arch of foliage and flowers. The boxes were very high, and the children knew that they must not creep over them; so they often obtained permission to get out of the windows to each other, and to sit on their little stools among the roses, where they could play delightfully. In winter there was an end of this pleasure. The windows were often frozen over; but then they heated copper farthings on the stove, and laid the hot farthing on the windowpane, and then they had a capital peep-hole, quite nicely rounded; and out of each peeped a gentle friendly eye—it was the little boy and the little girl who were looking out. His name was Kay, hers was Gerda. In summer, with one jump, they could get to each other; but in winter they were obliged first to go down the long stairs, and then up the long stairs again: and out-of-doors there was quite a snow-storm.

"It is the white bees that are swarming," said Kay's old grandmother.

"Do the white bees choose a queen?" asked the little boy; for he knew that the honey-bees always have one.

"Yes," said the grandmother, "she flies where the swarm hangs in the thickest clusters. She is the largest of all; and she can never remain quietly on the earth, but goes up again into the black clouds.

Many a winter's night she flies through the streets of the town, and peeps in at the windows; and they then freeze in so wondrous a manner that they look like flowers."

"Yes, I have seen it," said both the children; and so they knew that it was true.

"Can the Snow Queen come in?" said the little girl.

"Only let her come in!" said the little boy. "Then I'd put her on the stove, and she'd melt."

And then his grandmother patted his head and told him other stories.

In the evening, when little Kay was at home, and half undressed, he climbed up on the chair by the window, and peeped out of the little hole. A few snow-flakes were falling, and one, the largest of all, remained lying on the edge of a flower-pot.

The flake of snow grew larger and larger; and at last it was like a young lady, dressed in the finest white gauze, made of a million little flakes like stars. She was so beautiful and delicate, but she was of ice, of dazzling, sparkling ice; yet she lived; her eyes gazed fixedly, like two stars; but there was neither quiet nor repose in them. She nodded towards the window, and beckoned with her hand. The little boy was frightened, and jumped down from the chair; it seemed to him as if, at the same moment, a large bird flew past the window.

The next day it was a sharp frost—and then the spring came; the sun shone, the green leaves appeared, the swallows built their nests, the windows were opened, and the little children again sat in their pretty garden, high up on the leads at the top of the house.

That summer the roses flowered in unwonted beauty. The little girl had learned a hymn, in which there was something about roses; and then she thought of her own flowers; and she sang the verse to the little boy, who then sang it with her:

> "The rose in the valley is blooming so sweet,
> And angels descend there the children to greet."

And the children held each other by the hand, kissed the roses, looked up at the clear sunshine, and spoke as though they really saw angels there. What lovely summer-days those were! How delightful to be out in the air, near the fresh rose-bushes, that seem as if they would never finish blossoming!

Kay and Gerda looked at the picture-book full of beasts and of birds; and it was then—the clock in the church-tower was just striking five—that Kay said, "Oh! I feel such a sharp pain in my heart; and now something has got into my eye!"

The little girl put her arms around his neck. He winked his eyes; now there was nothing to be seen.

"I think it is out now," said he; but it was not. It was just one of those pieces of glass from the magic mirror that had got into his eye; and poor Kay had got another piece right in his heart. It will soon become like ice. It did not hurt any longer, but there it was.

"What are you crying for?" asked he. "You look so ugly! There's nothing the matter with me. Ah," said he at once, "that rose is cankered! And look, this one is quite crooked! After all, these roses are very ugly! They are just like the box they are planted in!" And then he gave the box a good kick with his foot, and pulled both the roses up.

"What are you doing?" cried the little girl; and as he perceived her fright, he pulled up another rose, got in at the window, and hastened off from dear little Gerda.

Afterwards, when she brought her picture-book, he asked, "What horrid beasts have you there?" And if his grandmother told them stories, he always interrupted her; besides, if he could manage it, he would get behind her, put on her spectacles, and imitate her way of speaking; he copied all her ways, and then everybody laughed at him. He was soon able to imitate the gait and manner of everyone in the street. Everything that was peculiar and displeasing in them—that Kay knew how to imitate: and at such times all the people said, "The boy is certainly very clever!" But it was the glass he had got in his eye; the glass that was sticking in his heart, which made him tease even little Gerda, whose whole soul was devoted to him.

His games now were quite different to what they had formerly been, they were so very knowing. One winter's day, when the flakes of snow were flying about, he spread the skirts of his blue coat, and caught the snow as it fell.

"Look through this glass, Gerda," said he. And every flake seemed larger, and appeared like a magnificent flower, or beautiful star; it was splendid to look at!

"Look, how clever!" said Kay. "That's much more interesting than real flowers! They are as exact as possible; there is not a fault in them, if they did not melt!"

It was not long after this, that Kay came one day with large gloves on, and his little sledge at his back, and bawled right into Gerda's ears, "I have permission to go out into the square where the others are playing"; and off he was in a moment.

There, in the market-place, some of the boldest of the boys used to tie their sledges to the carts as they passed by, and so they were pulled along, and got a good ride. It was so capital! Just as they were in the very height of their amusement, a large sledge passed by: it was painted quite white, and there was someone in it wrapped up in a rough white mantle of fur, with a rough white fur cap on his head. The sledge drove round the square twice, and Kay tied on his sledge as quickly as he could, and off he drove with it. On they went quicker and quicker into the next street; and the person who drove turned round to Kay, and nodded to him in a friendly manner, just as if they knew each other. Every time he was going to untie his sledge, the person nodded to him, and then Kay sat quiet; and so on they went till they came outside the gates of the town. Then the snow began to fall so thickly that the little boy could not see an arm's length before him, but still on he went: when suddenly he let go the string he held in his hand in order to get loose from the sledge, but it was of no use; still the little vehicle rushed on with the quickness of the wind. He then cried as loud as he could, but no one heard him; the snow drifted and the sledge flew on, and sometimes it gave a jerk as though they were driving over hedges and ditches. He was quite frightened, and he tried to repeat the Lord's Prayer; but all he could do, he was only able to remember the multiplication table.

The snow-flakes grew larger and larger, till at last they looked just like great white fowls. Suddenly they flew on one side; the large sledge stopped, and the person who drove rose up. It was a lady; her cloak and cap were of snow. She was tall and of slender figure, and of a dazzling whiteness. It was the Snow Queen.

"We have travelled fast," said she; "but it is freezingly cold. Come under my bearskin." And she put him in the sledge beside her, wrapped the fur round him, and he felt as though he were sinking in a snow-wreath.

"COME UNDER MY BEARSKIN," SAID THE SNOW-QUEEN

"Are you still cold?" asked she; and then she kissed his forehead. Ah! it was colder than ice; it penetrated to his very heart, which was already almost a frozen lump; it seemed to him as if he were about to die—but a moment more and it was quite congenial to him, and he did not remark the cold that was around him.

"My sledge! Do not forget my sledge!" It was the first thing he thought of. It was there tied to one of the white chickens, who flew along with it on his back behind the large sledge. The Snow Queen kissed Kay once more, and then he forgot little Gerda, grandmother, and all whom he had left at his home.

"Now you will have no more kisses," said she, "or else I should kiss you to death!"

Kay looked at her. She was very beautiful; a more clever, or a more lovely countenance he could not fancy to himself; and she no longer appeared of ice as before, when she sat outside the window, and beckoned to him; in his eyes she was perfect, he did not fear her at all, and told her that he could calculate in his head and with fractions, even; that he knew the number of square miles there were in the different countries, and how many inhabitants they contained; and she smiled while he spoke. It then seemed to him as if what he knew was not enough, and he looked upwards in the large huge empty space above him, and on she flew with him; flew high over the black clouds, while the storm moaned and whistled as though it were singing some old tune. On they flew over woods and lakes, over seas, and many lands; and beneath them the chilling storm rushed fast, the wolves howled, the snow crackled; above them flew large screaming crows, but higher up appeared the moon, quite large and bright; and it was on it that Kay gazed during the long long winter's night; while by day he slept at the feet of the Snow Queen.

THIRD STORY.

Of the Flower-Garden At the Old Woman's Who Understood Witchcraft

But what became of little Gerda when Kay did not return? Where could he be? Nobody knew; nobody could give any intelligence. All the boys knew was, that they had seen him tie his sledge to another large and splendid one, which drove down the street and out of the town. Nobody knew where he was; many sad tears were shed, and little Gerda wept long and bitterly; at last she said he must be dead; that he had been drowned in the river which flowed close to the town. Oh! those were very long and dismal winter evenings!

At last spring came, with its warm sunshine.

"Kay is dead and gone!" said little Gerda.

"That I don't believe," said the Sunshine.

"Kay is dead and gone!" said she to the Swallows.

"That I don't believe," said they: and at last little Gerda did not think so any longer either.

"I'll put on my red shoes," said she, one morning; "Kay has never seen them, and then I'll go down to the river and ask there."

It was quite early; she kissed her old grandmother, who was still asleep, put on her red shoes, and went alone to the river.

"Is it true that you have taken my little playfellow? I will make you a present of my red shoes, if you will give him back to me."

And, as it seemed to her, the blue waves nodded in a strange manner; then she took off her red shoes, the most precious things she possessed, and threw them both into the river. But they fell close to the bank, and the little waves bore them immediately to land; it was as if the stream would not take what was dearest to her; for in reality it had not got little Kay; but Gerda thought that she had not thrown the shoes out far enough, so she clambered into a boat which lay among the rushes, went to the farthest end, and threw out the shoes. But the boat was not fastened, and the motion which she occasioned, made it drift from the shore. She observed this, and hastened to get back; but before she could do so, the boat was more than a yard from the land, and was gliding quickly onward.

Little Gerda was very frightened, and began to cry; but no one heard her except the sparrows, and they could not carry her to land; but they flew along the bank, and sang as if to comfort her, "Here we are! Here we are!" The boat drifted with the stream, little Gerda sat quite still without shoes, for they were swimming behind the boat, but she could not reach them, because the boat went much faster than they did.

The banks on both sides were beautiful; lovely flowers, venerable trees, and slopes with sheep and cows, but not a human being was to be seen.

"Perhaps the river will carry me to little Kay," said she; and then she grew less sad. She rose, and looked for many hours at the beautiful green banks. Presently she sailed by a large cherry-orchard, where was a little cottage with curious red and blue windows; it was thatched, and before it two wooden soldiers stood sentry, and presented arms when anyone went past.

Gerda called to them, for she thought they were alive; but they, of course, did not answer. She came close to them, for the stream drifted the boat quite near the land.

Gerda called still louder, and an old woman then came out of the cottage, leaning upon a crooked stick. She had a large broad-brimmed hat on, painted with the most splendid flowers.

"Poor little child!" said the old woman. "How did you get upon the large rapid river, to be driven about so in the wide world!" And then the old woman went into the water, caught hold of the boat with her crooked stick, drew it to the bank, and lifted little Gerda out.

And Gerda was so glad to be on dry land again; but she was rather afraid of the strange old woman.

"But come and tell me who you are, and how you came here," said she.

And Gerda told her all; and the old woman shook her head and said, "A-hem! a-hem!" and when Gerda had told her everything, and asked her if she had not seen little Kay, the woman answered that he had not passed there, but he no doubt would come; and she told her not to be cast down, but taste her cherries, and look at her flowers, which were finer than any in a picture-book, each of which could tell a whole story. She then took Gerda by the hand, led her into the little cottage, and locked the door.

The windows were very high up; the glass was red, blue, and green, and the sunlight shone through quite wondrously in all sorts of colors. On the table stood the most exquisite cherries, and Gerda ate as many as she chose, for she had permission to do so. While she was eating, the old woman combed her hair with a golden comb, and her hair curled and shone with a lovely golden color around that sweet little face, which was so round and so like a rose.

"I have often longed for such a dear little girl," said the old woman. "Now you shall see how well we agree together"; and while she combed little Gerda's hair, the child forgot her foster-brother Kay more and more, for the old woman understood magic; but she was no evil being, she only practised witchcraft a little for her own private amusement, and now she wanted very much to keep little Gerda. She therefore went out in the garden, stretched out her crooked stick towards the rose-bushes, which, beautifully as they were blowing, all sank into the earth and no one could tell where they had stood. The old woman feared that if Gerda should see the roses, she would then think of her own, would remember little Kay, and run away from her.

She now led Gerda into the flower-garden. Oh, what odour and what loveliness was there! Every flower that one could think of, and of every season, stood there in fullest bloom; no picture-book could be gayer or more beautiful. Gerda jumped for joy, and played till the sun set behind the tall cherry-tree; she then had a pretty bed, with a red silken coverlet filled with blue violets. She fell asleep, and had as pleasant dreams as ever a queen on her wedding-day.

The next morning she went to play with the flowers in the warm sunshine, and thus passed away a day. Gerda knew every flower; and, numerous as they were, it still seemed to Gerda that one was wanting, though she did not know which. One day while she was looking at the hat of the old woman painted with flowers, the most beautiful of them all seemed to her to be a rose. The old woman had forgotten to take it from her hat when she made the others vanish in the earth. But so it is when one's thoughts are not collected. "What!" said Gerda. "Are there no roses here?" and she ran about amongst the flowerbeds, and looked, and looked, but there was not one to be found. She then sat down and wept; but her hot tears fell just where a rose-bush had sunk; and when her warm tears watered the ground, the tree shot up suddenly as fresh and blooming as when it had been swallowed up. Gerda kissed the roses, thought of her own dear roses at home, and with them of little Kay.

"Oh, how long I have stayed!" said the little girl. "I intended to look for Kay! Don't you know where he is?" she asked of the roses. "Do you think he is dead and gone?"

"Dead he certainly is not," said the Roses. "We have been in the earth where all the dead are, but Kay was not there."

SHE CAUGHT HOLD OF THE BOAT WITH HER CROOKED STICK

"Many thanks!" said little Gerda; and she went to the other flowers, looked into their cups, and asked, "Don't you know where little Kay is?"

But every flower stood in the sunshine, and dreamed its own fairy tale or its own story: and they all told her very many things, but not one knew anything of Kay.

Well, what did the Tiger-Lily say?

"Hearest thou not the drum? Bum! Bum! Those are the only two tones. Always bum! Bum! Hark to the plaintive song of the old woman, to the call of the priests! The Hindoo woman in her long robe stands upon the funeral pile; the flames rise around her and her dead husband, but the Hindoo woman thinks on the living one in the surrounding circle; on him whose eyes burn hotter than the flames—on him, the fire of whose eyes pierces her heart more than the flames which soon will burn her body to ashes. Can the heart's flame die in the flame of the funeral pile?"

"I don't understand that at all," said little Gerda.

"That is my story," said the Lily.

What did the Convolvulus say?

"Projecting over a narrow mountain-path there hangs an old feudal castle. Thick evergreens grow on the dilapidated walls, and around the altar, where a lovely maiden is standing: she bends over the railing and looks out upon the rose. No fresher rose hangs on the branches than she; no appleblossom carried away by the wind is more buoyant! How her silken robe is rustling!

"'Is he not yet come?'"

"Is it Kay that you mean?" asked little Gerda.

"I am speaking about my story—about my dream," answered the Convolvulus.

What did the Snowdrops say?

"Between the trees a long board is hanging—it is a swing. Two little girls are sitting in it, and swing themselves backwards and forwards; their frocks are as white as snow, and long green silk ribands flutter from their bonnets. Their brother, who is older than they are, stands up in the swing; he twines his arms round the cords to hold himself fast, for in one hand he has a little cup, and in the other a clay-pipe. He is blowing soap-bubbles. The swing moves, and the bubbles float in charming changing colors: the last is still hanging to the end of the pipe, and rocks in the breeze. The swing moves. The little black dog, as light as a soap-bubble, jumps up on his hind legs to try to get into the swing. It moves, the dog falls down, barks, and is angry. They tease him; the bubble bursts! A swing, a bursting bubble—such is my song!"

"What you relate may be very pretty, but you tell it in so melancholy a manner, and do not mention Kay."

What do the Hyacinths say?

"There were once upon a time three sisters, quite transparent, and very beautiful. The robe of the one was red, that of the second blue, and that of the third white. They danced hand in hand beside the calm lake in the clear moonshine. They were not elfin maidens, but mortal children. A sweet fragrance was smelt, and the maidens vanished in the wood; the fragrance grew stronger—three coffins, and in them three lovely maidens, glided out of the forest and across the lake: the shining glow-worms flew around like little floating lights. Do the dancing maidens sleep, or are they dead? The odour of the flowers says they are corpses; the evening bell tolls for the dead!"

"You make me quite sad," said little Gerda. "I cannot help thinking of the dead maidens. Oh! is little Kay really dead? The Roses have been in the earth, and they say no."

"Ding, dong!" sounded the Hyacinth bells. "We do not toll for little Kay; we do not know him. That is our way of singing, the only one we have."

And Gerda went to the Ranunculuses, that looked forth from among the shining green leaves.

"You are a little bright sun!" said Gerda. "Tell me if you know where I can find my playfellow."

And the Ranunculus shone brightly, and looked again at Gerda. What song could the Ranunculus sing? It was one that said nothing about Kay either.

"In a small court the bright sun was shining in the first days of spring. The beams glided down the white walls of a neighbor's house, and close by the fresh yellow flowers were growing, shining like gold in the warm sun-rays. An old grandmother was sitting in the air; her grand-daughter, the poor and lovely servant just come for a short visit. She knows her grandmother. There was gold, pure virgin gold in that blessed kiss. There, that is my little story," said the Ranunculus.

"My poor old grandmother!" sighed Gerda. "Yes, she is longing for me, no doubt: she is sorrowing for me, as she did for little Kay. But I will soon come home, and then I will bring Kay with me. It is of no use asking the flowers; they only know their own old rhymes, and can tell me nothing." And she tucked up her frock, to enable her to run quicker; but the Narcissus gave her a knock on the leg, just as she was going to jump over it. So she stood still, looked at the long yellow flower, and asked, "You perhaps know something?" and she bent down to the Narcissus. And what did it say?

"I can see myself—I can see myself! Oh, how odorous I am! Up in the little garret there stands, half-dressed, a little Dancer. She stands now on one leg, now on both; she despises the whole world; yet she lives only in imagination. She pours water out of the teapot over a piece of stuff which she holds in her hand; it is the bodice; cleanliness is a fine thing. The white dress is hanging on the hook; it was washed in the teapot, and dried on the roof. She puts it on, ties a saffron-colored kerchief round her neck, and then the gown looks whiter. I can see myself—I can see myself!"

"That's nothing to me," said little Gerda. "That does not concern me." And then off she ran to the further end of the garden.

The gate was locked, but she shook the rusted bolt till it was loosened, and the gate opened; and little Gerda ran off barefooted into the wide world. She looked round her thrice, but no one followed her. At last she could run no longer; she sat down on a large stone, and when she looked about her, she saw that the summer had passed; it was late in the autumn, but that one could not remark in the beautiful garden, where there was always sunshine, and where there were flowers the whole year round.

"Dear me, how long I have staid!" said Gerda. "Autumn is come. I must not rest any longer." And she got up to go further.

Oh, how tender and wearied her little feet were! All around it looked so cold and raw: the long willow-leaves were quite yellow, and the fog dripped from them like water; one leaf fell after the other:

the sloes only stood full of fruit, which set one's teeth on edge. Oh, how dark and comfortless it was in the dreary world!

FOURTH STORY.

The Prince and Princess

GERDA was obliged to rest herself again, when, exactly opposite to her, a large Raven came hopping over the white snow. He had long been looking at Gerda and shaking his head; and now he said, "Caw! Caw!" Good day! Good day! He could not say it better; but he felt a sympathy for the little girl, and asked her where she was going all alone. The word "alone" Gerda understood quite well, and felt how much was expressed by it; so she told the Raven her whole history, and asked if he had not seen Kay.

The Raven nodded very gravely, and said, "It may be—it may be!"

"What, do you really think so?" cried the little girl; and she nearly squeezed the Raven to death, so much did she kiss him.

"Gently, gently," said the Raven. "I think I know; I think that it may be little Kay. But now he has forgotten you for the Princess."

"Does he live with a Princess?" asked Gerda.

"Yes—listen," said the Raven; "but it will be difficult for me to speak your language. If you understand the Raven language I can tell you better."

"No, I have not learnt it," said Gerda; "but my grandmother understands it, and she can speak gibberish too. I wish I had learnt it."

"No matter," said the Raven; "I will tell you as well as I can; however, it will be bad enough." And then he told all he knew.

"In the kingdom where we now are there lives a Princess, who is extraordinarily clever; for she has read all the newspapers in the whole world, and has forgotten them again—so clever is she. She was lately, it is said, sitting on her throne—which is not very amusing after all—when she began humming an old tune, and it was just, 'Oh, why should I not be married?' 'That song is not without its meaning,' said she, and so then she was determined to marry; but she would have a husband who knew how to give an answer when he was spoken to—not one who looked only as if he were a great personage, for that is so tiresome. She then had all the ladies of the court drummed together; and when they heard her intention, all were very pleased, and said, 'We are very glad to hear it; it is the very thing we were thinking of.' You may believe every word I say," said the Raven; "for I have a tame sweetheart that hops about in the palace quite free, and it was she who told me all this.

"The newspapers appeared forthwith with a border of hearts and the initials of the Princess; and therein you might read that every good-looking young man was at liberty to come to the palace and speak to the Princess; and he who spoke in such wise as showed he felt himself at home there, that one the Princess would choose for her husband.

"Yes, Yes," said the Raven, "you may believe it; it is as true as I am sitting here. People came in crowds; there was a crush and a hurry, but no one was successful either on the first or second day. They could all talk well enough when they were out in the street; but as soon as they came inside the palace gates, and saw the guard richly dressed in silver, and the lackeys in gold on the staircase, and the large illuminated saloons, then they were abashed; and when they stood before the throne on which the Princess was sitting, all they could do was to repeat the last word they had uttered, and to hear it again did not interest her very much. It was just as if the people within were under a charm, and had fallen into a trance till they came out again into the street; for then—oh, then—they could chatter enough. There was a whole row of them standing from the town-gates to the palace. I was there myself to look," said the Raven. "They grew hungry and thirsty; but from the palace they got nothing whatever, not even a glass of water. Some of the cleverest, it is true, had taken bread and butter with them: but none shared it with his neighbor, for each thought, 'Let him look hungry, and then the Princess won't have him.'"

"But Kay—little Kay," said Gerda, "when did he come? Was he among the number?"

"Patience, patience; we are just come to him. It was on the third day when a little personage without horse or equipage, came marching right boldly up to the palace; his eyes shone like yours, he had beautiful long hair, but his clothes were very shabby."

"That was Kay," cried Gerda, with a voice of delight. "Oh, now I've found him!" and she clapped her hands for joy.

"He had a little knapsack at his back," said the Raven.

"No, that was certainly his sledge," said Gerda; "for when he went away he took his sledge with him."

"That may be," said the Raven; "I did not examine him so minutely; but I know from my tame sweetheart, that when he came into the court-yard of the palace, and saw the body-guard in silver, the lackeys on the staircase, he was not the least abashed; he nodded, and said to them, 'It must be very tiresome to stand on the stairs; for my part, I shall go in.' The saloons were gleaming with lustres—privy councillors and excellencies were walking about barefooted, and wore gold keys; it was enough to make any one feel uncomfortable. His boots creaked, too, so loudly, but still he was not at all afraid."

"That's Kay for certain," said Gerda. "I know he had on new boots; I have heard them creaking in grandmama's room."

"Yes, they creaked," said the Raven. "And on he went boldly up to the Princess, who was sitting on a pearl as large as a spinning-wheel. All the ladies of the court, with their attendants and attendants' attendants, and all the cavaliers, with their gentlemen and gentlemen's gentlemen, stood round; and the nearer they stood to the door, the prouder they looked. It was hardly possible to look at the gentleman's gentleman, so very haughtily did he stand in the doorway."

"It must have been terrible," said little Gerda. "And did Kay get the Princess?"

"Were I not a Raven, I should have taken the Princess myself, although I am promised. It is said he spoke as well as I speak when I talk Raven language; this I learned from my tame sweetheart. He was bold and nicely behaved; he had not come to woo the Princess, but only to hear her wisdom. She pleased him, and he pleased her."

"Yes, yes; for certain that was Kay," said Gerda. "He was so clever; he could reckon fractions in his head. Oh, won't you take me to the palace?"

"That is very easily said," answered the Raven. "But how are we to manage it? I'll speak to my tame sweetheart about it: she must advise us; for so much I must tell you, such a little girl as you are will never get permission to enter."

"Oh, yes I shall," said Gerda; "when Kay hears that I am here, he will come out directly to fetch me."

"Wait for me here on these steps," said the Raven. He moved his head backwards and forwards and flew away.

The evening was closing in when the Raven returned. "Caw—caw!" said he. "She sends you her compliments; and here is a roll for you. She took it out of the kitchen, where there is bread enough. You are hungry, no doubt. It is not possible for you to enter the palace, for you are barefooted: the guards in silver, and the lackeys in gold, would not allow it; but do not cry, you shall come in still. My sweetheart knows a little back stair that leads to the bedchamber, and she knows where she can get the key of it."

And they went into the garden in the large avenue, where one leaf was falling after the other; and when the lights in the palace had all gradually disappeared, the Raven led little Gerda to the back door, which stood half open.

Oh, how Gerda's heart beat with anxiety and longing! It was just as if she had been about to do something wrong; and yet she only wanted to know if little Kay was there. Yes, he must be there. She called to mind his intelligent eyes, and his long hair, so vividly, she could quite see him as he used to laugh when they were sitting under the roses at home. "He will, no doubt, be glad to see you—to hear what a long way you have come for his sake; to know how unhappy all at home were when he did not come back."

Oh, what a fright and a joy it was!

They were now on the stairs. A single lamp was burning there; and on the floor stood the tame Raven, turning her head on every side and looking at Gerda, who bowed as her grandmother had taught her to do.

"My intended has told me so much good of you, my dear young lady," said the tame Raven. "Your tale is very affecting. If you will take the lamp, I will go before. We will go straight on, for we shall meet no one."

"I think there is somebody just behind us," said Gerda; and something rushed past: it was like shadowy figures on the wall; horses with flowing manes and thin legs, huntsmen, ladies and gentlemen on horseback.

"They are only dreams," said the Raven. "They come to fetch the thoughts of the high personages to the chase; 'tis well, for now you can observe them in bed all the better. But let me find, when you enjoy honor and distinction, that you possess a grateful heart."

"Tut! That's not worth talking about," said the Raven of the woods.

They now entered the first saloon, which was of rose-colored satin, with artificial flowers on the wall. Here the dreams were rushing past, but they hastened by so quickly that Gerda could not see the high personages. One hall was more magnificent than the other; one might indeed well be abashed; and at last they came into the bedchamber. The ceiling of the room resembled a large palm-tree with leaves of glass, of costly glass; and in the middle, from a thick golden stem, hung two beds, each of which resembled a lily. One was white, and in this lay the Princess; the other was red, and it was here that Gerda was to look for little Kay. She bent back one of the red leaves, and saw a brown neck. Oh! that was Kay! She called him quite loud by name, held the lamp towards him—the dreams rushed back again into the chamber—he awoke, turned his head, and—it was not little Kay!

The Prince was only like him about the neck; but he was young and handsome. And out of the white lily leaves the Princess peeped, too, and asked what was the matter. Then little Gerda cried, and told her her whole history, and all that the Ravens had done for her.

"Poor little thing!" said the Prince and the Princess. They praised the Ravens very much, and told them they were not at all angry with them, but they were not to do so again. However, they should have a reward. "Will you fly about here at liberty," asked the Princess; "or would you like to have a fixed appointment as court ravens, with all the broken bits from the kitchen?"

And both the Ravens nodded, and begged for a fixed appointment; for they thought of their old age, and said, "It is a good thing to have a provision for our old days."

And the Prince got up and let Gerda sleep in his bed, and more than this he could not do. She folded her little hands and thought,

"How good men and animals are!" and she then fell asleep and slept soundly. All the dreams flew in again, and they now looked like the angels; they drew a little sledge, in which little Kay sat and nodded his head; but the whole was only a dream, and therefore it all vanished as soon as she awoke.

The next day she was dressed from head to foot in silk and velvet. They offered to let her stay at the palace, and lead a happy life; but she begged to have a little carriage with a horse in front, and for a small pair of shoes; then, she said, she would again go forth in the wide world and look for Kay.

Shoes and a muff were given her; she was, too, dressed very nicely; and when she was about to set off, a new carriage stopped before the door. It was of pure gold, and the arms of the Prince and Princess shone like a star upon it; the coachman, the footmen, and the outriders, for outriders were there, too, all wore golden crowns. The Prince and the Princess assisted her into the carriage themselves, and wished her all success. The Raven of the woods, who was now married, accompanied her for the first three miles. He sat beside Gerda, for he could not bear riding backwards; the other Raven stood in the doorway, and flapped her wings; she could not accompany Gerda, because she suffered from headache since she had had a fixed appointment and ate so much. The carriage was lined inside with sugar-plums, and in the seats were fruits and gingerbread.

"Farewell! Farewell!" cried Prince and Princess; and Gerda wept, and the Raven wept. Thus passed the first miles; and then the Raven bade her farewell, and this was the most painful separation of all. He flew into a tree, and beat his black wings as long as he could see the carriage, that shone from afar like a sunbeam.

FIFTH STORY.

The Little Robber Maiden

They drove through the dark wood; but the carriage shone like a torch, and it dazzled the eyes of the robbers, so that they could not bear to look at it.

"'Tis gold! 'Tis gold!" they cried; and they rushed forward, seized the horses, knocked down the little postilion, the coachman, and the servants, and pulled little Gerda out of the carriage.

"How plump, how beautiful she is! She must have been fed on nut-kernels," said the old female robber, who had a long, scrubby beard, and bushy eyebrows that hung down over her eyes. "She is as good as a fatted lamb! How nice she will be!" And then she drew out a knife, the blade of which shone so that it was quite dreadful to behold.

"Oh!" cried the woman at the same moment. She had been bitten in the ear by her own little daughter, who hung at her back; and who was so wild and unmanageable, that it was quite amusing to see her. "You naughty child!" said the mother: and now she had not time to kill Gerda.

"She shall play with me," said the little robber child. "She shall give me her muff, and her pretty frock; she shall sleep in my bed!" And then she gave her mother another bite, so that she jumped, and ran round with the pain; and the Robbers laughed, and said, "Look, how she is dancing with the little one!"

"I will go into the carriage," said the little robber maiden; and she would have her will, for she was very spoiled and very headstrong. She and Gerda got in; and then away they drove over the stumps of felled trees, deeper and deeper into the woods. The little robber maiden was as tall as Gerda, but stronger, broader-shouldered, and of dark complexion; her eyes were quite black; they looked almost melancholy. She embraced little Gerda, and said, "They shall not kill you as long as I am not displeased with you. You are, doubtless, a Princess?"

"No," said little Gerda; who then related all that had happened to her, and how much she cared about little Kay.

The little robber maiden looked at her with a serious air, nodded her head slightly, and said, "They shall not kill you, even if I am angry with you: then I will do it myself"; and she dried Gerda's eyes, and put both her hands in the handsome muff, which was so soft and warm.

At length the carriage stopped. They were in the midst of the court-yard of a robber's castle. It was full of cracks from top to bottom; and out of the openings magpies and rooks were flying; and the great bull-dogs, each of which looked as if he could swallow a man, jumped up, but they did not bark, for that was forbidden.

In the midst of the large, old, smoking hall burnt a great fire on the stone floor. The smoke disappeared under the stones, and had to seek its own egress. In an immense caldron soup was boiling; and rabbits and hares were being roasted on a spit.

"You shall sleep with me to-night, with all my animals," said the little robber maiden. They had something to eat and drink; and then went into a corner, where straw and carpets were lying. Beside them, on laths and perches, sat nearly a hundred pigeons, all asleep, seemingly; but yet they moved a little when the robber maiden came. "They are all mine," said she, at the same time seizing one that was next to her by the legs and shaking it so that its wings fluttered. "Kiss it," cried the little girl, and flung the pigeon in Gerda's face. "Up there is the rabble of the wood," continued she, pointing to several laths which were fastened before a hole high up in the wall; "that's the rabble; they would all fly away immediately, if they were not well fastened in. And here is my dear old Bac"; and she laid hold of the horns of a reindeer, that had a bright copper ring round its neck, and was tethered to the spot. "We are obliged to lock this fellow in too, or he would make his escape. Every evening I tickle his neck with my sharp knife; he is so frightened at it!" and the little girl drew forth a long knife, from a crack in the wall, and let it glide over the Reindeer's neck. The poor animal kicked; the girl laughed, and pulled Gerda into bed with her.

"Do you intend to keep your knife while you sleep?" asked Gerda; looking at it rather fearfully.

"I always sleep with the knife," said the little robber maiden. "There is no knowing what may happen. But tell me now, once more, all about little Kay; and why you have started off in the wide world alone." And Gerda related all, from the very beginning: the Wood-pigeons cooed above in their cage, and the others slept. The little robber maiden wound her arm round Gerda's neck, held the knife in the other hand, and snored so loud that everybody could hear her; but Gerda could not close her eyes, for she did not know whether she was to live or die. The robbers sat round the fire, sang and drank; and the old female robber jumped about so, that it was quite dreadful for Gerda to see her.

Then the Wood-pigeons said, "Coo! Coo! We have seen little Kay! A white hen carries his sledge; he himself sat in the carriage of the

Snow Queen, who passed here, down just over the wood, as we lay in our nest. She blew upon us young ones; and all died except we two. Coo! Coo!"

"What is that you say up there?" cried little Gerda. "Where did the Snow Queen go to? Do you know anything about it?"

"She is no doubt gone to Lapland; for there is always snow and ice there. Only ask the Reindeer, who is tethered there."

"Ice and snow is there! There it is, glorious and beautiful!" said the Reindeer. "One can spring about in the large shining valleys! The Snow Queen has her summer-tent there; but her fixed abode is high up towards the North Pole, on the Island called Spitzbergen."

"Oh, Kay! Poor little Kay!" sighed Gerda.

"Do you choose to be quiet?" said the robber maiden. "If you don't, I shall make you."

In the morning Gerda told her all that the Wood-pigeons had said; and the little maiden looked very serious, but she nodded her head, and said, "That's no matter—that's no matter. Do you know where Lapland lies!" she asked of the Reindeer.

"Who should know better than I?" said the animal; and his eyes rolled in his head. "I was born and bred there—there I leapt about on the fields of snow."

"Listen," said the robber maiden to Gerda. "You see that the men are gone; but my mother is still here, and will remain. However, towards morning she takes a draught out of the large flask, and then she sleeps a little: then I will do something for you." She now jumped out of bed, flew to her mother; with her arms round her neck, and pulling her by the beard, said, "Good morrow, my own sweet nanny-goat of a mother." And her mother took hold of her nose, and pinched it till it was red and blue; but this was all done out of pure love.

When the mother had taken a sup at her flask, and was having a nap, the little robber maiden went to the Reindeer, and said, "I should very much like to give you still many a tickling with the sharp knife, for then you are so amusing; however, I will untether you, and help you out, so that you may go back to Lapland. But you must make good use of your legs; and take this little girl for me to the palace of the Snow Queen, where her playfellow is. You have heard, I suppose, all she said; for she spoke loud enough, and you were listening."

The Reindeer gave a bound for joy. The robber maiden lifted up little Gerda, and took the precaution to bind her fast on the Reindeer's back; she even gave her a small cushion to sit on. "Here are your worsted leggins, for it will be cold; but the muff I shall keep for myself, for it is so very pretty. But I do not wish you to be cold. Here is a pair of lined gloves of my mother's; they just reach up to your elbow. On with them! Now you look about the hands just like my ugly old mother!"

And Gerda wept for joy.

"I can't bear to see you fretting," said the little robber maiden. "This is just the time when you ought to look pleased. Here are two loaves and a ham for you, so that you won't starve." The bread and the meat were fastened to the Reindeer's back; the little maiden opened the door, called in all the dogs, and then with her knife cut the rope that fastened the animal, and said to him, "Now, off with you; but take good care of the little girl!"

And Gerda stretched out her hands with the large wadded gloves towards the robber maiden, and said, "Farewell!" and the Reindeer flew on over bush and bramble through the great wood, over moor and heath, as fast as he could go.

"Ddsa! Ddsa!" was heard in the sky. It was just as if somebody was sneezing.

"These are my old northern-lights," said the Reindeer, "look how they gleam!" And on he now sped still quicker—day and night on he went: the loaves were consumed, and the ham too; and now they were in Lapland.

SIXTH STORY.

The Lapland Woman and the Finland Woman

SUDDENLY they stopped before a little house, which looked very miserable. The roof reached to the ground; and the door was so low, that the family were obliged to creep upon their stomachs when they went in or out. Nobody was at home except an old Lapland woman, who was dressing fish by the light of an oil lamp. And the Reindeer told her the whole of Gerda's history, but first of all his own; for that seemed to him of much greater importance. Gerda was so chilled that she could not speak.

"Poor thing," said the Lapland woman, "you have far to run still. You have more than a hundred miles to go before you get to Finland; there the Snow Queen has her country-house, and burns blue lights every evening. I will give you a few words from me, which I will write on a dried haberdine, for paper I have none; this you can take with you to the Finland woman, and she will be able to give you more information than I can."

When Gerda had warmed herself, and had eaten and drunk, the Lapland woman wrote a few words on a dried haberdine, begged Gerda to take care of them, put her on the Reindeer, bound her fast, and away sprang the animal. "Ddsa! Ddsa!" was again heard in the air; the most charming blue lights burned the whole night in the sky, and at last they came to Finland. They knocked at the chimney of the Finland woman; for as to a door, she had none.

There was such a heat inside that the Finland woman herself went about almost naked. She was diminutive and dirty. She immediately loosened little Gerda's clothes, pulled off her thick gloves and boots; for otherwise the heat would have been too great—and after laying a piece of ice on the Reindeer's head, read what was written on the fish-skin. She read it three times: she then knew it by heart; so she put the fish into the cupboard—for it might very well be eaten, and she never threw anything away.

Then the Reindeer related his own story first, and afterwards that of little Gerda; and the Finland woman winked her eyes, but said nothing.

"You are so clever," said the Reindeer; "you can, I know, twist all the winds of the world together in a knot. If the seaman loosens one knot, then he has a good wind; if a second, then it blows pretty stiffly; if he undoes the third and fourth, then it rages so that the forests are upturned. Will you give the little maiden a potion, that she may possess the strength of twelve men, and vanquish the Snow Queen?"

"The strength of twelve men!" said the Finland woman. "Much good that would be!" Then she went to a cupboard, and drew out a large skin rolled up. When she had unrolled it, strange characters were to be seen written thereon; and the Finland woman read at such a rate that the perspiration trickled down her forehead.

GERDA SAID FARTEWELL TO THE ROBBER-MAIDEN

But the Reindeer begged so hard for little Gerda, and Gerda looked so imploringly with tearful eyes at the Finland woman, that she winked, and drew the Reindeer aside into a corner, where they whispered together, while the animal got some fresh ice put on his head.

"'Tis true little Kay is at the Snow Queen's, and finds everything there quite to his taste; and he thinks it the very best place in the world; but the reason of that is, he has a splinter of glass in his eye, and in his heart. These must be got out first; otherwise he will never go back to mankind, and the Snow Queen will retain her power over him."

"But can you give little Gerda nothing to take which will endue her with power over the whole?"

"I can give her no more power than what she has already. Don't you see how great it is? Don't you see how men and animals are forced to serve her; how well she gets through the world barefooted? She must not hear of her power from us; that power lies in her heart, because she is a sweet and innocent child! If she cannot get to the Snow Queen by herself, and rid little Kay of the glass, we cannot help her. Two miles hence the garden of the Snow Queen begins; thither you may carry the little girl. Set her down by the large bush with red berries, standing in the snow; don't stay talking, but hasten back as fast as possible." And now the Finland woman placed little Gerda on the Reindeer's back, and off he ran with all imaginable speed.

"Oh! I have not got my boots! I have not brought my gloves!" cried little Gerda. She remarked she was without them from the cutting frost; but the Reindeer dared not stand still; on he ran till he came to the great bush with the red berries, and there he set Gerda down, kissed her mouth, while large bright tears flowed from the animal's eyes, and then back he went as fast as possible. There stood poor Gerda now, without shoes or gloves, in the very middle of dreadful icy Finland.

She ran on as fast as she could. There then came a whole regiment of snow-flakes, but they did not fall from above, and they were quite bright and shining from the Aurora Borealis. The flakes ran along the ground, and the nearer they came the larger they grew.

Gerda well remembered how large and strange the snow-flakes appeared when she once saw them through a magnifying-glass; but now they were large and terrific in another manner—they were all alive. They were the outposts of the Snow Queen. They had the most wondrous shapes; some looked like large ugly porcupines; others like snakes knotted together, with their heads sticking out; and others, again, like small fat bears, with the hair standing on end: all were of dazzling whiteness—all were living snow-flakes.

Little Gerda repeated the Lord's Prayer. The cold was so intense that she could see her own breath, which came like smoke out of her mouth. It grew thicker and thicker, and took the form of little angels, that grew more and more when they touched the earth. All had helms on their heads, and lances and shields in their hands; they increased in numbers; and when Gerda had finished the Lord's Prayer, she was surrounded by a whole legion. They thrust at the horrid snow-flakes with their spears, so that they flew into a thousand pieces; and little Gerda walked on bravely and in security. The angels patted her hands and feet; and then she felt the cold less, and went on quickly towards the palace of the Snow Queen.

But now we shall see how Kay fared. He never thought of Gerda, and least of all that she was standing before the palace.

SEVENTH STORY.

What Took Place in the Palace of the Snow Queen, and What Happened Afterward.

The walls of the palace were of driving snow, and the windows and doors of cutting winds. There were more than a hundred halls there, according as the snow was driven by the winds. The largest was many miles in extent; all were lighted up by the powerful Aurora Borealis, and all were so large, so empty, so icy cold, and so resplendent! Mirth never reigned there; there was never even a little bear-ball, with the storm for music, while the polar bears went on their hind legs and showed off their steps. Never a little tea-party of white young lady foxes; vast, cold, and empty were the halls of the Snow Queen. The northern-lights shone with such precision that one could tell exactly when they were at their highest or lowest degree of brightness. In the middle of the empty, endless hall of snow, was a frozen lake; it was cracked in a thousand pieces, but each piece was so like the other, that it seemed the work of a cunning artificer. In the middle of this lake sat the Snow Queen when she was at home; and then she said she was sitting in the Mirror of Understanding, and that this was the only one and the best thing in the world.

Little Kay was quite blue, yes nearly black with cold; but he did not observe it, for she had kissed away all feeling of cold from his body, and his heart was a lump of ice. He was dragging along some pointed flat pieces of ice, which he laid together in all possible ways, for he wanted to make something with them; just as we have little flat pieces of wood to make geometrical figures with, called the Chinese Puzzle. Kay made all sorts of figures, the most complicated, for it was an ice-puzzle for the understanding. In his eyes the figures were extraordinarily beautiful, and of the utmost importance; for the bit of glass which was in his eye caused this. He found whole figures which represented a written word; but he never could manage to represent just the word he wanted—that word was "eternity"; and the Snow Queen had said, "If you can discover that figure, you shall be your own master, and I will make you a present of the whole world and a pair of new skates." But he could not find it out.

"I am going now to warm lands," said the Snow Queen. "I must have a look down into the black caldrons." It was the volcanoes Vesuvius and Etna that she meant. "I will just give them a coating of white, for that is as it ought to be; besides, it is good for the oranges and the grapes." And then away she flew, and Kay sat quite alone in the empty halls of ice that were miles long, and looked at the blocks of ice, and thought and thought till his skull was almost cracked. There he sat quite benumbed and motionless; one would have imagined he was frozen to death.

Suddenly little Gerda stepped through the great portal into the palace. The gate was formed of cutting winds; but Gerda repeated her evening prayer, and the winds were laid as though they slept; and the little maiden entered the vast, empty, cold halls. There she beheld Kay: she recognised him, flew to embrace him, and cried out, her arms firmly holding him the while, "Kay, sweet little Kay! Have I then found you at last?"

But he sat quite still, benumbed and cold. Then little Gerda shed burning tears; and they fell on his bosom, they penetrated to his heart, they thawed the lumps of ice, and consumed the splinters of the looking-glass; he looked at her, and she sang the hymn:

> "The rose in the valley is blooming so sweet,
> And angels descend there the children to greet."

Hereupon Kay burst into tears; he wept so much that the splinter rolled out of his eye, and he recognised her, and shouted, "Gerda, sweet little Gerda! Where have you been so long? And where have I been?" He looked round him. "How cold it is here!" said he. "How empty and cold!" And he held fast by Gerda, who laughed and wept for joy. It was so beautiful, that even the blocks of ice danced about for joy; and when they were tired and laid themselves down, they formed exactly the letters which the Snow Queen had told him to find out; so now he was his own master, and he would have the whole world and a pair of new skates into the bargain.

Gerda kissed his cheeks, and they grew quite blooming; she kissed his eyes, and they shone like her own; she kissed his hands and feet, and he was again well and merry. The Snow Queen might come back as soon as she liked; there stood his discharge written in resplendent masses of ice.

They took each other by the hand, and wandered forth out of the large hall; they talked of their old grandmother, and of the roses upon the roof; and wherever they went, the winds ceased raging, and the sun burst forth. And when they reached the bush with the red berries, they found the Reindeer waiting for them. He had brought another, a young one, with him, whose udder was filled with milk, which he gave to the little ones, and kissed their lips. They then carried Kay and Gerda—first to the Finland woman, where they warmed themselves in the warm room, and learned what they were to do on their journey home; and they went to the Lapland woman, who made some new clothes for them and repaired their sledges.

The Reindeer and the young hind leaped along beside them, and accompanied them to the boundary of the country. Here the first vegetation peeped forth; here Kay and Gerda took leave of the Lapland woman. "Farewell! Farewell!" they all said. And the first green buds appeared, the first little birds began to chirrup; and out of the wood came, riding on a magnificent horse, which Gerda knew (it was one of the leaders in the golden carriage), a young damsel with a bright-red cap on her head, and armed with pistols. It was the little robber maiden, who, tired of being at home, had determined to make a journey to the north; and afterwards in another direction, if that did not please her. She recognised Gerda immediately, and Gerda knew her too. It was a joyful meeting.

"You are a fine fellow for tramping about," said she to little Kay; "I should like to know, faith, if you deserve that one should run from one end of the world to the other for your sake?"

But Gerda patted her cheeks, and inquired for the Prince and Princess.

"They are gone abroad," said the other.

"But the Raven?" asked little Gerda.

"Oh! The Raven is dead," she answered. "His tame sweetheart is a widow, and wears a bit of black worsted round her leg; she laments most piteously, but it's all mere talk and stuff! Now tell me what you've been doing and how you managed to catch him."

And Gerda and Kay both told their story.

And "Schnipp-schnapp-schnurre-basselurre," said the robber maiden; and she took the hands of each, and promised that if she should some day pass through the town where they lived, she would come and visit them; and then away she rode. Kay and Gerda took each other's hand: it was lovely spring weather, with abundance of flowers and of verdure. The church-bells rang, and the children recognised the high towers, and the large town; it was that in which they dwelt. They entered and hastened up to their grandmother's room, where everything was standing as formerly. The clock said "tick! tack!" and the finger moved round; but as they entered, they remarked that they were now grown up. The roses on the leads hung blooming in at the open window; there stood the little children's chairs, and Kay and Gerda sat down on them, holding each other by the hand; they both had forgotten the cold empty splendor of the Snow Queen, as though it had been a dream. The grandmother sat in the bright sunshine, and read aloud from the Bible: "Unless ye become as little children, ye cannot enter the kingdom of heaven."

And Kay and Gerda looked in each other's eyes, and all at once they understood the old hymn:

"The rose in the valley is blooming so sweet,
And angels descend there the children to greet."

There sat the two grown-up persons; grown-up, and yet children; children at least in heart; and it was summer-time; summer, glorious summer!

IV

LITTLE CLAUS AND BIG CLAUS

IN A VILLAGE there once lived two men of the same name. Both of them were called Claus. But because one of them owned four horses while the other had but one, people called the one who had the four horses Big, or Great, Claus and the one who owned but a single horse Little Claus. Now I shall tell you what happened to each of them, for this is a true story.

All the days of the week Little Claus was obliged to plow for Great Claus and to lend him his one horse; then once a week, on Sunday, Great Claus helped Little Claus with his four horses, but always on a holiday.

"Hurrah!" How Little Claus would crack his whip over the five, for they were as good as his own on that one day.

The sun shone brightly, and the church bells rang merrily as the people passed by. The people were dressed in their best, with their prayer books under their arms, for they were going to church to hear the clergyman preach. They looked at Little Claus plowing with five horses, and he was so proud and merry that he cracked his whip and cried, "Gee-up, my fine horses."

"You mustn't say that," said Great Claus, "for only one of them is yours."

But Little Claus soon forgot what it was that he ought not to say, and when any one went by he would call out, "Gee-up, my fine horses."

"I must really beg you not to say that again," said Great Claus as he passed; "for if you do, I shall hit your horse on the head so that he will drop down dead on the spot, and then it will be all over with him."

"I will certainly not say it again, I promise you," said Little Claus. But as soon as any one came by, nodding good day to him, he was so pleased, and felt so grand at having five horses plowing his field, that again he cried out, "Gee-up, all my horses."

"I'll gee-up your horses for you," said Great Claus, and he caught up the tethering mallet and struck Little Claus's one horse on the head, so that it fell down dead.

"Oh, now I haven't any horse at all!" cried Little Claus, and he began to weep. But after a while he flayed the horse and hung up the skin to dry in the wind.

Then he put the dried skin into a bag, and hanging it over his shoulder, went off to the next town to sell it. He had a very long way to go and was obliged to pass through a great, gloomy wood. A dreadful storm came up. He lost his way, and before he found it again, evening was drawing on. It was too late to get to the town, and too late to get home before nightfall.

Near the road stood a large farmhouse. The shutters outside the windows were closed, but lights shone through the crevices and at the top. "They might let me stay here for the night," thought Little Claus. So he went up to the door and knocked. The door was opened by the farmer's wife, but when he explained what it was that he wanted, she told him to go away; her husband, she said, was not at home, and she could not let any strangers in.

"Then I shall have to lie out here," said Little Claus to himself, as the farmer's wife shut the door in his face.

Close to the farmhouse stood a tall haystack, and between it and the house was a small shed with a thatched roof. "I can lie up there," said Little Claus, when he saw the roof. "It will make a capital bed, but I hope the stork won't fly down and bite my legs." A stork was just then standing near his nest on the house roof.

So Little Claus climbed onto the roof of the shed and proceeded to make himself comfortable. As he turned round to settle himself, he discovered that the wooden shutters did not reach to the tops of the windows. He could look over them straight into the room, in which a large table was laid with wine, roast meat, and a fine, great fish. The farmer's wife and the sexton were sitting at the table all by themselves, and she was pouring out wine for him, while his fork was in the fish, which he seemed to like the best.

"If I could only get some too," thought Little Claus, and as he stretched his neck toward the window he spied a large, beautiful cake. Goodness! what a glorious feast they had before them.

At that moment some one came riding down the road towards the farm. It was the farmer himself, returning. He was a good man enough, but he had one very singular prejudice—he could not bear the sight of a sexton, and if he came on one he fell into a terrible rage. This was the reason that the sexton had gone to visit the farmer's wife during his absence from home and that the good wife had put before him the best she had.

When they heard the farmer they were frightened, and the woman begged the sexton to creep into a large empty chest which stood in a corner. He did so with all haste, for he well knew how the farmer felt toward a sexton. The woman hid the wine and all the good things in the oven, for if her husband were to see them, he would certainly ask why they had been provided.

"O dear!" sighed Little Claus, on the shed roof, as he saw the good things disappear.

"Is any one up there?" asked the farmer, looking up where Little Claus was. "What are you doing up there? You had better come with me into the house."

Then Little Claus told him how he had lost his way, and asked if he might have shelter for the night.

"Certainly," replied the farmer; "but the first thing is to have something to eat."

The wife received them both in a friendly way, and laid the table, bringing to it a large bowl of porridge. The farmer was hungry and ate with a good appetite. But Little Claus could not help thinking of the capital roast meat, fish, and cake, which he knew were hidden in the oven.

He had put his sack with the hide in it under the table by his feet, for, we must remember, he was on his way to the town to sell it. He did not relish the porridge, so he trod on the sack and made the dried skin squeak quite loudly.

"Hush!" said Little Claus to his bag, at the same time treading upon it again, to make it squeak much louder than before.

"Hollo! what's that you've got in your bag?" asked the farmer.

"Oh, it's a magician," said Little Claus, "and he says we needn't eat the porridge, for he has charmed the oven full of roast meat, fish, and cake."

"What?" cried the farmer, and he opened the oven with all speed and saw all the nice things the woman had hidden, but which he believed the magician had conjured up for their special benefit.

The farmer's wife did not say a word, but set the food before them; and they both made a hearty meal of the fish, the meat, and the cake. Little Claus now trod again upon his sack and made the skin squeak.

"What does he say now?" inquired the farmer.

"He says," promptly answered Little Claus, "that he has conjured up three bottles of wine, which are standing in the corner near the stove." So the woman was obliged to bring the wine which she had hidden, and the farmer and Little Claus became right merry. Would not the farmer like to have such a conjurer as Little Claus carried about in his sack?

"Can he conjure up the Evil One?" inquired the farmer. "I shouldn't mind seeing him now, when I'm in such a merry mood."

"Yes," said Little Claus, "he will do anything that I please"; and he trod on the bag till it squeaked. "You hear him answer, 'Yes, only the Evil One is so ugly that you had better not see him.'"

"Oh, I'm not afraid. What will he look like?"

"Well, he will show himself to you in the image of a sexton."

"Nay, that's bad indeed. You must know that I can't abide a sexton. However, it doesn't matter, for I know he's a demon, and I shan't mind so much. Now my courage is up! Only he mustn't come too close."

"I'll ask him about it," said Little Claus, putting his ear down as he trod close to the bag.

"What does he say?"

"He says you can go along and open the chest in the corner, and there you'll see him cowering in the dark. But hold the lid tight, so that he doesn't get out."

"Will you help me to hold the lid," asked the farmer, going along to the chest in which his wife had hidden the sexton, who was shivering with fright.

The farmer opened the lid a wee little way and peeped in. "Ha!" he cried, springing backward. "I saw him, and he looks exactly like our sexton. It was a shocking sight!"

They must needs drink after this, and there they sat till far into the night.

"You must sell me your conjurer," said the farmer. "Ask anything you like for him. Nay, I'll give you a bushel of money for him."

"No, I can't do that," said Little Claus. "You must remember how much benefit I can get from such a conjurer."

"Oh, but I should so like to have him!" said the farmer, and he went on begging for him.

"Well," said Little Claus at last, "since you have been so kind as to give me a night's shelter, I won't say nay. You must give me a bushel of money, only I must have it full to the brim."

"You shall have it," said the farmer; "but you must take that chest away with you. I won't have it in the house an hour longer. You could never know that he might not still be inside."

So Little Claus gave his sack with the dried hide of the horse in it and received a full bushel of money in return, and the measure was full to the brim. The farmer also gave him a large wheelbarrow, with which to take away the chest and the bushel of money.

"Good-by," said Little Claus, and off he went with his money and the chest with the sexton in it.

On the other side of the forest was a wide, deep river, whose current was so strong that it was almost impossible to swim against it. A large, new bridge had just been built over it, and when they came to the middle of the bridge Little Claus said in a voice loud enough to be heard by the sexton: "What shall I do with this stupid old chest? It might be full of paving stones, it is so heavy. I am tired of wheeling it. I'll just throw it into the river. If it floats down to my home, well and good; if not, I don't care. It will be no great matter." And he took hold of the chest and lifted it a little, as if he were going to throw it into the river.

"No, no! let be!" shouted the sexton. "Let me get out."

"Ho!" said Little Claus, pretending to be frightened. "Why, he is still inside. Then I must heave it into the river to drown him."

"Oh, no, no, no!" shouted the sexton; "I'll give you a whole bushelful of money if you'll let me out."

"Oh, that's another matter," said Little Claus, opening the chest. He pushed the empty chest into the river and then went home with the sexton to get his bushelful of money. He had already had one from the farmer, you know, so now his wheelbarrow was quite full of money.

"I got a pretty fair price for that horse, I must admit," said he to himself, when he got home and turned the money out of the wheelbarrow into a heap in the middle of the floor. "What a rage Great Claus will be in when he discovers how rich I am become through my one horse. But I won't tell him just how it happened." So he sent a boy to Great Claus to borrow a bushel measure.

"What can he want with it?" thought Great Claus, and he rubbed some tallow on the bottom so that some part of whatever was measured might stick to it. And so it did, for when the measure came back, three new silver threepenny bits were sticking to it.

"What's this!" said Great Claus, and he ran off at once to Little Claus. "Where on earth did you get all this money?" he asked.

"Oh, that's for my horse's skin. I sold it yesterday morning."

"That was well paid for, indeed," said Great Claus. He ran home, took an ax, and hit all his four horses on the head; then he flayed them and carried their skins off to the town.

"Hides! hides! who'll buy my hides?" he cried through the streets.

All the shoemakers and tanners in the town came running up and asked him how much he wanted for his hides.

"A bushel of money for each," said Great Claus.

"Are you mad?" they all said. "Do you think we have money by the bushel?"

THE FARMER LIFTED THE LID AND PEEPED IN

"Skins! skins! who'll buy them?" he shouted again, and the shoemakers took up their straps, and the tanners their leather aprons, and began to beat Great Claus.

"Hides! hides!" they called after him. "Yes, we'll hide you and tan you. Out of the town with him," they shouted. And Great Claus made the best haste he could to get out of the town, for he had never yet been thrashed as he was being thrashed now.

"Little Claus shall pay for this," he said, when he got home. "I'll kill him for it."

Little Claus's old grandmother had just died in his house. She had often been harsh and unkind to him, but now that she was dead he felt quite grieved. He took the dead woman and laid her in his warm bed to see if she would not come to life again. He himself intended to sit in a corner all night. He had slept that way before.

As he sat there in the night, the door opened and in came Great Claus with his ax. He knew where Little Claus's bed stood, and he went straight to it and hit the dead grandmother a blow on the forehead, thinking it was Little Claus.

"Just see if you'll make a fool of me again," said he, and then he went home.

"What a bad, wicked man he is!" said Little Claus. "He was going to kill me. What a good thing that poor grandmother was dead already! He would have taken her life."

He now dressed his grandmother in her best Sunday clothes, borrowed a horse of his neighbor, harnessed it to a cart, and set his grandmother on the back seat, so that she could not fall when the cart moved. Then he started off through the woods. When the sun rose, he was just outside a big inn, and he drew up his horse and went in to get something to eat.

The landlord was a very rich man and a very good man, but he was hot-tempered, as if he were made of pepper and snuff. "Good morning!" said he to Little Claus; "you have your best clothes on very early this morning."

"Yes," said Little Claus, "I'm going to town with my old grandmother. She's sitting out there in the cart; I can't get her to come in. Won't you take her out a glass of beer? You'll have to shout at her, she's very hard of hearing."

"Yes, that I'll do," said the host, and he poured a glass and went out with it to the dead grandmother, who had been placed upright in the cart.

"Here is a glass of beer your son has sent," said the landlord but she sat quite still and said not a word.

"Don't you hear?" cried he as loud as he could. "Here is a glass of beer from your son."

But the dead woman replied not a word, and at last he became quite angry and threw the beer in her face—and at that moment she fell backwards out of the cart, for she was only set upright and not bound fast.

"Now!" shouted Little Claus, as he rushed out of the inn and seized the landlord by the neck, "you have killed my grandmother! Just look at the big hole in her forehead!"

"Oh! what a misfortune!" cried the man, "and all because of my quick temper. Good Little Claus, I will pay you a bushel of money, and I will have your poor grandmother buried as if she were my own, if only you will say nothing about it. Otherwise I shall have my head cut off—and that is so dreadful."

So Little Claus again received a whole bushel of money, and the landlord buried the old grandmother as if she had been his own.

When Little Claus got home again with all his money, he immediately sent his boy to Great Claus to ask to borrow his bushel measure.

"What!" said Great Claus, "is he not dead? I must go and see about this myself." So he took the measure over to Little Claus himself.

"I say, where did you get all that money?" asked he, his eyes big and round with amazement at what he saw.

"It was grandmother you killed instead of me," said Little Claus. "I have sold her and got a bushel of money for her."

"That's being well paid, indeed," said Great Claus, and he hurried home, took an ax and killed his own old grandmother.

He then put her in a carriage and drove off to the town where the apothecary lived, and asked him if he would buy a dead person.

"Who is it and where did you get him?" asked the apothecary.

"It is my grandmother, and I have killed her so as to sell her for a bushel of money."

"Heaven preserve us!" cried the apothecary. "You talk like a madman. Pray don't say such things, you may lose your head." And he told him earnestly what a horribly wicked thing he had done, and that he deserved punishment. Great Claus was so frightened that he rushed out of the shop, jumped into his cart, whipped up his horse, and galloped home through the wood. The apothecary and all the people who saw him thought he was mad, and so they let him drive away.

"You shall be paid for this!" said Great Claus, when he got out on the highroad. "You shall be paid for this, Little Claus!"

Directly after he got home, Great Claus took the biggest sack he could find and went over to Little Claus.

"You have deceived me again," he said. "First I killed my horses, and then my old grandmother. That is all your fault; but you shall never have the chance to trick me again." And he seized Little Claus around the body and thrust him into the sack; then he threw the sack over his back, calling out to Little Claus, "Now I'm going to the river to drown you."

It was a long way that he had to travel before he came to the river, and Little Claus was not light to carry. The road came close to the church, and the people within were singing beautifully. Great Claus put down his sack, with Little Claus in it, at the church door. He thought it would be a very good thing to go in and hear a psalm before he went further, for Little Claus could not get out. So he went in.

"O dear! O dear!" moaned Little Claus in the sack, and he turned and twisted, but found it impossible to loosen the cord. Then there came by an old drover with snow-white hair and a great staff in his hand. He was driving a whole herd of cows and oxen before him, and they jostled against the sack in which Little Claus was confined, so that it was upset.

"O dear," again sighed Little Claus, "I'm so young to be going directly to the kingdom of heaven!"

"And I, poor fellow," said the drover, "am so old already, and cannot get there yet."

"Open the sack," cried Little Claus, "and creep into it in my place, and you'll be there directly."

"With all my heart," said the drover, and he untied the sack for Little Claus, who crept out at once. "You must look out for the cattle now," said the old man, as he crept in. Then Little Claus tied it up and went his way, driving the cows and the oxen.

In a little while Great Claus came out of the church. He took the sack upon his shoulders and thought as he did so that it had certainly grown lighter since he had put it down, for the old cattle-drover was not more than half as heavy as Little Claus.

"How light he is to carry now! That must be because I have heard a psalm in the church."

He went on to the river, which was both deep and broad, threw the sack containing the old drover into the water, and called after him, thinking it was Little Claus, "Now lie there! You won't trick me again!"

He turned to go home, but when he came to the place where there was a crossroad he met Little Claus driving his cattle.

"What's this?" cried he. "Haven't I drowned you?"

"Yes," said Little Claus, "you threw me into the river, half an hour ago."

"But where did you get all those fine cattle?" asked Great Claus.

"These beasts are sea cattle," said Little Claus, "and I thank you heartily for drowning me, for now I'm at the top of the tree. I'm a very rich man, I can tell you. But I was frightened when you threw me into the water huddled up in the sack. I sank to the bottom immediately, but I did not hurt myself, for the grass is beautifully soft down there. I fell upon it, and the sack was opened, and the most beautiful maiden in snow-white garments and a green wreath upon her hair took me by the hand, and said to me, 'Have you come, Little Claus? Here are cattle for you, and a mile further up the road there is another herd!'

"Then I saw that she meant the river and that it was the highway for the sea folk. Down at the bottom of it they walk directly from the sea, straight into the land where the river ends. Lovely flowers and beautiful fresh grass were there. The fishes which swam there glided about me like birds in the air. How nice the people were, and what fine herds of cattle there were, pasturing on the mounds and about the ditches!"

"But why did you come up so quickly then?" asked Great Claus. "I shouldn't have done that if it was so fine down there."

"Why, that was just my cunning. You know, I told you that the mermaid said there was a whole herd of cattle for me a mile further up the stream. Well, you see, I know how the river bends this way and that, and how long a distance it would have been to go that way. If you can come up on the land and take the short cuts, driving across fields and down to the river again, you save almost half a mile and get the cattle much sooner."

"Oh, you are a fortunate man!" cried Great Claus. "Do you think I could get some sea cattle if I were to go down to the bottom of the river?"

"I'm sure you would," said Little Claus. "But I cannot carry you. If you will walk to the river and creep into a sack yourself, I will help you into the water with a great deal of pleasure."

"Thanks!" said Great Claus. "But if I do not find sea cattle there, I shall beat you soundly, you may be sure."

"Oh! do not be so hard on me."

And so they went together to the river. When the cows and oxen saw the water, they ran to it as fast as they could. "See how they hurry!" cried Little Claus. "They want to get back to the bottom again."

"Yes, but help me first or I'll thrash you," said Great Claus. He then crept into a big sack, which had been lying across the back of one of the cows. "Put a big stone in or I'm afraid I shan't sink."

"Oh, that'll be all right," said Little Claus, but he put a big stone into the sack and gave it a push. Plump! and there lay Great Claus in the river. He sank at once to the bottom.

"I'm afraid he won't find the cattle," said Little Claus. Then he drove homeward with his herd.

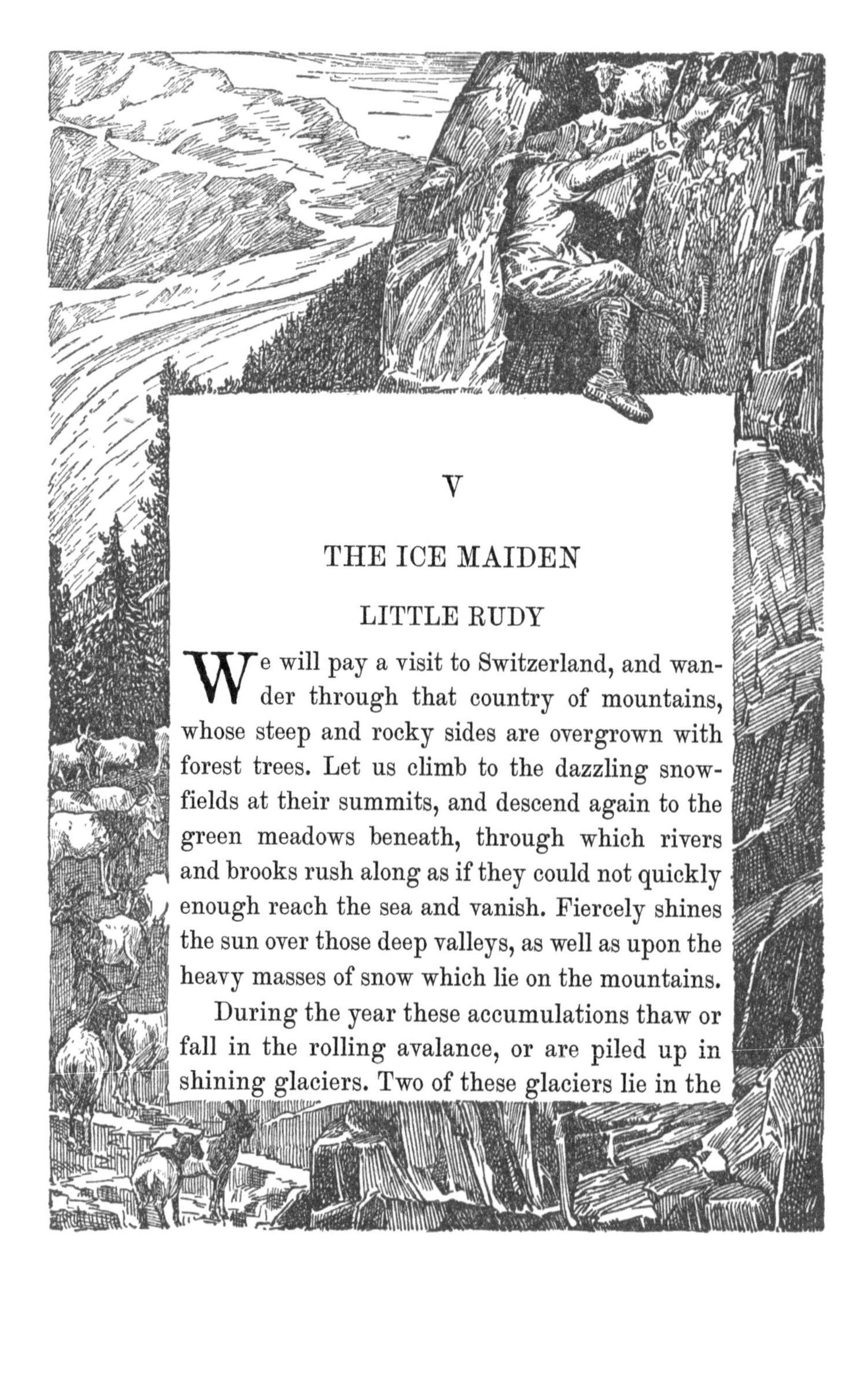

V

THE ICE MAIDEN

LITTLE RUDY

We will pay a visit to Switzerland, and wander through that country of mountains, whose steep and rocky sides are overgrown with forest trees. Let us climb to the dazzling snow-fields at their summits, and descend again to the green meadows beneath, through which rivers and brooks rush along as if they could not quickly enough reach the sea and vanish. Fiercely shines the sun over those deep valleys, as well as upon the heavy masses of snow which lie on the mountains.

During the year these accumulations thaw or fall in the rolling avalance, or are piled up in shining glaciers. Two of these glaciers lie in the broad, rocky cliffs, between the Schreckhorn and the Wetterhorn, near the little town of Grindelwald. They are wonderful to behold, and therefore in the summer time strangers come here from all parts of the world to see them. They cross snow-covered mountains, and travel through the deep valleys, or ascend for hours, higher and still higher, the valleys appearing to sink lower and lower as they proceed, and become as small as if seen from an air balloon. Over the lofty summits of these mountains the clouds often hang like a dark veil; while beneath in the valley, where many brown, wooden houses are scattered about, the bright rays of the sun may be shining upon a little brilliant patch of green, making it appear almost transparent. The waters foam and dash along in the valleys beneath; the streams from above trickle and murmur as they fall down the rocky mountain's side, looking like glittering silver bands.

On both sides of the mountain-path stand these little wooden houses; and, as within, there are many children and many mouths to feed, each house has its own little potato garden. These children rush out in swarms, and surround travellers, whether on foot or in carriages. They are all clever at making a bargain. They offer for sale the sweetest little toy-houses, models of the mountain cottages in Switzerland. Whether it be rain or sunshine, these crowds of children are always to be seen with their wares.

About twenty years ago, there might be seen occasionally, standing at a short distance from the other children, a little boy, who was also anxious to sell his curious wares. He had an earnest, expressive countenance, and held the box containing his carved toys tightly with both hands, as if unwilling to part with it. His earnest look, and being also a very little boy, made him noticed by the strangers; so that he often sold the most, without knowing why. An hour's walk farther up the ascent lived his grandfather, who cut and carved the pretty little toy-houses; and in the old man's room stood a large press, full of all sorts of carved things—nut-crackers, knives and forks, boxes with beautifully carved foliage, leaping chamois. It contained everything that could delight the eyes of a child. But the boy, who was named Rudy, looked with still greater pleasure and longing at some old fire-arms which hung upon the rafters, under the ceiling of the room. His grandfather promised him that he should have them some day, but that he must first grow big and strong, and learn how to use them. Small as he was, the goats were placed in his care, and a good goat-keeper should also be a good climber, and such Rudy was; he sometimes, indeed, climbed higher than the goats, for he was fond of seeking for birds'-nests at the top of high trees; he was bold and daring, but was seldom seen to smile, excepting when he stood by the roaring cataract, or heard the descending roll of the avalanche. He never played with the other children, and was not seen with them, unless his grandfather sent him down to sell his curious workmanship. Rudy did not much like trade; he loved to climb the mountains, or to sit by his grandfather and listen to his tales of olden times, or of the people in Meyringen, the place of his birth.

"In the early ages of the world," said the old man, "these people could not be found in Switzerland. They are a colony from the north, where their ancestors still dwell, and are called Swedes."

This was something for Rudy to know, but he learnt more from other sources, particularly from the domestic animals who belonged to the house. One was a large dog, called Ajola, which had belonged to his father; and the other was a tom-cat. This cat stood very high in Rudy's favor, for he had taught him to climb.

"Come out on the roof with me," said the cat; and Rudy quite understood him, for the language of fowls, ducks, cats, and dogs, is as easily understood by a young child as his own native tongue. But it must be at the age when grandfather's stick becomes a neighing horse, with head, legs, and tail. Some children retain these ideas later than others, and they are considered backwards and childish for their age. People say so; but is it so?

"Come out on the roof with me, little Rudy," was the first thing he heard the cat say, and Rudy understood him. "What people say about falling down is all nonsense," continued the cat; "you will not fall, unless you are afraid. Come, now, set one foot here and another there, and feel your way with your fore-feet. Keep your eyes wide open, and move softly, and if you come to a hole jump over it, and cling fast as I do." And this was just what Rudy did. He was often on the sloping roof with the cat, or on the tops of high trees. But, more frequently, higher still on the ridges of the rocks where puss never came.

"Higher, higher!" cried the trees and the bushes, "see to what height we have grown, and how fast we hold, even to the narrow edges of the rocks."

Rudy often reached the top of the mountain before the sunrise, and there inhaled his morning draught of the fresh, invigorating mountain air,—God's own gift, which men call the sweet fragrance of plant and herb on the mountain-side, and the mint and wild thyme in the valleys. The overhanging clouds absorb all heaviness from the air, and the winds convey them away over the pine-tree summits. The spirit of fragrance, light and fresh, remained behind, and this was Rudy's morning draught. The sunbeams—those blessing-bringing daughters of the sun—kissed his cheeks. Vertigo might be lurking on the watch, but he dared not approach him. The swallows, who had not less than seven nests in his grandfather's house, flew up to him and his goats, singing, "We and you, you and we." They brought him greetings from his grandfather's house, even from two hens, the only birds of the household; but Rudy was not intimate with them.

Although so young and such a little fellow, Rudy had travelled a great deal. He was born in the canton of Valais, and brought to his grandfather over the mountains. He had walked to Staubbach—a little town that seems to flutter in the air like a silver veil—the glittering, snow-clad mountain Jungfrau. He had also been to the great glaciers; but this is connected with a sad story, for here his mother met her death, and his grandfather used to say that all Rudy's childish merriment was lost from that time. His mother had written in a letter, that before he was a year old he had laughed more than he cried; but after his fall into the snow-covered crevasse, his disposition had completely changed. The grandfather seldom spoke of this, but the fact was generally known. Rudy's father had been a postilion, and the large dog which now lived in his grandfather's cottage had always followed him on his journeys over the Simplon to the lake of Geneva. Rudy's relations, on his father's side, lived in the canton of Valais, in the valley of the Rhone. His uncle was a chamois hunter, and a well-known guide. Rudy was only a year old when his father died, and his mother was anxious to return with her child to her own relations, who lived in the Bernese Oberland. Her father dwelt at a few hours' distance from Grindelwald; he was a carver in wood, and gained so much by it that he had plenty to live upon. She set out homewards in the month of June, carrying her infant in her arms, and, accompanied by two chamois hunters, crossed the Gemmi on her way to Grindelwald. They had already left more than half the journey behind them. They had crossed high ridges, and traversed snow-fields; they could even see her native valley, with its familiar wooden cottages. They had only one more glacier to climb. Some newly fallen snow concealed a cleft which, though it did not extend to the foaming waters in the depths beneath, was still much deeper than the height of a man. The young woman, with the child in her arms, slipped upon it, sank in, and disappeared. Not a shriek, not a groan was heard; nothing but the whining of a little child. More than an hour elapsed before her two companions could obtain from the nearest house ropes and poles to assist in raising them; and it was with much exertion that they at last succeeded in raising from the crevasse what appeared to be two dead bodies. Every means was used to restore them to life. With the child they were successful, but not with the mother; so the old grandfather received his daughter's little son into his house an orphan,—a little boy who laughed more than he cried; but it seemed as if laughter had left him in the cold ice-world into which he had fallen, where, as the Swiss peasants say, the souls of the lost are confined till the judgment-day.

The glaciers appear as if a rushing stream had been frozen in its course, and pressed into blocks of green crystal, which, balanced one upon another, form a wondrous palace of crystal for the Ice Maiden—the queen of the glaciers. It is she whose mighty power can crush the traveller to death, and arrest the flowing river in its course. She is also a child of the air, and with the swiftness of the chamois she can reach the snow-covered mountain tops, where the boldest mountaineer has to cut footsteps in the ice to ascend. She will sail on a frail pine-twig over the raging torrents beneath, and spring lightly from one iceberg to another, with her long, snow-white hair flowing around her, and her dark-green robe glittering like the waters of the deep Swiss lakes. "Mine is the power to seize and crush," she cried. "Once a beautiful boy was stolen from me by man,—a boy whom I had kissed, but had not kissed to death. He is again among mankind, and tends the goats on the mountains. He is always climbing higher and higher, far away from all others, but

NOTHING BUT THE CRYING OF A LITTLE CHILD

not from me. He is mine; I will send for him." And she gave Vertigo the commission.

It was summer, and the Ice Maiden was melting amidst the green verdure, when Vertigo swung himself up and down. Vertigo has many brothers, quite a troop of them, and the Ice Maiden chose the strongest among them. They exercise their power in different ways, and everywhere. Some sit on the banisters of steep stairs, others on the outer rails of lofty towers, or spring like squirrels along the ridges of the mountains. Others tread the air as a swimmer treads the water, and lure their victims here and there till they fall into the deep abyss. Vertigo and the Ice Maiden clutch at human beings, as the polypus seizes upon all that comes within its reach. And now Vertigo was to seize Rudy.

"Seize him, indeed," cried Vertigo; "I cannot do it. That monster of a cat has taught him her tricks. That child of the human race has a power within him which keeps me at a distance; I cannot possibly reach the boy when he hangs from the branches of trees, over the precipice; or I would gladly tickle his feet, and send him heels over head through the air; but I cannot accomplish it."

"We must accomplish it," said the Ice Maiden; "either you or I must; and I will—I will!"

"No, no!" sounded through the air, like an echo on the mountain church bells chime. It was an answer in song, in the melting tones of a chorus from others of nature's spirits—good and loving spirits, the daughters of the sunbeam. They who place themselves in a circle every evening on the mountain peaks; there they spread out their rose-colored wings, which, as the sun sinks, become more flaming red, until the lofty Alps seem to burn with fire. Men call this the Alpine glow. After the sun has set, they disappear within the white snow on the mountain-tops, and slumber there till sunrise, when they again come forth. They have great love for flowers, for butterflies, and for mankind; and from among the latter they had chosen little Rudy. "You shall not catch him; you shall not seize him!" they sang.

"Greater and stronger than he have I seized!" said the Ice Maiden.

Then the daughters of the sun sang a song of the traveller, whose cloak had been carried away by the wind. "The wind took the covering, but not the man; it could even seize upon him, but not hold him fast. The children of strength are more powerful, more ethereal, even than we are. They can rise higher than our parent, the sun. They have the magic words that rule the wind and the waves, and compel them to serve and obey; and they can, at last, cast off the heavy, oppressive weight of mortality, and soar upwards." Thus sweetly sounded the bell-like tones of the chorus.

And each morning the sun's rays shone through the one little window of the grandfather's house upon the quiet child. The daughters of the sunbeam kissed him; they wished to thaw, and melt, and obliterate the ice kiss which the queenly maiden of the glaciers had given him as he lay in the lap of his dead mother, in the deep crevasse of ice from which he had been so wonderfully rescued.

THE JOURNEY TO THE NEW HOME

RUDY was just eight years old, when his uncle, who lived on the other side of the mountain, wished to have the boy, as he thought he might obtain a better education with him, and learn something more. His grandfather thought the same, so he consented to let him go. Rudy had many to say farewell to, as well as his grandfather. First, there was Ajola, the old dog.

"Your father was the postilion, and I was the postilion's dog," said Ajola. "We have often travelled the same journey together; I knew all the dogs and men on this side of the mountain. It is not my habit to talk much; but now that we have so little time to converse together, I will say something more than usual. I will relate to you a story, which I have reflected upon for a long time. I do not understand it, and very likely you will not, but that is of no consequence. I have, however, learnt from it that in this world things are not equally divided, neither for dogs nor for men. All are not born to lie on the lap and to drink milk: I have never been petted in this way, but I have seen a little dog seated in the place of a gentleman or lady, and travelling inside a post-chaise. The lady, who was his mistress, or of whom he was master, carried a bottle of milk, of which the little dog now and then drank; she also offered him pieces of sugar to crunch. He sniffed at them proudly, but would not eat one, so she ate them herself. I was running along the dirty road by the side of the carriage as hungry as a dog could be, chewing the cud of my own thoughts, which were rather in confusion. But many other things seemed in confusion also. Why was not I lying on a lap and travelling in a coach? I could not tell; yet I knew I could not alter my own condition, either by barking or growling."

This was Ajola's farewell speech, and Rudy threw his arms round the dog's neck and kissed his cold nose. Then he took the cat in his arms, but he struggled to get free.

"You are getting too strong for me," he said; "but I will not use my claws against you. Clamber away over the mountains; it was I who taught you to climb. Do not fancy you are going to fall, and you will be quite safe." Then the cat jumped down and ran away; he did not wish Rudy to see that there were tears in his eyes.

The hens were hopping about the floor; one of them had no tail; a traveller, who fancied himself a sportsman, had shot off her tail, he had mistaken her for a bird of prey.

"Rudy is going away over the mountains," said one of the hens.

"He is always in such a hurry," said the other; "and I don't like taking leave," so they both hopped out.

But the goats said farewell; they bleated and wanted to go with him, they were so very sorry.

Just at this time two clever guides were going to cross the mountains to the other side of the Gemmi, and Rudy was to go with them on foot. It was a long walk for such a little boy, but he had plenty of strength and invincible courage. The swallows flew with him a little way, singing, "We and you—you and we." The way led across the rushing Lutschine, which falls in numerous streams from the dark clefts of the Grindelwald glaciers. Trunks of fallen trees and blocks of stone form bridges over these streams. After passing a forest of alders, they began to ascend, passing by some blocks of ice that had loosened themselves from the side of the mountain and lay across their path; they had to step over these ice-blocks or walk round them. Rudy crept here and ran there, his eyes sparkling with joy, and he stepped so firmly with his iron-tipped mountain shoe, that he left a mark behind him wherever he placed his foot.

The earth was black where the mountain torrents or the melted ice had poured upon it, but the bluish green, glassy ice sparkled and glittered. They had to go round little pools, like lakes, enclosed between large masses of ice; and, while thus wandering out of their path, they came near an immense stone, which lay balanced on the edge of an icy peak. The stone lost its balance just as they reached it, and rolled over into the abyss beneath, while the noise of its fall was echoed back from every hollow cliff of the glaciers.

They were always going upwards. The glaciers seemed to spread above them like a continued chain of masses of ice, piled up in wild confusion between bare and rugged rocks. Rudy thought for a moment of what had been told him, that he and his mother had once lain buried in one of these cold, heart-chilling fissures; but he soon banished such thoughts, and looked upon the story as fabulous, like many other stories which had been told him. Once or twice, when the men thought the way was rather difficult for such a little boy, they held out their hands to assist him; but he would not accept their assistance, for he stood on the slippery ice as firmly as if he had been a chamois. They came at length to rocky ground; sometimes stepping upon moss-covered stones, sometimes passing beneath stunted fir-trees, and again through green meadows. The landscape was always changing, but ever above them towered the lofty snow-clad mountains, whose names not only Rudy but every other child knew—"The Jungfrau," "The Monk and the Eiger."

Rudy had never been so far away before; he had never trodden on the wide-spreading ocean of snow that lay here with its immovable billows, from which the wind blows off the snowflake now and then, as it cuts the foam from the waves of the sea. The glaciers stand here so close together it might almost be said they are hand-in-hand; and each is a crystal palace for the Ice Maiden, whose power and will it is to seize and imprison the unwary traveller.

The sun shone warmly, and the snow sparkled as if covered with glittering diamonds. Numerous insects, especially butterflies and bees, lay dead in heaps on the snow. They had ventured too high, or the wind had carried them here and left them to die of cold.

Around the Wetterhorn hung a feathery cloud, like a woolbag, and a threatening cloud too, for as it sunk lower it increased in size, and concealed within was a *fohn*,[1] fearful in its violence should it break loose. This journey, with its varied incidents,—the wild paths, the night passed on the mountain, the steep rocky precipices,

[1] *Fohn*, a humid south wind on the Swiss mountains and lakes, the forerunner of a storm.

the hollow clefts, in which the rustling waters from time immemorial had worn away passages for themselves through blocks of stone,—all these were firmly impressed on Rudy's memory.

In a forsaken stone building, which stood just beyond the seas of snow, they one night took shelter. Here they found some charcoal and pine branches, so that they soon made a fire. They arranged couches to lie on as well as they could, and then the men seated themselves by the fire, took out their pipes, and began to smoke. They also prepared a warm, spiced drink, of which they partook and Rudy was not forgotten—he had his share. Then they began to talk of those mysterious beings with which the land of the Alps abounds; the hosts of apparitions which come in the night, and carry off the sleepers through the air, to the wonderful floating town of Venice; of the wild herds-man, who drives the black sheep across the meadows. These flocks are never seen, yet the tinkle of their little bells has often been heard, as well as their unearthly bleating. Rudy listened eagerly, but without fear, for he knew not what fear meant; and while he listened, he fancied he could hear the roaring of the spectral herd. It seemed to come nearer and roar louder, till the men heard it also and listened in silence, till, at length, they told Rudy that he must not dare to sleep. It was a "fohn," that violent storm-wind which rushes from the mountain to the valley beneath, and in its fury snaps asunder the trunks of large trees as if they were but slender reeds, and carries the wooden houses from one side of a river to the other as easily as we could move the pieces on a chess-board. After an hour had passed, they told Rudy that it was all over, and he might go to sleep; and, fatigued with his long walk, he readily slept at the word of command.

Very early the following morning they again set out. The sun on this day lighted up for Rudy new mountains, new glaciers, and new snow-fields. They had entered the Canton Valais, and found themselves on the ridge of the hills which can be seen from Grindelwald; but he was still far from his new home. They pointed out to him other clefts, other meadows, other woods and rocky paths, and other houses. Strange men made their appearance before him, and what men! They were misshapen, wretched-looking creatures, with yellow complexions; and on their necks were dark, ugly lumps of flesh, hanging down like bags. They were called cretins. They dragged themselves along painfully, and stared at the strangers with vacant eyes. The women looked more dreadful than the men. Poor Rudy! were these the sort of people he should see at his new home?

THE UNCLE

Rudy arrived at last at his uncle's house, and was thankful to find the people like those he had been accustomed to see. There was only one cretin amongst them, a poor idiot boy, one of those unfortunate beings who, in their neglected conditions, go from house to house, and are received and taken care of in different families, for a month or two at a time.

Poor Saperli had just arrived at his uncle's house when Rudy came. The uncle was an experienced hunter; he also followed the trade of a cooper; his wife was a lively little person, with a face like a bird, eyes like those of an eagle, and a long, hairy throat. Everything was new to Rudy—the fashion of the dress, the manners, the employments, and even the language; but the latter his childish ear would soon learn. He saw also that there was more wealth here, when compared with his former home at his grandfather's. The rooms were larger, the walls were adorned with the horns of the chamois, and brightly polished guns. Over the door hung a painting of the Virgin Mary, fresh alpine roses and a burning lamp stood near it. Rudy's uncle was, as we have said, one of the most noted chamois hunters in the whole district, and also one of the best guides. Rudy soon became the pet of the house; but there was another pet, an old hound, blind and lazy, who would never more follow the hunt, well as he had once done so. But his former good qualities were not forgotten, and therefore the animal was kept in the family and treated with every indulgence. Rudy stroked the old hound, but he did not like strangers, and Rudy was as yet a stranger; he did not, however, long remain so, he soon endeared himself to every heart, and became like one of the family.

"We are not very badly off, here in the canton Valais," said his uncle one day; "we have the chamois, they do not die so fast as the wild goats, and it is certainly much better here now than in former times. How highly the old times have been spoken of, but ours is better. The bag has been opened, and a current of air now blows through our once confined valley. Something better always makes its appearance when old, worn-out things fail."

When his uncle became communicative, he would relate stories of his youthful days, and farther back still of the warlike times in which his father had lived. Valais was then, as he expressed it, only a closed-up bag, quite full of sick people, miserable cretins; but the French soldiers came, and they were capital doctors, they soon killed the disease and the sick people, too. The French people knew how to fight in more ways than one, and the girls knew how to conquer too; and when he said this the uncle nodded at his wife, who was a French woman by birth, and laughed. The French could also do battle on the stones. "It was they who cut a road out of the solid rock over the Simplon—such a road, that I need only say to a child of three years old, 'Go down to Italy, you have only to keep in the high road,' and the child will soon arrive in Italy, if he followed my directions."

Then the uncle sang a French song, and cried, "Hurrah! long live Napoleon Buonaparte." This was the first time Rudy had ever heard of France, or of Lyons, that great city on the Rhone where his uncle had once lived. His uncle said that Rudy, in a very few years, would become a clever hunter, he had quite a talent for it; he taught the boy to hold a gun properly, and to load and fire it. In the hunting season he took him to the hills, and made him drink the warm blood of the chamois, which is said to prevent the hunter from becoming giddy; he taught him to know the time when, from the different mountains, the avalanche is likely to fall, namely, at noontide or in the evening, from the effects of the sun's rays; he made him observe the movements of the chamois when he gave a leap, so that he might fall firmly and lightly on his feet. He told him that when on the fissures of the rocks he could find no place for his feet, he must support himself on his elbows, and cling with his legs, and even lean firmly with his back, for this could be done when necessary. He told him also that the chamois are very cunning, they place lookers-out on the watch; but the hunter must be more cunning than they are, and find them out by the scent.

One day, when Rudy went out hunting with his uncle, he hung a coat and hat on an alpine staff, and the chamois mistook it for a man, as they generally do. The mountain path was narrow here;

indeed it was scarcely a path at all, only a kind of shelf, close to the yawning abyss. The snow that lay upon it was partially thawed, and the stones crumbled beneath the feet. Every fragment of stone broken off struck the sides of the rock in its fall, till it rolled into the depths beneath, and sunk to rest. Upon this shelf Rudy's uncle laid himself down, and crept forward. At about a hundred paces behind him stood Rudy, upon the highest point of the rock, watching a great vulture hovering in the air; with a single stroke of his wing the bird might easily cast the creeping hunter into the abyss beneath, and make him his prey. Rudy's uncle had eyes for nothing but the chamois, who, with its young kid, had just appeared round the edge of the rock. So Rudy kept his eyes fixed on the bird, he knew well what the great creature wanted; therefore he stood in readiness to discharge his gun at the proper moment. Suddenly the chamois made a spring, and his uncle fired and struck the animal with the deadly bullet; while the young kid rushed away, as if for a long life he had been accustomed to danger and practised flight. The large bird, alarmed at the report of the gun, wheeled off in another direction, and Rudy's uncle was saved from danger, of which he knew nothing till he was told of it by the boy.

While they were both in pleasant mood, wending their way homewards, and the uncle whistling the tune of a song he had learnt in his young days, they suddenly heard a peculiar sound which seemed to come from the top of the mountain. They looked up, and saw above them, on the over-hanging rock, the snow-covering heave and lift itself as a piece of linen stretched on the ground to dry raises itself when the wind creeps under it. Smooth as polished marble slabs, the waves of snow cracked and loosened themselves, and then suddenly, with the rumbling noise of distant thunder, fell like a foaming cataract into the abyss. An avalanche had fallen, not upon Rudy and his uncle, but very near them. Alas, a great deal too near!

"Hold fast, Rudy!" cried his uncle; "hold fast, with all your might."

Then Rudy clung with his arms to the trunk of the nearest tree, while his uncle climbed above him, and held fast by the branches. The avalanche rolled past them at some distance; but the gust of wind that followed, like the storm-wings of the avalanche, snapped asunder the trees and bushes over which it swept, as if they had been

AMID THE SHATTERED BRANCHES LAY HIS POOR UNCLE

but dry rushes, and threw them about in every direction. The tree to which Rudy clung was thus overthrown, and Rudy dashed to the ground. The higher branches were snapped off, and carried away to a great distance; and among these shattered branches lay Rudy's uncle, with his skull fractured. When they found him, his hand was still warm; but it would have been impossible to recognize his face. Rudy stood by, pale and trembling; it was the first shock of his life, the first time he had ever felt fear. Late in the evening he returned home with the fatal news,—to that home which was now to be so full of sorrow. His uncle's wife uttered not a word, nor shed a tear, till the corpse was brought in; then her agony burst forth. The poor cretin crept away to his bed, and nothing was seen of him during the whole of the following day. Towards evening, however, he came to Rudy, and said, "Will you write a letter for me? Saperli cannot write; Saperli can only take the letters to the post."

"A letter for you!" said Rudy; "who do you wish to write to?"

"To the Lord Christ," he replied.

"What do you mean?" asked Rudy.

Then the poor idiot, as the cretin was often called, looked at Rudy with a most touching expression in his eyes, clasped his hands, and said, solemnly and devoutly, "Saperli wants to send a letter to Jesus Christ, to pray Him to let Saperli die, and not the master of the house here."

Rudy pressed his hand, and replied, "A letter would not reach Him up above; it would not give him back whom we have lost."

It was not, however, easy for Rudy to convince Saperli of the impossibility of doing what he wished.

"Now you must work for us," said his foster-mother; and Rudy very soon became the entire support of the house.

BABETTE

Who was the best marksman in the canton Valais? The chamois knew well. "Save yourselves from Rudy," they might well say. And who is the handsomest marksman? "Oh, it is Rudy," said the maidens; but they did not say, "Save yourselves from Rudy." Neither did anxious mothers say so; for he bowed to them as pleasantly as to the young girls. He was so brave and cheerful. His cheeks were brown, his teeth white, and his eyes dark and sparkling. He was now a handsome young man of twenty years. The most icy water could not deter him from swimming; he could twist and turn like a fish. None could climb like he, and he clung as firmly to the edges of the rocks as a limpet. He had strong muscular power, as could be seen when he leapt from rock to rock. He had learnt this first from the cat, and more lately from the chamois. Rudy was considered the best guide over the mountains; every one had great confidence in him. He might have made a great deal of money as guide. His uncle had also taught him the trade of a cooper; but he had no inclination for either; his delight was in chamois-hunting, which also brought him plenty of money. Rudy would be a very good match, as people said, if he would not look above his own station. He was also such a famous partner in dancing, that the girls often dreamt about him, and one and another thought of him even when awake.

"He kissed me in the dance," said Annette, the schoolmaster's daughter, to her dearest friend; but she ought not to have told this, even to her dearest friend. It is not easy to keep such secrets; they are like sand in a sieve; they slip out. It was therefore soon known that Rudy, so brave and so good as he was, had kissed some one while dancing, and yet he had never kissed her who was dearest to him.

"Ah, ah," said an old hunter, "he has kissed Annette, has he? he has begun with A, and I suppose he will kiss through the whole alphabet."

But a kiss in the dance was all the busy tongues could accuse him of. He certainly had kissed Annette, but she was not the flower of his heart.

Down in the valley, near Bex, among the great walnut-trees, by the side of a little rushing mountain-stream, lived a rich miller. His dwelling-house was a large building, three storeys high, with little turrets. The roof was covered with chips, bound together with tin plates, that glittered in sunshine and in the moonlight. The largest of the turrets had a weather-cock, representing an apple pierced by a glittering arrow, in memory of William Tell. The mill was a neat and well-ordered place, that allowed itself to be sketched and written about; but the miller's daughter did not permit any to sketch or write about her. So, at least, Rudy would have said, for her image was pictured in his heart; her eyes shone in it so brightly, that quite a flame had been kindled there; and, like all other fires, it had burst forth so suddenly, that the miller's daughter, the beautiful Babette, was quite unaware of it. Rudy had never spoken a word to her on the subject. The miller was rich, and, on that account, Babette stood very high, and was rather difficult to aspire to. But said Rudy to himself, "Nothing is too high for a man to reach: he must climb with confidence in himself, and he will not fail." He had learnt this lesson in his youthful home.

It happened once that Rudy had some business to settle at Bex. It was a long journey at that time, for the railway had not been opened. From the glaciers of the Rhone, at the foot of the Simplon, between its ever-changing mountain summits, stretches the valley of the canton Valais. Through it runs the noble river of the Rhone, which often overflows its banks, covering fields and highways, and destroying everything in its course. Near the towns of Sion and St. Maurice, the valley takes a turn, and bends like an elbow, and behind St. Maurice becomes so narrow that there is only space enough for the bed of the river and a narrow carriage-road. An old tower stands here, as if it were guardian to the canton Valais, which ends at this point; and from it we can look across the stone bridge to the toll-house on the other side, where the canton Vaud commences. Not far from this spot stands the town of Bex, and at every step can be seen an increase of fruitfulness and verdure. It is like entering a grove of chestnut and walnut-trees. Here and there the cypress and pomegranate blossoms peep forth; and it is almost as warm as an Italian climate. Rudy arrived at Bex, and soon finished the business which had brought him there, and then walked about the town; but not even the miller's boy could be seen, nor any one belonging to the mill, not to mention Babette. This did not please him at all. Evening came on. The air was filled with the perfume of the wild thyme and the blossoms of the lime-trees, and the green woods on the mountains seemed to be covered with a shining veil, blue as the sky. Over everything reigned a stillness, not of sleep or of death, but as if Nature were holding her breath, that her image might be photographed on the blue vault of heaven. Here and there, amidst the trees of the silent valley, stood poles which supported the wires of the electric telegraph. Against one of these poles leaned an object so motionless that it might have been mistaken for the trunk of a tree; but it was Rudy, standing there as still as at that moment was everything around him. He was not asleep, neither was he dead; but just as the various events in the world—matters of momentous importance to individuals—were flying through the telegraph wires, without the quiver of a wire or the slightest tone, so, through the mind of Rudy, thoughts of overwhelming importance were passing, without an outward sign of emotion. The happiness of his future life depended upon the decision of his present reflections. His eyes were fixed on one spot in the distance—a light that twinkled through the foliage from the parlor of the miller's house, where Babette dwelt. Rudy stood so still, that it might have been supposed he was watching for a chamois; but he was in reality like a chamois, who will stand for a moment, looking as if it were chiselled out of the rock, and then, if only a stone rolled by, would suddenly bound forward with a spring, far away from the hunter. And so with Rudy: a sudden roll of his thoughts roused him from his stillness, and made him bound forward with determination to act.

"Never despair!" cried he. "A visit to the mill, to say good evening to the miller, and good evening to little Babette, can do no harm. No one ever fails who has confidence in himself. If I am to be Babette's husband, I must see her some time or other."

Then Rudy laughed joyously, and took courage to go to the mill. He knew what he wanted; he wanted to marry Babette. The clear water of the river rolled over its yellow bed, and willows and lime-trees were reflected in it, as Rudy stepped along the path to the miller's house. But, as the children sing—

> "Found to the miller's house his way;
> But there was nobody at home,
> Except a pussy cat at play!."

The cat standing on the steps put up its back and cried "mew." But Rudy had no inclination for this sort of conversation; he passed on, and knocked at the door. No one heard him, no one opened the door. "Mew," said the cat again; and had Rudy been still a child, he would have understood this language, and known that the cat wished to tell him there was no one at home. So he was obliged to go to the mill and make inquiries, and there he heard that the miller had gone on a journey to Interlachen, and taken Babette with him, to the great shooting festival, which began that morning, and would continue for eight days, and that people from all the German settlements would be there.

Poor Rudy! we may well say. It was not a fortunate day for his visit to Bex. He had just to return the way he came, through St. Maurice and Sion, to his home in the valley. But he did not despair. When the sun rose the next morning, his good spirits had returned; indeed he had never really lost them. "Babette is at Interlachen," said Rudy to himself, "many days' journey from here. It is certainly a long way for any one who takes the high-road, but not so far if he takes a short cut across the mountain, and that just suits a chamois-hunter. I have been that way before, for it leads to the home of my childhood, where, as a little boy, I lived with my grandfather. And there are shooting matches at Interlachen. I will go, and try to stand first in the match. Babette will be there, and I shall be able to make her acquaintance."

Carrying his light knapsack, which contained his Sunday clothes, on his back, and with his musket and his game-bag over his shoulder, Rudy started to take the shortest way across the mountain. Still it was a great distance. The shooting matches were to commence on that day, and to continue for a whole week. He had been told also that the miller and Babette would remain that time with some relatives at Interlachen. So over the Gemmi Rudy climbed bravely, and determined to descend the side of the Grindelwald. Bright and joyous were his feelings as he stepped lightly onwards, inhaling the invigorating mountain air. The valley sunk as he ascended, the circle of the horizon expanded. One snow-capped peak after another rose before him, till the whole of the glittering Alpine range became visible. Rudy knew each ice-clad peak, and he continued his course towards the Schreckhorn, with its white powdered stone finger raised high in the air. At length he had crossed the highest ridges, and before him lay the green pasture lands sloping down towards the valley, which was once his home. The buoyancy of the air made his heart light. Hill and valley were blooming in luxuriant beauty, and his thoughts were youthful dreams, in which old age or death were out of the question. Life, power, and enjoyment were in the future, and he felt free and light as a bird. And the swallows flew round him, as in the days of his childhood, singing "We and you—you and we." All was overflowing with joy. Beneath him lay the meadows, covered with velvety green, with the murmuring river flowing through them, and dotted here and there were small wooden houses. He could see the edges of the glaciers, looking like green glass against the soiled snow, and the deep chasms beneath the loftiest glacier. The church bells were ringing, as if to welcome him to his home with their sweet tones. His heart beat quickly, and for a moment he seemed to have foregotten Babette, so full were his thoughts of old recollections. He was, in imagination, once more wandering on the road where, when a little boy, he, with other children, came to sell their curiously carved toy houses. Yonder, behind the fir-trees, still stood his grandfather's house, his mother's father, but strangers dwelt in it now. Children came running to him, as he had once done, and wished to sell their wares. One of them offered him an Alpine rose. Rudy took the rose as a good omen, and thought of Babette. He quickly crossed the bridge where the two rivers flow into each other. Here he found a walk over-shadowed with large walnut-trees, and their thick foliage formed a pleasant shade. Very soon he perceived in the distance, waving flags, on which glittered a white cross on a red ground—the standard of the Danes as well as of the Swiss—and before him lay Interlachen.

"It is really a splendid town, like none other that I have ever seen," said Rudy to himself. It was indeed a Swiss town in its holiday dress. Not like the many other towns, crowded with heavy stone houses, stiff and foreign looking. No; here it seemed as if the wooden houses on the hills had run into the valley, and placed themselves in rows and ranks by the side of the clear river, which rushes like an arrow in its course. The streets were rather irregular, it is true, but still this added to their picturesque appearance. There was one street which Rudy thought the prettiest of them all; it had been built since he had visited the town when a little boy. It seemed to him as if all the neatest and most curiously carved toy houses which his grandfather once kept in the large cupboard at home, had been brought out and placed in this spot, and that they had increased in size since then, as the old chestnut trees had done. The houses were called hotels; the woodwork on the windows and balconies was curiously carved. The roofs were gayly painted, and before each house was a flower garden, which separated it from the macadamized high-road. These houses all stood on the same side of the road, so that the fresh, green meadows, in which were cows grazing, with bells on their necks, were not hidden. The sound of these bells is often heard amidst Alpine scenery. These meadows were encircled by lofty hills, which receded a little in the centre, so that the most beautifully formed of Swiss mountains—the snow-crowned Jungfrau—could be distinctly seen glittering in the distance. A number of elegantly dressed gentlemen and ladies from foreign lands, and crowds of country people from the neighboring cantons, were assembled in the town. Each marksman wore the number of hits he had made twisted in a garland round his hat. Here were music and singing of all descriptions: hand-organs, trumpets, shouting, and noise. The houses and bridges were adorned with verses and inscriptions. Flags and banners were waving. Shot after shot was fired, which was the best music to Rudy's ears. And amidst all this excitement he quite forgot Babette, on whose account only he had come. The shooters were thronging round the target, and Rudy was soon amongst them. But when he took his turn to fire, he proved himself the best shot, for he always struck the bull's-eye.

"Who may that young stranger be?" was the inquiry on all sides. "He speaks French as it is spoken in the Swiss cantons."

"And makes himself understood very well when he speaks German," said some.

"He lived here, when a child, with his grandfather, in a house on the road to Grindelwald," remarked one of the sportsmen.

And full of life was this young stranger; his eyes sparkled, his glance was steady, and his arm sure, therefore he always hit the mark. Good fortune gives courage, and Rudy was always courageous. He soon had a circle of friends gathered round him. Every one noticed him, and did him homage. Babette had quite vanished from his thoughts, when he was struck on the shoulder by a heavy hand, and a deep voice said to him in French, "You are from the canton Valais."

Rudy turned round, and beheld a man with a ruddy, pleasant face, and a stout figure. It was the rich miller from Bex. His broad, portly person, hid the slender, lovely Babette; but she came forward and glanced at him with her bright, dark eyes. The rich miller was very much flattered at the thought that the young man, who was acknowledged to be the best shot, and was so praised by every one, should be from his own canton. Now was Rudy really fortunate: he had travelled all this way to this place, and those he had forgotten were now come to seek him. When country people go far from home, they often meet with those they know, and improve their acquaintance. Rudy, by his shooting, had gained the first place in the shooting-match, just as the miller at home at Bex stood first, because of his money and his mill. So the two men shook hands, which they had never done before. Babette, too, held out her hand to Rudy frankly, and he pressed it in his, and looked at her so earnestly, that she blushed deeply. The miller talked of the long journey they had travelled, and of the many towns they had seen. It was his opinion that he had really made as great a journey as if he had travelled in a steamship, a railway carriage, or a post-chaise.

"I came by a much shorter way," said Rudy; "I came over the mountains. There is no road so high that a man may not venture upon it."

"Ah, yes; and break your neck," said the miller; "and you look like one who will break his neck some day, you are so daring."

"Oh, nothing ever happens to a man if he has confidence in himself," replied Rudy.

The miller's relations at Interlachen, with whom the miller and Babette were staying, invited Rudy to visit them, when they found he came from the same canton as the miller. It was a most pleasant visit. Good fortune seemed to follow him, as it does those who think and act for themselves, and who remember the proverb, "Nuts are given to us, but they are not cracked for us." And Rudy was treated by the miller's relations almost like one of the family, and glasses of wine were poured out to drink to the welfare of the best shooter. Babette clinked glasses with Rudy, and he returned thanks for the toast. In the evening they all took a delightful walk under the walnut-trees, in front of the stately hotels; there were so many people, and such crowding, that Rudy was obliged to offer his arm to Babette. Then he told her how happy it made him to meet people from the canton Vaud,—for Vaud and Valais were neighboring cantons. He spoke of this pleasure so heartily that Babette could not resist giving his arm a slight squeeze; and so they walked on together, and talked and chatted like old acquaintances. Rudy felt inclined to laugh sometimes at the absurd dress and walk of the foreign ladies; but Babette did not wish to make fun of them, for she knew there must be some good, excellent people amongst them; she, herself, had a godmother, who was a high-born English lady. Eighteen years before, when Babette was christened, this lady was staying at Bex, and she stood godmother for her, and gave her the valuable brooch she now wore in her bosom.

Her godmother had twice written to her, and this year she was expected to visit Interlachen with her two daughters; "but they are old-maids," added Babette, who was only eighteen: "they are nearly thirty." Her sweet little mouth was never still a moment, and all that she said sounded in Rudy's ears as matters of the greatest importance, and at last he told her what he was longing to tell. How often he had been at Bex, how well he knew the mill, and how often he had seen Babette, when most likely she had not noticed him; and lastly, that full of many thoughts which he could not tell her, he had been to the mill on the evening when she and her father has started on their long journey, but not too far for him to find a way to overtake them. He told her all this, and a great deal more; he told her how much he could endure for her; and that it was to see her, and not the shooting-match, which had brought him to Interlachen. Babette became quite silent after hearing all this; it was almost too much, and it troubled her.

And while they thus wandered on, the sun sunk behind the lofty mountains. The Jungfrau stood out in brightness and splendor, as a back-ground to the green woods of the surrounding hills. Every one stood still to look at the beautiful sight, Rudy and Babette among them.

"Nothing can be more beautiful than this," said Babette.

"Nothing!" replied Rudy, looking at Babette.

"To-morrow I must return home," remarked Rudy a few minutes afterwards.

"Come and visit us at Bex," whispered Babette; "my father will be pleased to see you."

ON THE WAY HOME

Oh, what a number of things Rudy had to carry over the mountains, when he set out to return home! He had three silver cups, two handsome pistols, and a silver coffee-pot. This latter would be useful when he began housekeeping. But all these were not the heaviest weight he had to bear; something mightier and more important he carried with him in his heart, over the high mountains, as he journeyed homeward.

The weather was dismally dark, and inclined to rain; the clouds hung low, like a mourning veil on the tops of the mountains, and shrouded their glittering peaks. In the woods could be heard the sound of the axe and the heavy fall of the trunks of the trees, as they rolled down the slopes of the mountains. When seen from the heights, the trunks of these trees looked like slender stems; but on a nearer inspection they were found to be large and strong enough for the masts of a ship. The river murmured monotonously, the wind whistled, and the clouds sailed along hurriedly.

Suddenly there appeared, close by Rudy's side, a young maiden; he had not noticed her till she came quite near to him. She was also going to ascend the mountain. The maiden's eyes shone with an unearthly power, which obliged you to look into them; they were strange eyes,—clear, deep, and unfathomable.

"Hast thou a lover?" asked Rudy; all his thoughts were naturally on love just then.

"I have none," answered the maiden, with a laugh; it was as if she had not spoken the truth.

"Do not let us go such a long way round," said she. "We must keep to the left; it is much shorter."

"Ah, yes," he replied; "and fall into some crevasse. Do you pretend to be a guide, and not know the road better than that?"

"I know every step of the way," said she; "and my thoughts are collected, while yours are down in the valley yonder. We should think of the Ice Maiden while we are up here; men say she is not kind to their race."

"I fear her not," said Rudy. "She could not keep me when I was a child; I will not give myself up to her now I am a man."

Darkness came on, the rain fell, and then it began to snow, and the whiteness dazzled the eyes.

"Give me your hand," said the maiden; "I will help you to mount." And he felt the touch of her icy fingers.

"You help me," cried Rudy; "I do not yet require a woman to help me to climb." And he stepped quickly forwards away from her.

The drifting snow-shower fell like a veil between them, the wind whistled, and behind him he could hear the maiden laughing and singing, and the sound was most strange to hear.

"It certainly must be a spectre or a servant of the Ice Maiden," thought Rudy, who had heard such things talked about when he was a little boy, and had stayed all night on the mountain with the guides.

The snow fell thicker than ever, the clouds lay beneath him; he looked back, there was no one to be seen, but he heard sounds of mocking laughter, which were not those of a human voice.

When Rudy at length reached the highest part of the mountain, where the path led down to the valley of the Rhone, the snow had ceased, and in the clear heavens he saw two bright stars twinkling. They reminded him of Babette and of himself, and of his future happiness, and his heart glowed at the thought.

THE VISIT TO THE MILL

"What beautiful things you have brought home!" said his old foster-mother; and her strange-looking eagle-eyes sparkled, while she wriggled and twisted her skinny neck more quickly and strangely than ever. "You have brought good luck with you, Rudy. I must give you a kiss, my dear boy."

Rudy allowed himself to be kissed; but it could be seen by his countenance that he only endured the infliction as a homely duty.

"How handsome you are, Rudy!" said the old woman.

"Don't flatter," said Rudy, with a laugh; but still he was pleased.

"I must say once more," said the old woman, "that you are very lucky."

"Well, in that I believe you are right," said he, as he thought of Babette. Never had he felt such a longing for that deep valley as he now had. "They must have returned home by this time," said he to himself, "it is already two days over the time which they fixed upon. I must go to Bex."

So Rudy set out to go to Bex; and when he arrived there, he found the miller and his daughter at home. They received him kindly, and brought him many greetings from their friends at Interlachen. Babette did not say much. She seemed to have become quite silent; but her eyes spoke, and that was quite enough for Rudy. The miller had generally a great deal to talk about, and seemed to expect that every one should listen to his jokes, and laugh at them; for was not he the rich miller? But now he was more inclined to hear Rudy's adventures while hunting and travelling, and to listen to his descriptions of the difficulties the chamois-hunter has to overcome on the mountain-tops, or of the dangerous snow-drifts which the wind and weather cause to cling to the edges of the rocks, or to lie in the form of a frail bridge over the abyss beneath. The eyes of the brave Rudy sparkled as he described the life of a hunter, or spoke of the cunning of the chamois and their wonderful leaps; also of the powerful fohn and the rolling avalanche. He noticed that the more he described, the more interested the miller became, especially when he spoke of the fierce vulture and of the royal eagle. Not far from Bex, in the canton Valais, was an eagle's nest, more curiously built under a high, overhanging rock. In this nest was a young eagle; but who would venture to take it? A young Englishman had offered Rudy a whole handful of gold, if he would bring him the young eagle alive.

"There is a limit to everything," was Rudy's reply. "The eagle could not be taken; it would be folly to attempt it."

The wine was passed round freely, and the conversation kept up pleasantly; but the evening seemed too short for Rudy, although it was midnight when he left the miller's house, after this his first visit.

While the lights in the windows of the miller's house still twinkled through the green foliage, out through the open skylight came the parlor-cat on to the roof, and along the water-pipe walked the kitchen-cat to meet her.

"What is the news at the mill?" asked the parlor-cat. "Here in the house there is secret love-making going on, which the father knows nothing about. Rudy and Babette have been treading on each other's paws, under the table, all the evening. They trod on my tail twice, but I did not mew; that would have attracted notice."

"Well, I should have mewed," said the kitchen-cat.

"What might suit the kitchen would not suit the parlor," said the other. "I am quite curious to know what the miller will say when he finds out this engagement."

Yes, indeed; what would the miller say? Rudy himself was anxious to know that; but to wait till the miller heard of it from others was out of the question. Therefore, not many days after this visit, he was riding in the omnibus that runs between the two cantons, Valais and Vaud. These cantons are separated by the Rhone, over which is a bridge that unites them. Rudy, as usual, had plenty of courage, and indulged in pleasant thoughts of the favorable answer he should receive that evening. And when the omnibus returned, Rudy was again seated in it, going homewards; and at the same time the parlor-cat at the miller's house ran out quickly, crying,—

"Here, you from the kitchen, what do you think? The miller knows all now. Everything has come to a delightful end. Rudy came here this evening, and he and Babette had much whispering and secret conversation together. They stood in the path near the miller's room. I lay at their feet; but they had no eyes or thoughts for me.

"'I will go to your father at once,' said he; 'it is the most honorable way.'

"'Shall I go with you?' asked Babette; 'it will give you courage.'

"'I have plenty of courage,' said Rudy; 'but if you are with me, he must be friendly, whether he says Yes or No.'

"So they turned to go in, and Rudy trod heavily on my tail; he certainly is very clumsy. I mewed; but neither he nor Babette had any ears for me. They opened the door, and entered together. I was before them, and jumped on the back of a chair. I hardly know what Rudy said; but the miller flew into a rage, and threatened to kick him out of the house. He told him he might go to the mountains, and look after the chamois, but not after our little Babette."

"And what did they say? Did they speak?" asked the kitchen-cat.

"What did they say! why, all that people generally do say when they go a-wooing—'I love her, and she loves me; and when there is milk in the can for one, there is milk in the can for two.'

"'But she is so far above you,' said the miller; 'she has heaps of gold, as you know. You should not attempt to reach her.'

"'There is nothing so high that a man cannot reach, if he will,' answered Rudy; for he is a brave youth.

"'Yet you could not reach the young eagle,' said the miller, laughing. 'Babette is higher than the eagle's nest.'

"'I will have them both,' said Rudy.

"'Very well; I will give her to you when you bring me the young eaglet alive,' said the miller; and he laughed till the tears stood in his eyes. 'But now I thank you for this visit, Rudy; and if you come to-morrow, you will find nobody at home. Good-bye, Rudy.'

"Babette also wished him farewell; but her voice sounded as mournful as the mew of a little kitten that has lost its mother.

"'A promise is a promise between man and man,' said Rudy. 'Do not weep, Babette; I shall bring the young eagle.'

"'You will break your neck, I hope,' said the miller, 'and we shall be relieved from your company.'

"I call that kicking him out of the house," said the parlor-cat. "And now Rudy is gone, and Babette sits and weeps, while the miller sings German songs that he learnt on his journey; but I do not trouble myself on the matter,—it would be of no use."

"Yet, for all that, it is a very strange affair," said the kitchen-cat.

THE EAGLE'S NEST

From the mountain-path came a joyous sound of some person whistling, and it betokened good humor and undaunted courage. It was Rudy, going to meet his friend Vesinaud. "You must come and help," said he. "I want to carry off the young eaglet from the top of the rock. We will take young Ragli with us."

"Had you not better first try to take down the moon? That would be quite as easy a task," said Vesinaud. "You seem to be in good spirits."

"Yes, indeed I am. I am thinking of my wedding. But to be serious, I will tell you all about it, and how I am situated."

Then he explained to Vesinaud and Ragli what he wished to do, and why.

"You are a daring fellow," said they; "but it is no use; you will break your neck."

"No one falls, unless he is afraid," said Rudy.

So at midnight they set out, carrying with them poles, ladders, and ropes. The road lay amidst brushwood and underwood, over rolling stones, always upwards higher and higher in the dark night. Waters roared beneath them, or fell in cascades from above. Humid clouds were driving through the air as the hunters reached the precipitous ledge of the rock. It was even darker here, for the sides of the rocks almost met, and the light penetrated only through a small opening at the top. At a little distance from the edge could be heard the sound of the roaring, foaming waters in the yawning abyss beneath them. The three seated themselves on a stone, to await in stillness the dawn of day, when the parent eagle would fly out, as it would be necessary to shoot the old bird before they could think of gaining possession of the young one. Rudy sat motionless, as if he had been part of the stone on which he sat. He held his gun ready to fire, with his eyes fixed steadily on the highest point of the cliff, where the eagle's nest lay concealed beneath the overhanging rock.

The three hunters had a long time to wait. At last they heard a rustling, whirring sound above them, and a large hovering object darkened the air. Two guns were ready to aim at the dark body of the eagle as it rose from the nest. Then a shot was fired; for an instant the bird fluttered its wide-spreading wings, and seemed as if it would fill up the whole of the chasm, and drag down the hunters in its fall. But it was not so; the eagle sunk gradually into the abyss beneath, and the branches of trees and bushes were broken by its weight. Then the hunters roused themselves: three of the longest ladders were brought and bound together; the topmost ring of these ladders would just reach the edge of the rock which hung over the abyss, but no farther. The point beneath which the eagle's nest lay sheltered was much higher, and the sides of the rock were as smooth as a wall. After consulting together, they determined to bind together two more ladders, and to hoist them over the cavity, and so form a communication with the three beneath them, by binding the upper ones to the lower. With great difficulty they contrived to drag the two ladders over the rock, and there they hung for some moments, swaying over the abyss; but no sooner had they fastened them together, than Rudy placed his foot on the lowest step.

It was a bitterly cold morning; clouds of mist were rising from beneath, and Rudy stood on the lower step of the ladder as a fly rests on a piece of swinging straw, which a bird may have dropped from the edge of the nest it was building on some tall factory chimney; but the fly could fly away if the straw were shaken, Rudy could only break his neck. The wind whistled around him, and beneath him the waters of the abyss, swelled by the thawing of the glaciers, those palaces of the Ice Maiden, foamed and roared in their rapid course. When Rudy began to ascend, the ladder trembled like the web of the spider, when it draws out the long, delicate threads; but as soon as he reached the fourth of the ladders, which had been bound together, he felt more confidence,—he knew that they had been fastened securely by skilful hands. The fifth ladder, that appeared to reach the nest, was supported by the sides of the rock, yet it swung to and fro, and flapped about like a slender reed, and as if it had been bound by fishing lines. It seemed a most dangerous undertaking to ascend it, but Rudy knew how to climb; he had learnt that from the cat, and he had no fear. He did not observe Vertigo, who stood in the air behind him, trying to lay hold of him with his outstretched polypous arms.

When at length he stood on the topmost step of the ladder, he found that he was still some distance below the nest, and not even able to see into it. Only by using his hands and climbing could he possibly reach it. He tried the strength of the stunted trees, and the thick underwood upon which the nest rested, and of which it was formed, and finding they would support his weight, he grasped them firmly, and swung himself up from the ladder till his head and breast were above the nest, and then what an overpowering stench came from it, for in it lay the putrid remains of lambs, chamois, and

HELD ON TILL HIS FOOT TOUCHED THE LADDER

birds. Vertigo, although he could not reach him, blew the poisonous vapor in his face, to make him giddy and faint; and beneath, in the dark, yawning deep, on the rushing waters, sat the Ice Maiden, with her long, pale, green hair falling around her, and her deathlike eyes fixed upon him, like the two barrels of a gun. "I have thee now," she cried.

In a corner of the eagle's nest sat the young eaglet, a large and powerful bird, though still unable to fly. Rudy fixed his eyes upon it, held on by one hand with all his strength, and with the other threw a noose round the young eagle. The string slipped to its legs. Rudy tightened it, and thus secured the bird alive. Then flinging the sling over his shoulder, so that the creature hung a good way down behind him, he prepared to descend with the help of a rope, and his foot soon touched safely the highest step of the ladder. Then Rudy, remembering his early lesson in climbing, "Hold fast, and do not fear," descended carefully down the ladders, and at last stood safely on the ground with the young living eaglet, where he was received with loud shouts of joy and congratulations.

WHAT FRESH NEWS THE PARLOR-CAT HAD TO TELL

"There is what you asked for," said Rudy, as he entered the miller's house at Bex, and placed on the floor a large basket. He removed the lid as he spoke, and a pair of yellow eyes, encircled by a black ring, stared forth with a wild, fiery glance, that seemed ready to burn and destroy all that came in its way. Its short, strong beak was open, ready to bite, and on its red throat were short feathers, like stubble.

"The young eaglet!" cried the miller.

Babette screamed, and started back, while her eyes wandered from Rudy to the bird in astonishment.

"You are not to be discouraged by difficulties, I see," said the miller.

"And you will keep your word," replied Rudy. "Each has his own characteristic, whether it is honor or courage."

"But how is it you did not break your neck?" asked the miller.

"Because I held fast," answered Rudy; "and I mean to hold fast to Babette."

"You must get her first," said the miller, laughing; and Babette thought this a very good sign.

"We must take the bird out of the basket," said she. "It is getting into a rage; how its eyes glare. How did you manage to conquer it?"

Then Rudy had to describe his adventure, and the miller's eyes opened wide as he listened.

"With your courage and your good fortune you might win three wives," said the miller.

"Oh, thank you," cried Rudy.

"But you have not won Babette yet," said the miller, slapping the young Alpine hunter on the shoulder playfully.

"Have you heard the fresh news at the mill?" asked the parlor-cat of the kitchen-cat. "Rudy has brought us the young eagle, and he is to take Babette in exchange. They kissed each other in the presence of the old man, which is as good as an engagement. He was quite civil about it; drew in his claws, and took his afternoon nap, so that the two were left to sit and wag their tails as much as they pleased. They have so much to talk about that it will not be finished till Christmas." Neither was it finished till Christmas.

The wind whirled the faded, fallen leaves; the snow drifted in the valleys, as well as upon the mountains, and the Ice Maiden sat in the stately palace which, in winter time, she generally occupied. The perpendicular rocks were covered with slippery ice, and where in summer the stream from the rocks had left a watery veil, icicles large and heavy hung from the trees, while the snow-powdered fir-trees were decorated with fantastic garlands of crystal. The Ice Maiden rode on the howling wind across the deep valleys, the country, as far as Bex, was covered with a carpet of snow, so that the Ice Maiden could follow Rudy, and see him, when he visited the mill; and while in the room at the miller's house, where he was accustomed to spend so much of his time with Babette. The wedding was to take place in the following summer, and they heard enough of it, for so many of their friends spoke of the matter.

Then came sunshine to the mill. The beautiful Alpine roses bloomed, and joyous, laughing Babette, was like the early spring, which makes all the birds sing of summer time and bridal days.

"How those two do sit and chatter together," said the parlor-cat; "I have had enough of their mewing."

THE ICE MAIDEN'S SCORN OF MANKIND

THE walnut and chestnut trees, which extend from the bridge of St. Maurice, by the river Rhone, to the shores of the lake of Geneva, were already covered with the delicate green garlands of early spring, just bursting into bloom, while the Rhone rushed wildly from its source among the green glaciers which form the ice palace of the Ice Maiden. She sometimes allows herself to be carried by the keen wind to the lofty snow-fields, where she stretches herself in the sunshine on the soft snowy-cushions. From thence she throws her far-seeing glance into the deep valley beneath, where human beings are busily moving about like ants on a stone in the sun. "Spirits of strength, as the children of the sun call you," cried the Ice Maiden, "ye are but worms! Let but a snow-ball roll, and you and your houses and your towns are crushed and swept away." And she raised her proud head, and looked around her with eyes that flashed death from their glance. From the valley came a rumbling sound; men were busily at work blasting the rocks to form tunnels, and laying down roads for the railway. "They are playing at work underground, like moles," said she. "They are digging passages beneath the earth, and the noise is like the reports of cannons. I shall throw down my palaces, for the clamor is louder than the roar of thunder." Then there ascended from the valley a thick vapor, which waved itself in the air like a fluttering veil. It rose, as a plume of feathers, from a steam engine, to which, on the lately-opened railway, a string of carriages was linked, carriage to carriage, looking like a winding serpent. The train shot past with the speed of an arrow. "They play at being masters down there, those spirits of strength!" exclaimed the Ice Maiden; "but the powers of nature are still the rulers." And she laughed and sang till her voice sounded through the valley, and people said it was the rolling of an avalanche. But the children of the sun sang in louder strains in praise of the mind of man, which can span the sea as with a yoke, can level mountains, and fill up valleys. It is the power of thought which gives man the mastery over nature.

HERE SHE SAT AND GAZED FIXEDLY DOWN

Just at this moment there came across the snow-field, where the Ice Maiden sat, a party of travellers. They had bound themselves fast to each other, so that they looked like one large body on the slippery plains of ice encircling the deep abyss.

"Worms!" exclaimed the Ice Maiden. "You, the lords of the powers of nature!" And she turned away and looked maliciously at the deep valley where the railway train was rushing by. "There they sit, these thoughts!" she exclaimed. "There they sit in their power over nature's strength. I see them all. One sits proudly apart, like a king; others sit together in a group; yonder, half of them are asleep; and when the steam dragon stops, they will get out and go their way. The thoughts go forth into the world," and she laughed.

"There goes another avalanche," said those in the valley beneath.

"It will not reach us," said two who sat together behind the steam dragon. "Two hearts and one beat," as people say. They were Rudy and Babette, and the miller was with them. "I am like the luggage," said he; "I am here as a necessary appendage."

"There sit those two," said the Ice Maiden. "Many a chamois have I crushed. Millions of Alpine roses have I snapped and broken off; not a root have I spared. I know them all, and their thoughts, those spirits of strength!" and again she laughed.

"There rolls another avalanche," said those in the valley.

THE GODMOTHER

At Montreux, one of the towns which encircle the northeast part of the lake of Geneva, lived Babette's godmother, the noble English lady, with her daughters and a young relative. They had only lately arrived, yet the miller had paid them a visit, and informed them of Babette's engagement to Rudy. The whole story of their meeting at Interlachen, and his brave adventure with the eaglet, were related to them, and they were all very much interested, and as pleased about Rudy and Babette as the miller himself. The three were invited to come to Montreux; it was but right for Babette to become acquainted with her godmother, who wished to see her very much. A steamboat started from the town of Villeneuve, at one end of the lake of Geneva, and arrived at Bernex, a little town beyond Montreux, in about half an hour. And in this boat, the miller, with his daughter and Rudy, set out to visit her godmother. They passed the coast which has been so celebrated in song. Here, under the walnut-trees, by the deep blue lake, sat Byron, and wrote his melodious verses about the prisoner confined in the gloomy castle of Chillon. Here, where Clarens, with its weeping-willows, is reflected in the clear water, wandered Rousseau, dreaming of Heloise. The river Rhone glides gently by beneath the lofty snow-capped hills of Savoy, and not far from its mouth lies a little island in the lake, so small that, seen from the shore, it looks like a ship. The surface of the island is rocky; and about a hundred years ago, a lady caused the ground to be covered with earth, in which three acacia-trees were planted, and the whole enclosed with stone walls. The acacia-trees now overshadow every part of the island. Babette was enchanted with the spot; it seemed to her the most beautiful object in the whole voyage, and she thought how much she should like to land there. But the steam-ship passed it by, and did not stop till it reached Bernex. The little party walked slowly from this place to Montreux, passing the sun-lit walls with which the vineyards of the little mountain town of Montreux are surrounded, and peasants' houses, overshadowed by fig-trees, with gardens in which grow the laurel and the cypress.

Halfway up the hill stood the boarding-house in which Babette's godmother resided. She was received most cordially; her godmother was a very friendly woman, with a round, smiling countenance. When a child, her head must have resembled one of Raphael's cherubs; it was still an angelic face, with its white locks of silvery hair. The daughters were tall, elegant, slender maidens.

The young cousin, whom they had brought with them, was dressed in white from head to foot; he had golden hair and golden whiskers, large enough to be divided amongst three gentlemen; and he began immediately to pay the greatest attention to Babette.

Richly bound books, note-paper, and drawings, lay on the large table. The balcony window stood open, and from it could be seen the beautiful wide extended lake, the water so clear and still, that the mountains of Savoy, with their villages, woods, and snow-crowned peaks, were clearly reflected in it.

Rudy, who was usually so lively and brave, did not in the least feel himself at home; he acted as if he were walking on peas, over a slippery floor. How long and wearisome the time appeared; it was like being in a treadmill. And then they went out for a walk, which was very slow and tedious. Two steps forward and one backwards had Rudy to take to keep pace with the others. They walked down to Chillon, and went over the old castle on the rocky island. They saw the implements of torture, the deadly dungeons, the rusty fetters in the rocky walls, the stone benches for those condemned to death, the trap-doors through which the unhappy creatures were hurled upon iron spikes, and impaled alive. They called looking at all these a pleasure. It certainly was the right place to visit. Byron's poetry had made it celebrated in the world. Rudy could only feel that it was a place of execution. He leaned against the stone framework of the window, and gazed down into the deep, blue water, and over to the little island with the three acacias, and wished himself there, away and free from the whole chattering party. But Babette was most unusually lively and good-tempered.

"I have been so amused," she said.

The cousin had found her quite perfect.

"He is a perfect fop," said Rudy; and this was the first time Rudy had said anything that did not please Babette.

The Englishman had made her a present of a little book, in remembrance of their visit to Chillon. It was Byron's poem, "The Prisoner of Chillon," translated into French, so that Babette could read it.

"The book may be very good," said Rudy; "but that finely combed fellow who gave it to you is not worth much."

"He looks something like a flour-sack without any flour," said the miller, laughing at his own wit. Rudy laughed, too, for so had he appeared to him.

THE COUSIN

When Rudy went a few days after to pay a visit to the mill, he found the young Englishman there. Babette was just thinking of preparing some trout to set before him. She understood well how to garnish the dish with parsley, and make it look quite tempting. Rudy thought all this quite unnecessary. What did the Englishman want there? What was he about? Why should he be entertained, and waited upon by Babette? Rudy was jealous, and that made Babette happy. It amused her to discover all the feelings of his heart; the strong points and weak ones. Love was to her as yet only a pastime, and she played with Rudy's whole heart. At the same time it must be acknowledged that her fortune, her whole life, her inmost thoughts, her best and most noble feelings in this world were all for him. Still the more gloomy he looked, the more her eyes laughed. She could almost have kissed the fair Englishman, with the golden whiskers, if by so doing she could have put Rudy in a rage, and made him run out of the house. That would have proved how much he loved her. All this was not right in Babette, but she was only nineteen years of age, and she did not reflect on what she did, neither did she think that her conduct would appear to the young Englishman as light, and not even becoming the modest and much-loved daughter of the miller.

The mill at Bex stood in the highway, which passed under the snow-clad mountains, and not far from a rapid mountain-stream, whose waters seemed to have been lashed into a foam like soap-suds. This stream, however, did not pass near enough to the mill, and therefore the mill-wheel was turned by a smaller stream which tumbled down the rocks on the opposite side, where it was opposed by a stone mill-dam, and obtained greater strength and speed, till it fell into a large basin, and from thence through a channel to the mill-wheel. This channel sometimes overflowed, and made the path so slippery that any one passing that way might easily fall in, and be carried towards the mill wheel with frightful rapidity. Such a catastrophe nearly happened to the young Englishman. He had dressed himself in white clothes, like a miller's man, and was climbing the path to the miller's house, but he had never been taught to climb, and therefore slipped, and nearly went in head-foremost. He managed, however, to scramble out with wet sleeves and bespattered trousers. Still, wet and splashed with mud, he contrived to reach Babette's window, to which he had been guided by the light that shone from it. Here he climbed the old linden-tree that stood near it, and began to imitate the voice of an owl, the only bird he could venture to mimic. Babette heard the noise, and glanced through the thin window curtain; but when she saw the man in white, and guessed who he was, her little heart beat with terror as well as anger. She quickly put out the light, felt if the fastening of the window was secure, and then left him to howl as long as he liked. How dreadful it would be, thought Babette, if Rudy were here in the house. But Rudy was not in the house. No, it was much worse, he was outside, standing just under the linden-tree. He was speaking loud, angry words. He could fight, and there might be murder! Babette opened the window in alarm, and called Rudy's name; she told him to go away, she did not wish him to remain there.

"You do not wish me to stay," cried he; "then this is an appointment you expected—this good friend whom you prefer to me. Shame on you, Babette!"

"You are detestable!" exclaimed Babette, bursting into tears. "Go away. I hate you."

"I have not deserved this," said Rudy, as he turned away, his cheeks burning, and his heart like fire.

Babette threw herself on the bed, and wept bitterly. "So much as I loved thee, Rudy, and yet thou canst think ill of me."

Thus her anger broke forth; it relieved her, however: otherwise she would have been more deeply grieved; but now she could sleep soundly, as youth only can sleep.

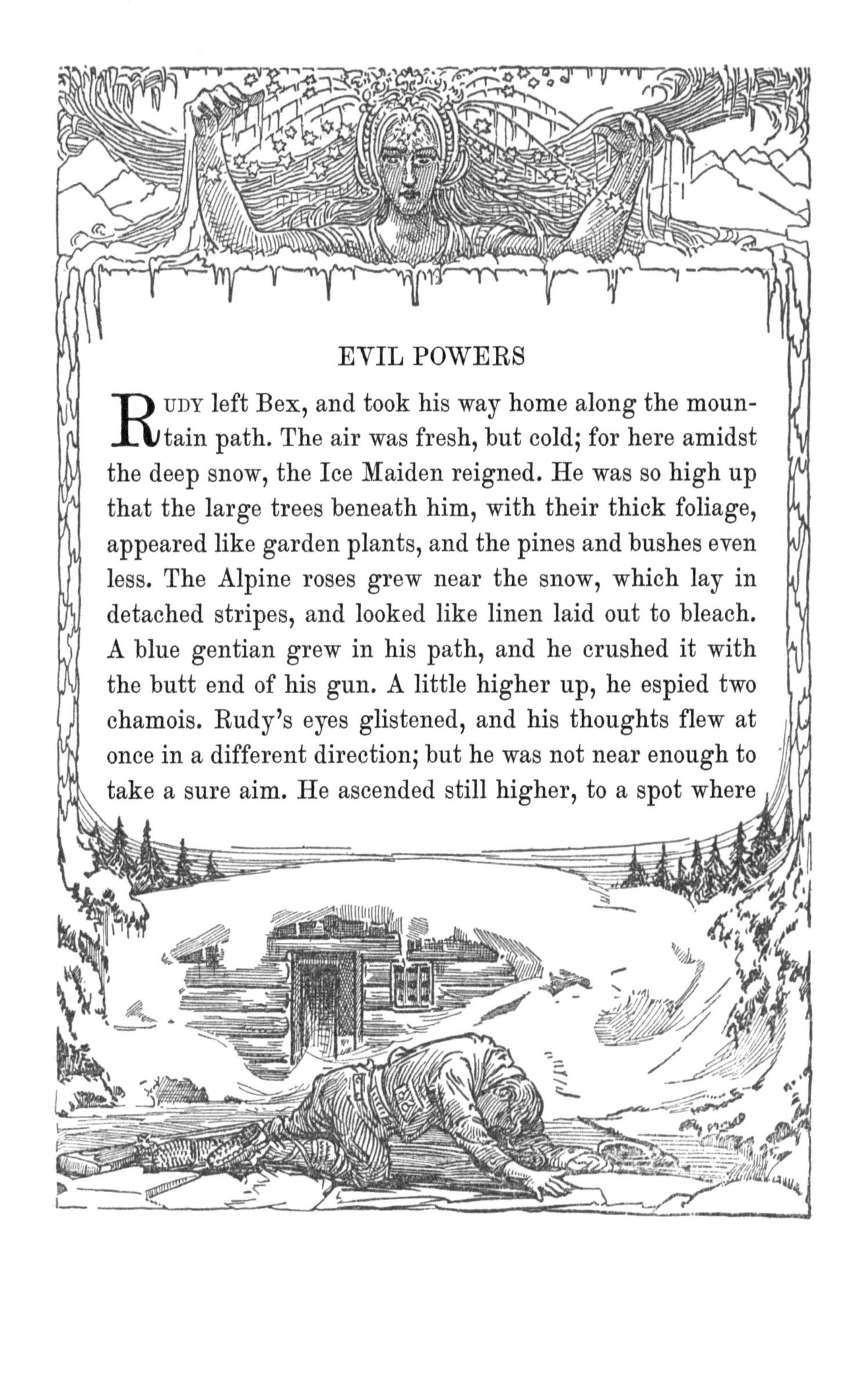

EVIL POWERS

RUDY left Bex, and took his way home along the mountain path. The air was fresh, but cold; for here amidst the deep snow, the Ice Maiden reigned. He was so high up that the large trees beneath him, with their thick foliage, appeared like garden plants, and the pines and bushes even less. The Alpine roses grew near the snow, which lay in detached stripes, and looked like linen laid out to bleach. A blue gentian grew in his path, and he crushed it with the butt end of his gun. A little higher up, he espied two chamois. Rudy's eyes glistened, and his thoughts flew at once in a different direction; but he was not near enough to take a sure aim. He ascended still higher, to a spot where a few rough blades of grass grew between the blocks of stone and the chamois passed quietly on over the snow-fields. Rudy walked hurriedly, while the clouds of mist gathered round him. Suddenly he found himself on the brink of a precipitous rock. The rain was falling in torrents. He felt a burning thirst, his head was hot, and his limbs trembled with cold. He seized his hunting-flask, but it was empty; he had not thought of filling it before ascending the mountain. He had never been ill in his life, nor ever experienced such sensations as those he now felt. He was so tired that he could scarcely resist lying down at his full length to sleep, although the ground was flooded with the rain. Yet when he tried to rouse himself a little, every object around him danced and trembled before his eyes.

Suddenly he observed in the doorway of a hut newly built under the rock, a young maiden. He did not remember having seen this hut before, yet there it stood; and he thought, at first, that the young maiden was Annette, the schoolmaster's daughter, whom he had once kissed in the dance. The maiden was not Annette; yet it seemed as if he had seen her somewhere before, perhaps near Grindelwald, on the evening of his return home from Interlachen, after the shooting-match.

"How did you come here?" he asked.

"I am at home," she replied; "I am watching my flocks."

"Your flocks!" he exclaimed; "where do they find pasture? There is nothing here but snow and rocks."

"Much you know of what grows here," she replied, laughing. "Not far beneath us there is beautiful pasture-land. My goats go there. I tend them carefully; I never miss one. What is once mine remains mine."

"You are bold," said Rudy.

"And so are you," she answered.

"Have you any milk in the house?" he asked; "if so, give me some to drink; my thirst is intolerable."

"I have something better than milk," she replied, "which I will give you. Some travellers who were here yesterday with their guide left behind them a half a flask of wine, such as you have never tasted. They will not come back to fetch it, I know, and I shall not drink it; so you shall have it."

Then the maiden went to fetch the wine, poured some into a wooden cup, and offered it to Rudy.

"How good it is!" said he; "I have never before tasted such warm, invigorating wine." And his eyes sparkled with new life; a glow diffused itself over his frame; it seemed as if every sorrow, every oppression were banished from his mind, and a fresh, free nature were stirring within him. "You are surely Annette, the schoolmaster's daughter," cried he; "will you give me a kiss?"

"Yes, if you will give me that beautiful ring which you wear on your finger."

"My betrothal ring?" he replied.

"Yes, just so," said the maiden, as she poured out some more wine, and held it to his lips. Again he drank, and a living joy streamed through every vein.

"The whole world is mine, why therefore should I grieve?" thought he. "Everything is created for our enjoyment and happiness. The stream of life is a stream of happiness; let us flow on with it to joy and felicity."

Rudy gazed on the young maiden; it was Annette, and yet it was not Annette; still less did he suppose it was the spectral phantom, whom he had met near Grindelwald. The maiden up here on the mountain was fresh as the new fallen snow, blooming as an Alpine rose, and as nimble-footed as a young kid. Still, she was one of Adam's race, like Rudy. He flung his arms round the beautiful being, and gazed into her wonderfully clear eyes,—only for a moment; but in that moment words cannot express the effect of his gaze. Was it the spirit of life or of death that overpowered him? Was he rising higher, or sinking lower and lower into the deep, deadly abyss? He knew not; but the walls of ice shone like blue-green glass; innumerable clefts yawned around him, and the water-drops tinkled like the chiming of church bells, and shone clearly as pearls in the light of a pale-blue flame. The Ice Maiden, for she it was, kissed him, and her kiss sent a chill as of ice through his whole frame. A cry of agony escaped from him; he struggled to get free, and tottered from her. For a moment all was dark before his eyes, but when he opened them again it was light, and the Alpine maiden had vanished. The powers of evil had played their game; the sheltering hut was no more to be seen. The water trickled down the naked sides of the rocks, and snow lay thickly all around. Rudy shivered with cold; he was wet through to the skin; and his ring was gone,—the betrothal ring that Babette had given him. His gun lay near him in the snow; he took it up and tried to discharge it, but it missed fire. Heavy clouds lay on the mountain clefts, like firm masses of snow. Upon one of these Vertigo sat, lurking after his powerless prey, and from beneath came a sound as if a piece of rock had fallen from the cleft, and was crushing everything that stood in its way or opposed its course.

But, at the miller's, Babette sat alone and wept. Rudy had not been to see her for six days. He who was in the wrong, and who ought to ask her forgiveness; for did she not love him with her whole heart?

AT THE MILLER'S HOUSE

"What strange creatures human beings are," said the parlor-cat to the kitchen-cat; "Babette and Rudy have fallen out with each other. She sits and cries, and he thinks no more about her."

"That does not please me to hear," said the kitchen-cat.

"Nor me either," replied the parlor-cat; "but I do not take it to heart. Babette may fall in love with the red whiskers, if she likes, but he has not been here since he tried to get on the roof."

The powers of evil carry on their game both around us and within us. Rudy knew this, and thought a great deal about it. What was it that had happened to him on the mountain? Was it really a ghostly apparition, or a fever dream? Rudy knew nothing of fever, or any other ailment. But, while he judged Babette, he began to examine his own conduct. He had allowed wild thoughts to chase each other in his heart, and a fierce tornado to break loose. Could he confess to Babette, indeed, every thought which in the hour of temptation might have led him to wrong doing? He had lost her ring, and that very loss had won him back to her. Could she expect him to confess? He felt as if his heart would break while he thought of it, and while so many memories lingered on his mind. He saw her again, as she once stood before him, a laughing, spirited child; many loving words, which she had spoken to him out of the fulness of her love, came like a ray of sunshine into his heart, and soon it was all sunshine as he thought of Babette. But she must also confess she was wrong; that she should do.

in her agony, and there, on the edge of the rock, she espied Rudy. She stretched out her arms to him, but she did not venture to call him or to pray; and had she called him, it would have been useless, for it was not Rudy, only his hunting coat and hat hanging on an alpenstock, as the hunters sometimes arrange them to deceive the chamois. "Oh!" she exclaimed in her agony; "oh, that I had died on the happiest day of my life, my wedding-day. O my God, it would have been a mercy and a blessing had Rudy travelled far away from me, and I had never known him. None know what will happen in the future." And then, in ungodly despair, she cast herself down into the deep rocky gulf. The spell was broken; a cry of terror escaped her, and she awoke.

The dream was over; it had vanished. But she knew she had dreamt something frightful about the young Englishman, yet months had passed since she had seen him or even thought of him. Was he still at Montreux, and should she meet him there on her wedding day? A slight shadow passed over her pretty mouth as she thought of this, and she knit her brows; but the smile soon returned to her lip, and joy sparkled in her eyes, for this was the morning of the day on which she and Rudy were to be married, and the sun was shining brightly. Rudy was already in the parlor when she entered it, and they very soon started for Villeneuve. Both of them were overflowing with happiness, and the miller was in the best of tempers, laughing and merry; he was a good, honest soul, and a kind father.

"Now we are masters of the house," said the parlor-cat.

THE CONCLUSION

It was early in the afternoon, and just at dinner-time, when the three joyous travellers reached Villeneuve. After dinner, the miller placed himself in the arm-chair, smoked his pipe, and had a little nap. The bridal pair went arm-in-arm out through the town and along the high road, at the foot of the wood-covered rocks, and by the deep, blue lake.

The gray walls, and the heavy clumsy-looking towers of the gloomy castle of Chillon, were reflected in the clear flood. The little island, on which grew the three acacias, lay at a short distance, looking like a bouquet rising from the lake. "How delightful it must be to live there," said Babette, who again felt the greatest wish to visit the island; and an opportunity offered to gratify her wish at once, for on the shore lay a boat, and the rope by which it was moored could be very easily loosened. They saw no one near, so they took possession of it without asking permission of any one, and Rudy could row very well. The oars divided the pliant water like the fins of a fish—that water which, with all its yielding softness, is so strong to bear and to carry, so mild and smiling when at rest, and yet so terrible in its destroying power. A white streak of foam followed in the wake of the boat, which, in a few minutes, carried them both to the little island, where they went on shore; but there was only just room enough for two to dance. Rudy swung Babette round two or three times; and then, hand-in-hand, they sat down on a little bench under the drooping acacia-tree, and looked into each other's eyes, while everything around them glowed in the rays of the setting sun.

The fir-tree forests on the mountains were covered with a purple hue like the heather bloom; and where the woods terminated, and the rocks became prominent, they looked almost transparent in the rich crimson glow of the evening sky. The surface of the lake was like a bed of pink rose-leaves.

As the evening advanced, the shadows fell upon the snow-capped mountains of Savoy painting them in colors of deep blue, while their topmost peaks glowed like red lava; and for a moment this light was reflected on the cultivated parts of the mountains, making them appear as if newly risen from the lap of earth, and giving to the snow-crested peak of the Dent du Midi the appearance of the full moon as it rises above the horizon.

Rudy and Babette felt that they had never seen the Alpine glow in such perfection before. "How very beautiful it is, and what happiness to be here!" exclaimed Babette.

"Earth has nothing more to bestow upon me," said Rudy; "an evening like this is worth a whole life. Often have I realized my good fortune, but never more than in this moment. I feel that if my existence were to end now, I should still have lived a happy life. What a glorious world this is; one day ends, and another begins even more beautiful than the last. How infinitely good God is, Babette!"

LOOKED INTO EACH OTHER'S EYES AND HELD EACH OTHER'S HANDS

"I have such complete happiness in my heart," said she.

"Earth has no more to bestow," answered Rudy. And then came the sound of the evening bells, borne upon the breeze over the mountains of Switzerland and Savoy, while still, in the golden splendor of the west, stood the dark blue mountains of Jura.

"God grant you all that is brightest and best!" exclaimed Babette.

"He will," said Rudy. "He will to-morrow. To-morrow you will be wholly mine, my own sweet wife."

"The boat!" cried Babette, suddenly. The boat in which they were to return had broken loose, and was floating away from the island.

"I will fetch it back," said Rudy; throwing off his coat and boots, he sprang into the lake, and swam with strong efforts towards it.

The dark-blue water, from the glaciers of the mountains, was icy cold and very deep. Rudy gave but one glance into the water beneath; but in that one glance he saw a gold ring rolling, glittering, and sparkling before him. His engaged ring came into his mind; but this was larger, and spread into a glittering circle, in which appeared a clear glacier. Deep chasms yawned around it, the waterdrops glittered as if lighted with blue flame, and tinkled like the chiming of church bells. In one moment he saw what would require many words to describe. Young hunters, and young maidens—men and women who had sunk in the deep chasms of the glaciers—stood before him here in lifelike forms, with eyes open and smiles on their lips; and far beneath them could be heard the chiming of the church bells of buried villages, where the villagers knelt beneath the vaulted arches of churches in which ice-blocks formed the organ pipes, and the mountain stream the music.

On the clear, transparent ground sat the Ice Maiden. She raised herself towards Rudy, and kissed his feet; and instantly a cold, deathly chill, like an electric shock, passed through his limbs. Ice or fire! It was impossible to tell, the shock was so instantaneous.

"Mine! mine!" sounded around him, and within him; "I kissed thee when thou wert a little child. I once kissed thee on the mouth, and now I have kissed thee from heel to toe; thou art wholly mine." And then he disappeared in the clear, blue water.

All was still. The church bells were silent; the last tone floated away with the last red glimmer on the evening clouds. "Thou art mine," sounded from the depths below: but from the heights above, from the eternal world, also sounded the words, "Thou art mine!" Happy was he thus to pass from life to life, from earth to heaven. A chord was loosened, and tones of sorrow burst forth. The icy kiss of death had overcome the perishable body; it was but the prelude before life's real drama could begin, the discord which was quickly lost in harmony. Do you think this a sad story? Poor Babette! for her it was unspeakable anguish.

The boat drifted farther and farther away. No one on the opposite shore knew that the betrothed pair had gone over to the little island. The clouds sunk as the evening drew on, and it became dark. Alone, in despair, she waited and trembled. The weather became fearful; flash after flash lighted up the mountains of Jura, Savoy, and Switzerland, while peals of thunder, that lasted for many minutes, rolled over her head. The lightning was so vivid that every single vine stem could be seen for a moment as distinctly as in the sunlight at noon-day; and then all was veiled in darkness. It flashed across the lake in winding, zigzag lines, lighting it up on all sides; while the echoes of the thunder grew louder and stronger. On land, the boats were all carefully drawn up on the beach, every living thing sought shelter, and at length the rain poured down in torrents.

"Where can Rudy and Babette be in this awful weather?" said the miller.

Poor Babette sat with her hands clasped, and her head bowed down, dumb with grief; she had ceased to weep and cry for help.

"In the deep water!" she said to herself; "far down he lies, as if beneath a glacier."

Deep in her heart rested the memory of what Rudy had told her of the death of his mother, and of his own recovery, even after he had been taken up as dead from the cleft in the glacier.

"Ah," she thought, "the Ice Maiden has him at last."

Suddenly there came a flash of lightning, as dazzling as the rays of the sun on the white snow. The lake rose for a moment like a shining glacier; and before Babette stood the pallid, glittering, majestic form of the Ice Maiden, and at her feet lay Rudy's corpse.

"Mine!" she cried, and again all was darkness around the heaving water.

"How cruel," murmured Babette; "why should he die just as the day of happiness drew near? Merciful God, enlighten my understanding, shed light upon my heart; for I cannot comprehend the arrangements of Thy providence, even while I bow to the decree of Thy almighty wisdom and power." And God did enlighten her heart.

A sudden flash of thought, like a ray of mercy, recalled her dream of the preceding night; all was vividly represented before her. She remembered the words and wishes she had then expressed, that what was best for her and for Rudy she might piously submit to.

"Woe is me," she said; "was the germ of sin really in my heart? was my dream a glimpse into the course of my future life, whose thread must be violently broken to rescue me from sin? Oh, miserable creature that I am!"

Thus she sat lamenting in the dark night, while through the deep stillness the last words of Rudy seemed to ring in her ears. "This earth has nothing more to bestow." Words, uttered in the fulness of joy, were again heard amid the depths of sorrow.

Years have passed since this sad event happened. The shores of the peaceful lake still smile in beauty. The vines are full of luscious grapes. Steamboats, with waving flags, pass swiftly by. Pleasure-boats, with their swelling sails, skim lightly over the watery mirror, like white butterflies. The railway is opened beyond Chillon, and goes far into the deep valley of the Rhone. At every station strangers alight with red-bound guide-books in their hands, in which they read of every place worth seeing. They visit Chillon, and observe on the lake the little island with the three acacias, and then read in their guide-book the story of the bridal pair who, in the year 1856, rowed over to it. They read that the two were missing till the next morning, when some people on the shore heard the despairing cries of the bride, and went to her assistance, and by her were told of the bridegroom's fate.

But the guide-book does not speak of Babette's quiet life afterwards with her father, not at the mill—strangers dwell there now—but in a pretty house in a row near the station. On many an evening she sits at her window, and looks out over the chestnut-trees to the snow-capped mountains on which Rudy once roamed. She looks at the Alpine glow in the evening sky, which is caused by the children of the sun retiring to rest on the mountain-tops; and again they breathe their song of the traveller whom the whirlwind could deprive of his cloak but not of his life. There is a rosy tint on the mountain snow, and there are rosy gleams in each heart in which dwells the thought, "God permits nothing to happen, which is not the best for us." But this is not often revealed to all, as it was revealed to Babette in her wonderful dream.

VI

THE LITTLE MERMAID

FAR out in the ocean, where the water is as blue as the prettiest cornflower and as clear as crystal, it is very, very deep; so deep, indeed, that no cable could sound it, and many church steeples, piled one upon another, would not reach from the ground beneath to the surface of the water above. There dwell the Sea King and his subjects.

We must not imagine that there is nothing at the bottom of the sea but bare yellow sand. No, indeed, for on this sand grow the strangest flowers and plants, the leaves and stems of which are so pliant that the slightest agitation of the water causes them to stir as if they had life. Fishes, both large and small, glide between the branches as birds fly among the trees here upon land.

In the deepest spot of all stands the castle of the Sea King. Its walls are built of coral, and the long Gothic windows are of the clearest amber. The roof is formed of shells that open and close as the water flows over them. Their appearance is very beautiful, for in each lies a glittering pearl which would be fit for the diadem of a queen.

The Sea King had been a widower for many years, and his aged mother kept house for him. She was a very sensible woman, but exceedingly proud of her high birth, and on that account wore twelve oysters on her tail, while others of high rank were only allowed to wear six.

She was, however, deserving of very great praise, especially for her care of the little sea princesses, her six granddaughters. They were beautiful children, but the youngest was the prettiest of them all. Her skin was as clear and delicate as a rose leaf, and her eyes as blue as the deepest sea; but, like all the others, she had no feet and her body ended in a fish's tail. All day long they played in the great halls of the castle or among the living flowers that grew out of the walls. The large amber windows were open, and the fish swam in, just as the swallows fly into our houses when we open the windows; only the fishes swam up to the princesses, ate out of their hands, and allowed themselves to be stroked.

Outside the castle there was a beautiful garden, in which grew bright-red and dark-blue flowers, and blossoms like flames of fire; the fruit glittered like gold, and the leaves and stems waved to and fro continually. The earth itself was the finest sand, but blue as the flame of burning sulphur. Over everything lay a peculiar blue radiance, as if the blue sky were everywhere, above and below, instead of the dark depths of the sea. In calm weather the sun could be seen, looking like a reddish-purple flower with light streaming from the calyx.

Each of the young princesses had a little plot of ground in the garden, where she might dig and plant as she pleased. One arranged her flower bed in the form of a whale; another preferred to make hers like the figure of a little mermaid; while the youngest child made hers round, like the sun, and in it grew flowers as red as his rays at sunset.

She was a strange child, quiet and thoughtful. While her sisters showed delight at the wonderful things which they obtained from the wrecks of vessels, she cared only for her pretty flowers, red like the sun, and a beautiful marble statue. It was the representation of a handsome boy, carved out of pure white stone, which had fallen to the bottom of the sea from a wreck.

She planted by the statue a rose-colored weeping willow. It grew rapidly and soon hung its fresh branches over the statue, almost down to the blue sands. The shadows had the color of violet and waved to and fro like the branches, so that it seemed as if the crown of the tree and the root were at play, trying to kiss each other.

Nothing gave her so much pleasure as to hear about the world above the sea. She made her old grandmother tell her all she knew of the ships and of the towns, the people and the animals. To her it seemed most wonderful and beautiful to hear that the flowers of the land had fragrance, while those below the sea had none; that the trees of the forest were green; and that the fishes among the trees could sing so sweetly that it was a pleasure to listen to them. Her grandmother called the birds fishes, or the little mermaid would not have understood what was meant, for she had never seen birds.

"When you have reached your fifteenth year," said the grandmother, "you will have permission to rise up out of the sea and sit on the rocks in the moonlight, while the great ships go sailing by. Then you will see both forests and towns."

In the following year, one of the sisters would be fifteen, but as each was a year younger than the other, the youngest would have to wait five years before her turn came to rise up from the bottom of the ocean to see the earth as we do. However, each promised to tell the others what she saw on her first visit and what she thought was most beautiful. Their grandmother could not tell them enough—there were so many things about which they wanted to know.

None of them longed so much for her turn to come as the youngest—she who had the longest time to wait and who was so quiet and thoughtful. Many nights she stood by the open window, looking up through the dark blue water and watching the fish as they splashed about with their fins and tails. She could see the moon and stars shining faintly, but through the water they looked larger than they do to our eyes. When something like a black cloud passed between her and them, she knew that it was either a whale swimming over her head, or a ship full of human beings who never imagined that a pretty little mermaid was standing beneath them, holding out her white hands towards the keel of their ship.

At length the eldest was fifteen and was allowed to rise to the surface of the ocean.

When she returned she had hundreds of things to talk about. But the finest thing, she said, was to lie on a sand bank in the quiet moonlit sea, near the shore, gazing at the lights of the nearby town, that twinkled like hundreds of stars, and listening to the sounds of music, the noise of carriages, the voices of human beings, and the merry pealing of the bells in the church steeples. Because she could not go near all these wonderful things, she longed for them all the more.

Oh, how eagerly did the youngest sister listen to all these descriptions! And afterwards, when she stood at the open window looking up through the dark-blue water, she thought of the great city, with all its bustle and noise, and even fancied she could hear the sound of the church bells down in the depths of the sea.

In another year the second sister received permission to rise to the surface of the water and to swim about where she pleased. She rose just as the sun was setting, and this, she said, was the most beautiful sight of all. The whole sky looked like gold, and violet and rose-colored clouds, which she could not describe, drifted across it. And more swiftly than the clouds, flew a large flock of wild swans toward the setting sun, like a long white veil across the sea. She also swam towards the sun, but it sank into the waves, and the rosy tints faded from the clouds and from the sea.

The third sister's turn followed, and she was the boldest of them all, for she swam up a broad river that emptied into the sea. On the banks she saw green hills covered with beautiful vines, and palaces and castles peeping out from amid the proud trees of the forest. She heard birds singing and felt the rays of the sun so strongly that she was obliged often to dive under the water to cool her burning face. In a narrow creek she found a large group of little human children, almost naked, sporting about in the water. She wanted to play with them, but they fled in a great fright; and then a little black animal—it was a dog, but she did not know it, for she had never seen one before—came to the water and barked at her so furiously that she became frightened and rushed back to the open sea. But she said she should never forget the beautiful forest, the green hills, and the pretty children who could swim in the water although they had no tails.

The fourth sister was more timid. She remained in the midst of the sea, but said it was quite as beautiful there as nearer the land.

She could see many miles around her, and the sky above looked like a bell of glass. She had seen the ships, but at such a great distance that they looked like sea gulls. The dolphins sported in the waves, and the great whales spouted water from their nostrils till it seemed as if a hundred fountains were playing in every direction.

The fifth sister's birthday occurred in the winter, so when her turn came she saw what the others had not seen the first time they went up. The sea looked quite green, and large icebergs were floating about, each like a pearl, she said, but larger and loftier than the churches built by men. They were of the most singular shapes and glittered like diamonds. She had seated herself on one of the largest and let the wind play with her long hair. She noticed that all the ships sailed past very rapidly, steering as far away as they could, as if they were afraid of the iceberg. Towards evening, as the sun went down, dark clouds covered the sky, the thunder rolled, and the flashes of lightning glowed red on the icebergs as they were tossed about by the heaving sea. On all the ships the sails were reefed with fear and trembling, while she sat on the floating iceberg, calmly watching the lightning as it darted its forked flashes into the sea.

Each of the sisters, when first she had permission to rise to the surface, was delighted with the new and beautiful sights. Now that they were grown-up girls and could go when they pleased, they had become quite indifferent about it. They soon wished themselves back again, and after a month had passed they said it was much more beautiful down below and pleasanter to be at home.

Yet often, in the evening hours, the five sisters would twine their arms about each other and rise to the surface together. Their voices were more charming than that of any human being, and before the approach of a storm, when they feared that a ship might be lost, they swam before the vessel, singing enchanting songs of the delights to be found in the depths of the sea and begging the voyagers not to fear if they sank to the bottom. But the sailors could not understand the song and thought it was the sighing of the storm. These things were never beautiful to them, for if the ship sank, the men were drowned and their dead bodies alone reached the palace of the Sea King.

THEY SWAM BEFORE THE SHIPS AND SANG LOVELY SONGS

When the sisters rose, arm in arm, through the water, their youngest sister would stand quite alone, looking after them, ready to cry—only, since mermaids have no tears, she suffered more acutely.

"Oh, were I but fifteen years old!" said she. "I know that I shall love the world up there, and all the people who live in it."

At last she reached her fifteenth year.

"Well, now you are grown up," said the old dowager, her grandmother. "Come, and let me adorn you like your sisters." And she placed in her hair a wreath of white lilies, of which every flower leaf was half a pearl. Then the old lady ordered eight great oysters to attach themselves to the tail of the princess to show her high rank.

"But they hurt me so," said the little mermaid.

"Yes, I know; pride must suffer pain," replied the old lady.

Oh, how gladly she would have shaken off all this grandeur and laid aside the heavy wreath! The red flowers in her own garden would have suited her much better. But she could not change herself, so she said farewell and rose as lightly as a bubble to the surface of the water.

The sun had just set when she raised her head above the waves. The clouds were tinted with crimson and gold, and through the glimmering twilight beamed the evening star in all its beauty. The sea was calm, and the air mild and fresh. A large ship with three masts lay becalmed on the water; only one sail was set, for not a breeze stirred, and the sailors sat idle on deck or amidst the rigging. There was music and song on board, and as darkness came on, a hundred colored lanterns were lighted, as if the flags of all nations waved in the air.

The little mermaid swam close to the cabin windows, and now and then, as the waves lifted her up, she could look in through glass window-panes and see a number of gayly dressed people.

Among them, and the most beautiful of all, was a young prince with large, black eyes. He was sixteen years of age, and his birthday was being celebrated with great display. The sailors were dancing on deck, and when the prince came out of the cabin, more than a hundred rockets rose in the air, making it as bright as day. The little mermaid was so startled that she dived under water, and when she again stretched out her head, it looked as if all the stars of heaven were falling around her.

She had never seen such fireworks before. Great suns spurted fire about, splendid fireflies flew into the blue air, and everything was reflected in the clear, calm sea beneath. The ship itself was so brightly illuminated that all the people, and even the smallest rope, could be distinctly seen. How handsome the young prince looked, as he pressed the hands of all his guests and smiled at them, while the music resounded through the clear night air!

It was very late, yet the little mermaid could not take her eyes from the ship or from the beautiful prince. The colored lanterns had been extinguished, no more rockets rose in the air, and the cannon had ceased firing; but the sea became restless, and a moaning, grumbling sound could be heard beneath the waves. Still the little mermaid remained by the cabin window, rocking up and down on the water, so that she could look within. After a while the sails were quickly set, and the ship went on her way. But soon the waves rose higher, heavy clouds darkened the sky, and lightning appeared in the distance. A dreadful storm was approaching. Once more the sails were furled, and the great ship pursued her flying course over the raging sea. The waves rose mountain high, as if they would overtop the mast, but the ship dived like a swan between them, then rose again on their lofty, foaming crests. To the little mermaid this was pleasant sport; but not so to the sailors. At length the ship groaned and creaked; the thick planks gave way under the lashing of the sea, as the waves broke over the deck; the mainmast snapped asunder like a reed, and as the ship lay over on her side, the water rushed in.

The little mermaid now perceived that the crew were in danger; even she was obliged to be careful, to avoid the beams and planks of the wreck which lay scattered on the water. At one moment it was pitch dark so that she could not see a single object, but when a flash of lightning came it revealed the whole scene; she could see every one who had been on board except the prince. When the ship parted, she had seen him sink into the deep waves, and she was glad, for she thought he would now be with her. Then she remembered that human beings could not live in the water, so that when he got down to her father's palace he would certainly be quite dead.

No, he must not die! So she swam about among the beams and planks which strewed the surface of the sea, forgetting that they could crush her to pieces. Diving deep under the dark waters, rising and falling with the waves, she at length managed to reach the young prince, who was fast losing the power to swim in that stormy sea. His limbs were failing him, his beautiful eyes were closed, and he would have died had not the little mermaid come to his assistance. She held his head above the water and let the waves carry them where they would.

In the morning the storm had ceased, but of the ship not a single fragment could be seen. The sun came up red and shining out of the water, and its beams brought back the hue of health to the prince's cheeks, but his eyes remained closed. The mermaid kissed his high, smooth forehead and stroked back his wet hair. He seemed to her like the marble statue in her little garden, so she kissed him again and wished that he might live.

Presently they came in sight of land, and she saw lofty blue mountains on which the white snow rested as if a flock of swans were lying upon them. Beautiful green forests were near the shore, and close by stood a large building, whether a church or a convent she could not tell. Orange and citron trees grew in the garden, and before the door stood lofty palms. The sea here formed a little bay, in which the water lay quiet and still, but very deep. She swam with the handsome prince to the beach, which was covered with fine white sand, and there she laid him in the warm sunshine, taking care to raise his head higher than his body. Then bells sounded in the large white building, and some young girls came into the garden. The little mermaid swam out farther from the shore and hid herself among some high rocks that rose out of the water. Covering her head and neck with the foam of the sea, she watched there to see what would become of the poor prince.

It was not long before she saw a young girl approach the spot where the prince lay. She seemed frightened at first, but only for a moment; then she brought a number of people, and the mermaid saw that the prince came to life again and smiled upon those who stood about him. But to her he sent no smile; he knew not that she had saved him. This made her very sorrowful, and when he was led away into the great building, she dived down into the water and returned to her father's castle.

She had always been silent and thoughtful, and now she was more so than ever. Her sisters asked her what she had seen during her first visit to the surface of the water, but she could tell them nothing. Many an evening and morning did she rise to the place where she had left the prince. She saw the fruits in the garden ripen and watched them gathered; she watched the snow on the mountain tops melt away; but never did she see the prince, and therefore she always returned home more sorrowful than before.

It was her only comfort to sit in her own little garden and fling her arm around the beautiful marble statue, which was like the prince. She gave up tending her flowers, and they grew in wild confusion over the paths, twining their long leaves and stems round the branches of the trees so that the whole place became dark and gloomy.

At length she could bear it no longer and told one of her sisters all about it. Then the others heard the secret, and very soon it became known to several mermaids, one of whom had an intimate friend who happened to know about the prince. She had also seen the festival on board ship, and she told them where the prince came from and where his palace stood.

"Come, little sister," said the other princesses. Then they entwined their arms and rose together to the surface of the water, near the spot where they knew the prince's palace stood. It was built of bright-yellow, shining stone and had long flights of marble steps, one of which reached quite down to the sea. Splendid gilded cupolas rose over the roof, and between the pillars that surrounded the whole building stood lifelike statues of marble. Through the clear crystal of the lofty windows could be seen noble rooms, with costly silk curtains and hangings of tapestry and walls covered with beautiful paintings. In the center of the largest salon a fountain threw its sparkling jets high up into the glass cupola of the ceiling, through which the sun shone in upon the water and upon the beautiful plants that grew in the basin of the fountain.

Now that the little mermaid knew where the prince lived, she spent many an evening and many a night on the water near the palace. She would swim much nearer the shore than any of the others had ventured, and once she went up the narrow channel under the marble balcony, which threw a broad shadow on the water. Here she sat and watched the young prince, who thought himself alone in the bright moonlight.

She often saw him evenings, sailing in a beautiful boat on which music sounded and flags waved. She peeped out from among the green rushes, and if the wind caught her long silvery-white veil, those who saw it believed it to be a swan, spreading out its wings.

Many a night, too, when the fishermen set their nets by the light of their torches, she heard them relate many good things about the young prince. And this made her glad that she had saved his life when he was tossed about half dead on the waves. She remembered how his head had rested on her bosom and how heartily she had kissed him, but he knew nothing of all this and could not even dream of her.

She grew more and more to like human beings and wished more and more to be able to wander about with those whose world seemed to be so much larger than her own. They could fly over the sea in ships and mount the high hills which were far above the clouds; and the lands they possessed, their woods and their fields, stretched far away beyond the reach of her sight. There was so much that she wished to know! but her sisters were unable to answer all her questions. She then went to her old grandmother, who knew all about the upper world, which she rightly called "the lands above the sea."

"If human beings are not drowned," asked the little mermaid, "can they live forever? Do they never die, as we do here in the sea?"

"Yes," replied the old lady, "they must also die, and their term of life is even shorter than ours. We sometimes live for three hundred years, but when we cease to exist here, we become only foam on the surface of the water and have not even a grave among those we love. We have not immortal souls, we shall never live again; like the green seaweed when once it has been cut off, we can never flourish more. Human beings, on the contrary, have souls which live forever, even after the body has been turned to dust. They rise up through the clear, pure air, beyond the glittering stars. As we rise out of the water and behold all the land of the earth, so do they rise to unknown and glorious regions which we shall never see."

"Why have not we immortal souls?" asked the little mermaid, mournfully. "I would gladly give all the hundreds of years that I have to live, to be a human being only for one day and to have the hope of knowing the happiness of that glorious world above the stars."

"You must not think that," said the old woman. "We believe that we are much happier and much better off than human beings."

"So I shall die," said the little mermaid, "and as the foam of the sea I shall be driven about, never again to hear the music of the waves or to see the pretty flowers or the red sun? Is there anything I can do to win an immortal soul?"

"No," said the old woman; "unless a man should love you so much that you were more to him than his father or his mother, and if all his thoughts and all his love were fixed upon you, and the priest placed his right hand in yours, and he promised to be true to you here and hereafter—then his soul would glide into your body, and you would obtain a share in the future happiness of mankind. He would give to you a soul and retain his own as well; but this can never happen. Your fish's tail, which among us is considered so beautiful, on earth is thought to be quite ugly. They do not know any better, and they think it necessary, in order to be handsome, to have two stout props, which they call legs."

Then the little mermaid sighed and looked sorrowfully at her fish's tail. "Let us be happy," said the old lady, "and dart and spring about during the three hundred years that we have to live, which is really quite long enough. After that we can rest ourselves all the better. This evening we are going to have a court ball."

It was one of those splendid sights which we can never see on earth. The walls and the ceiling of the large ballroom were of thick but transparent crystal. Many hundreds of colossal shells,—some of a deep red, others of a grass green,—with blue fire in them, stood in rows on each side. These lighted up the whole salon, and shone through the walls so that the sea was also illuminated. Innumerable fishes, great and small, swam past the crystal walls; on some of them the scales glowed with a purple brilliance, and on others shone like silver and gold. Through the halls flowed a broad stream, and in it danced the mermen and the mermaids to the music of their own sweet singing.

No one on earth has such lovely voices as they, but the little mermaid sang more sweetly than all. The whole court applauded her with hands and tails, and for a moment her heart felt quite gay, for she knew she had the sweetest voice either on earth or in the sea. But soon she thought again of the world above her; she could not forget the charming prince, nor her sorrow that she had not an immortal soul like his. She crept away silently out of her father's palace, and while everything within was gladness and song, she sat in her own little garden, sorrowful and alone. Then she heard the bugle sounding through the water and thought: "He is certainly sailing above, he in whom my wishes center and in whose hands I should like to place the happiness of my life. I will venture all for him and to win an immortal soul. While my sisters are dancing in my father's palace I will go to the sea witch, of whom I have always been so much afraid; she can give me counsel and help."

Then the little mermaid went out from her garden and took the road to the foaming whirlpools, behind which the sorceress lived. She had never been that way before. Neither flowers nor grass grew there; nothing but bare, gray, sandy ground stretched out to the whirlpool, where the water, like foaming mill wheels, seized everything that came within its reach and cast it into the fathomless deep. Through the midst of these crushing whirlpools the little mermaid was obliged to pass before she could reach the dominions of the sea witch. Then, for a long distance, the road lay across a stretch of warm, bubbling mire, called by the witch her turf moor.

Beyond this was the witch's house, which stood in the center of a strange forest, where all the trees and flowers were polypi, half animals and half plants. They looked like serpents with a hundred heads, growing out of the ground. The branches were long, slimy arms, with fingers like flexible worms, moving limb after limb from the root to the top. All that could be reached in the sea they seized upon and held fast, so that it never escaped from their clutches.

The little mermaid was so alarmed at what she saw that she stood still and her heart beat with fear. She came very near turning back, but she thought of the prince and of the human soul for which she longed, and her courage returned. She fastened her long, flowing hair round her head, so that the polypi should not lay hold of it. She crossed her hands on her bosom, and then darted forward as

ON THE WAY TO THE HOME OF THE SEA-WITCH

a fish shoots through the water, between the supple arms and fingers of the ugly polypi, which were stretched out on each side of her. She saw that they all held in their grasp something they had seized with their numerous little arms, which were as strong as iron bands. Tightly grasped in their clinging arms were white skeletons of human beings who had perished at sea and had sunk down into the deep waters; skeletons of land animals; and oars, rudders, and chests, of ships. There was even a little mermaid whom they had caught and strangled, and this seemed the most shocking of all to the little princess.

She now came to a space of marshy ground in the wood, where large, fat water snakes were rolling in the mire and showing their ugly, drab-colored bodies. In the midst of this spot stood a house, built of the bones of shipwrecked human beings. There sat the sea witch, allowing a toad to eat from her mouth just as people sometimes feed a canary with pieces of sugar. She called the ugly water snakes her little chickens and allowed them to crawl all over her bosom.

"I know what you want," said the sea witch. "It is very stupid of you, but you shall have your way, though it will bring you to sorrow, my pretty princess. You want to get rid of your fish's tail and to have two supports instead, like human beings on earth, so that the young prince may fall in love with you and so that you may have an immortal soul." And then the witch laughed so loud and so disgustingly that the toad and the snakes fell to the ground and lay there wriggling.

"You are but just in time," said the witch, "for after sunrise tomorrow I should not be able to help you till the end of another year. I will prepare a draft for you, with which you must swim to land to-morrow before sunrise; seat yourself there and drink it. Your tail will then disappear, and shrink up into what men call legs.

"You will feel great pain, as if a sword were passing through you. But all who see you will say that you are the prettiest little human being they ever saw. You will still have the same floating gracefulness of movement, and no dancer will ever tread so lightly. Every step you take, however, will be as if you were treading upon sharp knives and as if the blood must flow. If you will bear all this, I will help you."

"Yes, I will," said the little princess in a trembling voice, as she thought of the prince and the immortal soul.

"But think again," said the witch, "for when once your shape has become like a human being, you can no more be a mermaid. You will never return through the water to your sisters or to your father's palace again. And if you do not win the love of the prince, so that he is willing to forget his father and mother for your sake and to love you with his whole soul and allow the priest to join your hands that you may be man and wife, then you will never have an immortal soul. The first morning after he marries another, your heart will break and you will become foam on the crest of the waves."

"I will do it," said the little mermaid, and she became pale as death.

"But I must be paid, also," said the witch, "and it is not a trifle that I ask. You have the sweetest voice of any who dwell here in the depths of the sea, and you believe that you will be able to charm the prince with it. But this voice you must give to me. The best thing you possess will I have as the price of my costly draft, which must be mixed with my own blood so that it may be as sharp as a two-edged sword."

"But if you take away my voice," said the little mermaid, "what is left for me?"

"Your beautiful form, your graceful walk, and your expressive eyes. Surely with these you can enchain a man's heart. Well, have you lost your courage? Put out your little tongue, that I may cut it off as my payment; then you shall have the powerful draft."

"It shall be," said the little mermaid.

Then the witch placed her caldron on the fire, to prepare the magic draft.

"Cleanliness is a good thing," said she, scouring the vessel with snakes which she had tied together in a large knot. Then she pricked herself in the breast and let the black blood drop into the caldron. The steam that rose twisted itself into such horrible shapes that no one could look at them without fear. Every moment the witch threw a new ingredient into the vessel, and when it began to boil, the sound was like the weeping of a crocodile. When at last the magic draft was ready, it looked like the clearest water.

"There it is for you," said the witch. Then she cut off the mermaid's tongue, so that she would never again speak or sing. "If the polypi should seize you as you return through the wood," said the witch, "throw over them a few drops of the potion, and their fingers will be torn into a thousand pieces." But the little mermaid had no occasion to do this, for the polypi sprang back in terror when they caught sight of the glittering draft, which shone in her hand like a twinkling star.

So she passed quickly through the wood and the marsh and between the rushing whirlpools. She saw that in her father's palace the torches in the ballroom were extinguished and that all within were asleep. But she did not venture to go in to them, for now that she was dumb and going to leave them forever she felt as if her heart would break. She stole into the garden, took a flower from the flower bed of each of her sisters, kissed her hand towards the palace a thousand times, and then rose up through the dark-blue waters.

The sun had not risen when she came in sight of the prince's palace and approached the beautiful marble steps, but the moon shone clear and bright. Then the little mermaid drank the magic draft, and it seemed as if a two-edged sword went through her delicate body. She fell into a swoon and lay like one dead. When the sun rose and shone over the sea, she recovered and felt a sharp pain, but before her stood the handsome young prince.

He fixed his coal-black eyes upon her so earnestly that she cast down her own and then became aware that her fish's tail was gone and that she had as pretty a pair of white legs and tiny feet as any little maiden could have. But she had no clothes, so she wrapped herself in her long, thick hair. The prince asked her who she was and whence she came. She looked at him mildly and sorrowfully with her deep blue eyes, but could not speak. He took her by the hand and led her to the palace.

Every step she took was as the witch had said it would be; she felt as if she were treading upon the points of needles or sharp knives. She bore it willingly, however, and moved at the prince's side as lightly as a bubble, so that he and all who saw her wondered at her graceful, swaying movements. She was very soon arrayed in costly robes of silk and muslin and was the most beautiful creature in the palace; but she was dumb and could neither speak nor sing.

THE PRINCE ASKED HOW SHE CAME THERE

Beautiful female slaves, dressed in silk and gold, stepped forward and sang before the prince and his royal parents. One sang better than all the others, and the prince clapped his hands and smiled at her. This was a great sorrow to the little mermaid, for she knew how much more sweetly she herself once could sing, and she thought, "Oh, if he could only know that I have given away my voice forever, to be with him!"

The slaves next performed some pretty fairy-like dances, to the sound of beautiful music. Then the little mermaid raised her lovely white arms, stood on the tips of her toes, glided over the floor, and danced as no one yet had been able to dance. At each moment her beauty was more revealed, and her expressive eyes appealed more directly to the heart than the songs of the slaves. Every one was enchanted, especially the prince, who called her his little foundling. She danced again quite readily, to please him, though each time her foot touched the floor it seemed as if she trod on sharp knives.

The prince said she should remain with him always, and she was given permission to sleep at his door, on a velvet cushion. He had a page's dress made for her, that she might accompany him on horseback. They rode together through the sweet-scented woods, where the green boughs touched their shoulders, and the little birds sang among the fresh leaves. She climbed with him to the tops of high mountains, and although her tender feet bled so that even her steps were marked, she only smiled, and followed him till they could see the clouds beneath them like a flock of birds flying to distant lands. While at the prince's palace, and when all the household were asleep, she would go and sit on the broad marble steps, for it eased her burning feet to bathe them in the cold sea water. It was then that she thought of all those below in the deep.

Once during the night her sisters came up arm in arm, singing sorrowfully as they floated on the water. She beckoned to them, and they recognized her and told her how she had grieved them; after that, they came to the same place every night. Once she saw in the distance her old grandmother, who had not been to the surface of the sea for many years, and the old Sea King, her father, with his crown on his head. They stretched out their hands towards her, but did not venture so near the land as her sisters had.

As the days passed she loved the prince more dearly, and he loved her as one would love a little child. The thought never came to him to make her his wife. Yet unless he married her, she could not receive an immortal soul, and on the morning after his marriage with another, she would dissolve into the foam of the sea.

"Do you not love me the best of them all?" the eyes of the little mermaid seemed to say when he took her in his arms and kissed her fair forehead.

"Yes, you are dear to me," said the prince, "for you have the best heart and you are the most devoted to me. You are like a young maiden whom I once saw, but whom I shall never meet again. I was in a ship that was wrecked, and the waves cast me ashore near a holy temple where several young maidens performed the service. The youngest of them found me on the shore and saved my life. I saw her but twice, and she is the only one in the world whom I could love. But you are like her, and you have almost driven her image from my mind. She belongs to the holy temple, and good fortune has sent you to me in her stead. We will never part.

"Ah, he knows not that it was I who saved his life," thought the little mermaid. "I carried him over the sea to the wood where the temple stands; I sat beneath the foam and watched till the human beings came to help him. I saw the pretty maiden that he loves better than he loves me." The mermaid sighed deeply, but she could not weep. "He says the maiden belongs to the holy temple, therefore she will never return to the world—they will meet no more. I am by his side and see him every day. I will take care of him, and love him, and give up my life for his sake."

Very soon it was said that the prince was to marry and that the beautiful daughter of a neighboring king would be his wife, for a fine ship was being fitted out. Although the prince gave out that he intended merely to pay a visit to the king, it was generally supposed that he went to court the princess. A great company were to go with him. The little mermaid smiled and shook her head. She knew the prince's thoughts better than any of the others.

"I must travel," he had said to her; "I must see this beautiful princess. My parents desire it, but they will not oblige me to bring her home as my bride. I cannot love her, because she is not like the beautiful maiden in the temple, whom you resemble. If I were forced to choose a bride, I would choose you, my dumb foundling, with those expressive eyes." Then he kissed her rosy mouth, played with her long, waving hair, and laid his head on her heart, while she dreamed of human happiness and an immortal soul.

"You are not afraid of the sea, my dumb child, are you?" he said, as they stood on the deck of the noble ship which was to carry them to the country of the neighboring king. Then he told her of storm and of calm, of strange fishes in the deep beneath them, and of what the divers had seen there. She smiled at his descriptions, for she knew better than any one what wonders were at the bottom of the sea.

In the moonlight night, when all on board were asleep except the man at the helm, she sat on deck, gazing down through the clear water. She thought she could distinguish her father's castle, and upon it her aged grandmother, with the silver crown on her head, looking through the rushing tide at the keel of the vessel. Then her sisters came up on the waves and gazed at her mournfully, wringing their white hands. She beckoned to them, and smiled, and wanted to tell them how happy and well off she was. But the cabin boy approached, and when her sisters dived down, he thought what he saw was only the foam of the sea.

The next morning the ship sailed into the harbor of a beautiful town belonging to the king whom the prince was going to visit. The church bells were ringing, and from the high towers sounded a flourish of trumpets. Soldiers, with flying colors and glittering bayonets, lined the roads through which they passed. Every day was a festival, balls and entertainments following one another. But the princess had not yet appeared. People said that she had been brought up and educated in a religious house, where she was learning every royal virtue.

At last she came. Then the little mermaid, who was anxious to see whether she was really beautiful, was obliged to admit that she had never seen a more perfect vision of beauty. Her skin was delicately fair, and beneath her long, dark eyelashes her laughing blue eyes shone with truth and purity.

"It was you," said the prince, "who saved my life when I lay as if dead on the beach," and he folded his blushing bride in his arms.

"Oh, I am too happy!" said he to the little mermaid; "my fondest hopes are now fulfilled. You will rejoice at my happiness, for your devotion to me is great and sincere."

The little mermaid kissed his hand and felt as if her heart were already broken. His wedding morning would bring death to her, and she would change into the foam of the sea.

All the church bells rang, and the heralds rode through the town proclaiming the betrothal. Perfumed oil was burned in costly silver lamps on every altar. The priests waved the censers, while the bride and the bridegroom joined their hands and received the blessing of the bishop. The little mermaid, dressed in silk and gold, held up the bride's train; but her ears heard nothing of the festive music, and her eyes saw not the holy ceremony. She thought of the night of death which was coming to her, and of all she had lost in the world.

On the same evening the bride and bridegroom went on board the ship. Cannons were roaring, flags waving, and in the center of the ship a costly tent of purple and gold had been erected. It contained elegant sleeping couches for the bridal pair during the night. The ship, under a favorable wind, with swelling sails, glided away smoothly and lightly over the calm sea.

When it grew dark, a number of colored lamps were lighted and the sailors danced merrily on the deck. The little mermaid could not help thinking of her first rising out of the sea, when she had seen similar joyful festivities, so she too joined in the dance, poised herself in the air as a swallow when he pursues his prey, and all present cheered her wonderingly. She had never danced so gracefully before. Her tender feet felt as if cut with sharp knives, but she cared not for the pain; a sharper pang had pierced her heart.

She knew this was the last evening she should ever see the prince for whom she had forsaken her kindred and her home. She had given up her beautiful voice and suffered unheard-of pain daily for him, while he knew nothing of it. This was the last evening that she should breathe the same air with him or gaze on the starry sky and the deep sea. An eternal night, without a thought or a dream, awaited her. She had no soul, and now could never win one.

All was joy and gaiety on the ship until long after midnight. She smiled and danced with the rest, while the thought of death was in her heart. The prince kissed his beautiful bride and she played with his raven hair till they went arm in arm to rest in the sumptuous tent. Then all became still on board the ship, and only the pilot, who stood at the helm, was awake. The little mermaid leaned her white arms on the edge of the vessel and looked towards the east for the first blush of morning—for that first ray of the dawn which was to be her death. She saw her sisters rising out of the flood. They were as pale as she, but their beautiful hair no longer waved in the wind; it had been cut off.

"We have given our hair to the witch," said they, "to obtain help for you, that you may not die to-night. She has given us a knife; see, it is very sharp. Before the sun rises you must plunge it into the heart of the prince. When the warm blood falls upon your feet they will grow together again into a fish's tail, and you will once more be a mermaid and can return to us to live out your three hundred years before you are changed into the salt sea foam. Haste, then; either he or you must die before sunrise. Our old grandmother mourns so for you that her white hair is falling, as ours fell under the witch's scissors. Kill the prince, and come back. Hasten! Do you not see the first red streaks in the sky? In a few minutes the sun will rise, and you must die."

Then they sighed deeply and mournfully, and sank beneath the waves.

The little mermaid drew back the crimson curtain of the tent and beheld the fair bride, whose head was resting on the prince's breast. She bent down and kissed his noble brow, then looked at the sky, on which the rosy dawn grew brighter and brighter. She glanced at the sharp knife and again fixed her eyes on the prince, who whispered the name of his bride in his dreams.

She was in his thoughts, and the knife trembled in the hand of the little mermaid—but she flung it far from her into the waves. The water turned red where it fell, and the drops that spurted up looked like blood. She cast one more lingering, half-fainting glance at the prince, then threw herself from the ship into the sea and felt her body dissolving into foam.

The sun rose above the waves, and his warm rays fell on the cold foam of the little mermaid, who did not feel as if she were dying. She saw the bright sun, and hundreds of transparent, beautiful creatures floating around her—she could see through them the white sails of the ships and the red clouds in the sky. Their speech was melodious, but could not be heard by mortal ears—just as their bodies could not be seen by mortal eyes. The little mermaid perceived that she had a body like theirs and that she continued to rise higher and higher out of the foam. "Where am I?" asked she, and her voice sounded ethereal, like the voices of those who were with her. No earthly music could imitate it.

"Among the daughters of the air," answered one of them. "A mermaid has not an immortal soul, nor can she obtain one unless she wins the love of a human being. On the will of another hangs her eternal destiny. But the daughters of the air, although they do not possess an immortal soul, can, by their good deeds, procure one for themselves. We fly to warm countries and cool the sultry air that destroys mankind with the pestilence. We carry the perfume of the flowers to spread health and restoration.

"After we have striven for three hundred years to do all the good in our power, we receive an immortal soul and take part in the happiness of mankind. You, poor little mermaid, have tried with your whole heart to do as we are doing. You have suffered and endured, and raised yourself to the spirit world by your good deeds, and now, by striving for three hundred years in the same way, you may obtain an immortal soul."

The little mermaid lifted her glorified eyes toward the sun and, for the first time, felt them filling with tears.

On the ship in which she had left the prince there were life and noise, and she saw him and his beautiful bride searching for her. Sorrowfully they gazed at the pearly foam, as if they knew she had thrown herself into the waves. Unseen she kissed the forehead of the bride and fanned the prince, and then mounted with the other children of the air to a rosy cloud that floated above.

"After three hundred years, thus shall we float into the kingdom of heaven," said she. "And we may even get there sooner," whispered one of her companions. "Unseen we can enter the houses of men where there are children, and for every day on which we find a good child that is the joy of his parents and deserves their love, our time of probation is shortened. The child does not know, when we fly through the room, that we smile with joy at his good conduct—for we can count one year less of our three hundred years. But when we see a naughty or a wicked child we shed tears of sorrow, and for every tear a day is added to our time of trial."

VII

SOUP FROM A SAUSAGE SKEWER

I

WE HAD such an excellent dinner yesterday," said an old lady-mouse to another who had not been present at the feast. "I sat number twenty-one below the mouse-king, which was not a bad place. Shall I tell you what we had? Everything was excellent—moldy bread, tallow candle, and sausage.

"Then, when we had finished that course, the same came on all over again; it was as good as two feasts. We were very sociable, and there was as much joking and fun as if we had been all of one family circle. Nothing was left but the sausage skewers, and this formed a subject of conversation till at last some one used the expression, 'Soup from sausage sticks'; or, as the people in the neighboring country call it, 'Soup from a sausage skewer.'

"Every one had heard the expression, but no one had ever tasted the soup, much less prepared it. A capital toast was drunk to the inventor of the soup, and some one said he ought to be made a relieving officer to the poor. Was not that witty?

"Then the old mouse-king rose and promised that the young lady-mouse who should learn how best to prepare this much-admired and savory soup should be his queen, and a year and a day should be allowed for the purpose."

"That was not at all a bad proposal," said the other mouse; "but how is the soup made?"

"Ah, that is more than I can tell you. All the young lady-mice were asking the same question. They wish very much to be the queen, but they do not want to take the trouble to go out into the world to learn how to make soup, which it is absolutely necessary to do first.

"It is not every one who would care to leave her family or her happy corner by the fireside at home, even to be made queen. It is not always easy in foreign lands to find bacon and cheese rind every day, and, after all, it is not pleasant to endure hunger and perhaps be eaten alive by the cat."

Probably some such thoughts as these discouraged the majority from going out into the world to collect the required information. Only four mice gave notice that they were ready to set out on the journey.

They were young and sprightly, but poor. Each of them wished to visit one of the four divisions of the world, to see which of them would be most favored by fortune. Each took a sausage skewer as a traveler's staff and to remind her of the object of her journey.

They left home early in May, and none of them returned till the first of May in the following year, and then only three of them. Nothing was seen or heard of the fourth, although the day of decision was close at hand. "Ah, yes, there is always some trouble mingled with the greatest pleasure," said the mouse-king. But he gave orders that all the mice within a circle of many miles should be invited at once.

They were to assemble in the kitchen, and the three travelers were to stand in a row before them, and a sausage skewer covered with crape was to stand in the place of the missing mouse. No one dared express an opinion until the king spoke and desired one of them to proceed with her story. And now we shall hear what she said.

II

WHAT THE FIRST LITTLE MOUSE SAW AND HEARD ON HER TRAVELS

"When I first went out into the world," said the little mouse, "I fancied, as so many of my age do, that I already knew everything—but it was not so. It takes years to acquire great knowledge.

"I went at once to sea, in a ship bound for the north. I had been told that the ship's cook must know how to prepare every dish at sea, and it is easy enough to do that with plenty of sides of bacon, and large tubs of salt meat and musty flour. There I found plenty of delicate food but no opportunity to learn how to make soup from a sausage skewer.

"We sailed on for many days and nights; the ship rocked fearfully, and we did not escape without a wetting. As soon as we arrived at the port to which the ship was bound, I left it and went on shore at a place far towards the north. It is a wonderful thing to leave your own little corner at home, to hide yourself in a ship where there are sure to be some nice snug corners for shelter, then suddenly to find yourself thousands of miles away in a foreign land.

"I saw large, pathless forests of pine and birch trees, which smelt so strong that I sneezed and thought of sausage. There were great lakes also, which looked as black as ink at a distance but were quite clear when I came close to them. Large swans were floating upon them, and I thought at first they were only foam, they lay so still; but when I saw them walk and fly, I knew directly what they were. They belonged to the goose species. One could see that by their walk, for no one can successfully disguise his family descent.

"I kept with my own kind and associated with the forest and field mice, who, however, knew very little—especially about what I wanted to know and what had actually made me travel abroad.

"The idea that soup could be made from a sausage skewer was so startling to them that it was repeated from one to another through the whole forest. They declared that the problem would never be solved—that the thing was an impossibility. How little I thought that in this place, on the very first night, I should be initiated into the manner of its preparation!

"It was the height of summer, which the mice told me was the reason that the forest smelt so strong, and that the herbs were so fragrant, and that the lakes with the white, swimming swans were so dark and yet so clear.

"On the margin of the wood, near several houses, a pole as large as the mainmast of a ship had been erected, and from the summit hung wreaths of flowers and fluttering ribbons. It was the Maypole.

Lads and lasses danced round it and tried to outdo the violins of the musicians with their singing. They were as gay as ever at sunset and in the moonlight, but I took no part in the merrymaking. What has a little mouse to do with a Maypole dance? I sat in the soft moss and held my sausage skewer tight. The moon shone particularly bright on one spot where stood a tree covered with very fine moss. I may almost venture to say that it was as fine and soft as the fur of the mouse-king, but it was green, which is a color very agreeable to the eye.

"All at once I saw the most charming little people marching towards me. They did not reach higher than my knee, although they looked like human beings but were better proportioned. They called themselves elves, and wore clothes that were very delicate and fine, for they were made of the leaves of flowers, trimmed with the wings of flies and gnats. The effect was by no means bad.

"They seemed to be seeking something—I knew not what, till at last one of them espied me. They came towards me, and the foremost pointed to my sausage skewer, saying: 'There, that is just what we want. See, it is pointed at the top; is it not capital?' The longer he looked at my pilgrim's staff the more delighted he became.

"'I will lend it to you,' said I, 'but not to keep.'

"'Oh, no, we won't keep it!' they all cried. Then they seized the skewer, which I gave up to them, and dancing with it to the tree covered with delicate moss, set it up in the middle of the green. They wanted a Maypole, and the one they now had seemed made especially for them. This they decorated so beautifully that it was quite dazzling to look at. Little spiders spun golden threads around it, and it was hung with fluttering veils and flags, as delicately white as snow glittering in the moonlight. Then they took colors from the butterfly's wing, sprinkling them over the white drapery until it gleamed as if covered with flowers and diamonds, and I could no longer recognize my sausage skewer. Such a Maypole as this has never been seen in all the world.

"Then came a great company of real elves. Nothing could be finer than their clothes. They invited me to be present at the feast, but I was to keep at a certain distance because I was too large for them. Then began music that sounded like a thousand glass bells,

THEY INVITED MRS. MOUSE TO BE PRESENT AT THE FEAST

and was so full and strong that I thought it must be the song of the swans. I fancied also that I heard the voices of the cuckoo and the blackbird, and it seemed at last as if the whole forest sent forth glorious melodies—the voices of children, the tinkling of bells, and the songs of the birds. And all this wonderful melody came from the elfin Maypole. My sausage peg was a complete peal of bells. I could scarcely believe that so much could have been produced from it, till I remembered into what hands it had fallen. I was so much affected that I wept tears such as a little mouse can weep, but they were tears of joy.

"The night was far too short for me; there are no long nights there in summer, as we often have in this part of the world. When the morning dawned and the gentle breeze rippled the glassy mirror of the forest lake, all the delicate veils and flags fluttered away into thin air. The waving garlands of the spider's web, the hanging bridges and galleries, or whatever else they may be called, vanished away as if they had never been. Six elves brought me back my sausage skewer and at the same time asked me to make any request, which they would grant if it lay in their power. So I begged them, if they could, to tell me how to make soup from a sausage skewer.

"'How do *we* make it?' asked the chief of the elves, with a smile. 'Why, you have just seen us. You scarcely knew your sausage skewer again, I am sure.'

"'They think themselves very wise,' thought I to myself. Then I told them all about it, and why I had traveled so far, and also what promise had been made at home to the one who should discover the method of preparing this soup.

"'What good will it do the mouse-king or our whole mighty kingdom,' I asked, 'for me to have seen all these beautiful things? I cannot shake the sausage peg and say, "Look, here is the skewer, and now the soup will come." That would only produce a dish to be served when people were keeping a fast.'

"Then the elf dipped his finger into the cup of a violet and said, 'Look, I will anoint your pilgrim's staff, so that when you return to your home and enter the king's castle, you have only to touch the king with your staff and violets will spring forth, even in the coldest winter time. I think I have given you something worth carrying home, and a little more than something.'"

Before the little mouse explained what this something more was, she stretched her staff toward the king, and as it touched him the most beautiful bunch of violets sprang forth and filled the place with their perfume. The smell was so powerful that the mouse-king ordered the mice who stood nearest the chimney to thrust their tails into the fire that there might be a smell of burning, for the perfume of the violets was overpowering and not the sort of scent that every one liked.

"But what was the something more, of which you spoke just now?" asked the mouse-king.

"Why," answered the little mouse, "I think it is what they call 'effect.'" Thereupon she turned the staff round, and behold, not a single flower was to be seen on it! She now held only the naked skewer, and lifted it up as a conductor lifts his baton at a concert.

"Violets, the elf told me," continued the mouse, "are for the sight, the smell, and the touch; so we have only to produce the effect of hearing and tasting." Then, as the little mouse beat time with her staff, there came sounds of music; not such music as was heard in the forest, at the elfin feast, but such as is often heard in the kitchen—the sounds of boiling and roasting. It came quite suddenly, like wind rushing through the chimneys, and it seemed as if every pot and kettle were boiling over.

The fire shovel clattered down on the brass fender, and then, quite as suddenly, all was still,—nothing could be heard but the light, vapory song of the teakettle, which was quite wonderful to hear, for no one could rightly distinguish whether the kettle was just beginning to boil or just going to stop. And the little pot steamed, and the great pot simmered, but without any regard for each other; indeed, there seemed no sense in the pots at all. As the little mouse waved her baton still more wildly, the pots foamed and threw up bubbles and boiled over, while again the wind roared and whistled through the chimney, and at last there was such a terrible hubbub that the little mouse let her stick fall.

"That is a strange sort of soup," said the mouse-king. "Shall we not now hear about the preparation?"

"That is all," answered the little mouse, with a bow.

"That all!" said the mouse-king; "then we shall be glad to hear what information the next may have to give us."

III

WHAT THE SECOND MOUSE HAD TO TELL

"I WAS born in the library, at a castle," said the second mouse. "Very few members of our family ever had the good fortune to get into the dining room, much less into the storeroom. To-day and while on my journey are the only times I have ever seen a kitchen. We were often obliged to suffer hunger in the library, but we gained a great deal of knowledge. The rumor reached us of the royal prize offered to those who should be able to make soup from a sausage skewer.

"Then my old grandmother sought out a manuscript,—which she herself could not read, to be sure, but she had heard it read,—and in it were written these words, 'Those who are poets can make soup of sausage skewers.' She asked me if I was a poet. I told her I felt myself quite innocent of any such pretensions. Then she said I must go out and make myself a poet. I asked again what I should be required to do, for it seemed to me quite as difficult as to find out how to make soup of a sausage skewer. My grandmother had heard a great deal of reading in her day, and she told me that three principal qualifications were necessary—understanding, imagination, and feeling. 'If you can manage to acquire these three, you will be a poet, and the sausage-skewer soup will seem quite simple to you.'

"So I went forth into the world and turned my steps toward the west, that I might become a poet. Understanding is the most important matter of all. I was sure of that, for the other two qualifications are not thought much of; so I went first to seek understanding. Where was I to find it?

"'Go to the ant and learn wisdom,' said the great Jewish king. I learned this from living in a library. So I went straight on till I came to the first great ant hill. There I set myself to watch, that I might become wise. The ants are a very respectable people; they are wisdom itself. All they do is like the working of a sum in arithmetic, which comes right. 'To work, and to lay eggs,' say they, 'and to provide for posterity, is to live out your time properly.' This they truly do. They are divided into clean and dirty ants, and their rank is indicated by a number. The ant-queen is number ONE. Her opinion is the only correct one on everything, and she seems to have in her the wisdom of the whole world. This was just what I wished to acquire. She said a great deal that was no doubt very clever—yet it sounded like nonsense to me. She said the ant hill was the loftiest thing in the world, although close to the mound stood a tall tree which no one could deny was loftier, much loftier. Yet she made no mention of the tree.

"One evening an ant lost herself on this tree. She had crept up the stem, not nearly to the top but higher than any ant had ever ventured, and when at last she returned home she said that she had found something in her travels much higher than the ant hill. The rest of the ants considered this an insult to the whole community, and condemned her to wear a muzzle and live in perpetual solitude.

"A short time afterwards another ant got on the tree and made the same journey and the same discovery. But she spoke of it cautiously and indefinitely, and as she was one of the superior ants and very much respected, they believed her. And when she died they erected an egg-shell as a monument to her memory, for they cultivated a great respect for science.

"I saw," said the little mouse, "that the ants were always running to and fro with their burdens on their backs. Once I saw one of them, who had dropped her load, try very hard to raise it again, but she did not succeed. Two others came up and tried with all their strength to help her, till they nearly dropped their own burdens. Then they were obliged to stop a moment, for every one must think of himself first. The ant-queen remarked that their conduct that day showed that they possessed kind hearts and good understanding. 'These two qualities,' she continued, 'place us ants in the highest degree above all other reasonable beings. Understanding must therefore stand out prominently among us, and my wisdom is greatest.' So saying, she raised herself on her two hind legs, that no one else might be mistaken for her. I could not, therefore, have made a mistake, so I ate her up. We are to go to the ants to learn wisdom, and I had secured the queen.

"I now turned and went nearer to the lofty tree already mentioned, which was an oak. It had a tall trunk, with a wide-spreading top, and was very old. I knew that a living being dwelt here, a dryad, as she is called, who is born with the tree and dies with it. I had heard this in the library, and here was just such a tree and in it an oak maiden. She uttered a terrible scream when she caught sight of me so near to her. Like women, she was very much afraid of mice, and she had more real cause for fear than they have, for I might have gnawed through the tree on which her life depended.

"I spoke to her in a friendly manner and begged her to take courage. At last she took me up in her delicate hand, and I told her what had brought me out into the world. She told me that perhaps on that very evening she would be able to obtain for me one of the two treasures for which I was seeking. She told me that Phantæsus, the genius of the imagination, was her very dear friend; that he was as beautiful as the god of love; that he rested many an hour with her under the leafy boughs of the tree, which then rustled and waved more than ever. He called her his dryad, she said, and the tree his tree, for the grand old oak with its gnarled trunk was just to his taste. The root, which spread deep into the earth, and the top, which rose high in the fresh air, knew the value of the drifting snow, the keen wind, and the warm sunshine, as it ought to be known. 'Yes,' continued the dryad, 'the birds sing up above in the branches and talk to each other about the beautiful fields they have visited in foreign lands. On one of the withered boughs a stork has built his nest—it is beautifully arranged, and, besides, it is pleasant to hear a little about the land of the pyramids. All this pleases Phantæsus, but it is not enough for him. I am obliged to relate to him of my life in the woods and to go back to my childhood, when I was little and the tree so small and delicate that a stinging nettle could overshadow it, and I have to tell everything that has happened since then until now, when the tree is so large and strong. Sit you down now under the green bindwood and pay attention. When Phantæsus comes I will find an opportunity to lay hold of his wing and to pull out one of the little feathers. That feather you shall have. A better was never given to any poet, and it will be quite enough for you.'

"And when Phantæsus came the feather was plucked," said the little mouse, "and I seized and put it in water and kept it there till it was quite soft. It was very heavy and indigestible, but I managed to nibble it up at last. It is not so easy to nibble oneself into a poet, there are so many things to get through. Now, however, I had two of them, understanding and imagination, and through these I knew that the third was to be found in the library.

"A great man has said and written that there are novels whose sole and only use appears to be to attempt to relieve mankind of overflowing tears—a kind of sponge, in fact, for sucking up feelings and emotions. I remembered a few of these books. They had always appeared tempting to the appetite, for they had been much read and were so greasy that they must have absorbed no end of emotions in themselves.

"I retraced my steps to the library and literally devoured a whole novel—that is, properly speaking, the interior, or soft part of it. The crust, or binding, I left. When I had digested not only this, but a second, I felt a stirring within me. I then ate a small piece of a third romance and felt myself a poet. I said it to myself and told others the same. I had headache and backache and I cannot tell what aches besides. I thought over all the stories that may be said to be connected with sausage pegs; and all that has ever been written about skewers, and sticks, and staves, and splinters came to my thoughts—the ant-queen must have had a wonderfully clear understanding. I remembered the man who placed in his mouth a white stick, by which he could make himself and the stick invisible. I thought of sticks as hobbyhorses, staves of music or rime, of breaking a stick over a man's back, and of Heaven knows how many more phrases of the same sort, relating to sticks, staves, and skewers. All my thoughts ran on skewers, sticks of wood, and staves. As I am at last a poet and have worked terribly hard to make myself one, I can of course make poetry on anything. I shall therefore be able to wait upon you every day in the week with a poetical history of a skewer. And that is my soup."

"In that case," said the mouse-king, "we will hear what the third mouse has to say."

"Squeak, squeak," cried a little mouse at the kitchen door. It was the fourth, and not the third, of the four who were contending for the prize, the one whom the rest supposed to be dead. She shot in like an arrow and overturned the sausage peg that had been covered with crape. She had been running day and night, for although she had traveled in a baggage train, by railway, yet she had arrived almost too late. She pressed forward, looking very much ruffled.

She had lost her sausage skewer but not her voice, and she began to speak at once, as if they waited only for her and would hear her only—as if nothing else in the world were of the least consequence. She spoke out so clearly and plainly, and she had come in so suddenly, that no one had time to stop her or to say a word while she was speaking. This is what she said.

IV

WHAT THE FOURTH MOUSE, WHO SPOKE BEFORE THE THIRD, HAD TO TELL

"I STARTED off at once to the largest town," said she, "but the name of it has escaped me. I have a very bad memory for names. I was carried from the railway, with some goods on which duties had not been paid, to the jail, and on arriving I made my escape, running into the house of the keeper. He was speaking of his prisoners, especially of one who had uttered thoughtless words. These words had given rise to other words, and at length they were written down and registered. 'The whole affair is like making soup of sausage skewers,' said he, 'but the soup may cost him his neck.'

"Now this raised in me an interest for the prisoner," continued the little mouse, "and I watched my opportunity and slipped into his apartment, for there is a mousehole to be found behind every closed door.

"The prisoner, who had a great beard and large, sparkling eyes, looked pale. There was a lamp burning, but the walls were so black that they only looked the blacker for it. The prisoner scratched pictures and verses with white chalk on the black walls, but I did not read the verses. I think he found his confinement wearisome, so that I was a welcome guest. He enticed me with bread crumbs, with whistling, and with gentle words, and seemed so friendly towards me that by degrees I gained confidence in him and we became friends. He divided his bread and water with me and gave me cheese and sausage, and I began to love him. Altogether, I must own that it was a very pleasant intimacy. He let me run about on his hand, on his arm, into his sleeve, and even into his beard. He called me his little friend, and I forgot for what I had come out into the world; forgot my sausage skewer, which I had laid in a crack in the floor, where it is still lying. I wished to stay with him always, for I knew that if I went away, the poor prisoner would have no one to be his friend, which is a sad thing.

"I stayed, but he did not. He spoke to me so mournfully for the last time, gave me double as much bread and cheese as usual, and kissed his hand to me. Then he went away and never came back. I know nothing more of his history.

"The jailer took possession of me now. He said something about soup from a sausage skewer, but I could not trust him. He took me in his hand, certainly, but it was to place me in a cage like a tread-mill. Oh, how dreadful it was! I had to run round and round without getting any farther, and only to make everybody laugh.

"The jailer's granddaughter was a charming little thing. She had merry eyes, curly hair like the brightest gold, and such a smiling mouth.

"'You poor little mouse,' said she one day, as she peeped into my cage, 'I will set you free.' She then drew forth the iron fastening, and I sprang out on the window-sill, and from thence to the roof. Free! free! that was all I could think of, and not of the object of my journey.

"It grew dark, and as night was coming on I found a lodging in an old tower, where dwelt a watchman and an owl. I had no confidence in either of them, least of all in the owl, which is like a cat and has a great failing, for she eats mice. One may, however, be mistaken sometimes, and I was now, for this was a respectable and well-educated old owl, who knew more than the watchman and even as much as I did myself. The young owls made a great fuss about everything, but the only rough words she would say to them were, 'You had better go and try to make some soup from sausage skewers.' She was very indulgent and loving to her own children. Her conduct gave me such confidence in her that from the crack where I sat I called out 'Squeak.'

"This confidence pleased her so much that she assured me she would take me under her own protection and that not a creature should do me harm. The fact was, she wickedly meant to keep me in reserve for her own eating in the winter, when food would be scarce. Yet she was a very clever lady-owl. She explained to me that the watchman could only hoot with the horn that hung loose at his side and that he was so terribly proud of it that he imagined himself an owl in the tower, wanted to do great things, but only succeeded in small—soup from a sausage skewer.

"Then I begged the owl to give me the recipe for this soup. 'Soup from a sausage skewer,' said she, 'is only a proverb amongst mankind and may be understood in many ways. Each believes his own way the best, and, after all, the proverb signifies nothing.' 'Nothing!' I exclaimed. I was quite struck. Truth is not always agreeable, but truth is above everything else, as the old owl said. I thought over all this and saw quite plainly that if truth was really so far above everything else, it must be much more valuable than soup from a sausage skewer. So I hastened to get away, that I might be in time and bring what was highest and best and above everything—namely, the truth.

"The mice are enlightened people, and the mouse-king is above them all. He is therefore capable of making me queen for the sake of truth."

"Your truth is a falsehood," said the mouse who had not yet spoken. "I can prepare the soup, and I mean to do so."

V

HOW IT WAS PREPARED

"I did not travel," said the third mouse, "I stayed in this country; that was the right way. One gains nothing by traveling. Everything can be acquired here quite as easily, so I stayed at home. I have not obtained what I know from supernatural beings; I have neither swallowed it nor learned it from conversing with owls. I have gained it all from my own reflections and thoughts. Will you now set the kettle on the fire—so? Now pour the water in, quite full up to the brim; place it on the fire; make up a good blaze; keep it burning, that the water may boil, for it must boil over and over. There, now I throw in the skewer. Will the mouse-king be pleased now to dip his tail into the boiling water and stir it round with the tail? The longer the king stirs it the stronger the soup will become. Nothing more is necessary, only to stir it."

"Can no one else do this?" asked the king.

"No," said the mouse; "only in the tail of the mouse-king is this power contained."

And the water boiled and bubbled, as the mouse-king stood close beside the kettle. It seemed rather a dangerous performance, but he turned round and put out his tail, as mice do in a dairy when they wish to skim the cream from a pan of milk with their tails and afterwards lick it off. But the mouse-king's tail had only just touched the hot steam when he sprang away from the chimney in a great hurry, exclaiming:

"Oh, certainly, by all means, you must be my queen. We will let the soup question rest till our golden wedding, fifty years hence, so that the poor in my kingdom who are then to have plenty of food will have something to look forward to for a long time, with great joy."

And very soon the wedding took place. Many of the mice, however, as they were returning home, said that the soup could not be properly called "soup from a sausage skewer," but "soup from a mouse's tail." They acknowledged that some of the stories were very well told, but thought that the whole might have been managed differently.

VIII

THE WILD SWANS

FAR away, in the land to which the swallows fly when it is winter, dwelt a king who had eleven sons, and one daughter, named Eliza. The eleven brothers were princes, and each went to school with a star on his breast and a sword by his side. They wrote with diamond pencils on golden slates and learned their lessons so quickly and read so easily that every one knew they were princes. Their sister Eliza sat on a little stool of plate-glass and had a book full of pictures, which had cost as much as half a kingdom.

Happy, indeed, were these children; but they were not long to remain so, for their father, the king, married a queen who did not love the children, and who proved to be a wicked sorceress.

The queen began to show her unkindness the very first day. While the great festivities were taking place in the palace, the children played at receiving company; but the queen, instead of sending them the cakes and apples that were left from the feast, as was customary, gave them some sand in a teacup and told them to pretend it was something good. The next week she sent the little Eliza into the country to a peasant and his wife. Then she told the king so many untrue things about the young princes that he gave himself no more trouble about them.

"Go out into the world and look after yourselves," said the queen. "Fly like great birds without a voice." But she could not make it so bad for them as she would have liked, for they were turned into eleven beautiful wild swans.

With a strange cry, they flew through the windows of the palace, over the park, to the forest beyond. It was yet early morning when they passed the peasant's cottage where their sister lay asleep in her room. They hovered over the roof, twisting their long necks and flapping their wings, but no one heard them or saw them, so they at last flew away, high up in the clouds, and over the wide world they sped till they came to a thick, dark wood, which stretched far away to the seashore.

Poor little Eliza was alone in the peasant's room playing with a green leaf, for she had no other playthings. She pierced a hole in the leaf, and when she looked through it at the sun she seemed to see her brothers' clear eyes, and when the warm sun shone on her cheeks she thought of all the kisses they had given her.

One day passed just like another. Sometimes the winds rustled through the leaves of the rosebush and whispered to the roses, "Who can be more beautiful than you?" And the roses would shake their heads and say, "Eliza is." And when the old woman sat at the cottage door on Sunday and read her hymn book, the wind would flutter the leaves and say to the book, "Who can be more pious than you?" And then the hymn book would answer, "Eliza." And the roses and the hymn book told the truth.

When she was fifteen she returned home, but because she was so beautiful the witch-queen became full of spite and hatred toward her. Willingly would she have turned her into a swan like her brothers, but she did not dare to do so for fear of the king.

Early one morning the queen went into the bathroom; it was built of marble and had soft cushions trimmed with the most beautiful tapestry. She took three toads with her, and kissed them, saying to the first, "When Eliza comes to bathe seat yourself upon her head, that she may become as stupid as you are." To the second toad she said, "Place yourself on her forehead, that she may become as ugly as you are, and that her friends may not know her." "Rest on her heart," she whispered to the third; "then she will have evil inclinations and suffer because of them." So she put the toads into the clear water, which at once turned green. She next called Eliza and helped her undress and get into the bath.

As Eliza dipped her head under the water one of the toads sat on her hair, a second on her forehead, and a third on her breast. But she did not seem to notice them, and when she rose from the water there were three red poppies floating upon it. Had not the creatures been venomous or had they not been kissed by the witch, they would have become red roses. At all events they became flowers, because they had rested on Eliza's head and on her heart. She was too good and too innocent for sorcery to have any power over her.

When the wicked queen saw this, she rubbed Eliza's face with walnut juice, so that she was quite brown; then she tangled her beautiful hair and smeared it with disgusting ointment until it was quite impossible to recognize her.

The king was shocked, and declared she was not his daughter. No one but the watchdog and the swallows knew her, and they were only poor animals and could say nothing. Then poor Eliza wept and thought of her eleven brothers who were far away. Sorrowfully she stole from the palace and walked the whole day over fields and moors, till she came to the great forest. She knew not in what direction to go, but she was so unhappy and longed so for her brothers, who, like herself, had been driven out into the world, that she was determined to seek them.

She had been in the wood only a short time when night came on and she quite lost the path; so she laid herself down on the soft moss, offered up her evening prayer, and leaned her head against the stump of a tree. All nature was silent, and the soft, mild air fanned her forehead. The light of hundreds of glowworms shone amidst the grass and the moss like green fire, and if she touched a twig with her hand, ever so lightly, the brilliant insects fell down around her like shooting stars.

All night long she dreamed of her brothers. She thought they were all children again, playing together. She saw them writing with their diamond pencils on golden slates, while she looked at the beautiful picture book which had cost half a kingdom. They were not writing lines and letters, as they used to do, but descriptions of the noble deeds they had performed and of all that they had discovered and seen. In the picture book, too, everything was living. The birds sang, and the people came out of the book and spoke to Eliza and her brothers; but as the leaves were turned over they darted back again to their places, that all might be in order.

When she awoke, the sun was high in the heavens. She could not see it, for the lofty trees spread their branches thickly overhead, but its gleams here and there shone through the leaves like a gauzy golden mist. There was a sweet fragrance from the fresh verdure, and the birds came near and almost perched on her shoulders. She heard water rippling from a number of springs, all flowing into a lake with golden sands. Bushes grew thickly round the lake, and at one spot, where an opening had been made by a deer, Eliza went down to the water.

The lake was so clear that had not the wind rustled the branches of the trees and the bushes so that they moved, they would have seemed painted in the depths of the lake; for every leaf, whether in the shade or in the sunshine, was reflected in the water.

When Eliza saw her own face she was quite terrified at finding it so brown and ugly, but after she had wet her little hand and rubbed her eyes and forehead, the white skin gleamed forth once more; and when she had undressed and dipped herself in the fresh water, a more beautiful king's daughter could not have been found anywhere in the wide world.

As soon as she had dressed herself again and braided her long hair, she went to the bubbling spring and drank some water out of the hollow of her hand. Then she wandered far into the forest, not knowing whither she went. She thought of her brothers and of her father and mother and felt sure that God would not forsake her. It is God who makes the wild apples grow in the wood to satisfy the hungry, and He now showed her one of these trees, which was so loaded with fruit that the boughs bent beneath the weight. Here she ate her noonday meal, and then placing props under the boughs, she went into the gloomiest depths of the forest.

It was so still that she could hear the sound of her own footsteps, as well as the rustling of every withered leaf which she crushed under her feet. Not a bird was to be seen, not a sunbeam could penetrate the large, dark boughs of the trees. The lofty trunks stood so close together that when she looked before her it seemed as if she were enclosed within trelliswork. Here was such solitude as she had never known before!

The night was very dark. Not a glowworm was glittering in the moss. Sorrowfully Eliza laid herself down to sleep. After a while it seemed to her as if the branches of the trees parted over her head and the mild eyes of angels looked down upon her from heaven.

In the morning, when she awoke, she knew not whether this had really been so or whether she had dreamed it. She continued her wandering, but she had not gone far when she met an old woman who had berries in her basket and who gave her a few to eat. Eliza asked her if she had not seen eleven princes riding through the forest.

"No," replied the old woman, "but I saw yesterday eleven swans with gold crowns on their heads, swimming in the river close by." Then she led Eliza a little distance to a sloping bank, at the foot of which ran a little river. The trees on its banks stretched their long leafy branches across the water toward each other, and where they did not meet naturally the roots had torn themselves away from the ground, so that the branches might mingle their foliage as they hung over the water.

Eliza bade the old woman farewell and walked by the flowing river till she reached the shore of the open sea. And there, before her eyes, lay the glorious ocean, but not a sail appeared on its surface; not even a boat could be seen. How was she to go farther? She noticed how the countless pebbles on the shore had been smoothed and rounded by the action of the water. Glass, iron, stones, everything that lay there mingled together, had been shaped by the same power until they were as smooth as her own delicate hand.

"The water rolls on without weariness," she said, "till all that is hard becomes smooth; so will I be unwearied in my task. Thanks for your lesson, bright rolling waves; my heart tells me you will one day lead me to my dear brothers."

On the foam-covered seaweeds lay eleven white swan feathers, which she gathered and carried with her. Drops of water lay upon them; whether they were dewdrops or tears no one could say. It was lonely on the seashore, but she did not know it, for the ever-moving sea showed more changes in a few hours than the most varying lake could produce in a whole year. When a black, heavy cloud arose, it was as if the sea said, "I can look dark and angry too"; and then the wind blew, and the waves turned to white foam as they rolled. When the wind slept and the clouds glowed with the red sunset, the sea looked like a rose leaf. Sometimes it became green and sometimes white. But, however quietly it lay, the waves were always restless on the shore and rose and fell like the breast of a sleeping child.

When the sun was about to set, Eliza saw eleven white swans, with golden crowns on their heads, flying toward the land, one behind the other, like a long white ribbon. She went down the slope from the shore and hid herself behind the bushes. The swans alighted quite close to her, flapping their great white wings. As soon as the sun had disappeared under the water, the feathers of the swans fell off and eleven beautiful princes, Eliza's brothers, stood near her.

She uttered a loud cry, for, although they were very much changed, she knew them immediately. She sprang into their arms and called them each by name. Very happy the princes were to see their little sister again; they knew her, although she had grown so tall and beautiful. They laughed and wept and told each other how cruelly they had been treated by their stepmother.

"We brothers," said the eldest, "fly about as wild swans while the sun is in the sky, but as soon as it sinks behind the hills we recover our human shape. Therefore we must always be near a resting place before sunset; for if we were flying toward the clouds when we recovered our human form, we should sink deep into the sea.

"We do not dwell here, but in a land just as fair that lies far across the ocean; the way is long, and there is no island upon which we can pass the night—nothing but a little rock rising out of the sea, upon which, even crowded together, we can scarcely stand with safety. If the sea is rough, the foam dashes over us; yet we thank God for this rock. We have passed whole nights upon it, or we should never have reached our beloved fatherland, for our flight across the sea occupies two of the longest days in the year.

"We have permission to visit our home once every year and to remain eleven days. Then we fly across the forest to look once more at the palace where our father dwells and where we were born, and at the church beneath whose shade our mother lies buried. The very trees and bushes here seem related to us. The wild horses leap over the plains as we have seen them in our childhood. The charcoal burners sing the old songs to which we have danced as children. This is our fatherland, to which we are drawn by loving ties; and here we have found you, our dear little sister. Two days longer we can remain here, and then we must fly away to a beautiful land which is not our home. How can we take you with us? We have neither ship nor boat."

"How can I break this spell?" asked the sister. And they talked about it nearly the whole night, slumbering only a few hours.

Eliza was awakened by the rustling of the wings of swans soaring above her. Her brothers were again changed to swans. They flew in circles, wider and wider, till they were far away; but one of them, the youngest, remained behind and laid his head in his sister's lap, while she stroked his wings. They remained together the whole day.

Towards evening the rest came back, and as the sun went down they resumed their natural forms. "To-morrow," said one, "we shall fly away, not to return again till a whole year has passed. But we cannot leave you here. Have you courage to go with us? My arm is strong enough to carry you through the wood, and will not all our wings be strong enough to bear you over the sea?"

"Yes, take me with you," said Eliza. They spent the whole night in weaving a large, strong net of the pliant willow and rushes. On this Eliza laid herself down to sleep, and when the sun rose and her brothers again became wild swans, they took up the net with their beaks, and flew up to the clouds with their dear sister, who still slept. When the sunbeams fell on her face, one of the swans soared over her head so that his broad wings might shade her.

They were far from the land when Eliza awoke. She thought she must still be dreaming, it seemed so strange to feel herself being carried high in the air over the sea. By her side lay a branch full of beautiful ripe berries and a bundle of sweet-tasting roots; the youngest of her brothers had gathered them and placed them there. She smiled her thanks to him; she knew it was the same one that was hovering over her to shade her with his wings. They were now so high that a large ship beneath them looked like a white sea gull skimming the waves. A great cloud floating behind them appeared like a vast mountain, and upon it Eliza saw her own shadow and those of the eleven swans, like gigantic flying things. Altogether it formed a more beautiful picture than she had ever before seen; but as the sun rose higher and the clouds were left behind, the picture vanished.

SHE SAW THE LITTLE ROCK BENEATH HER

Onward the whole day they flew through the air like winged arrows, yet more slowly than usual, for they had their sister to carry. The weather grew threatening, and Eliza watched the sinking sun with great anxiety, for the little rock in the ocean was not yet in sight. It seemed to her as if the swans were exerting themselves to the utmost. Alas! she was the cause of their not advancing more quickly. When the sun set they would change to men, fall into the sea, and be drowned.

Then she offered a prayer from her inmost heart, but still no rock appeared. Dark clouds came nearer, the gusts of wind told of the coming storm, while from a thick, heavy mass of clouds the lightning burst forth, flash after flash. The sun had reached the edge of the sea, when the swans darted down so swiftly that Eliza's heart trembled; she believed they were falling, but they again soared onward.

Presently, and by this time the sun was half hidden by the waves, she caught sight of the rock just below them. It did not look larger than a seal's head thrust out of the water. The sun sank so rapidly that at the moment their feet touched the rock it shone only like a star, and at last disappeared like the dying spark in a piece of burnt paper. Her brothers stood close around her with arms linked together, for there was not the smallest space to spare. The sea dashed against the rock and covered them with spray. The heavens were lighted up with continual flashes, and thunder rolled from the clouds. But the sister and brothers stood holding each other's hands, and singing hymns.

In the early dawn the air became calm and still, and at sunrise the swans flew away from the rock, bearing their sister with them. The sea was still rough, and from their great height the white foam on the dark-green waves looked like millions of swans swimming on the water. As the sun rose higher, Eliza saw before her, floating in the air, a range of mountains with shining masses of ice on their summits. In the center rose a castle that seemed a mile long, with rows of columns rising one above another, while around it palm trees waved and flowers as large as mill wheels bloomed. She asked if this was the land to which they were hastening. The swans shook their heads, for what she beheld were the beautiful, ever-changing cloud-palaces of the Fata Morgana, into which no mortal can enter.

Eliza was still gazing at the scene, when mountains, forests, and castles melted away, and twenty stately churches rose in their stead, with high towers and pointed Gothic windows. She even fancied she could hear the tones of the organ, but it was the music of the murmuring sea. As they drew nearer to the churches, these too were changed and became a fleet of ships, which seemed to be sailing beneath her; but when she looked again she saw only a sea mist gliding over the ocean.

One scene melted into another, until at last she saw the real land to which they were bound, with its blue mountains, its cedar forests, and its cities and palaces. Long before the sun went down she was sitting on a rock in front of a large cave, the floor of which was overgrown with delicate green creeping plants, like an embroidered carpet.

"Now we shall expect to hear what you dream of to-night," said the youngest brother, as he showed his sister her bedroom.

"Heaven grant that I may dream how to release you!" she replied. And this thought took such hold upon her mind that she prayed earnestly to God for help, and even in her sleep she continued to pray. Then it seemed to her that she was flying high in the air toward the cloudy palace of the Fata Morgana, and that a fairy came out to meet her, radiant and beautiful, yet much like the old woman who had given her berries in the wood, and who had told her of the swans with golden crowns on their heads.

"Your brothers can be released," said she, "if you only have courage and perseverance. Water is softer than your own delicate hands, and yet it polishes and shapes stones. But it feels no pain such as your fingers will feel; it has no soul and cannot suffer such agony and torment as you will have to endure. Do you see the stinging nettle which I hold in my hand? Quantities of the same sort grow round the cave in which you sleep, but only these, and those that grow on the graves of a churchyard, will be of any use to you. These you must gather, even while they burn blisters on your hands. Break them to pieces with your hands and feet, and they will become flax, from which you must spin and weave eleven coats with long sleeves; if these are then thrown over the eleven swans, the spell will be broken. But remember well, that from the moment you commence your task until it is finished, even though it occupy years of your life, you must not speak. The first word you utter will pierce the hearts of your brothers like a deadly dagger. Their lives hang upon your tongue. Remember all that I have told you."

And as she finished speaking, she touched Eliza's hand lightly with the nettle, and a pain as of burning fire awoke her.

It was broad daylight, and near her lay a nettle like the one she had seen in her dream. She fell on her knees and offered thanks to God. Then she went forth from the cave to begin work with her delicate hands. She groped in amongst the ugly nettles, which burned great blisters on her hands and arms, but she determined to bear the pain gladly if she could only release her dear brothers. So she bruised the nettles with her bare feet and spun the flax.

At sunset her brothers returned, and were much frightened when she did not speak. They believed her to be under the spell of some new sorcery, but when they saw her hands they understood what she was doing in their behalf. The youngest brother wept, and where his tears touched her the pain ceased and the burning blisters vanished. Eliza kept to her work all night, for she could not rest till she had released her brothers. During the whole of the following day, while her brothers were absent, she sat in solitude, but never before had the time flown so quickly.

One coat was already finished and she had begun the second, when she heard a huntsman's horn and was struck with fear. As the sound came nearer and nearer, she also heard dogs barking, and fled with terror into the cave. She hastily bound together the nettles she had gathered, and sat upon them. In a moment there came bounding toward her out of the ravine a great dog, and then another and another; they ran back and forth barking furiously, until in a few minutes all the huntsmen stood before the cave. The handsomest of them was the king of the country, who, when he saw the beautiful maiden, advanced toward her, saying, "How did you come here, my sweet child?"

Eliza shook her head. She dared not speak, for it would cost her brothers their deliverance and their lives. And she hid her hands under her apron, so that the king might not see how she was suffering.

"Come with me," he said; "here you cannot remain. If you are as

ARM IN ARM STOOD THE BROTHERS AROUND HER

good as you are beautiful, I will dress you in silk and velvet, I will place a golden crown on your head, and you shall rule and make your home in my richest castle." Then he lifted her onto his horse. She wept and wrung her hands, but the king said: "I wish only your happiness. A time will come when you will thank me for this."

He galloped away over the mountains, holding her before him on his horse, and the hunters followed behind them. As the sun went down they approached a fair, royal city, with churches and cupolas. On arriving at the castle, the king led her into marble halls, where large fountains played and where the walls and the ceilings were covered with rich paintings. But she had no eyes for all these glorious sights; she could only mourn and weep. Patiently she allowed the women to array her in royal robes, to weave pearls in her hair, and to draw soft gloves over her blistered fingers. As she stood arrayed in her rich dress, she looked so dazzlingly beautiful that the court bowed low in her presence.

Then the king declared his intention of making her his bride, but the archbishop shook his head and whispered that the fair young maiden was only a witch, who had blinded the king's eyes and ensnared his heart. The king would not listen to him, however, and ordered the music to sound, the daintiest dishes to be served, and the loveliest maidens to dance before them.

Afterwards he led her through fragrant gardens and lofty halls, but not a smile appeared on her lips or sparkled in her eyes. She looked the very picture of grief. Then the king opened the door of a little chamber in which she was to sleep. It was adorned with rich green tapestry and resembled the cave in which he had found her. On the floor lay the bundle of flax which she had spun from the nettles, and under the ceiling hung the coat she had made. These things had been brought away from the cave as curiosities, by one of the huntsmen.

"Here you can dream yourself back again in the old home in the cave," said the king; "here is the work with which you employed yourself. It will amuse you now, in the midst of all this splendor, to think of that time."

When Eliza saw all these things which lay so near her heart, a smile played around her mouth, and the crimson blood rushed to her cheeks. The thought of her brothers and their release made her so joyful that she kissed the king's hand. Then he pressed her to his heart.

Very soon the joyous church bells announced the marriage feast; the beautiful dumb girl of the woods was to be made queen of the country. A single word would cost her brothers their lives, but she loved the kind, handsome king, who did everything to make her happy, more and more each day; she loved him with her whole heart, and her eyes beamed with the love she dared not speak. Oh! if she could only confide in him and tell him of her grief. But dumb she must remain till her task was finished.

Therefore at night she crept away into her little chamber which had been decked out to look like the cave and quickly wove one coat after another. But when she began the seventh, she found she had no more flax. She knew that the nettles she wanted to use grew in the churchyard and that she must pluck them herself. How should she get out there? "Oh, what is the pain in my fingers to the torment which my heart endures?" thought she. "I must venture; I shall not be denied help from heaven."

Then with a trembling heart, as if she were about to perform a wicked deed, Eliza crept into the garden in the broad moonlight, and passed through the narrow walks and the deserted streets till she reached the churchyard. She prayed silently, gathered the burning nettles, and carried them home with her to the castle.

One person only had seen her, and that was the archbishop—he was awake while others slept. Now he felt sure that his suspicions were correct; all was not right with the queen; she was a witch and had bewitched the king and all the people. Secretly he told the king what he had seen and what he feared, and as the hard words came from his tongue, the carved images of the saints shook their heads as if they would say, "It is not so; Eliza is innocent."

But the archbishop interpreted it in another way; he believed that they witnessed against her and were shaking their heads at her wickedness. Two tears rolled down the king's cheeks. He went home with doubt in his heart, and at night pretended to sleep. But no real sleep came to his eyes, for every night he saw Eliza get up and disappear from her chamber. Day by day his brow became darker, and Eliza saw it, and although she did not understand the reason, it alarmed her and made her heart tremble for her brothers. Her hot tears glittered like pearls on the regal velvet and diamonds, while all who saw her were wishing they could be queen.

In the meantime she had almost finished her task; only one of her brothers' coats was wanting, but she had no flax left and not a single nettle. Once more only, and for the last time, must she venture to the churchyard and pluck a few handfuls. She went, and the king and the archbishop followed her. The king turned away his head and said, "The people must condemn her." Quickly she was condemned to suffer death by fire.

Away from the gorgeous regal halls she was led to a dark, dreary cell, where the wind whistled through the iron bars. Instead of the velvet and silk dresses, they gave her the ten coats which she had woven, to cover her, and the bundle of nettles for a pillow. But they could have given her nothing that would have pleased her more. She continued her task with joy and prayed for help, while the street boys sang jeering songs about her and not a soul comforted her with a kind word.

Toward evening she heard at the grating the flutter of a swan's wing; it was her youngest brother. He had found his sister, and she sobbed for joy, although she knew that probably this was the last night she had to live. Still, she had hope, for her task was almost finished and her brothers were come.

Then the archbishop arrived, to be with her during her last hours as he had promised the king. She shook her head and begged him, by looks and gestures, not to stay; for in this night she knew she must finish her task, otherwise all her pain and tears and sleepless nights would have been suffered in vain. The archbishop withdrew, uttering bitter words against her, but she knew that she was innocent and diligently continued her work.

Little mice ran about the floor, dragging the nettles to her feet, to help as much as they could; and a thrush, sitting outside the grating of the window, sang to her the whole night long as sweetly as possible, to keep up her spirits.

It was still twilight, and at least an hour before sunrise, when the eleven brothers stood at the castle gate and demanded to be brought

"HOW DID YOU COME HITHER, YOU DELIGHTFUL CHILD?"

before the king. They were told it could not be; it was yet night; the king slept and could not be disturbed. They threatened, they entreated, until the guard appeared, and even the king himself, inquiring what all the noise meant. At this moment the sun rose, and the eleven brothers were seen no more, but eleven wild swans flew away over the castle.

Now all the people came streaming forth from the gates of the city to see the witch burned. An old horse drew the cart on which she sat. They had dressed her in a garment of coarse sackcloth. Her lovely hair hung loose on her shoulders, her cheeks were deadly pale, her lips moved silently while her fingers still worked at the green flax. Even on the way to death she would not give up her task. The ten finished coats lay at her feet; she was working hard at the eleventh, while the mob jeered her and said: "See the witch; how she mutters! She has no hymn book in her hand; she sits there with her ugly sorcery. Let us tear it into a thousand pieces."

They pressed toward her, and doubtless would have destroyed the coats had not, at that moment, eleven wild swans flown over her and alighted on the cart. They flapped their large wings, and the crowd drew back in alarm.

"It is a sign from Heaven that she is innocent," whispered many of them; but they did not venture to say it aloud.

As the executioner seized her by the hand to lift her out of the cart, she hastily threw the eleven coats over the eleven swans, and they immediately became eleven handsome princes; but the youngest had a swan's wing instead of an arm, for she had not been able to finish the last sleeve of the coat.

"Now I may speak," she exclaimed. "I am innocent."

Then the people, who saw what had happened, bowed to her as before a saint; but she sank unconscious in her brothers' arms, overcome with suspense, anguish, and pain.

"Yes, she is innocent," said the eldest brother, and related all that had taken place. While he spoke, there rose in the air a fragrance as from millions of roses. Every piece of fagot in the pile made to burn her had taken root, and threw out branches until the whole appeared like a thick hedge, large and high, covered with roses; while above all bloomed a white, shining flower that glittered like a star. This flower the king plucked, and when he placed it in Eliza's bosom she awoke from her swoon with peace and happiness in her heart. Then all the church bells rang of themselves, and the birds came in great flocks. And a marriage procession, such as no king had ever before seen, returned to the castle.

IX

THE CONSTANT TIN SOLDIER

THERE were once five-and-twenty tin soldiers, who were all brothers, for they had been made out of the same old tin spoon. They shouldered arms and looked straight before them, and wore a splendid uniform, red and blue. The first thing in the world they ever heard were the words, "Tin soldiers!" uttered by a little boy, who clapped his hands with delight when the lid of the box, in which they lay, was taken off. They were given him for a birthday present, and he stood at the table to set them up. The soldiers were all exactly alike, excepting one, who had only one leg; he had been left to the last, and then there was not enough of the melted tin to finish him, so they made him to stand firmly on one leg, and this caused him to be very remarkable. The table on which the tin soldiers stood, was covered with other playthings, but the most attractive to the eye was a pretty little paper castle. Through the small windows the rooms could be seen. In front of the castle a number of little trees surrounded a piece of looking-glass, which was intended to represent a transparent lake. Swans, made of wax, swam on the lake, and were reflected in it. All this was very pretty, but the prettiest of all was a tiny little lady, who stood at the open door of the castle; she, also, was made of paper, and she wore a dress of clear muslin, with a narrow blue ribbon over her shoulders just like a scarf. In front of these was fixed a glittering tinsel rose, as large as her whole face. The little lady was a dancer, and she stretched out both her arms, and raised one of her legs so high, that the tin soldier could not see it at all, and he thought that she, like himself, had only one leg. "That is the wife for me," he thought; "but she is too grand, and lives in a castle, while I have only a box to live in, five-and-twenty of us altogether, that is no place for her. Still I must try and make her acquaintance." Then he laid himself at full length on the table behind a snuff-box that stood upon it, so that he could peep at the little delicate lady, who continued to stand on one leg without losing her balance. When evening came, the other tin soldiers were all placed in the box, and the people of the house went to bed. Then the playthings began to have their own games together, to pay visits, to have sham fights, and to give balls. The tin soldiers rattled in their box; they wanted to get out and join the amusements, but they could not open the lid. The nut-crackers played at leap-frog, and the pencil jumped about the table. There was such a noise that the canary woke up and began to talk, and in poetry too. Only the tin soldier and the dancer remained in their places. She stood on tiptoe, with her legs stretched out, as firmly as he did on his one leg. He never took his eyes from her for even a moment. The clock struck twelve, and, with a bounce, up sprang the lid of the snuff-box; but, instead of snuff, there jumped up a little black goblin; for the snuff-box was a toy puzzle.

"Tin soldier," said the goblin, "don't wish for what does not belong to you."

But the tin soldier pretended not to hear.

"Very well; wait till to-morrow, then," said the goblin.

When the children came in the next morning, they placed the tin soldier in the window. Now, whether it was the goblin who did it, or the draught, is not known, but the window flew open, and out fell the tin soldier, heels over head, from the third story, into the street beneath. It was a terrible fall; for he came head downwards, his helmet and his bayonet stuck in between the flagstones, and his one leg up in the air. The servant maid and the little boy went down stairs directly to look for him; but he was nowhere to be seen, although once they nearly trod upon him. If he had called out, "Here I am," it would have been all right, but he was too proud to cry out for help while he wore a uniform.

Presently it began to rain, and the drops fell faster and faster, till there was a heavy shower. When it was over, two boys happened to pass by, and one of them said, "Look, there is a tin soldier. He ought to have a boat to sail in."

So they made a boat out of a newspaper, and placed the tin soldier in it, and sent him sailing down the gutter, while the two boys ran by the side of it, and clapped their hands. Good gracious, what large waves arose in that gutter! and how fast the stream rolled on! for the rain had been very heavy. The paper boat rocked up and down, and turned itself round sometimes so quickly that the tin soldier trembled; yet he remained firm; his countenance did not change; he looked straight before him, and shouldered his musket. Suddenly the boat shot under a bridge which formed a part of a drain, and then it was as dark as the tin soldier's box.

"Where am I going now?" thought he. "This is the black goblin's fault, I am sure. Ah, well, if the little lady were only here with me in the boat, I should not care for any darkness."

Suddenly there appeared a great water-rat, who lived in the drain.

"Have you a passport?" asked the rat, "give it to me at once." But the tin soldier remained silent and held his musket tighter than ever. The boat sailed on and the rat followed it. How he did gnash his teeth and cry out to the bits of wood and straw, "Stop him, stop him; he has not paid toll, and has not shown his pass." But the stream rushed on stronger and stronger. The tin soldier could already see daylight shining where the arch ended. Then he heard a roaring sound quite terrible enough to frighten the bravest man. At the end of the tunnel the drain fell into a large canal over a steep place, which made it as dangerous for him as a waterfall would be to us. He was too close to it to stop, so the boat rushed on, and the poor tin soldier could only hold himself as stiffly as possible, without moving an eyelid, to show that he was not afraid. The boat whirled round three or four times, and then filled with water to the very edge; nothing could save it from sinking. He now stood up to his neck in water, while deeper and deeper sank the boat, and the paper became soft and loose with the wet, till at last the water closed over the soldier's head. He thought of the elegant little dancer whom he should never see again, and the words of the song sounded in his ears—

"Farewell, warrior! ever brave,
Drifting onward to thy grave."

Then the paper boat fell to pieces, and the soldier sank into the water and immediately afterwards was swallowed up by a great fish. Oh how dark it was inside the fish! A great deal darker than in the tunnel, and narrower too, but the tin soldier continued firm, and lay at full length shouldering his musket. The fish swam to and fro, making the most wonderful movements, but at last he became quite still. After a while, a flash of lightning seemed to pass through him, and then the daylight approached, and a voice cried out, "I declare here is the tin soldier." The fish had been caught, taken to the market and sold to the cook, who took him into the kitchen and cut him open with a large knife. She picked up the soldier and held him by the waist between her finger and thumb, and carried him into the room. They were all anxious to see this wonderful soldier who had travelled about inside a fish; but he was not at all proud. They placed him on the table, and—how many curious things do happen in the world!—there he was in the very same room from the window of which he had fallen, there were the same children, the same playthings, standing on the table, and the pretty castle with the elegant little dancer at the door; she still balanced herself on one leg, and held up the other, so she was as firm as himself. It touched the tin soldier so much to see her that he almost wept tin tears, but he kept them back. He only looked at her and they both remained silent. Presently one of the little boys took up the tin soldier, and threw him into the stove. He had no reason for doing so, therefore it must have been the fault of the black goblin who lived in the snuff-box. The flames lighted up the tin soldier, as he stood, the heat was very terrible, but whether it proceeded from the real fire or from the fire of love he could not tell. Then he could see that the bright colors were faded from his uniform, but whether they had been washed off during his journey or from the effects of his sorrow, no one could say. He looked at the little lady, and she looked at him.

He felt himself melting away, but he still remained firm with his gun on his shoulder. Suddenly the door of the room flew open and the draught of air caught up the little dancer, she fluttered like a sylph right into the stove by the side of the tin soldier, and was instantly in flames and was gone. The tin soldier melted down into a lump, and the next morning, when the maid servant took the ashes out of the stove, she found him in the shape of a little tin heart. But of the little dancer nothing remained but the tinsel rose, which was burnt black as a cinder.

X

SUNSHINE STORIES

"NOW I am going to tell a story," said the Wind.

"Excuse me," said the Rain, "but now it is my turn—, you have been howling round the corner as hard as ever you could, this long time past."

"Is that your gratitude toward me?" said the Wind. "I who, in honor of you, turn inside out—yes, even break—all the umbrellas, when people won't have anything to do with you."

"I am going to speak!" said the Sunshine. "Silence!"

And the Sunshine said it with such glory and majesty, that the long, weary

Wind fell prostrate, and the Rain beat against him, and shook him, and said,—"We won't stand it! She always breaks through, that Madam Sunshine; we won't listen to her. What she says is not worth hearing."

But the Sunshine said,—"A beautiful swan flew over the rolling, tumbling waves of the ocean. Every one of its feathers shone like gold: one feather drifted down on the great merchant vessel that, with all sail set, was sailing away. The feather dropped on the curly light hair of a young man, whose business it was to have a care for the goods—,supercargo they called him. The bird of Fortune's feather touched his forehead, became a pen in his hand, and brought him such luck, that very soon he became a wealthy merchant,—rich enough to have bought for himself spurs of gold; rich enough to change a golden dish into a nobleman's shield; and I shone on it," said the Sunshine.

"The swan flew further, away over the bright green meadow, where the little shepherd-boy, only seven years old, had lain down in the shadow of the old and only tree there was. The swan, in its flight, kissed one of the leaves of the tree. The leaf fell into the boy's hand, and it was changed to three leaves, to ten,—yes, to a whole book,—and in it he read about all the wonders of nature, about his native language, about faith and knowledge. At night he laid the book under his head, that he might not forget what he had been reading. The wonderful book led him to the school-bench, and thence in search of knowledge. I have read his name among the names of learned men," said the Sunshine.

"The swan flew into the quiet, lonely forest, rested awhile on the dark, deep lake, where the water-lilies grow; where the wild apples are to be found on the shore; where the cuckoo and wild pigeon have their homes.

"A poor woman was in the wood, gathering firewood branches that had fallen down, and dry sticks; she carried them in a bundle on her back, and in her arms she held her little child. She saw the golden swan, the bird of Fortune, rise from among the reeds on the shore. What was that that glittered? A golden egg, quite warm yet. She laid it in her bosom, and the warmth remained in it. Surely there was life in the egg! She heard a gentle picking inside of the shell, but mistook the sound, and thought it was her own heart that she heard beating.

"At home, in the poor cottage, she took out the egg; 'tick, tick,' it said, as if it had been a valuable gold watch; but that it was not, only an egg—a real, living egg. The egg cracked and opened, and a dear little baby-swan, all feathered as with purest gold, put out its little head; round its neck it had four rings, and as the poor woman had four boys,—three at home, and the little one that she had had with her in the lonely wood,—she understood at once that here was a ring for each boy and just as she thought of that, the little gold-bt here was a ring for each boy and just as she thought of that, the little gold-biird took flight She kissed each ring, made each of the children kiss one of the rings, laid it next to the child's heart, then put it on his finger. I saw it all," said the Sunshine, "and I saw what followed.

"One of the boys was playing in a ditch, and took a lump of clay in his hand, turned and twisted and pressed it between his fingers, till it took shape, and was like Jason, who went in search of and found the golden fleece.

"The second boy ran out on the meadow, where the flowers stood,—flowers of all imaginable colors; he gathered a handful, and squeezed them so tight that all the juice spurted into his eyes, and some of it wetted the ring. It cribbled and crawled in his thoughts, and in his hands, and after many a day, and many a year, people in the great city talked of the great painter.

"The third child held the ring so tight in his teeth, that it gave forth sound, an echo of the song in the depth of his heart. Thoughts and feelings rose in beautiful sounds; rose like singing swans; plunged, like swans, into the deep, deep sea. He became a great master, a great composer, of whom every country has the right to say, 'He was mine!'

"And the fourth little one was—yes, he was—the 'ugly duck' of the family; they said he had the pip, and must have pepper and butter, like the little sick chickens, and that he got; but of me he got a warm, sunny kiss," said the Sunshine. "He got ten kisses for one; he was a poet, and was buffeted and kissed, alternately, all his life. But he held what no one could take from him,—the Ring of Fortune, from Dame Fortune's golden swan. His thoughts took wings, and flew up and away, like singing butterflies,—the emblem of immortality!"

"That was a dreadfully long story," said the Wind.

"And O, how stupid and tiresome!" said the Rain. "Blow on me, please, that I may revive a little."

And the Wind blew, and the Sunshine said,—"The swan of Fortune flew over the beautiful bay, where the fishermen had set their nets; the poorest of them wanted to get married, and marry he did. To him the swan brought a piece of amber; amber draws things toward it, and it drew hearts to the house. Amber is the most wonderful incense, and there came a soft perfume, as from a church; there came a sweet breath from out of beautiful nature, that God has made. They were so happy and grateful for their peaceful home, and content even in their poverty. Their life became a real Sunshine story!"

"I think we had better stop now," said the Wind, "the Sunshine has talked long enough, and I am dreadfully bored."

"And I also," said the Rain.

And what do we others, who have heard the story, say?

We say, "Now my story's done."

XI

THE DAISY

NOW listen. Out in the country, close by the roadside, stood a pleasant house; you have seen one like it, no doubt, very often. In front lay a little fenced-in garden, full of blooming flowers. Near the hedge, in the soft green grass, grew a little daisy. The sun shone as brightly and warmly upon her as upon the large and beautiful garden flowers, so the daisy grew from hour to hour. Every morning she unfolded her little white petals, like shining rays round the little golden sun in the center of the flower. She never seemed to think that she was unseen down in the grass or that she was only a poor, insignificant flower. She felt too happy to care for that. Merrily she turned toward the warm sun, looked up to the blue sky, and listened to the lark singing high in the air.

One day the little flower was as joyful as if it had been a great holiday, although it was only Monday. All the children were at school, and while they sat on their benches learning their lessons, she, on her little stem, learned also from the warm sun and from everything around her how good God is, and it made her happy to hear the lark expressing in his song her own glad feelings. The daisy admired the happy bird who could warble so sweetly and fly so high, and she was not at all sorrowful because she could not do the same.

"I can see and hear," thought she; "the sun shines upon me, and the wind kisses me; what else do I need to make me happy?"

Within the garden grew a number of aristocratic flowers; the less scent they had the more they flaunted. The peonies considered it a grand thing to be so large, and puffed themselves out to be larger than the roses. The tulips knew that they were marked with beautiful colors, and held themselves bolt upright so that they might be seen more plainly.

They did not notice the little daisy outside, but she looked at them and thought: "How rich and beautiful they are! No wonder the pretty bird flies down to visit them. How glad I am that I grow so near them, that I may admire their beauty!"

Just at this moment the lark flew down, crying "Tweet," but he did not go to the tall peonies and tulips; he hopped into the grass near the lowly daisy. She trembled for joy and hardly knew what to think. The little bird hopped round the daisy, singing, "Oh, what sweet, soft grass, and what a lovely little flower, with gold in its heart and silver on its dress!" For the yellow center in the daisy looked like gold, and the leaves around were glittering white, like silver.

How happy the little daisy felt, no one can describe. The bird kissed her with his beak, sang to her, and then flew up again into the blue air above. It was at least a quarter of an hour before the daisy could recover herself. Half ashamed, yet happy in herself, she glanced at the other flowers; they must have seen the honor she had received, and would understand her delight and pleasure.

But the tulips looked prouder than ever; indeed, they were evidently quite vexed about it. The peonies were disgusted, and could they have spoken, the poor little daisy would no doubt have received a good scolding. She could see they were all out of temper, and it made her very sorry.

At this moment there came into the garden a girl with a large, glittering knife in her hand. She went straight to the tulips and cut off several of them.

"O dear," sighed the daisy, "how shocking! It is all over with them now." The girl carried the tulips away, and the daisy felt very glad to grow outside in the grass and to be only a poor little flower.

When the sun set, she folded up her leaves and went to sleep. She dreamed the whole night long of the warm sun and the pretty little bird.

The next morning, when she joyfully stretched out her white leaves once more to the warm air and the light, she recognized the voice of the bird, but his song sounded mournful and sad.

Alas! he had good reason to be sad: he had been caught and made a prisoner in a cage that hung close by the open window. He sang of the happy time when he could fly in the air, joyous and free; of the young green corn in the fields, from which he would spring higher and higher to sing his glorious song—but now he was a prisoner in a cage.

The little daisy wished very much to help him. But what could she do? In her anxiety she forgot all the beautiful things around her, the warm sunshine, and her own pretty, shining, white leaves. Alas! she could think of nothing but the captive bird and her own inability to help him.

Two boys came out of the garden; one of them carried a sharp knife in his hand, like the one with which the girl had cut the tulips. They went straight to the little daisy, who could not think what they were going to do.

"We can cut out a nice piece of turf for the lark here," said one of the boys; and he began to cut a square piece round the daisy, so that she stood just in the center.

"Pull up the flower," said the other boy; and the daisy trembled with fear, for to pluck her up would destroy her life and she wished so much to live and to be taken to the captive lark in his cage.

"No, let it stay where it is," said the boy, "it looks so pretty." So the daisy remained, and was put with the turf in the lark's cage. The poor bird was complaining loudly about his lost freedom, beating his wings against the iron bars of his prison. The little daisy could make no sign and utter no word to console him, as she would gladly have done. The whole morning passed in this manner.

"There is no water here," said the captive lark; "they have all gone out and have forgotten to give me a drop to drink. My throat is hot and dry; I feel as if I had fire and ice within me, and the air is so heavy. Alas! I must die. I must bid farewell to the warm sunshine, the fresh green, and all the beautiful things which God has created." And then he thrust his beak into the cool turf to refresh himself a little with the fresh grass, and, as he did so, his eye fell upon the daisy. The bird nodded to her and kissed her with his beak and said: "You also will wither here, you poor little flower! They have given you to me, with the little patch of green grass on which you grow, in exchange for the whole world which was mine out there. Each little blade of grass is to me as a great tree, and each of your white leaves a flower. Alas! you only show me how much I have lost."

"Oh, if I could only comfort him!" thought the daisy, but she could not move a leaf. The perfume from her leaves was stronger than is usual in these flowers, and the bird noticed it, and though he was fainting with thirst, and in his pain pulled up the green blades of grass, he did not touch the flower.

The evening came, and yet no one had come to bring the bird a drop of water. Then he stretched out his pretty wings and shook convulsively; he could only sing "Tweet, tweet," in a weak, mournful tone. His little head bent down toward the flower; the bird's heart was broken with want and pining. Then the flower could not fold her leaves as she had done the evening before when she went to sleep, but, sick and sorrowful, drooped toward the earth.

Not till morning did the boys come, and when they found the bird dead, they wept many and bitter tears. They dug a pretty grave for him and adorned it with leaves of flowers. The bird's lifeless body was placed in a smart red box and was buried with great honor.

Poor bird! while he was alive and could sing, they forgot him and allowed him to sit in his cage and suffer want, but now that he was dead, they mourned for him with many tears and buried him in royal state.

But the turf with the daisy on it was thrown out into the dusty road. No one thought of the little flower that had felt more for the poor bird than had any one else and that would have been so glad to help and comfort him if she had been able.

XII

THE SNOW MAN

"IT IS so delightfully cold that it makes my whole body crackle," said the Snow Man. "This is just the kind of wind to blow life into one. How that great red thing up there is staring at me!" He meant the sun, which was just setting. "It shall not make me wink. I shall manage to keep the pieces."

He had two triangular pieces of tile in his head instead of eyes, and his mouth, being made of an old broken rake, was therefore furnished with teeth. He had been brought into existence amid the joyous shouts of boys, the jingling of sleigh bells, and the slashing of whips.

The sun went down, and the full moon rose, large, round, and clear, shining in the deep blue.

"There it comes again, from the other side," said the Snow Man, who supposed the sun was showing itself once more. "Ah, I have cured it of staring. Now it may hang up there and shine, so that I may see myself. If I only knew how to manage to move away from this place—I should so like to move! If I could, I would slide along yonder on the ice, as I have seen the boys do; but I don't understand how. I don't even know how to run."

"Away, away!" barked the old yard dog. He was quite hoarse and could not pronounce "Bow-wow" properly. He had once been an indoor dog and lain by the fire, and he had been hoarse ever since. "The sun will make you run some day. I saw it, last winter, make your predecessor run, and his predecessor before him. Away, away! They all have to go."

"I don't understand you, comrade," said the Snow Man. "Is that thing up yonder to teach me to run? I saw it running itself, a little while ago, and now it has come creeping up from the other side."

"You know nothing at all," replied the yard dog. "But then, you've only lately been patched up. What you see yonder is the moon, and what you saw before was the sun. It will come again to-morrow and most likely teach you to run down into the ditch by the well, for I think the weather is going to change. I can feel such pricks and stabs in my left leg that I am sure there is going to be a change."

"I don't understand him," said the Snow Man to himself, "but I have a feeling that he is talking of something very disagreeable. The thing that stared so hard just now, which he calls the sun, is not my friend; I can feel that too."

"Away, away!" barked the yard dog, and then he turned round three times and crept into his kennel to sleep.

There really was a change in the weather. Toward morning a thick fog covered the whole country and a keen wind arose, so that the cold seemed to freeze one's bones. But when the sun rose, a splendid sight was to be seen. Trees and bushes were covered with hoarfrost and looked like a forest of white coral, while on every twig glittered frozen dewdrops. The many delicate forms, concealed in summer by luxuriant foliage, were now clearly defined and looked like glittering lacework. A white radiance glistened from every twig. The birches, waving in the wind, looked as full of life as in summer and as wondrously beautiful. Where the sun shone, everything glittered and sparkled as if diamond dust had been strewn about; and the snowy carpet of the earth seemed covered with diamonds from which gleamed countless lights, whiter even than the snow itself.

"This is really beautiful," said a girl who had come into the garden with a young friend; and they both stood still near the Snow Man, contemplating the glittering scene. "Summer cannot show a more beautiful sight," she exclaimed, while her eyes sparkled.

"And we can't have such a fellow as this in the summer-time," replied the young man, pointing to the Snow Man. "He is capital."

The girl laughed and nodded at the Snow Man, then tripped away over the snow with her friend. The snow creaked and crackled beneath her feet, as if she had been treading on starch.

"Who are those two?" asked the Snow Man of the yard dog. "You have been here longer than I; do you know them?"

"Of course I know them," replied the yard dog; "the girl has stroked my back many times, and the young man has often given me a bone of meat. I never bite those two."

"But what are they?" asked the Snow Man.

"They are lovers," he replied. "They will go and live in the same kennel, by and by, and gnaw at the same bone. Away, away!"

"Are they the same kind of beings as you and I?" asked the Snow Man.

"Well, they belong to the master," retorted the yard dog. "Certainly people know very little who were only born yesterday. I can see that in you. I have age and experience. I know every one here in the house, and I know there was once a time when I did not lie out here in the cold, fastened to a chain. Away, away!"

"The cold is delightful," said the Snow Man. "But do tell me, tell me; only you must not clank your chain so, for it jars within me when you do that."

"Away, away!" barked the yard dog. "I'll tell you: they said I was a pretty little fellow, once; then I used to lie in a velvet-covered chair, up at the master's house, and sit in the mistress's lap; they used to kiss my nose, and wipe my paws with an embroidered handkerchief, and I was called 'Ami, dear Ami, sweet Ami.' But after a while I grew too big for them, and they sent me away to the housekeeper's room; so I came to live on the lower story. You can look into the room from where you stand, and see where I was once master—for I was, indeed, master to the housekeeper. It was a much smaller room than those upstairs, but I was more comfortable, for I was not continually being taken hold of and pulled about by the children, as I had been. I received quite as good food and even better. I had my own cushion, and there was a stove—it is the finest thing in the world at this season of the year. I used to go under the stove and lie down. Ah, I still dream of that stove. Away, away!"

"Does a stove look beautiful?" asked the Snow Man. "Is it at all like me?"

"It is just the opposite of you," said the dog. "It's as black as a crow and has a long neck and a brass knob; it eats firewood, and that makes fire spurt out of its mouth. One has to keep on one side or under it, to be comfortable. You can see it through the window from where you stand."

Then the Snow Man looked, and saw a bright polished thing with a brass knob, and fire gleaming from the lower part of it. The sight of this gave the Snow Man a strange sensation; it was very odd, he knew not what it meant, and he could not account for it. But there are people who are not men of snow who understand what the feeling is. "And why did you leave her?" asked the Snow Man, for it seemed to him that the stove must be of the female sex. "How could you give up such a comfortable place?"

"I was obliged to," replied the yard dog. "They turned me out of doors and chained me up here. I had bitten the youngest of my master's sons in the leg, because he kicked away the bone I was gnawing. 'Bone for bone,' I thought. But they were very angry, and since that time I have been fastened to a chain and have lost my voice. Don't you hear how hoarse I am? Away, away! I can't talk like other dogs any more. Away, away! That was the end of it all."

But the Snow Man was no longer listening. He was looking into the housekeeper's room on the lower story, where the stove, which was about the same size as the Snow Man himself, stood on its four iron legs. "What a strange crackling I feel within me," he said. "Shall I ever get in there? It is an innocent wish, and innocent wishes are sure to be fulfilled. I must go in there and lean against her, even if I have to break the window."

"You must never go in there," said the yard dog, "for if you approach the stove, you will melt away, away."

"I might as well go," said the Snow Man, "for I think I am breaking up as it is."

During the whole day the Snow Man stood looking in through the window, and in the twilight hour the room became still more inviting, for from the stove came a gentle glow, not like the sun or the moon; it was only the kind of radiance that can come from a stove when it has been well fed. When the door of the stove was opened, the flames darted out of its mouth,—as is customary with all stoves,—and the light of the flames fell with a ruddy gleam directly on the face and breast of the Snow Man. "I can endure it no longer," said he. "How beautiful it looks when it stretches out its tongue!"

The night was long, but it did not appear so to the Snow Man, who stood there enjoying his own reflections and crackling with the cold. In the morning the window-panes of the housekeeper's room were covered with ice. They were the most beautiful ice flowers any Snow Man could desire, but they concealed the stove. These window-panes would not thaw, and he could see nothing of the stove, which he pictured to himself as if it had been a beautiful human being. The snow crackled and the wind whistled around him; it was just the kind of frosty weather a Snow Man ought to enjoy thoroughly. But he did not enjoy it. How, indeed, could he enjoy anything when he was so stove-sick?

"That is a terrible disease for a Snow Man to have," said the yard dog. "I have suffered from it myself, but I got over it. Away, away!" he barked, and then added, "The weather is going to change."

The weather did change. It began to thaw, and as the warmth increased, the Snow Man decreased. He said nothing and made no complaint, which is a sure sign.

One morning he broke and sank down altogether; and behold! where he had stood, something that looked like a broomstick remained sticking up in the ground. It was the pole round which the boys had built him.

"Ah, now I understand why he had such a great longing for the stove," said the yard dog. "Why, there's the shovel that is used for cleaning out the stove, fastened to the pole. The Snow Man had a stove scraper in his body; that was what moved him so. But it is all over now. Away, away!"

And soon the winter passed. "Away, away!" barked the hoarse yard dog, but the girls in the house sang:

"Come from your fragrant home, green thyme;
Stretch your soft branches, willow tree;
The months are bringing the sweet spring-time,
When the lark in the sky sings joyfully.
Come, gentle sun, while the cuckoo sings,
And I'll mock his note in my wanderings."

And nobody thought any more of the Snow Man.

XIII

THE NIGHTINGALE

In China, you know, the emperor is a Chinese, and all those about him are Chinamen also. The story I am going to tell you happened a great many years ago, so it is well to hear it now before it is forgotten. The emperor's palace was the most beautiful in the world. It was built entirely of porcelain, and very costly, but so delicate and brittle that whoever touched it was obliged to be careful. In the garden could be seen the most singular flowers, with pretty silver bells tied to them, which tinkled so that every one who passed could not help noticing the flowers. Indeed, everything in the emperor's garden was remarkable, and it extended so far that the gardener himself did not know where it ended. Those who travelled beyond its limits knew that there was a noble forest, with lofty trees, sloping down to the deep blue sea, and the great ships sailed under the shadow of its branches. In one of these trees lived a nightingale, who sang so beautifully that even the poor fishermen, who had so many other things to do, would stop and listen. Sometimes, when they went at night to spread their nets, they would hear her sing, and say, "Oh, is not that beautiful?" But when they returned to their fishing, they forgot the bird until the next night. Then they would hear it again, and exclaim "Oh, how beautiful is the nightingale's song!"

Travellers from every country in the world came to the city of the emperor, which they admired very much, as well as the palace and gardens; but when they heard the nightingale, they all declared it to be the best of all. And the travellers, on their return home, related what they had seen; and learned men wrote books, containing descriptions of the town, the palace, and the gardens; but they did not forget the nightingale, which was really the greatest wonder. And those who could write poetry composed beautiful verses about the nightingale, who lived in a forest near the deep sea. The books travelled all over the world, and some of them came into the hands of the emperor; and he sat in his golden chair, and, as he read, he nodded his approval every moment, for it pleased him to find such a beautiful description of his city, his palace, and his gardens. But when he came to the words, "the nightingale is the most beautiful of all," he exclaimed, "What is this? I know nothing of any nightingale. Is there such a bird in my empire? and even in my garden? I have never heard of it. Something, it appears, may be learnt from books."

Then he called one of his lords-in-waiting, who was so high-bred, that when any in an inferior rank to himself spoke to him, or asked him a question, he would answer, "Pooh," which means nothing.

"There is a very wonderful bird mentioned here, called a nightingale," said the emperor; "they say it is the best thing in my large kingdom. Why have I not been told of it?"

"I have never heard the name," replied the cavalier; "she has not been presented at court."

"It is my pleasure that she shall appear this evening." said the emperor; "the whole world knows what I possess better than I do myself."

"I have never heard of her," said the cavalier; "yet I will endeavor to find her."

But where was the nightingale to be found? The nobleman went up stairs and down, through halls and passages; yet none of those whom he met had heard of the bird. So he returned to the emperor, and said that it must be a fable, invented by those who had written the book. "Your imperial majesty," said he, "cannot believe everything contained in books; sometimes they are only fiction, or what is called the black art."

"But the book in which I have read this account," said the emperor, "was sent to me by the great and mighty emperor of Japan, and therefore it cannot contain a falsehood. I will hear the nightingale, she must be here this evening; she has my highest favor; and if she does not come, the whole court shall be trampled upon after supper is ended."

"Tsing-pe!" cried the lord-in-waiting, and again he ran up and down stairs, through all the halls and corridors; and half the court ran with him, for they did not like the idea of being trampled upon. There was a great inquiry about this wonderful nightingale, whom all the world knew, but who was unknown to the court.

At last they met with a poor little girl in the kitchen, who said, "Oh, yes, I know the nightingale quite well; indeed, she can sing. Every evening I have permission to take home to my poor sick mother the scraps from the table; she lives down by the sea-shore, and as I come back I feel tired, and I sit down in the wood to rest, and listen to the nightingale's song. Then the tears come into my eyes, and it is just as if my mother kissed me."

"Little maiden," said the lord-in-waiting, "I will obtain for you constant employment in the kitchen, and you shall have permission to see the emperor dine, if you will lead us to the nightingale; for she is invited for this evening to the palace." So she went into the wood where the nightingale sang, and half the court followed her. As they went along, a cow began lowing.

"Oh," said a young courtier, "now we have found her; what wonderful power for such a small creature; I have certainly heard it before."

"No, that is only a cow lowing," said the little girl; "we are a long way from the place yet."

Then some frogs began to croak in the marsh.

"Beautiful," said the young courtier again. "Now I hear it, tinkling like little church bells."

"No, those are frogs," said the little maiden; "but I think we shall soon hear her now:" and presently the nightingale began to sing.

"Hark, hark! there she is," said the girl, "and there she sits," she added, pointing to a little gray bird who was perched on a bough.

"Is it possible?" said the lord-in-waiting, "I never imagined it would be a little, plain, simple thing like that. She has certainly changed color at seeing so many grand people around her."

"Little nightingale," cried the girl, raising her voice, "our most gracious emperor wishes you to sing before him."

"With the greatest pleasure," said the nightingale, and began to sing most delightfully.

"It sounds like tiny glass bells," said the lord-in-waiting, "and see how her little throat works. It is surprising that we have never heard this before; she will be a great success at court."

"Shall I sing once more before the emperor?" asked the nightingale, who thought he was present.

"My excellent little nightingale," said the courtier, "I have the great pleasure of inviting you to a court festival this evening, where you will gain imperial favor by your charming song."

"My song sounds best in the green wood," said the bird; but still she came willingly when she heard the emperor's wish.

The palace was elegantly decorated for the occasion. The walls and floors of porcelain glittered in the light of a thousand lamps. Beautiful flowers, round which little bells were tied, stood in the corridors: what with the running to and fro and the draught, these bells tinkled so loudly that no one could speak to be heard. In the centre of the great hall, a golden perch had been fixed for the nightingale to sit on. The whole court was present, and the little kitchen-maid had received permission to stand by the door. She was not installed as a real court cook. All were in full dress, and every eye was turned to the little gray bird when the emperor nodded to her to begin. The nightingale sang so sweetly that the tears came into the emperor's eyes, and then rolled down his cheeks, as her song became still more touching and went to every one's heart. The emperor was so delighted that he declared the nightingale should have his gold slipper to wear round her neck, but she declined the honor with thanks: she had been sufficiently rewarded already. "I have seen tears in an emperor's eyes," she said, "that is my richest reward. An emperor's tears have wonderful power, and are quite sufficient honor for me;" and then she sang again more enchantingly than ever.

"That singing is a lovely gift;" said the ladies of the court to each other; and then they took water in their mouths to make them utter the gurgling sounds of the nightingale when they spoke to any one, so that they might fancy themselves nightingales. And the footmen and chambermaids also expressed their satisfaction, which is saying a great deal, for they are very difficult to please. In fact the nightingale's visit was most successful. She was now to remain at court, to have her own cage, with liberty to go out twice a day, and once during the night. Twelve servants were appointed to attend her on these occasions, who each held her by a silken string fastened to her leg. There was certainly not much pleasure in this kind of flying.

The whole city spoke of the wonderful bird, and when two people met, one said "nightin," and the other said "gale," and they understood what was meant, for nothing else was talked of. Eleven peddlers' children were named after her, but not of them could sing a note.

One day the emperor received a large packet on which was written "The Nightingale." "Here is no doubt a new book about our celebrated bird," said the emperor. But instead of a book, it was a work of art contained in a casket, an artificial nightingale made to look like a living one, and covered all over with diamonds, rubies, and sapphires. As soon as the artificial bird was wound up, it could sing like the real one, and could move its tail up and down, which sparkled with silver and gold. Round its neck hung a piece of ribbon, on which was written "The Emperor of China's nightingale is poor compared with that of the Emperor of Japan's."

"This is very beautiful," exclaimed all who saw it, and he who had brought the artificial bird received the title of "Imperial nightingale-bringer-in-chief."

"Now they must sing together," said the court, "and what a duet it will be." But they did not get on well, for the real nightingale sang in its own natural way, but the artificial bird sang only waltzes.

"That is not a fault," said the music-master, "it is quite perfect to my taste," so then it had to sing alone, and was as successful as the real bird; besides, it was so much prettier to look at, for it sparkled like bracelets and breast-pins. Three and thirty times did it sing the same tunes without being tired; the people would gladly have heard it again, but the emperor said the living nightingale ought to sing something. But where was she? No one had noticed her when she flew out at the open window, back to her own green woods.

"What strange conduct," said the emperor, when her flight had been discovered; and all the courtiers blamed her, and said she was a very ungrateful creature.

"But we have the best bird after all," said one, and then they would have the bird sing again, although it was the thirty-fourth time they had listened to the same piece, and even then they had not learnt it, for it was rather difficult. But the music-master praised the bird in the highest degree, and even asserted that it was better than a real nightingale, not only in its dress and the beautiful diamonds, but also in its musical power. "For you must perceive, my chief lord and emperor, that with a real nightingale we can never tell what is going to be sung, but with this bird everything is settled. It can be opened and explained, so that people may understand how the waltzes are formed, and why one note follows upon another."

"This is exactly what we think," they all replied, and then the music-master received permission to exhibit the bird to the people on the following Sunday, and the emperor commanded that they should be present to hear it sing. When they heard it they were like people intoxicated; however it must have been with drinking tea, which is quite a Chinese custom. They all said "Oh!" and held up their forefingers and nodded, but a poor fisherman, who had heard the real nightingale, said, "it sounds prettily enough, and the melodies are all alike; yet there seems something wanting, I cannot exactly tell what."

And after this the real nightingale was banished from the empire, and the artificial bird placed on a silk cushion close to the emperor's bed. The presents of gold and precious stones which had been received with it were round the bird, and it was now advanced to the title of "Little Imperial Toilet Singer," and to the rank of No. 1 on the left hand; for the emperor considered the left side, on which the heart lies, as the most noble, and the heart of an emperor is in the same place as that of other people.

The music-master wrote a work, in twenty-five volumes, about the artificial bird, which was very learned and very long, and full of the most difficult Chinese words; yet all the people said they had read it, and understood it, for fear of being thought stupid and having their bodies trampled upon.

So a year passed, and the emperor, the court, and all the other Chinese knew every little turn in the artificial bird's song; and for that same reason it pleased them better. They could sing with the bird, which they often did. The street-boys sang, "Zi-zi-zi, cluck,

cluck, cluck," and the emperor himself could sing it also. It was really most amusing.

One evening, when the artificial bird was singing its best, and the emperor lay in bed listening to it, something inside the bird sounded "whizz." Then a spring cracked. "Whir-r-r-r" went all the wheels, running round, and then the music stopped. The emperor immediately sprang out of bed, and called for his physician; but what could he do? Then they sent for a watchmaker; and, after a great deal of talking and examination, the bird was put into something like order; but he said that it must be used very carefully, as the barrels were worn, and it would be impossible to put in new ones without injuring the music. Now there was great sorrow, as the bird could only be allowed to play once a year; and even that was dangerous for the works inside it. Then the music-master made a little speech, full of hard words, and declared that the bird was as good as ever; and, of course no one contradicted him.

Five years passed, and then a real grief came upon the land. The Chinese really were fond of their emperor, and he now lay so ill that he was not expected to live. Already a new emperor had been chosen and the people who stood in the street asked the lord-in-waiting how the old emperor was; but he only said, "Pooh!" and shook his head.

Cold and pale lay the emperor in his royal bed; the whole court thought he was dead, and every one ran away to pay homage to his successor. The chamberlains went out to have a talk on the matter, and the ladies'-maids invited company to take coffee. Cloth had been laid down on the halls and passages, so that not a footstep should be heard, and all was silent and still. But the emperor was not yet dead, although he lay white and stiff on his gorgeous bed, with the long velvet curtains and heavy gold tassels. A window stood open, and the moon shone in upon the emperor and the artificial bird. The poor emperor, finding he could scarcely breathe with a strange weight on his chest, opened his eyes, and saw Death sitting there. He had put on the emperor's golden crown, and held in one hand his sword of state, and in the other his beautiful banner. All around the bed and peeping through the long velvet curtains, were a number of strange heads, some very ugly, and others lovely and gentle-looking. These were the emperor's good and bad deeds, which stared him in the face now Death sat at his heart.

DEATH SAT UPON THE EMPEROR'S CHEST

"Do you remember this?" "Do you recollect that?" they asked one after another, thus bringing to his remembrance circumstances that made the perspiration stand on his brow.

"I know nothing about it," said the emperor. "Music! music!" he cried; "the large Chinese drum! that I may not hear what they say." But they still went on, and Death nodded like a Chinaman to all they said. "Music! music!" shouted the emperor. "You little precious golden bird, sing, pray sing! I have given you gold and costly presents; I have even hung my golden slipper round your neck. Sing! sing!" But the bird remained silent. There was no one to wind it up, and therefore it could not sing a note.

Death continued to stare at the emperor with his cold, hollow eyes, and the room was fearfully still. Suddenly there came through the open window the sound of sweet music. Outside, on the bough of a tree, sat the living nightingale. She had heard of the emperor's illness, and was therefore come to sing to him of hope and trust. And as she sung, the shadows grew paler and paler; the blood in the emperor's veins flowed more rapidly, and gave life to his weak limbs; and even Death himself listened, and said, "Go on, little nightingale, go on."

"Then will you give me the beautiful golden sword and that rich banner? and will you give me the emperor's crown?" said the bird.

So Death gave up each of these treasures for a song; and the nightingale continued her singing. She sung of the quiet churchyard, where the white roses grow, where the elder-tree wafts its perfume on the breeze, and the fresh, sweet grass is moistened by the mourners' tears. Then Death longed to go and see his garden, and floated out through the window in the form of a cold, white mist.

"Thanks, thanks, you heavenly little bird. I know you well. I banished you from my kingdom once, and yet you have charmed away the evil faces from my bed, and banished Death from my heart, with your sweet song. How can I reward you?"

"You have already rewarded me," said the nightingale. "I shall never forget that I drew tears from your eyes the first time I sang to you. These are the jewels that rejoice a singer's heart. But now sleep, and grow strong and well again. I will sing to you again."

And as she sung, the emperor fell into a sweet sleep; and how mild and refreshing that slumber was! When he awoke, strengthened and restored, the sun shone brightly through the window; but not one of his servants had returned—they all believed he was dead; only the nightingale still sat beside him, and sang.

"You must always remain with me," said the emperor. "You shall sing only when it pleases you; and I will break the artificial bird into a thousand pieces."

"No; do not do that," replied the nightingale; "the bird did very well as long as it could. Keep it here still. I cannot live in the palace, and build my nest; but let me come when I like. I will sit on a bough outside your window, in the evening, and sing to you, so that you may be happy, and have thoughts full of joy. I will sing to you of those who are happy, and those who suffer; of the good and the evil, who are hidden around you. The little singing bird flies far from you and your court to the home of the fisherman and the peasant's cot. I love your heart better than your crown; and yet something holy lingers round that also. I will come, I will sing to you; but you must promise me one thing."

"Everything," said the emperor, who, having dressed himself in his imperial robes, stood with the hand that held the heavy golden sword pressed to his heart.

"I only ask one thing," she replied; "let no one know that you have a little bird who tells you everything. It will be best to conceal it." So saying, the nightingale flew away.

The servants now came in to look after the dead emperor; when, lo! there he stood, and, to their astonishment, said, "Good morning."

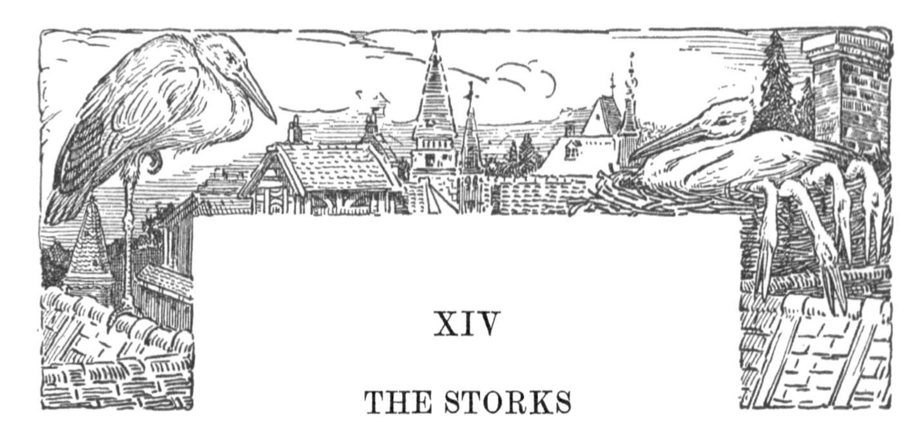

XIV

THE STORKS

ON the last house in the village there lay a stork's nest. The mother stork sat in it with her four little ones, who were stretching out their heads with their pointed black bills that had not yet turned red. At a little distance, on the top of the roof, stood the father stork, bolt upright and as stiff as could be. That he might not appear quite idle while standing sentry, he had drawn one leg up under him, as is the manner of storks. One might have taken him to be carved in marble, so still did he stand.

"It must look very grand for my wife to have a sentinel to guard her nest," he thought. "They can't know that I am her husband and will, of course, conclude that I am commanded to stand here by her nest. It looks aristocratic!"

Below, in the street, a crowd of children were playing. When they chanced to catch sight of the storks, one of the boldest of the boys began to sing the old song about the stork. The others soon joined him, but each sang the words that he happened to have heard. This is one of the ways:

"Stork, stork, fly away;
Stand not on one leg to-day.
Thy dear wife sits in the nest,
To lull the little ones to rest.

"There's a halter for one,
There's a stake for another,
For the third there's a gun,
And a spit for his brother!"

"Only listen," said the young storks, "to what the boys are singing. Do you hear them say we're to be hanged and shot?"

"Don't listen to what they say; if you don't mind, it won't hurt you," said the mother.

But the boys went on singing, and pointed mockingly at the sentinel stork. Only one boy, whom they called Peter, said it was a shame to make game of animals, and he would not join in the singing at all.

The mother stork tried to comfort her young ones. "Don't mind them," she said; "see how quiet your father stands on one leg there."

"But we are afraid," said the little ones, drawing back their beaks into the nest.

The children assembled again on the next day, and no sooner did they see the storks than they again began their song:

"The first will be hanged,
The second be hit."

"Tell us, are we to be hanged and burned?" asked the young storks.

"No, no; certainly not," replied the mother. "You are to learn to fly, and then we shall pay a visit to the frogs. They will bow to us in the water and sing 'Croak! croak!' and we shall eat them up, and that will be a great treat."

"And then what?" questioned the young storks.

"Oh, then all the storks in the land will assemble, and the autumn sports will begin; only then one must be able to fly well, for that is very important. Whoever does not fly as he should will be pierced to death by the general's beak, so mind that you learn well, when the drill begins."

"Yes, but then, after that, we shall be killed, as the boys say. Hark! they are singing it again."

"Attend to me and not to them," said the mother stork. "After the great review we shall fly away to warm countries, far from here, over hills and forests. To Egypt we shall fly, where are the three-cornered houses of stone, one point of which reaches to the clouds; they are called pyramids and are older than a stork can imagine. In that same land there is a river which overflows its banks and turns the whole country into mire. We shall go into the mire and eat frogs."

"Oh! oh!" exclaimed all the youngsters.

"Yes, it is indeed a delightful place. We need do nothing all day long but eat; and while we are feasting there so comfortably, in this country there is not a green leaf left on the trees. It is so cold here that the very clouds freeze in lumps or fall down in little white rags." It was hail and snow that she meant, but she did not know how to say it better.

"And will the naughty boys freeze in lumps?" asked the young storks.

"No, they will not freeze in lumps, but they will come near it, and they will sit moping and cowering in gloomy rooms while you are flying about in foreign lands, amid bright flowers and warm sunshine."

Some time passed, and the nestlings had grown so large and strong that they could stand upright in the nest and look all about them. Every day the father stork came with delicious frogs, nice little snakes, and other such dainties that storks delight in. How funny it was to see the clever feats he performed to amuse them! He would lay his head right round upon his tail; and sometimes he would clatter with his beak, as if it were a little rattle; or he would tell them stories, all relating to swamps and fens.

"Come, children," said the mother stork one day, "now you must learn to fly." And all the four young storks had to go out on the ridge of the roof. How they did totter and stagger about! They tried to balance themselves with their wings, but came very near falling to the ground.

"Look at me!" said the mother. "This is the way to hold your head. And thus you must place your feet. Left! right! left! right! that's what will help you on in the world."

Then she flew a little way, and the young ones took a clumsy little leap. Bump! plump! down they fell, for their bodies were still too heavy for them.

"I will not fly," said one of the young storks, as he crept back to the nest. "I don't care about going to warm countries."

"Do you want to stay here and freeze when the winter comes? Will you wait till the boys come to hang, to burn, or to roast you? Well, then, I'll call them."

"Oh, no!" cried the timid stork, hopping back to the roof with the rest.

By the third day they actually began to fly a little. Then they had no doubt that they could soar or hover in the air, upborne by their wings. And this they attempted to do, but down they fell, flapping their wings as fast as they could.

Again the boys came to the street, singing their song,

"Storks, storks, fly home and rest."

"Shall we fly down and peck them?" asked the young ones.

"No, leave them alone. Attend to me; that's far more important. One—two—three! now we fly round to the right. One—two—three! now to the left, round the chimney. There! that was very good. That last flap with your wings and the kick with your feet were so graceful and proper that to-morrow you shall fly with me to the marsh. Several of the nicest stork families will be there with their children. Let me see that mine are the best bred of all. Carry your heads high and mind you strut about proudly, for that looks well and helps to make one respected."

"But shall we not take revenge upon the naughty boys?" asked the young storks.

"No, no; let them scream away, as much as they please. You are to fly up to the clouds and away to the land of the pyramids, while they are freezing and can neither see a green leaf nor taste a sweet apple."

"But we will revenge ourselves," they whispered one to another. And then the training began again.

Among all the children down in the street the one that seemed most bent upon singing the song that made game of the storks was the boy who had begun it, and he was a little fellow hardly more than six years old. The young storks, to be sure, thought he was at least a hundred, for he was much bigger than their parents, and, besides, what did they know about the ages of either children or grown men? Their whole vengeance was to be aimed at this one boy. It was always he who began the song and persisted in mocking them. The young storks were very angry, and as they grew larger they also grew less patient under insult, and their mother was at last obliged to promise them that they might be revenged—but not until the day of their departure.

"We must first see how you carry yourselves at the great review. If you do so badly that the general runs his beak through you, then the boys will be in the right—at least in one way. We must wait and see!"

"Yes, you shall see!" cried all the young storks; and they took the greatest pains, practicing every day, until they flew so evenly and so lightly that it was a pleasure to see them.

The autumn now set in; all the storks began to assemble, in order to start for the warm countries and leave winter behind them. And such exercises as there were! Young fledglings were set to fly over forests and villages, to see if they were equal to the long journey that was before them. So well did our young storks acquit themselves, that, as a proof of the satisfaction they had given, the mark they got was, "Remarkably well," with a present of a frog and a snake, which they lost no time in eating.

"Now," said they, "we will be revenged."

"Yes, certainly," said their mother; "and I have thought of a way that will surely be the fairest. I know a pond where all the little human children lie till the stork comes to take them to their parents. There lie the pretty little babies, dreaming more sweetly than they ever dream afterwards. All the parents are wishing for one of these little ones, and the children all want a sister or a brother. Now we'll fly to the pond and bring back a baby for every child who did not sing the naughty song that made game of the storks."

"But the very naughty boy who was the first to begin the song," cried the young storks, "what shall we do with him?"

"There is a little dead child in the pond—one that has dreamed itself to death. We will bring that for him. Then he will cry because we have brought a little dead brother to him.

"But that good boy,—you have not forgotten him!—the one who said it was a shame to mock at the animals; for him we will bring both a brother and a sister. And because his name is Peter, all of you shall be called Peter, too."

All was done as the mother had said; the storks were named Peter, and so they are called to this day.

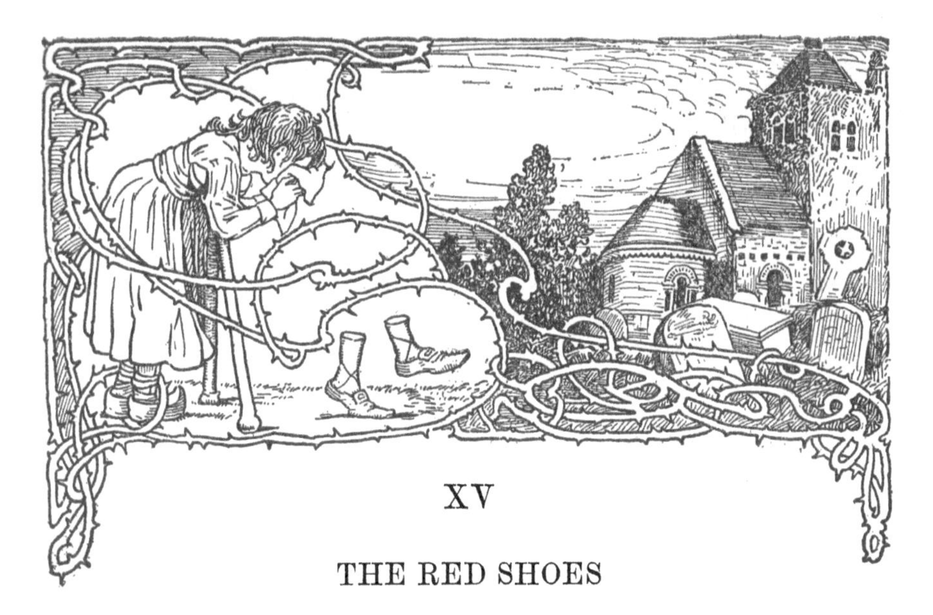

XV

THE RED SHOES

THERE was once a pretty, delicate little girl, who was so poor that she had to go barefoot in summer and wear coarse wooden shoes in winter, which made her little instep quite red.

In the center of the village there lived an old shoemaker's wife. One day this good woman made, as well as she could, a little pair of shoes out of some strips of old red cloth. The shoes were clumsy enough, to be sure, but they fitted the little girl tolerably well, and anyway the woman's intention was kind. The little girl's name was Karen.

On the very day that Karen received the shoes, her mother was to be buried. They were not at all suitable for mourning, but she had no others, so she put them on her little bare feet and followed the poor plain coffin to its last resting place.

Just at that time a large, old-fashioned carriage happened to pass by, and the old lady who sat in it saw the little girl and pitied her.

"Give me the little girl," she said to the clergyman, "and I will take care of her."

Karen supposed that all this happened because of the red shoes, but the old lady thought them frightful and ordered them to be burned. Karen was then dressed in neat, well-fitting clothes and taught to read and sew. People told her she was pretty, but the mirror said, "You are much more than pretty—you are beautiful."

It happened not long afterwards that the queen and her little daughter, the princess, traveled through the land. All the people, Karen among the rest, flocked toward the palace and crowded around it, while the little princess, dressed in white, stood at the window for every one to see. She wore neither a train nor a golden crown, but on her feet were beautiful red morocco shoes, which, it must be admitted, were prettier than those the shoemaker's wife had given to little Karen. Surely nothing in the world could be compared to those red shoes.

Now that Karen was old enough to be confirmed, she of course had to have a new frock and new shoes. The rich shoemaker in the town took the measure of her little feet in his own house, in a room where stood great glass cases filled with all sorts of fine shoes and elegant, shining boots. It was a pretty sight, but the old lady could not see well and naturally did not take so much pleasure in it as Karen. Among the shoes were a pair of red ones, just like those worn by the little princess. Oh, how gay they were! The shoemaker said they had been made for the child of a count, but had not fitted well.

"Are they of polished leather, that they shine so?" asked the old lady.

"Yes, indeed, they do shine," replied Karen. And since they fitted her, they were bought. But the old lady had no idea that they were red, or she would never in the world have allowed Karen to go to confirmation in them, as she now did. Every one, of course, looked at Karen's shoes; and when she walked up the nave to the chancel it seemed to her that even the antique figures on the monuments, the portraits of clergymen and their wives, with their stiff ruffs and long black robes, were fixing their eyes on her red shoes. Even when the bishop laid his hand upon her head and spoke of her covenant with God and how she must now begin to be a full-grown Christian, and when the organ pealed forth solemnly and the children's fresh, sweet voices joined with those of the choir—still Karen thought of nothing but her shoes.

In the afternoon, when the old lady heard every one speak of the red shoes, she said it was very shocking and improper and that, in the future, when Karen went to church it must always be in black shoes, even if they were old.

The next Sunday was Karen's first Communion day. She looked at her black shoes, and then at her red ones, then again at the black and at the red—and the red ones were put on.

The sun shone very brightly, and Karen and the old lady walked to church through the cornfields, for the road was very dusty.

At the door of the church stood an old soldier, who leaned upon a crutch and had a marvelously long beard that was not white but red. He bowed almost to the ground and asked the old lady if he might dust her shoes. Karen, in her turn, put out her little foot.

"Oh, look, what smart little dancing pumps!" said the old soldier. "Mind you do not let them slip off when you dance," and he passed his hands over them. The old lady gave the soldier a halfpenny and went with Karen into the church.

As before, every one saw Karen's red shoes, and all the carved figures too bent their gaze upon them. When Karen knelt at the chancel she thought only of the shoes; they floated before her eyes, and she forgot to say her prayer or sing her psalm.

At last all the people left the church, and the old lady got into her carriage. As Karen lifted her foot to step in, the old soldier said, "See what pretty dancing shoes!" And Karen, in spite of herself, made a few dancing steps. When she had once begun, her feet went on of themselves; it was as though the shoes had received power over her. She danced round the church corner,—she could not help it,—and the coachman had to run behind and catch her to put her into the carriage. Still her feet went on dancing, so, that she trod upon the good lady's toes. It was not until the shoes were taken from her feet that she had rest.

The shoes were put away in a closet, but Karen could not resist going to look at them every now and then.

Soon after this the old lady lay ill in bed, and it was said that she could not recover. She had to be nursed and waited on, and this, of course, was no one's duty so much as it was Karen's, as Karen herself well knew. But there happened to be a great ball in the town, and Karen was invited. She looked at the old lady, who was very ill, and she looked at the red shoes. She put them on, for she thought there could not be any sin in that, and of course there was not—but she went next to the ball and began to dance.

AN ANGEL IN LONG WHITE GARMENTS

Strange to say, when she wanted to move to the right the shoes bore her to the left; and when she wished to dance up the room the shoes persisted in going down the room. Down the stairs they carried her at last, into the street, and out through the town gate. On and on she danced, for dance she must, straight out into the gloomy wood. Up among the trees something glistened. She thought it was the round, red moon, for she saw a face; but no, it was the old soldier with the red beard, who sat and nodded, saying, "See what pretty dancing shoes!"

She was dreadfully frightened and tried to throw away the red shoes, but they clung fast and she could not unclasp them. They seemed to have grown fast to her feet. So dance she must, and dance she did, over field and meadow, in rain and in sunshine, by night and by day—and by night it was by far more dreadful.

She danced out into the open churchyard, but the dead there did not dance; they were at rest and had much better things to do. She would have liked to sit down on the poor man's grave, where the bitter tansy grew, but for her there was no rest.

She danced past the open church door, and there she saw an angel in long white robes and with wings that reached from his shoulders to the earth. His look was stern and grave, and in his hand he held a broad, glittering sword.

"Thou shalt dance," he said, "in thy red shoes, till thou art pale and cold, and till thy body is wasted like a skeleton. Thou shalt dance from door to door, and wherever proud, haughty children dwell thou shalt knock, that, hearing thee, they may take warning. Dance thou shalt—dance on!"

"Mercy!" cried Karen; but she did not hear the answer of the angel, for the shoes carried her past the door and on into the fields.

One morning she danced past a well-known door. Within was the sound of a psalm, and presently a coffin strewn with flowers was borne out. She knew that her friend, the old lady, was dead, and in her heart she felt that she was abandoned by all on earth and condemned by God's angel in heaven.

Still on she danced—for she could not stop—through thorns and briers, while her feet bled. Finally, she danced to a lonely little house where she knew that the executioner dwelt, and she tapped at the window, saying, "Come out, come out! I cannot come in, for I must dance."

The man said, "Do you know who I am and what I do?"

"Yes," said Karen; "but do not strike off my head, for then I could not live to repent of my sin. Strike off my feet, that I may be rid of my red shoes."

Then she confessed her sin, and the executioner struck off the red shoes, which danced away over the fields and into the deep wood. To Karen it seemed that the feet had gone with the shoes, for she had almost lost the power of walking.

"Now I have suffered enough for the red shoes," she said; "I will go to the church, that people may see me." But no sooner had she hobbled to the church door than the shoes danced before her and frightened her back.

All that week she endured the keenest sorrow and shed many bitter tears. When Sunday came, she said: "I am sure I must have suffered and striven enough by this time. I am quite as good, I dare say, as many who are holding their heads high in the church." So she took courage and went again. But before she reached the churchyard gate the red shoes were dancing there, and she turned back again in terror, more deeply sorrowful than ever for her sin.

She then went to the pastor's house and begged as a favor to be taken into the family's service, promising to be diligent and faithful. She did not want wages, she said, only a home with good people. The clergyman's wife pitied her and granted her request, and she proved industrious and very thoughtful.

Earnestly she listened when at evening the preacher read aloud the Holy Scriptures. All the children came to love her, but when they spoke of beauty and finery, she would shake her head and turn away.

On Sunday, when they all went to church, they asked her if she would not go, too, but she looked sad and bade them go without her. Then she went to her own little room, and as she sat with the psalm book in her hand, reading its pages with a gentle, pious mind, the wind brought to her the notes of the organ. She raised her tearful eyes and said, "O God, do thou help me!"

Then the sun shone brightly, and before her stood the white angel that she had seen at the church door. He no longer bore the glittering sword, but in his hand was a beautiful branch of roses.

He touched the ceiling with it, and the ceiling rose, and at each place where the branch touched it there shone a star. He touched the walls, and they widened so that Karen could see the organ that was being played at the church. She saw, too, the old pictures and statues on the walls, and the congregation sitting in the seats and singing psalms, for the church itself had come to the poor girl in her narrow room, or she in her chamber had come to it. She sat in the seat with the rest of the clergyman's household, and when the psalm was ended, they nodded and said, "Thou didst well to come, Karen!"

"This is mercy," said she. "It is the grace of God."

The organ pealed, and the chorus of children's voices mingled sweetly with it. The bright sunshine shed its warm light, through the windows, over the pew in which Karen sat. Her heart was so filled with sunshine, peace, and joy that it broke, and her soul was borne by a sunbeam up to God, where there was nobody to ask about the red shoes.

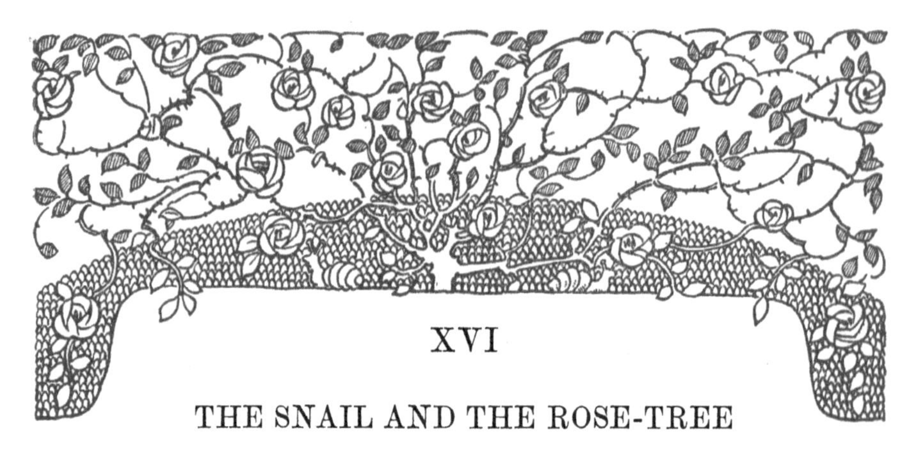

XVI

THE SNAIL AND THE ROSE-TREE

Round about the garden ran a hedge of hazel-bushes; beyond the hedge were fields and meadows with cows and sheep; but in the middle of the garden stood a Rose-tree in bloom, under which sat a Snail, whose shell contained a great deal—that is, himself.

"Only wait till my time comes," he said; "I shall do more than grow roses, bear nuts, or give milk, like the hazel-bush, the cows and the sheep."

"I expect a great deal from you," said the rose-tree. "May I ask when it will appear?"

"I take my time," said the snail. "You're always in such a hurry. That does not excite expectation."

The following year the snail lay in almost the same spot, in the sunshine under the rose-tree, which was again budding and bearing roses as fresh and beautiful as ever. The snail crept half out of his shell, stretched out his horns, and drew them in again.

"Everything is just as it was last year! No progress at all; the rose-tree sticks to its roses and gets no farther."

The summer and the autumn passed; the rose-tree bore roses and buds till the snow fell and the weather became raw and wet; then it bent down its head, and the snail crept into the ground.

A new year began; the roses made their appearance, and the snail made his too.

"You are an old rose-tree now," said the snail. "You must make haste and die. You have given the world all that you had in you; whether it was of much importance is a question that I have not had time to think about. But this much is clear and plain, that you have not done the least for your inner development, or you would have produced something else. Have you anything to say in defence? You will now soon be nothing but a stick. Do you understand what I say?"

"You frighten me," said the rose—tree. "I have never thought of that."

"No, you have never taken the trouble to think at all. Have you ever given yourself an account why you bloomed, and how your blooming comes about—why just in that way and in no other?"

"No," said the rose-tree. "I bloom in gladness, because I cannot do otherwise. The sun shone and warmed me, and the air refreshed me; I drank the clear dew and the invigorating rain. I breathed and I lived! Out of the earth there arose a power within me, whilst from above I also received strength; I felt an ever-renewed and ever-increasing happiness, and therefore I was obliged to go on blooming. That was my life; I could not do otherwise."

"You have led a very easy life," remarked the snail.

"Certainly. Everything was given me," said the rose-tree. "But still more was given to you. Yours is one of those deep-thinking natures, one of those highly gifted minds that astonishes the world."

"I have not the slightest intention of doing so," said the snail. "The world is nothing to me. What have I to do with the world? I have enough to do with myself, and enough in myself."

"But must we not all here on earth give up our best parts to others, and offer as much as lies in our power? It is true, I have only given roses. But you—you who are so richly endowed—what have you given to the world? What will you give it?"

"What have I given? What am I going to give? I spit at it; it's good for nothing, and does not concern me. For my part, you may go on bearing roses; you cannot do anything else. Let the hazel bush bear nuts, and the cows and sheep give milk; they have each their public. I have mine in myself. I retire within myself and there I stop. The world is nothing to me."

With this the snail withdrew into his house and blocked up the entrance.

"That's very sad," said the rose tree. "I cannot creep into myself, however much I might wish to do so; I have to go on bearing roses. Then they drop their leaves, which are blown away by the wind. But

I once saw how a rose was laid in the mistress's hymn-book, and how one of my roses found a place in the bosom of a young beautiful girl, and how another was kissed by the lips of a child in the glad joy of life. That did me good; it was a real blessing. Those are my recollections, my life."

And the rose tree went on blooming in innocence, while the snail lay idling in his house—the world was nothing to him.

Years passed by.

The snail had turned to earth in the earth, and the rose tree too. Even the souvenir rose in the hymn-book was faded, but in the garden there were other rose trees and other snails. The latter crept into their houses and spat at the world, for it did not concern them.

Shall we read the story all over again? It will be just the same.

XVII

LITTLE IDA'S FLOWERS

My poor flowers are quite dead," said little Ida, "they were so pretty yesterday evening, and now all the leaves are hanging down quite withered. What do they do that for," she asked, of the student who sat on the sofa; she liked him very much, he could tell the most amusing stories, and cut out the prettiest pictures; hearts, and ladies dancing, castles with doors that opened, as well as flowers; he was a delightful student. "Why do the flowers look so faded today?" she asked again, and pointed to her nosegay, which was quite withered.

"Don't you know what is the matter with them?" said the student. "The flowers were at a ball last night, and therefore, it is no wonder they hang their heads."

"But flowers cannot dance?" cried little Ida.

"Yes indeed, they can," replied the student. "When it grows dark, and everybody is asleep, they jump about quite merrily. They have a ball almost every night."

"Can children go to these balls?"

"Yes," said the student, "little daisies and lilies of the valley."

"Where do the beautiful flowers dance?" asked little Ida.

"Have you not often seen the large castle outside the gates of the town, where the king lives in summer, and where the beautiful garden is full of flowers? And have you not fed the swans with bread when they swam towards you? Well, the flowers have capital balls there, believe me."

"I was in the garden out there yesterday with my mother," said Ida, "but all the leaves were off the trees, and there was not a single flower left. Where are they? I used to see so many in the summer."

"They are in the castle," replied the student. "You must know that as soon as the king and all the court are gone into the town, the flowers run out of the garden into the castle, and you should see how merry they are. The two most beautiful roses seat themselves on the throne, and are called the king and queen, then all the red cocks-combs range themselves on each side, and bow, these are the lords-in-waiting. After that the pretty flowers come in, and there is a grand ball. The blue violets represent little naval cadets, and dance with hyacinths and crocuses which they call young ladies. The tu-lips and tiger-lilies are the old ladies who sit and watch the dancing, so that everything may be conducted with order and propriety."

"But," said little Ida, "is there no one there to hurt the flowers for dancing in the king's castle?"

"No one knows anything about it," said the student. "The old steward of the castle, who has to watch there at night, sometimes comes in; but he carries a great bunch of keys, and as soon as the flowers hear the keys rattle, they run and hide themselves behind the long curtains, and stand quite still, just peeping their heads out. Then the old steward says, 'I smell flowers here,' but he cannot see them."

"Oh how capital," said little Ida, clapping her hands. "Should I be able to see these flowers?"

"Yes," said the student, "mind you think of it the next time you go out, no doubt you will see them, if you peep through the window. I did so to-day, and I saw a long yellow lily lying stretched out on the sofa. She was a court lady."

"Can the flowers from the Botanical Gardens go to these balls?" asked Ida. "It is such a distance!"

"Oh yes," said the student, "whenever they like, for they can fly. Have you not seen those beautiful red, white, and yellow butterflies, that look like flowers? They were flowers once. They have flown off their stalks into the air, and flap their leaves as if they were little wings to make them fly. Then, if they behave well, they obtain permission to fly about during the day, instead of being obliged to sit still on their stems at home, and so in time their leaves become real wings. It may be, however, that the flowers in the Botanical Gardens have never been to the king's palace, and, therefore, they know nothing of the merry doings at night, which take place there. I will tell you what to do, and the botanical professor, who lives close by here, will be so surprised. You know him very well, do you not? Well, next time you go into his garden, you must tell one of the flowers that there is going to be a grand ball at the castle, then that flower will tell all the others, and they will fly away to the castle as soon as possible. And when the professor walks into his garden, there will not be a single flower left. How he will wonder what has become of them!"

"But how can one flower tell another? Flowers cannot speak?"

"No, certainly not," replied the student; "but they can make signs. Have you not often seen that when the wind blows they nod at one another, and rustle all their green leaves?"

"Can the professor understand the signs?" asked Ida.

"Yes, to be sure he can. He went one morning into his garden, and saw a stinging nettle making signs with its leaves to a beautiful red carnation. It was saying, 'You are so pretty, I like you very much.' But the professor did not approve of such nonsense, so he clapped his hands on the nettle to stop it. Then the leaves, which are its fingers, stung him so sharply that he has never ventured to touch a nettle since."

"Oh how funny!" said Ida, and she laughed.

"How can anyone put such notions into a child's head?" said a tiresome lawyer, who had come to pay a visit, and sat on the sofa. He did not like the student, and would grumble when he saw him cutting out droll or amusing pictures. Sometimes it would be a man hanging on a gibbet and holding a heart in his hand as if he had been stealing hearts. Sometimes it was an old witch riding through the air on a broom and carrying her husband on her nose. But the lawyer did not like such jokes, and he would say as he had just said,

"How can anyone put such nonsense into a child's head! what absurd fancies there are!"

But to little Ida, all these stories which the student told her about the flowers, seemed very droll, and she thought over them a great deal. The flowers did hang their heads, because they had been dancing all night, and were very tired, and most likely they were ill. Then she took them into the room where a number of toys lay on a pretty little table, and the whole of the table drawer besides was full of beautiful things. Her doll Sophy lay in the doll's bed asleep, and little Ida said to her, "You must really get up Sophy, and be content to lie in the drawer to-night; the poor flowers are ill, and they must lie in your bed, then perhaps they will get well again."

So she took the doll out, who looked quite cross, and said not a single word, for she was angry at being turned out of her bed. Ida placed the flowers in the doll's bed, and drew the quilt over them. Then she told them to lie quite still and be good, while she made some tea for them, so that they might be quite well and able to get up the next morning. And she drew the curtains close round the little bed, so that the sun might not shine in their eyes. During the whole evening she could not help thinking of what the student had told her. And before she went to bed herself, she was obliged to peep behind the curtains into the garden where all her mother's beautiful flowers grew, hyacinths and tulips, and many others. Then she whispered to them quite softly, "I know you are going to a ball to-night."

But the flowers appeared as if they did not understand, and not a leaf moved; still Ida felt quite sure she knew all about it. She lay awake a long time after she was in bed, thinking how pretty it must be to see all the beautiful flowers dancing in the king's garden. "I wonder if my flowers have really been there," she said to herself, and then she fell asleep. In the night she awoke; she had been dreaming of the flowers and of the student, as well as of the tiresome lawyer who found fault with him. It was quite still in Ida's bedroom; the night-lamp burnt on the table, and her father and mother were asleep. "I wonder if my flowers are still lying in Sophy's bed," she thought to herself; "how much I should like to know."

She raised herself a little, and glanced at the door of the room where all her flowers and playthings lay; it was partly open, and as she listened, it seemed as if some one in the room was playing the piano, but softly and more prettily than she had ever before heard it. "Now all the flowers are certainly dancing in there," she thought, "oh how much I should like to see them," but she did not dare move for fear of disturbing her father and mother.

"If they would only come in here," she thought; but they did not come, and the music continued to play so beautifully, and was so pretty, that she could resist no longer. She crept out of her little bed, went softly to the door and looked into the room. Oh what a splendid sight there was to be sure! There was no night-lamp burning, but the room appeared quite light, for the moon shone through the window upon the floor, and made it almost like day. All the hyacinths and tulips stood in two long rows down the room, not a single flower remained in the window, and the flower-pots were all empty. The flowers were dancing gracefully on the floor, making turns and holding each other by their long green leaves as they swung round.

At the piano sat a large yellow lily which little Ida was sure she had seen in the summer, for she remembered the student saying she was very much like Miss Lina, one of Ida's friends. They all laughed at him then, but now it seemed to little Ida as if the tall, yellow flower was really like the young lady. She had just the same manners while playing, bending her long yellow face from side to side, and nodding in time to the beautiful music. Then she saw a large purple crocus jump into the middle of the table where the playthings stood, go up to the doll's bedstead and draw back the curtains; there lay the sick flowers, but they got up directly, and nodded to the others as a sign that they wished to dance with them. The old rough doll, with the broken mouth, stood up and bowed to the pretty flowers. They did not look ill at all now, but jumped about and were very merry, yet none of them noticed little Ida.

Presently it seemed as if something fell from the table. Ida looked that way, and saw a slight carnival rod jumping down among the flowers as if it belonged to them; it was, however, very smooth and neat, and a little wax doll with a broad brimmed hat on her head, like the one worn by the lawyer, sat upon it. The carnival rod hopped about among the flowers on its three red stilted feet, and stamped quite loud when it danced the Mazurka; the flowers could not perform this dance, they were too light to stamp in that manner. All at once the wax doll which rode on the carnival rod seemed to grow larger and taller, and it turned round and said to the paper flowers, "How can you put such things in a child's head? they are all foolish fancies;" and then the doll was exactly like the lawyer with the broad brimmed hat, and looked as yellow and as cross as he did; but the paper dolls struck him on his thin legs, and he shrunk up again and became quite a little wax doll.

This was very amusing, and Ida could not help laughing. The carnival rod went on dancing, and the lawyer was obliged to dance also. It was no use, he might make himself great and tall, or remain a little wax doll with a large black hat; still he must dance. Then at last the other flowers interceded for him, especially those who had lain in the doll's bed, and the carnival rod gave up his dancing. At the same moment a loud knocking was heard in the drawer, where Ida's doll Sophy lay with many other toys. Then the rough doll ran to the end of the table, laid himself flat down upon it, and began to pull the drawer out a little way.

Then Sophy raised himself, and looked round quite astonished, "There must be a ball here to-night," said Sophy. "Why did not somebody tell me?"

"Will you dance with me?" said the rough doll.

"You are the right sort to dance with, certainly," said she, turning her back upon him.

Then she seated herself on the edge of the drawer, and thought that perhaps one of the flowers would ask her to dance; but none of them came. Then she coughed, "Hem, hem, a-hem;" but for all that not one came. The shabby doll now danced quite alone, and not very badly, after all. As none of the flowers seemed to notice Sophy, she let herself down from the drawer to the floor, so as to make a very great noise. All the flowers came round her directly, and asked if she had hurt herself, especially those who had lain in her bed. But she was not hurt at all, and Ida's flowers thanked her for the use of the nice bed, and were very kind to her. They led her into the middle of the room, where the moon shone, and danced with her, while all the other flowers formed a circle round them. Then Sophy was very happy, and said they might keep her bed; she did not mind lying in the drawer at all. But the flowers thanked her very much, and said,—

SHOT WITH THEIR CROSSBOWS OVER THE GRAVE

"We cannot live long. To-morrow morning we shall be quite dead; and you must tell little Ida to bury us in the garden, near to the grave of the canary; then, in the summer we shall wake up and be more beautiful than ever."

"No, you must not die," said Sophy, as she kissed the flowers.

Then the door of the room opened, and a number of beautiful flowers danced in. Ida could not imagine where they could come from, unless they were the flowers from the king's garden. First came two lovely roses, with little golden crowns on their heads; these were the king and queen. Beautiful stocks and carnations followed, bowing to every one present. They had also music with them. Large poppies and peonies had pea-shells for instruments, and blew into them till they were quite red in the face. The bunches of blue hyacinths and the little white snowdrops jingled their bell-like flowers, as if they were real bells. Then came many more flowers: blue violets, purple heart's-ease, daisies, and lilies of the valley, and they all danced together, and kissed each other. It was very beautiful to behold.

At last the flowers wished each other good-night. Then little Ida crept back into her bed again, and dreamt of all she had seen. When she arose the next morning, she went quickly to the little table, to see if the flowers were still there. She drew aside the curtains of the little bed. There they all lay, but quite faded; much more so than the day before. Sophy was lying in the drawer where Ida had placed her; but she looked very sleepy.

"Do you remember what the flowers told you to say to me?" said little Ida. But Sophy looked quite stupid, and said not a single word.

"You are not kind at all," said Ida; "and yet they all danced with you."

Then she took a little paper box, on which were painted beautiful birds, and laid the dead flowers in it.

"This shall be your pretty coffin," she said; "and by and by, when my cousins come to visit me, they shall help me to bury you out in the garden; so that next summer you may grow up again more beautiful than ever."

Her cousins were two good-tempered boys, whose names were James and Adolphus. Their father had given them each a bow and arrow, and they had brought them to show Ida. She told them about the poor flowers which were dead; and as soon as they obtained permission, they went with her to bury them. The two boys walked first, with their crossbows on their shoulders, and little Ida followed, carrying the pretty box containing the dead flowers. They dug a little grave in the garden. Ida kissed her flowers and then laid them, with the box, in the earth. James and Adolphus then fired their crossbows over the grave, as they had neither guns nor cannons.

XVIII

THE FLYING TRUNK

There was once a merchant who was so rich that he could have paved the whole street with gold, and would even then have had enough for a small alley. But he did not do so; he knew the value of money better than to use it in this way. So clever was he, that every shilling he put out brought him a crown; and so he continued till he died.

His son inherited his wealth, and he lived a merry life with it; he went to a masquerade every night, made kites out of five pound notes, and threw pieces of gold into the sea instead of stones, making ducks and drakes of them. In this manner he soon lost all his money. At last he had nothing left but a pair of slippers, an old dressing-gown, and four shillings. And now all his friends deserted him, they could not walk with him in the streets; but one of them, who was very good-natured, sent him an old trunk with this message, "Pack up!" "Yes," he said, "it is all very well to say 'pack up,'" but he had nothing left to pack up, therefore he seated himself in the trunk.

It was a very wonderful trunk; no sooner did any one press on the lock than the trunk could fly. He shut the lid and pressed the lock, when away flew the trunk up the chimney with the merchant's son in it, right up into the clouds. Whenever the bottom of the trunk cracked, he was in a great fright, for if the trunk fell to pieces he would have made a tremendous somerset over the trees. However, he got safely in his trunk to the land of Turkey. He hid the trunk in the wood under some dry leaves, and then went into the town:

he could so this very well, for the Turks always go about dressed in dressing-gowns and slippers, as he was himself. He happened to meet a nurse with a little child. "I say, you Turkish nurse," cried he, "what castle is that near the town, with the windows placed so high?"

"The king's daughter lives there," she replied; "it has been prophesied that she will be very unhappy about a lover, and therefore no one is allowed to visit her, unless the king and queen are present."

"Thank you," said the merchant's son. So he went back to the wood, seated himself in his trunk, flew up to the roof of the castle, and crept through the window into the princess's room. She lay on the sofa asleep, and she was so beautiful that the merchant's son could not help kissing her. Then she awoke, and was very much frightened; but he told her he was a Turkish angel, who had come down through the air to see her, which pleased her very much. He sat down by her side and talked to her: he said her eyes were like beautiful dark lakes, in which the thoughts swam about like little mermaids, and he told her that her forehead was a snowy mountain, which contained splendid halls full of pictures. And then he related to her about the stork who brings the beautiful children from the rivers. These were delightful stories; and when he asked the princess if she would marry him, she consented immediately.

"But you must come on Saturday," she said; "for then the king and queen will take tea with me. They will be very proud when they find that I am going to marry a Turkish angel; but you must think of some very pretty stories to tell them, for my parents like to hear stories better than anything. My mother prefers one that is deep and moral; but my father likes something funny, to make him laugh."

"Very well," he replied; "I shall bring you no other marriage portion than a story," and so they parted. But the princess gave him a sword which was studded with gold coins, and these he could use.

Then he flew away to the town and bought a new dressing-gown, and afterwards returned to the wood, where he composed a story, so as to be ready for Saturday, which was no easy matter. It was ready however by Saturday, when he went to see the princess. The king, and queen, and the whole court, were at tea with the princess; and he was received with great politeness.

"Will you tell us a story?" said the queen,—"one that is instructive and full of deep learning."

"Yes, but with something in it to laugh at," said the king.

"Certainly," he replied, and commenced at once, asking them to listen attentively. "There was once a bundle of matches that were exceedingly proud of their high descent. Their genealogical tree, that is, a large pine-tree from which they had been cut, was at one time a large, old tree in the wood. The matches now lay between a tinder-box and an old iron saucepan, and were talking about their youthful days. 'Ah! then we grew on the green boughs, and were as green as they; every morning and evening we were fed with diamond drops of dew. Whenever the sun shone, we felt his warm rays, and the little birds would relate stories to us as they sung. We knew that we were rich, for the other trees only wore their green dress in summer, but our family were able to array themselves in green, summer and winter. But the wood-cutter came, like a great revolution, and our family fell under the axe. The head of the house obtained a situation as mainmast in a very fine ship, and can sail round the world when he will. The other branches of the family were taken to different places, and our office now is to kindle a light for common people. This is how such high-born people as we came to be in a kitchen.'

"'Mine has been a very different fate,' said the iron pot, which stood by the matches; 'from my first entrance into the world I have been used to cooking and scouring. I am the first in this house, when anything solid or useful is required. My only pleasure is to be made clean and shining after dinner, and to sit in my place and have a little sensible conversation with my neighbors. All of us, excepting the water-bucket, which is sometimes taken into the courtyard, live here together within these four walls. We get our news from the market-basket, but he sometimes tells us very unpleasant things about the people and the government. Yes, and one day an old pot was so alarmed, that he fell down and was broken to pieces. He was a liberal, I can tell you.'

"'You are talking too much,' said the tinder-box, and the steel struck against the flint till some sparks flew out, crying, 'We want a merry evening, don't we?'

"'Yes, of course,' said the matches, 'let us talk about those who are the highest born.'

"'No, I don't like to be always talking of what we are,' remarked the saucepan; 'let us think of some other amusement; I will begin. We will tell something that has happened to ourselves; that will be very easy, and interesting as well. On the Baltic Sea, near the Danish shore'—

"'What a pretty commencement!' said the plates; 'we shall all like that story, I am sure.'

"'Yes; well in my youth, I lived in a quiet family, where the furniture was polished, the floors scoured, and clean curtains put up every fortnight.'

"'What an interesting way you have of relating a story,' said the carpet-broom; 'it is easy to perceive that you have been a great deal in women's society, there is something so pure runs through what you say.'

"'That is quite true,' said the water-bucket; and he made a spring with joy, and splashed some water on the floor.

"Then the saucepan went on with his story, and the end was as good as the beginning.

"The plates rattled with pleasure, and the carpet-broom brought some green parsley out of the dust-hole and crowned the saucepan, for he knew it would vex the others; and he thought, 'If I crown him to-day he will crown me to-morrow.'

"'Now, let us have a dance,' said the fire-tongs; and then how they danced and stuck up one leg in the air. The chair-cushion in the corner burst with laughter when she saw it.

"'Shall I be crowned now?' asked the fire-tongs; so the broom found another wreath for the tongs.

"'They were only common people after all,' thought the matches. The tea-urn was now asked to sing, but she said she had a cold, and could not sing without boiling heat. They all thought this was affectation, and because she did not wish to sing excepting in the parlor, when on the table with the grand people.

"In the window sat an old quill-pen, with which the maid generally wrote. There was nothing remarkable about the pen, excepting that it had been dipped too deeply in the ink, but it was proud of that.

"'If the tea-urn won't sing,' said the pen, 'she can leave it alone; there is a nightingale in a cage who can sing; she has not been taught much, certainly, but we need not say anything this evening about that.'

"'I think it highly improper,' said the tea-kettle, who was kitchen singer, and half-brother to the tea-urn, 'that a rich foreign bird should be listened to here. Is it patriotic? Let the market-basket decide what is right.'

"'I certainly am vexed,' said the basket; 'inwardly vexed, more than any one can imagine. Are we spending the evening properly? Would it not be more sensible to put the house in order? If each were in his own place I would lead a game; this would be quite another thing.'

"'Let us act a play,' said they all. At the same moment the door opened, and the maid came in. Then not one stirred; they all remained quite still; yet, at the same time, there was not a single pot amongst them who had not a high opinion of himself, and of what he could do if he chose.

"'Yes, if we had chosen,' they each thought, 'we might have spent a very pleasant evening.'

"The maid took the matches and lighted them; dear me, how they sputtered and blazed up!

"'Now then,' they thought, 'every one will see that we are the first. How we shine; what a light we give!' Even while they spoke their light went out.

"What a capital story," said the queen, "I feel as if I were really in the kitchen, and could see the matches; yes, you shall marry our daughter."

"Certainly," said the king, "thou shalt have our daughter." The king said thou to him because he was going to be one of the family. The wedding-day was fixed, and, on the evening before, the whole city was illuminated. Cakes and sweetmeats were thrown among the people. The street boys stood on tiptoe and shouted "hurrah," and whistled between their fingers; altogether it was a very splendid affair.

"CRACK!" HOW THEY WENT OFF!

"I will give them another treat," said the merchant's son. So he went and bought rockets and crackers, and all sorts of fire-works that could be thought of, packed them in his trunk, and flew up with it into the air. What a whizzing and popping they made as they went off! The Turks, when they saw such a sight in the air, jumped so high that their slippers flew about their ears. It was easy to believe after this that the princess was really going to marry a Turkish angel.

As soon as the merchant's son had come down in his flying trunk to the wood after the fireworks, he thought, "I will go back into the town now, and hear what they think of the entertainment." It was very natural that he should wish to know. And what strange things people did say, to be sure! every one whom he questioned had a different tale to tell, though they all thought it very beautiful.

"'I saw the Turkish angel myself," said one; "he had eyes like glittering stars, and a head like foaming water."

"He flew in a mantle of fire," cried another, "and lovely little cherubs peeped out from the folds."

He heard many more fine things about himself, and that the next day he was to be married. After this he went back to the forest to rest himself in his trunk. It had disappeared! A spark from the fireworks which remained had set it on fire; it was burnt to ashes! So the merchant's son could not fly any more, nor go to meet his bride. She stood all day on the roof waiting for him, and most likely she is waiting there still; while he wanders through the world telling fairy tales, but none of them so amusing as the one he related about the matches.

XIX

THE TINDER BOX

There came a soldier marching down the high road-one, two! one, two! He had his knapsack on his back and his sword at his side as he came home from the wars. On the road he met a witch, an ugly old witch, a witch whose lower lip dangled right down on her chest.

"Good evening, soldier," she said. "What a fine sword you've got there, and what a big knapsack. Aren't you every inch a soldier! And now you shall have money, as much as you please."

"That's very kind, you old witch," said the soldier.

"See that big tree." The witch pointed to one near by them. "It's hollow to the roots. Climb to the top of the trunk and you'll find a hole through which you can let yourself down deep under the tree. I'll tie a rope around your middle, so that when you call me I can pull you up again."

"What would I do deep down under that tree?" the soldier wanted to know.

"Fetch money," the witch said. "Listen. When you touch bottom you'll find yourself in a great hall. It is very bright there, because more than a hundred lamps are burning. By their light you will see three doors. Each door has a key in it, so you can open them all.

"If you walk into the first room, you'll see a large chest in the middle of the floor. On it sits a dog, and his eyes are as big as saucers. But don't worry about that. I'll give you my blue checked apron to spread out on the floor. Snatch up that dog and set him on my apron. Then you can open the chest and take out as many pieces of money as you please. They are all copper.

"But if silver suits you better, then go into the next room. There sits a dog and his eyes are as big as mill wheels. But don't you care about that. Set the dog on my apron while you line your pockets with silver.

"Maybe you'd rather have gold. You can, you know. You can have all the gold you can carry if you go into the third room. The only hitch is that there on the money-chest sits a dog, and each of his eyes is as big as the Round Tower of Copenhagen. That's the sort of dog he is. But never you mind how fierce he looks. Just set him on my apron and he'll do you no harm as you help yourself from the chest to all the gold you want."

"That suits me," said the soldier. "But what do you get out of all this, you old witch? I suppose that you want your share."

"No indeed," said the witch. "I don't want a penny of it. All I ask is for you to fetch me an old tinder box that my grandmother forgot the last time she was down there."

"Good," said the soldier. "Tie the rope around me."

"Here it is," said the witch, "and here's my blue checked apron."

The soldier climbed up to the hole in the tree and let himself slide through it, feet foremost down into the great hall where the hundreds of lamps were burning, just as the witch had said. Now he threw open the first door he came to. Ugh! There sat a dog glaring at him with eyes as big as saucers.

"You're a nice fellow," the soldier said, as he shifted him to the witch's apron and took all the coppers that his pockets would hold. He shut up the chest, set the dog back on it, and made for the second room. Alas and alack! There sat the dog with eyes as big as mill wheels.

"Don't you look at me like that." The soldier set him on the witch's apron. "You're apt to strain your eyesight." When he saw the chest brimful of silver, he threw away all his coppers and filled both his pockets and knapsack with silver alone. Then he went into the third room. Oh, what a horrible sight to see! The dog in there really did have eyes as big as the Round Tower, and when he rolled them they spun like wheels.

"Good evening," the soldier said, and saluted, for such a dog he had never seen before. But on second glance he thought to himself, "This won't do." So he lifted the dog down to the floor, and threw open the chest. What a sight! Here was gold and to spare. He could buy out all Copenhagen with it. He could buy all the cake-woman's sugar pigs, and all the tin soldiers, whips, and rocking horses there are in the world. Yes, there was really money!

In short order the soldier got rid of all the silver coins he had stuffed in his pockets and knapsack, to put gold in their place. Yes sir, he crammed all his pockets, his knapsack, his cap, and his boots so full that he scarcely could walk. Now he was made of money. Putting the dog back on the chest he banged out the door and called up through the hollow tree:

"Pull me up now, you old witch."

"Have you got the tinder box?" asked the witch.

"Confound the tinder box," the soldier shouted. "I clean forgot it."

When he fetched it, the witch hauled him up. There he stood on the highroad again, with his pockets, boots, knapsack and cap full of gold.

"What do you want with the tinder box?" he asked the old witch.

"None of your business," she told him. "You've had your money, so hand over my tinder box."

"Nonsense," said the soldier. "I'll take out my sword and I'll cut your head off if you don't tell me at once what you want with it."

"I won't," the witch screamed at him.

So he cut her head off. There she lay! But he tied all his money in her apron, slung it over his shoulder, stuck the tinder box in his pocket, and struck out for town.

It was a splendid town. He took the best rooms at the best inn, and ordered all the good things he liked to eat, for he was a rich man now because he had so much money. The servant who cleaned his boots may have thought them remarkably well worn for a man of such means, but that was before he went shopping. Next morning he bought boots worthy of him, and the best clothes. Now that he had turned out to be such a fashionable gentleman, people told him all about the splendors of their town-all about their King, and what a pretty Princess he had for a daughter.

"Where can I see her?" the soldier inquired.

"You can't see her at all," everyone said. "She lives in a great copper castle inside all sorts of walls and towers. Only the King can come in or go out of it, for it's been foretold that the Princess will marry a common soldier. The King would much rather she didn't."

"I'd like to see her just the same," the soldier thought. But there was no way to manage it,

Now he lived a merry life. He went to the theatre, drove about in the

King's garden, and gave away money to poor people. This was to his credit, for he remembered from the old days what it feels like to go without a penny in your pocket. Now that he was wealthy and well dressed, he had all too many who called him their friend and a genuine gentleman. That pleased him

But he spent money every day without making any, and wound up with only two coppers to his name. He had to quit his fine quarters to live in a garret, clean his own boots, and mend them himself with a darning needle. None of his friends came to see him, because there were too many stairs to climb.

One evening when he sat in the dark without even enough money to buy a candle, he suddenly remembered there was a candle end in the tinder box that he had picked up when the witch sent him down the hollow tree. He got out the tinder box, and the moment he struck sparks from the flint of it his door burst open and there stood a dog from down under the tree. It was the one with eyes as big as saucers.

"What," said the dog, "is my lord's command?"

"What's this?" said the soldier. "Have I got the sort of tinder box that will get me whatever I want? Go get me some money," he ordered the dog. Zip! The dog was gone. Zip! He was back again, with a bag full of copper in his mouth.

Now the soldier knew what a remarkable tinder box he had. Strike it once and there was the dog from the chest of copper coins. Strike it twice and here came the dog who had the silver. Three times brought the dog who guarded gold.

Back went the soldier to his comfortable quarters. Out strode the soldier in fashionable clothes. Immediately his friends knew him again, because they liked him so much.

SHE SAT UPON THE DOG'S BACK AND SLEPT

Then the thought occurred to him, "Isn't it odd that no one ever gets to see the Princess? They say she's very pretty, but what's the good of it as long as she stays locked up in that large copper castle with so many towers? Why can't I see her? Where's my tinder box?" He struck a light and, zip! came the dog with eyes as big as saucers.

"It certainly is late," said the soldier. "Practically midnight. But I do want a glimpse of the Princess, if only for a moment."

Out the door went the dog, and before the soldier could believe it, here came the dog with the Princess on his back. She was sound asleep, and so pretty that everyone could see she was a Princess. The soldier couldn't keep from kissing her, because he was every inch a soldier. Then the dog took the Princess home.

Next morning when the King and Queen were drinking their tea, the Princess told them about the strange dream she'd had-all about a dog and a soldier. She'd ridden on the dog's back, and the soldier had kissed her.

"Now that was a fine story," said the Queen. The next night one of the old ladies of the court was under orders to sit by the Princess's bed, and see whether this was a dream or something else altogether. The soldier was longing to see the pretty Princess again, so the dog came by night to take her up and away as fast as he could run. But the old lady pulled on her storm boots and ran right after them. When she saw them disappear into a large house she thought, "Now I know where it is," and drew a big cross on the door with a piece of chalk. Then she went home to bed, and before long the dog brought the Princess home too. But when the dog saw that cross marked on the soldier's front door, he got himself a piece of chalk and cross-marked every door in the town. This was a clever thing to do, because now the old lady couldn't tell the right door from all the wrong doors he had marked.

Early in the morning along came the King and the Queen, the old lady, and all the officers, to see where the Princess had been.

"Here it is," said the King when he saw the first cross mark.

"No, my dear. There it is," said the Queen who was looking next door.

"Here's one, there's one, and yonder's another one!" said they all. Wherever they looked they saw chalk marks, so they gave up searching.

The Queen, though, was an uncommonly clever woman, who could do more than ride in a coach. She took her big gold scissors, cut out a piece of silk, and made a neat little bag. She filled it with fine buckwheat flour and tied it on to the Princess's back. Then she pricked a little hole in it so that the flour would sift out along the way, wherever the Princess might go.

Again the dog came in the night, took the Princess on his back, and ran with her to the soldier, who loved her so much that he would have been glad to be a Prince just so he could make his wife.

The dog didn't notice how the flour made a trail from the castle right up to the soldier's window, where he ran up the wall with the Princess. So in the morning it was all too plain to the King and Queen just where their daughter had been.

They took the soldier and they put him in prison. There he sat. It was dark, and it was dismal, and they told him, "Tomorrow is the day for you to hang." That didn't cheer him up any, and as for his tinder box he'd left it behind at the inn. In the morning he could see through his narrow little window how the people all hurried out of town to see him hanged. He heard the drums beat and he saw the soldiers march. In the crowd of running people he saw a shoemaker's boy in a leather apron and slippers. The boy galloped so fast that off flew one slipper, which hit the wall right where the soldier pressed his face to the iron bars.

"Hey there, you shoemaker's boy, there's no hurry," the soldier shouted. "Nothing can happen till I get there. But if you run to where I live and bring me my tinder box, I'll give you four coppers. Put your best foot foremost."

The shoemaker's boy could use four coppers, so he rushed the tinder box to the soldier, and-well, now we shall hear what happened!

Outside the town a high gallows had been built. Around it stood soldiers and many hundred thousand people. The King and Queen sat on a splendid throne, opposite the judge and the whole council. The soldier already stood upon the ladder, but just as they were about to put the rope around his neck he said the custom was to grant a poor criminal one last small favor. He wanted to smoke a pipe of tobacco-the last he'd be smoking in this world.

The King couldn't refuse him, so the soldier struck fire from his tinder box, once-twice-and a third time. Zip! There stood all the dogs, one with eyes as big as saucers, one with eyes as big as mill wheels, one with eyes as big as the Round Tower of Copenhagen.

"Help me. Save me from hanging!" said the soldier. Those dogs took the judges and all the council, some by the leg and some by the nose, and tossed them so high that they came down broken to bits.

"Don't!" cried the King, but the biggest dog took him and the Queen too, and tossed them up after the others. Then the soldiers trembled and the people shouted, "Soldier, be our King and marry the pretty Princess."

So they put the soldier in the King's carriage. All three of his dogs danced in front of it, and shouted "Hurrah!" The boys whistled through their fingers, and the soldiers saluted. The Princess came out of the copper castle to be Queen, and that suited her exactly. The wedding lasted all of a week, and the three dogs sat at the table, with their eyes opened wider than ever before.

XX

THE PEA BLOSSOM

THERE were once five peas in one shell; they were green, and the shell was green, and so they believed that the whole world must be green also, which was a very natural conclusion.

The shell grew, and the peas grew; and as they grew they arranged themselves all in a row. The sun shone without and warmed the shell, and the rain made it clear and transparent; it looked mild and agreeable in broad daylight and dark at night, just as it should. And the peas, as they sat there, grew bigger and bigger, and more thoughtful as they mused, for they felt there must be something for them to do.

"Are we to sit here forever?" asked one. "Shall we not become hard, waiting here so long? It seems to me there must be something outside; I feel sure of it."

Weeks passed by; the peas became yellow, and the shell became yellow.

"All the world is turning yellow, I suppose," said they—and perhaps they were right.

Suddenly they felt a pull at the shell. It was torn off and held in human hands; then it was slipped into the pocket of a jacket, together with other full pods.

"Now we shall soon be let out," said one, and that was just what they all wanted.

"I should like to know which of us will travel farthest," said the smallest of the five; "and we shall soon see."

"What is to happen will happen," said the largest pea.

"Crack!" went the shell, and the five peas rolled out into the bright sunshine. There they lay in a child's hand. A little boy was holding them tightly. He said they were fine peas for his pea-shooter, and immediately he put one in and shot it out.

"Now I am flying out into the wide world," said the pea. "Catch me if you can." And he was gone in a moment.

"I intend to fly straight to the sun," said the second. "That is a shell that will suit me exactly, for it lets itself be seen." And away he went.

"We will go to sleep wherever we find ourselves," said the next two; "we shall still be rolling onwards." And they did fall to the floor and roll about, but they got into the pea-shooter for all that. "We will go farthest of any," said they.

"What is to happen will happen," exclaimed the last one, as he was shot out of the pea-shooter. Up he flew against an old board under a garret window and fell into a little crevice which was almost filled with moss and soft earth. The moss closed itself about him, and there he lay—a captive indeed, but not unnoticed by God.

"What is to happen will happen," said he to himself.

Within the little garret lived a poor woman, who went out to clean stoves, chop wood into small pieces, and do other hard work, for she was both strong and industrious. Yet she remained always poor, and at home in the garret lay her only daughter, not quite grown up and very delicate and weak. For a whole year she had kept her bed, and it seemed as if she could neither die nor get well.

"She is going to her little sister," said the woman. "I had only the two children, and it was not an easy thing to support them; but the good God provided for one of them by taking her home to himself. The other was left to me, but I suppose they are not to be separated, and my sick girl will soon go to her sister in heaven."

All day long the sick girl lay quietly and patiently, while her mother went out to earn money.

Spring came, and early one morning the sun shone through the little window and threw his rays mildly and pleasantly over the floor of the room. Just as the mother was going to her work, the sick girl fixed her gaze on the lowest pane of the window. "Mother," she exclaimed, "what can that little green thing be that peeps in at the window? It is moving in the wind."

The mother stepped to the window and half opened it. "Oh!" she said, "there is actually a little pea that has taken root and is putting out its green leaves. How could it have got into this crack? Well, now, here is a little garden for you to amuse yourself with." So the bed of the sick girl was drawn nearer to the window, that she might see the budding plant; and the mother went forth to her work.

"Mother, I believe I shall get well," said the sick child in the evening. "The sun has shone in here so bright and warm to-day, and the little pea is growing so fast, that I feel better, too, and think I shall get up and go out into the warm sunshine again."

"God grant it!" said the mother, but she did not believe it would be so. She took a little stick and propped up the green plant which had given her daughter such pleasure, so that it might not be broken by the winds. She tied the piece of string to the window-sill and to the upper part of the frame, so that the pea tendrils might have something to twine round. And the plant shot up so fast that one could almost see it grow from day to day.

"A flower is really coming," said the mother one morning. At last she was beginning to let herself hope that her little sick daughter might indeed recover. She remembered that for some time the child had spoken more cheerfully, and that during the last few days she had raised herself in bed in the morning to look with sparkling eyes at her little garden which contained but a single pea plant.

A week later the invalid sat up by the open window a whole hour, feeling quite happy in the warm sunshine, while outside grew the little plant, and on it a pink pea blossom in full bloom. The little maiden bent down and gently kissed the delicate leaves. This day was like a festival to her.

"Our heavenly Father himself has planted that pea and made it grow and flourish, to bring joy to you and hope to me, my blessed child," said the happy mother, and she smiled at the flower as if it had been an angel from God.

But what became of the other peas? Why, the one who flew out into the wide world and said, "Catch me if you can," fell into a gutter on the roof of a house and ended his travels in the crop of a pigeon. The two lazy ones were carried quite as far and were of some use, for they also were eaten by pigeons; but the fourth, who wanted to reach the sun, fell into a sink and lay there in the dirty water for days and weeks, till he had swelled to a great size.

"I am getting beautifully fat," said the pea; "I expect I shall burst at last; no pea could do more than that, I think. I am the most remarkable of all the five that were in the shell." And the sink agreed with the pea.

But the young girl, with sparkling eyes and the rosy hue of health upon her cheeks, stood at the open garret window and, folding her thin hands over the pea blossom, thanked God for what He had done.

XXI

WHAT THE OLD MAN DOES IS ALWAYS RIGHT

I will tell you a story that was told me when I was a little boy. Every time I thought of this story, it seemed to me more and more charming; for it is with stories as it is with many people—they become better as they grow older.

I have no doubt that you have been in the country, and seen a very old farmhouse, with a thatched roof, and mosses and small plants growing wild upon it. There is a stork's nest on the ridge of the gable, for we cannot do without the stork. The walls of the house are sloping, and the windows are low, and only one of the latter is made to open. The baking-oven sticks out of the wall like a great knob. An elder-tree hangs over the palings; and beneath its branches, at the foot of the paling, is a pool of water, in which a few ducks are disporting themselves. There is a yard-dog too, who barks at all corners. Just such a farmhouse as this stood in a country lane; and in it dwelt an old couple, a peasant and his wife. Small as their possessions were, they had one article they could not do without, and that was a horse, which contrived to live upon the grass which it found by the side of the high road. The old peasant rode into the town upon this horse, and his neighbors often borrowed it of him, and paid for the loan of it by rendering some service to the old couple. After a time they thought it would be as well to sell the horse, or exchange it for something which might be more useful to them. But what might this something be?

"You'll know best, old man," said the wife. "It is fair-day to-day; so ride into town, and get rid of the horse for money, or make a good exchange; whichever you do will be right to me, so ride to the fair."

And she fastened his neckerchief for him; for she could do that better than he could, and she could also tie it very prettily in a double bow. She also smoothed his hat round and round with the palm of her hand, and gave him a kiss. Then he rode away upon the horse that was to be sold or bartered for something else. Yes, the old man knew what he was about. The sun shone with great heat, and not a cloud was to be seen in the sky. The road was very dusty; for a number of people, all going to the fair, were driving, riding, or walking upon it. There was no shelter anywhere from the hot sunshine. Among the rest a man came trudging along, and driving a cow to the fair. The cow was as beautiful a creature as any cow could be.

"She gives good milk, I am certain," said the peasant to himself. "That would be a very good exchange: the cow for the horse. Hallo there! you with the cow," he said. "I tell you what; I dare say a horse is of more value than a cow; but I don't care for that,—a cow will be more useful to me; so, if you like, we'll exchange."

"To be sure I will," said the man.

Accordingly the exchange was made; and as the matter was settled, the peasant might have turned back; for he had done the business he came to do. But, having made up his mind to go to the fair, he determined to do so, if only to have a look at it; so on he went to the town with his cow. Leading the animal, he strode on sturdily, and, after a short time, overtook a man who was driving a sheep. It was a good fat sheep, with a fine fleece on its back.

"I should like to have that fellow," said the peasant to himself. "There is plenty of grass for him by our palings, and in the winter we could keep him in the room with us. Perhaps it would be more profitable to have a sheep than a cow. Shall I exchange?" The man with the sheep was quite ready, and the bargain was quickly made. And then our peasant continued his way on the high-road with his sheep. Soon after this, he overtook another man, who had come into the road from a field, and was carrying a large goose under his arm.

SO SHE TIED ON HIS NECKERCHIEF AND
MADE HIM LOOK QUITE SPRUCE

"What a heavy creature you have there!" said the peasant; "it has plenty of feathers and plenty of fat, and would look well tied to a string, or paddling in the water at our place. That would be very useful to my old woman; she could make all sorts of profits out of it. How often she has said, 'If now we only had a goose!' Now here is an opportunity, and, if possible, I will get it for her. Shall we exchange? I will give you my sheep for your goose, and thanks into the bargain."

The other had not the least objection, and accordingly the exchange was made, and our peasant became possessor of the goose. By this time he had arrived very near the town. The crowd on the high road had been gradually increasing, and there was quite a rush of men and cattle. The cattle walked on the path and by the palings, and at the turnpike-gate they even walked into the toll-keeper's potato-field, where one fowl was strutting about with a string tied to its leg, for fear it should take fright at the crowd, and run away and get lost. The tail-feathers of the fowl were very short, and it winked with both its eyes, and looked very cunning, as it said "Cluck, cluck." What were the thoughts of the fowl as it said this I cannot tell you; but directly our good man saw it, he thought, "Why that's the finest fowl I ever saw in my life; it's finer than our parson's brood hen, upon my word. I should like to have that fowl. Fowls can always pick up a few grains that lie about, and almost keep themselves. I think it would be a good exchange if I could get it for my goose. Shall we exchange?" he asked the toll-keeper.

"Exchange," repeated the man; "well, it would not be a bad thing."

And so they made an exchange,—the toll-keeper at the turnpike-gate kept the goose, and the peasant carried off the fowl. Now he had really done a great deal of business on his way to the fair, and he was hot and tired. He wanted something to eat, and a glass of ale to refresh himself; so he turned his steps to an inn. He was just about to enter when the ostler came out, and they met at the door. The ostler was carrying a sack. "What have you in that sack?" asked the peasant.

"Rotten apples," answered the ostler; "a whole sackful of them. They will do to feed the pigs with."

"Why that will be terrible waste," he replied; "I should like to take them home to my old woman. Last year the old apple-tree by the grass-plot only bore one apple, and we kept it in the cupboard till it was quite withered and rotten. It was always property, my old woman said; and here she would see a great deal of property—a whole sackful; I should like to show them to her."

"What will you give me for the sackful?" asked the ostler.

"What will I give? Well, I will give you my fowl in exchange."

So he gave up the fowl, and received the apples, which he carried into the inn parlor. He leaned the sack carefully against the stove, and then went to the table. But the stove was hot, and he had not thought of that. Many guests were present—horse dealers, cattle drovers, and two Englishmen. The Englishmen were so rich that their pockets quite bulged out and seemed ready to burst; and they could bet too, as you shall hear. "Hiss-s-s, hiss-s-s." What could that be by the stove? The apples were beginning to roast. "What is that?" asked one.

"Why, do you know"—said our peasant. And then he told them the whole story of the horse, which he had exchanged for a cow, and all the rest of it, down to the apples.

"Well, your old woman will give it you well when you get home," said one of the Englishmen. "Won't there be a noise?"

"What! Give me what?" said the peasant. "Why, she will kiss me, and say, 'what the old man does is always right.'"

"Let us lay a wager on it," said the Englishmen. "We'll wager you a ton of coined gold, a hundred pounds to the hundred-weight."

"No; a bushel will be enough," replied the peasant. "I can only set a bushel of apples against it, and I'll throw myself and my old woman into the bargain; that will pile up the measure, I fancy."

"Done! taken!" and so the bet was made.

Then the landlord's coach came to the door, and the two Englishmen and the peasant got in, and away they drove, and soon arrived and stopped at the peasant's hut. "Good evening, old woman." "Good evening, old man." "I've made the exchange."

"Ah, well, you understand what you're about," said the woman. Then she embraced him, and paid no attention to the strangers, nor did she notice the sack.

"I got a cow in exchange for the horse."

"Thank Heaven," said she. "Now we shall have plenty of milk, and butter, and cheese on the table. That was a capital exchange."

"Yes, but I changed the cow for a sheep."

"Ah, better still!" cried the wife. "You always think of everything; we have just enough pasture for a sheep. Ewe's milk and cheese, woollen jackets and stockings! The cow could not give all these, and her hair only falls off. How you think of everything!"

"But I changed away the sheep for a goose."

"Then we shall have roast goose to eat this year. You dear old man, you are always thinking of something to please me. This is delightful. We can let the goose walk about with a string tied to her leg, so she will be fatter still before we roast her."

"But I gave away the goose for a fowl."

"A fowl! Well, that was a good exchange," replied the woman. "The fowl will lay eggs and hatch them, and we shall have chickens; we shall soon have a poultry-yard. Oh, this is just what I was wishing for."

"Yes, but I exchanged the fowl for a sack of shrivelled apples."

"What! I really must give you a kiss for that!" exclaimed the wife. "My dear, good husband, now I'll tell you something. Do you know, almost as soon as you left me this morning, I began to think of what I could give you nice for supper this evening, and then I thought of fried eggs and bacon, with sweet herbs; I had eggs and bacon, but I wanted the herbs; so I went over to the schoolmaster's: I knew they had plenty of herbs, but the schoolmistress is very mean, although she can smile so sweetly. I begged her to lend me a handful of herbs. 'Lend!' she exclaimed, 'I have nothing to lend; nothing at all grows in our garden, not even a shrivelled apple; I could not even lend you a shrivelled apple, my dear woman. But now I can lend her ten, or a whole sackful, which I'm very glad of; it makes me laugh to think about it;" and then she gave him a hearty kiss.

"Well, I like all this," said both the Englishmen; "always going down the hill, and yet always merry; it's worth the money to see it." So they paid a hundred-weight of gold to the peasant, who, whatever he did, was not scolded but kissed.

Yes, it always pays best when the wife sees and maintains that her husband knows best, and whatever he does is right.

That is a story which I heard when I was a child; and now you have heard it too, and know that "What the old man does is always right."

XXII

THE ELF OF THE ROSE

IN the midst of a garden grew a rose-tree, in full blossom, and in the prettiest of all the roses lived an elf. He was such a little wee thing, that no human eye could see him. Behind each leaf of the rose he had a sleeping chamber. He was as well formed and as beautiful as a little child could be, and had wings that reached from his shoulders to his feet. Oh, what sweet fragrance there was in his chambers! and how clean and beautiful were the walls! for they were the blushing leaves of the rose.

During the whole day he enjoyed himself in the warm sunshine, flew from flower to flower, and danced on the wings of the flying butterflies. Then he took it into his head to measure how many steps he would have to go through the roads and cross-roads that are on the leaf of a linden-tree. What we call the veins on a leaf, he took for roads; ay, and very long roads they were for him; for before he had half finished his task, the sun went down: he had commenced his work too late. It became very cold, the dew fell, and the wind blew; so he thought the best thing he could do would be to return home. He hurried himself as much as he could; but he found the roses all closed up, and he could not get in; not a single rose stood open. The poor little elf was very much frightened. He had never before been out at night, but had always slumbered secretly behind the warm rose-leaves. Oh, this would certainly be his death. At the other end of the garden, he knew there was an arbor, overgrown with beautiful honey-suckles. The blossoms looked like large painted horns; and he thought to himself, he would go and sleep in one of these till the morning. He flew thither; but "hush!" two people were in the arbor,—a handsome young man and a beautiful lady. They sat side by side, and wished that they might never be obliged to part. They loved each other much more than the best child can love its father and mother.

"But we must part," said the young man; "your brother does not like our engagement, and therefore he sends me so far away on business, over mountains and seas. Farewell, my sweet bride; for so you are to me."

And then they kissed each other, and the girl wept, and gave him a rose; but before she did so, she pressed a kiss upon it so fervently that the flower opened. Then the little elf flew in, and leaned his head on the delicate, fragrant walls. Here he could plainly hear them say, "Farewell, farewell;" and he felt that the rose had been placed on the young man's breast. Oh, how his heart did beat! The little elf could not go to sleep, it thumped so loudly. The young man took it out as he walked through the dark wood alone, and kissed the flower so often and so violently, that the little elf was almost crushed. He could feel through the leaf how hot the lips of the young man were, and the rose had opened, as if from the heat of the noonday sun.

There came another man, who looked gloomy and wicked. He was the wicked brother of the beautiful maiden. He drew out a sharp knife, and while the other was kissing the rose, the wicked man stabbed him to death; then he cut off his head, and buried it with the body in the soft earth under the linden-tree.

"Now he is gone, and will soon be forgotten," thought the wicked brother; "he will never come back again. He was going on a long journey over mountains and seas; it is easy for a man to lose his life in such a journey. My sister will suppose he is dead; for he cannot come back, and she will not dare to question me about him."

Then he scattered the dry leaves over the light earth with his foot, and went home through the darkness; but he went not alone, as he thought,—the little elf accompanied him. He sat in a dry rolled-up linden-leaf, which had fallen from the tree on to the wicked man's head, as he was digging the grave. The hat was on the head now, which made it very dark, and the little elf shuddered with fright and indignation at the wicked deed.

It was the dawn of morning before the wicked man reached home; he took off his hat, and went into his sister's room. There lay the beautiful, blooming girl, dreaming of him whom she loved so, and who was now, she supposed, travelling far away over mountain and sea. Her wicked brother stopped over her, and laughed hideously, as fiends only can laugh. The dry leaf fell out of his hair upon the counterpane; but he did not notice it, and went to get a little sleep during the early morning hours. But the elf slipped out of the withered leaf, placed himself by the ear of the sleeping girl, and told her, as in a dream, of the horrid murder; described the place where her brother had slain her lover, and buried his body; and told her of the linden-tree, in full blossom, that stood close by.

"That you may not think this is only a dream that I have told you," he said, "you will find on your bed a withered leaf."

Then she awoke, and found it there. Oh, what bitter tears she shed! and she could not open her heart to any one for relief.

The window stood open the whole day, and the little elf could easily have reached the roses, or any of the flowers; but he could not find it in his heart to leave one so afflicted. In the window stood a bush bearing monthly roses. He seated himself in one of the flowers, and gazed on the poor girl. Her brother often came into the room, and would be quite cheerful, in spite of his base conduct; so she dare not say a word to him of her heart's grief.

As soon as night came on, she slipped out of the house, and went into the wood, to the spot where the linden-tree stood; and after removing the leaves from the earth, she turned it up, and there found him who had been murdered. Oh, how she wept and prayed that she also might die! Gladly would she have taken the body home with her; but that was impossible; so she took up the poor head with the closed eyes, kissed the cold lips, and shook the mould out of the beautiful hair.

STANDING WEEPING BY THE FLOWER-POT

"I will keep this," said she; and as soon as she had covered the body again with the earth and leaves, she took the head and a little sprig of jasmine that bloomed in the wood, near the spot where he was buried, and carried them home with her. As soon as she was in her room, she took the largest flower-pot she could find, and in this she placed the head of the dead man, covered it up with earth, and planted the twig of jasmine in it.

"Farewell, farewell," whispered the little elf. He could not any longer endure to witness all this agony of grief, he therefore flew away to his own rose in the garden. But the rose was faded; only a few dry leaves still clung to the green hedge behind it.

"Alas! how soon all that is good and beautiful passes away," sighed the elf.

After a while he found another rose, which became his home, for among its delicate fragrant leaves he could dwell in safety. Every morning he flew to the window of the poor girl, and always found her weeping by the flower pot. The bitter tears fell upon the jasmine twig, and each day, as she became paler and paler, the sprig appeared to grow greener and fresher. One shoot after another sprouted forth, and little white buds blossomed, which the poor girl fondly kissed. But her wicked brother scolded her, and asked her if she was going mad. He could not imagine why she was weeping over that flower-pot, and it annoyed him. He did not know whose closed eyes were there, nor what red lips were fading beneath the earth. And one day she sat and leaned her head against the flower-pot, and the little elf of the rose found her asleep. Then he seated himself by her ear, talked to her of that evening in the arbor, of the sweet perfume of the rose, and the loves of the elves. Sweetly she dreamed, and while she dreamt, her life passed away calmly and gently, and her spirit was with him whom she loved, in heaven. And the jasmine opened its large white bells, and spread forth its sweet fragrance; it had no other way of showing its grief for the dead. But the wicked brother considered the beautiful blooming plant as his own property, left to him by his sister, and he placed it in his sleeping room, close by his bed, for it was very lovely in appearance, and the fragrance sweet and delightful. The little elf of the rose followed it, and flew from flower to flower, telling each little spirit that dwelt in them the story of the murdered young man, whose head now formed part of the earth beneath them, and of the wicked brother and the poor sister. "We know it," said each little spirit in the flowers, "we know it, for have we not sprung from the eyes and lips of the murdered one. We know it, we know it," and the flowers nodded with their heads in a peculiar manner.

The elf of the rose could not understand how they could rest so quietly in the matter, so he flew to the bees, who were gathering honey, and told them of the wicked brother. And the bees told it to their queen, who commanded that the next morning they should go and kill the murderer. But during the night, the first after the sister's death, while the brother was sleeping in his bed, close to where he had placed the fragrant jasmine, every flower cup opened, and invisibly the little spirits stole out, armed with poisonous spears. They placed themselves by the ear of the sleeper, told him dreadful dreams and then flew across his lips, and pricked his tongue with their poisoned spears.

"Now have we revenged the dead," said they, and flew back into the white bells of the jasmine flowers.

When the morning came, and as soon as the window was opened, the rose elf, with the queen bee, and the whole swarm of bees, rushed in to kill him. But he was already dead. People were standing round the bed, and saying that the scent of the jasmine had killed him. Then the elf of the rose understood the revenge of the flowers, and explained it to the queen bee, and she, with the whole swarm, buzzed about the flower-pot. The bees could not be driven away. Then a man took it up to remove it, and one of the bees stung him in the hand, so that he let the flower-pot fall, and it was broken to pieces.

Then every one saw the whitened skull, and they knew the dead man in the bed was a murderer.

And the queen bee hummed in the air, and sang of the revenge of the flowers, and of the elf of the rose and said that behind the smallest leaf dwells One, who can discover evil deeds, and punish them also.

XXIII

THE LITTLE MATCH-SELLER

It was terribly cold and nearly dark on the last evening of the old year, and the snow was falling fast. In the cold and the darkness, a poor little girl, with bare head and naked feet, roamed through the streets. It is true she had on a pair of slippers when she left home, but they were not of much use. They were very large, so large, indeed, that they had belonged to her mother, and the poor little creature had lost them in running across the street to avoid two carriages that were rolling along at a terrible rate. One of the slippers she could not find, and a boy seized upon the other and ran away with it, saying that he could use it as a cradle, when he had children of his own. So the little girl went on with her little naked feet, which were quite red and blue with the cold. In an old apron she carried a number of matches, and had a bundle of them in her hands. No one had bought anything of her the whole day, nor had any one given here even a penny.

Shivering with cold and hunger, she crept along; poor little child, she looked the picture of misery. The snowflakes fell on her long, fair hair, which hung in curls on her shoulders, but she regarded them not.

Lights were shining from every window, and there was a savory smell of roast goose, for it was New-year's eve—yes, she remembered that. In a corner, between two houses, one of which projected beyond the other, she sank down and huddled herself together. She had drawn her little feet under her, but she could not keep off the cold; and she dared not go home, for she had sold no matches, and could not take home even a penny of money. Her father would certainly beat her; besides, it was almost as cold at home as here, for they had only the roof to cover them, through which the wind howled, although the largest holes had been stopped up with straw and rags. Her little hands were almost frozen with the cold. Ah! perhaps a burning match might be some good, if she could draw it from the bundle and strike it against the wall, just to warm her fingers. She drew one out-"scratch!" how it sputtered as it burnt! It gave a warm, bright light, like a little candle, as she held her hand over it. It was really a wonderful light. It seemed to the little girl that she was sitting by a large iron stove, with polished brass feet and a brass ornament. How the fire burned! and seemed so beautifully warm that the child stretched out her feet as if to warm them, when, lo! the flame of the match went out, the stove vanished, and she had only the remains of the half-burnt match in her hand.

She rubbed another match on the wall. It burst into a flame, and where its light fell upon the wall it became as transparent as a veil, and she could see into the room. The table was covered with a snowy white table-cloth, on which stood a splendid dinner service, and a steaming roast goose, stuffed with apples and dried plums. And what was still more wonderful, the goose jumped down from the dish and waddled across the floor, with a knife and fork in its breast, to the little girl. Then the match went out, and there remained nothing but the thick, damp, cold wall before her.

She lighted another match, and then she found herself sitting under a beautiful Christmas-tree. It was larger and more beautifully decorated than the one which she had seen through the glass door at the rich merchant's. Thousands of tapers were burning upon the green branches, and colored pictures, like those she had seen in the show-windows, looked down upon it all. The little one stretched out her hand towards them, and the match went out.

The Christmas lights rose higher and higher, till they looked to her like the stars in the sky. Then she saw a star fall, leaving behind it a bright streak of fire. "Some one is dying," thought the little girl, for her old grandmother, the only one who had ever loved her, and who was now dead, had told her that when a star falls, a soul was going up to God.

She again rubbed a match on the wall, and the light shone round her; in the brightness stood her old grandmother, clear and shining, yet mild and loving in her appearance. "Grandmother," cried the little one, "O take me with you; I know you will go away when the match burns out; you will vanish like the warm stove, the roast goose, and the large, glorious Christmas-tree." And she made haste to light the whole bundle of matches, for she wished to keep her grandmother there. And the matches glowed with a light that was brighter than the noon-day, and her grandmother had never appeared so large or so beautiful. She took the little girl in her arms, and they both flew upwards in brightness and joy far above the earth, where there was neither cold nor hunger nor pain, for they were with God.

In the dawn of morning there lay the poor little one, with pale cheeks and smiling mouth, leaning against the wall; she had been frozen to death on the last evening of the year; and the New-year's sun rose and shone upon a little corpse! The child still sat, in the stiffness of death, holding the matches in her hand, one bundle of which was burnt. "She tried to warm herself," said some. No one imagined what beautiful things she had seen, nor into what glory she had entered with her grandmother, on New-year's day.

XXIV

THE FIR TREE

Out in the woods stood a nice little Fir Tree. The place he had was a very good one: the sun shone on him: as to fresh air, there was enough of that, and round him grew many large-sized comrades, pines as well as firs. But the little Fir wanted so very much to be a grown-up tree.

He did not think of the warm sun and of the fresh air; he did not care for the little cottage children that ran about and prattled when they were in the woods looking for wild-strawberries. The children often came with a whole pitcher full of berries, or a long row of them threaded on a straw, and sat down near the young tree and said, "Oh, how pretty he is! What a nice little fir!" But this was what the Tree could not bear to hear.

At the end of a year he had shot up a good deal, and after another year he was another long bit taller; for with fir trees one can always tell by the shoots how many years old they are.

"Oh! Were I but such a high tree as the others are," sighed he. "Then I should be able to spread out my branches, and with the tops to look into the wide world! Then would the birds build nests among my branches: and when there was a breeze, I could bend with as much stateliness as the others!"

Neither the sunbeams, nor the birds, nor the red clouds which morning and evening sailed above him, gave the little Tree any pleasure.

In winter, when the snow lay glittering on the ground, a hare would often come leaping along, and jump right over the little Tree. Oh, that made him so angry! But two winters were past, and in the third the Tree was so large that the hare was obliged to go round it. "To grow and grow, to get older and be tall," thought the Tree—"that, after all, is the most delightful thing in the world!"

In autumn the wood-cutters always came and felled some of the largest trees. This happened every year; and the young Fir Tree, that had now grown to a very comely size, trembled at the sight; for the magnificent great trees fell to the earth with noise and cracking, the branches were lopped off, and the trees looked long and bare; they were hardly to be recognised; and then they were laid in carts, and the horses dragged them out of the wood.

Where did they go to? What became of them?

In spring, when the swallows and the storks came, the Tree asked them, "Don't you know where they have been taken? Have you not met them anywhere?"

The swallows did not know anything about it; but the Stork looked musing, nodded his head, and said, "Yes; I think I know; I met many ships as I was flying hither from Egypt; on the ships were magnificent masts, and I venture to assert that it was they that smelt so of fir. I may congratulate you, for they lifted themselves on high most majestically!"

"Oh, were I but old enough to fly across the sea! But how does the sea look in reality? What is it like?"

"That would take a long time to explain," said the Stork, and with these words off he went.

"Rejoice in thy growth!" said the Sunbeams. "Rejoice in thy vigorous growth, and in the fresh life that moveth within thee!"

And the Wind kissed the Tree, and the Dew wept tears over him; but the Fir understood it not.

When Christmas came, quite young trees were cut down: trees which often were not even as large or of the same age as this Fir Tree, who could never rest, but always wanted to be off. These young trees, and they were always the finest looking, retained their branches; they were laid on carts, and the horses drew them out of the wood.

LOUIS RHEAD

"Where are they going to?" asked the Fir. "They are not taller than I; there was one indeed that was considerably shorter; and why do they retain all their branches? Whither are they taken?"

"We know! We know!" chirped the Sparrows. "We have peeped in at the windows in the town below! We know whither they are taken! The greatest splendor and the greatest magnificence one can imagine await them. We peeped through the windows, and saw them planted in the middle of the warm room and ornamented with the most splendid things, with gilded apples, with gingerbread, with toys, and many hundred lights!"

"And then?" asked the Fir Tree, trembling in every bough. "And then? What happens then?"

"We did not see anything more: it was incomparably beautiful."

"I would fain know if I am destined for so glorious a career," cried the Tree, rejoicing. "That is still better than to cross the sea! What a longing do I suffer! Were Christmas but come! I am now tall, and my branches spread like the others that were carried off last year! Oh! were I but already on the cart! Were I in the warm room with all the splendor and magnificence! Yes; then something better, something still grander, will surely follow, or wherefore should they thus ornament me? Something better, something still grander must follow—but what? Oh, how I long, how I suffer! I do not know myself what is the matter with me!"

"Rejoice in our presence!" said the Air and the Sunlight. "Rejoice in thy own fresh youth!"

But the Tree did not rejoice at all; he grew and grew, and was green both winter and summer. People that saw him said, "What a fine tree!" and towards Christmas he was one of the first that was cut down. The axe struck deep into the very pith; the Tree fell to the earth with a sigh; he felt a pang—it was like a swoon; he could not think of happiness, for he was sorrowful at being separated from his home, from the place where he had sprung up. He well knew that he should never see his dear old comrades, the little bushes and flowers around him, anymore; perhaps not even the birds! The departure was not at all agreeable.

The Tree only came to himself when he was unloaded in a courtyard with the other trees, and heard a man say, "That one is splendid! We don't want the others." Then two servants came in rich livery and carried the Fir Tree into a large and splendid drawing-room. Portraits were hanging on the walls, and near the white porcelain stove stood two large Chinese vases with lions on the covers. There, too, were large easy-chairs, silken sofas, large tables full of picture-books and full of toys, worth hundreds and hundreds of crowns—at least the children said so. And the Fir Tree was stuck upright in a cask that was filled with sand; but no one could see that it was a cask, for green cloth was hung all round it, and it stood on a large gaily-colored carpet. Oh! how the Tree quivered! What was to happen? The servants, as well as the young ladies, decorated it. On one branch there hung little nets cut out of colored paper, and each net was filled with sugarplums; and among the other boughs gilded apples and walnuts were suspended, looking as though they had grown there, and little blue and white tapers were placed among the leaves. Dolls that looked for all the world like men—the Tree had never beheld such before—were seen among the foliage, and at the very top a large star of gold tinsel was fixed. It was really splendid—beyond description splendid.

"This evening!" they all said. "How it will shine this evening!"

"Oh!" thought the Tree. "If the evening were but come! If the tapers were but lighted! And then I wonder what will happen! Perhaps the other trees from the forest will come to look at me! Perhaps the sparrows will beat against the windowpanes! I wonder if I shall take root here, and winter and summer stand covered with ornaments!"

He knew very much about the matter—but he was so impatient that for sheer longing he got a pain in his back, and this with trees is the same thing as a headache with us.

The candles were now lighted—what brightness! What splendor! The Tree trembled so in every bough that one of the tapers set fire to the foliage. It blazed up famously.

"Help! Help!" cried the young ladies, and they quickly put out the fire.

Now the Tree did not even dare tremble. What a state he was in! He was so uneasy lest he should lose something of his splendor, that he was quite bewildered amidst the glare and brightness; when suddenly both folding-doors opened and a troop of children rushed in as if they would upset the Tree. The older persons followed quietly; the little ones stood quite still. But it was only for a moment; then they shouted that the whole place re-echoed with their rejoicing; they danced round the Tree, and one present after the other was pulled off.

"What are they about?" thought the Tree. "What is to happen now!" And the lights burned down to the very branches, and as they burned down they were put out one after the other, and then the children had permission to plunder the Tree. So they fell upon it with such violence that all its branches cracked; if it had not been fixed firmly in the ground, it would certainly have tumbled down.

The children danced about with their beautiful playthings; no one looked at the Tree except the old nurse, who peeped between the branches; but it was only to see if there was a fig or an apple left that had been forgotten.

"A story! A story!" cried the children, drawing a little fat man towards the Tree. He seated himself under it and said, "Now we are in the shade, and the Tree can listen too. But I shall tell only one story. Now which will you have; that about Ivedy-Avedy, or about Humpy-Dumpy, who tumbled downstairs, and yet after all came to the throne and married the princess?"

"Ivedy-Avedy," cried some; "Humpy-Dumpy," cried the others. There was such a bawling and screaming—the Fir Tree alone was silent, and he thought to himself, "Am I not to bawl with the rest? Am I to do nothing whatever?" for he was one of the company, and had done what he had to do.

And the man told about Humpy-Dumpy that tumbled down, who notwithstanding came to the throne, and at last married the princess. And the children clapped their hands, and cried. "Oh, go on! Do go on!" They wanted to hear about Ivedy-Avedy too, but the little man only told them about Humpy-Dumpy. The Fir Tree stood quite still and absorbed in thought; the birds in the wood had never related the like of this. "Humpy-Dumpy fell downstairs, and yet he married the princess! Yes, yes! That's the way of the world!" thought the Fir Tree, and believed it all, because the man who told the story was so good-looking. "Well, well! who knows, perhaps I

"NOW WE WILL HAVE A STORY, AND THE TREE CAN LISTEN TOO"

may fall downstairs, too, and get a princess as wife!" And he looked forward with joy to the morrow, when he hoped to be decked out again with lights, playthings, fruits, and tinsel.

"I won't tremble to-morrow!" thought the Fir Tree. "I will enjoy to the full all my splendor! To-morrow I shall hear again the story of Humpy-Dumpy, and perhaps that of Ivedy-Avedy too." And the whole night the Tree stood still and in deep thought.

In the morning the servant and the housemaid came in.

"Now then the splendor will begin again," thought the Fir. But they dragged him out of the room, and up the stairs into the loft: and here, in a dark corner, where no daylight could enter, they left him. "What's the meaning of this?" thought the Tree. "What am I to do here? What shall I hear now, I wonder?" And he leaned against the wall lost in reverie. Time enough had he too for his reflections; for days and nights passed on, and nobody came up; and when at last somebody did come, it was only to put some great trunks in a corner, out of the way. There stood the Tree quite hidden; it seemed as if he had been entirely forgotten.

"'Tis now winter out-of-doors!" thought the Tree. "The earth is hard and covered with snow; men cannot plant me now, and therefore I have been put up here under shelter till the spring-time comes! How thoughtful that is! How kind man is, after all! If it only were not so dark here, and so terribly lonely! Not even a hare! And out in the woods it was so pleasant, when the snow was on the ground, and the hare leaped by; yes—even when he jumped over me; but I did not like it then! It is really terribly lonely here!"

"Squeak! Squeak!" said a little Mouse, at the same moment, peeping out of his hole. And then another little one came. They snuffed about the Fir Tree, and rustled among the branches.

"It is dreadfully cold," said the Mouse. "But for that, it would be delightful here, old Fir, wouldn't it?"

"I am by no means old," said the Fir Tree. "There's many a one considerably older than I am."

"Where do you come from," asked the Mice; "and what can you do?" They were so extremely curious. "Tell us about the most beautiful spot on the earth. Have you never been there? Were you never in the larder, where cheeses lie on the shelves, and hams hang from above; where one dances about on tallow candles: that place where one enters lean, and comes out again fat and portly?"

"I know no such place," said the Tree. "But I know the wood, where the sun shines and where the little birds sing." And then he told all about his youth; and the little Mice had never heard the like before; and they listened and said,

"Well, to be sure! How much you have seen! How happy you must have been!"

"I!" said the Fir Tree, thinking over what he had himself related. "Yes, in reality those were happy times." And then he told about Christmas-eve, when he was decked out with cakes and candles.

"Oh," said the little Mice, "how fortunate you have been, old Fir Tree!"

"I am by no means old," said he. "I came from the wood this winter; I am in my prime, and am only rather short for my age."

"What delightful stories you know," said the Mice: and the next night they came with four other little Mice, who were to hear what the Tree recounted: and the more he related, the more he remembered himself; and it appeared as if those times had really been happy times. "But they may still come—they may still come! Humpy-Dumpy fell downstairs, and yet he got a princess!" and he thought at the moment of a nice little Birch Tree growing out in the woods: to the Fir, that would be a real charming princess.

"Who is Humpy-Dumpy?" asked the Mice. So then the Fir Tree told the whole fairy tale, for he could remember every single word of it; and the little Mice jumped for joy up to the very top of the Tree. Next night two more Mice came, and on Sunday two Rats even; but they said the stories were not interesting, which vexed the little Mice; and they, too, now began to think them not so very amusing either.

"Do you know only one story?" asked the Rats.

"Only that one," answered the Tree. "I heard it on my happiest evening; but I did not then know how happy I was."

"It is a very stupid story! Don't you know one about bacon and tallow candles? Can't you tell any larder stories?"

"No," said the Tree.

"Then good-bye," said the Rats; and they went home.

At last the little Mice stayed away also; and the Tree sighed: "After all, it was very pleasant when the sleek little Mice sat round me, and listened to what I told them. Now that too is over. But I will take good care to enjoy myself when I am brought out again."

But when was that to be? Why, one morning there came a quantity of people and set to work in the loft. The trunks were moved, the tree was pulled out and thrown—rather hard, it is true—down on the floor, but a man drew him towards the stairs, where the daylight shone.

"Now a merry life will begin again," thought the Tree. He felt the fresh air, the first sunbeam—and now he was out in the court-yard. All passed so quickly, there was so much going on around him, the Tree quite forgot to look to himself. The court adjoined a garden, and all was in flower; the roses hung so fresh and odorous over the balustrade, the lindens were in blossom, the Swallows flew by, and said, "Quirre-vit! My husband is come!" but it was not the Fir Tree that they meant.

"Now, then, I shall really enjoy life," said he exultingly, and spread out his branches; but, alas, they were all withered and yellow! It was in a corner that he lay, among weeds and nettles. The golden star of tinsel was still on the top of the Tree, and glittered in the sunshine.

In the court-yard some of the merry children were playing who had danced at Christmas round the Fir Tree, and were so glad at the sight of him. One of the youngest ran and tore off the golden star.

"Only look what is still on the ugly old Christmas tree!" said he, trampling on the branches, so that they all cracked beneath his feet.

And the Tree beheld all the beauty of the flowers, and the freshness in the garden; he beheld himself, and wished he had remained in his dark corner in the loft; he thought of his first youth in the wood, of the merry Christmas-eve, and of the little Mice who had listened with so much pleasure to the story of Humpy-Dumpy.

"'Tis over—'tis past!" said the poor Tree. "Had I but rejoiced when I had reason to do so! But now 'tis past, 'tis past!"

And the gardener's boy chopped the Tree into small pieces; there was a whole heap lying there. The wood flamed up splendidly under the large brewing copper, and it sighed so deeply! Each sigh was like a shot.

The boys played about in the court, and the youngest wore the gold star on his breast which the Tree had had on the happiest evening of his life. However, that was over now—the Tree gone, the story at an end. All, all was over—every tale must end at last.

XXV

THUMBELINA

THERE was once a woman who wished very much to have a little child, but she could not obtain her wish. At last she went to a fairy, and said, "I should so very much like to have a little child; can you tell me where I can find one?"

"Oh, that can be easily managed," said the fairy. "Here is a barleycorn of a different kind to those which grow in the farmer's fields, and which the chickens eat; put it into a flower-pot, and see what will happen."

"Thank you," said the woman, and she gave the fairy twelve shillings, which was the price of the barleycorn. Then she went home and planted it, and immediately there grew up a large handsome flower, something like a tulip in appearance, but with its leaves tightly closed as if it were still a bud.

"It is a beautiful flower," said the woman, and she kissed the red and golden-colored leaves, and while she did so the flower opened, and she could see that it was a real tulip. Within the flower, upon the green velvet stamens, sat a very delicate and graceful little maiden. She was scarcely half as long as a thumb, and they gave her the name of "Thumbelina," or Tiny, because she was so small.

A walnut-shell, elegantly polished, served her for a cradle; her bed was formed of blue violet-leaves, with a rose-leaf for a counterpane. Here she slept at night, but during the day she amused herself on a table, where the woman had placed a plateful of water.

Round this plate were wreaths of flowers with their stems in the water, and upon it floated a large tulip-leaf, which served Tiny for a boat. Here the little maiden sat and rowed herself from side to side, with two oars made of white horse-hair. It really was a very pretty sight. Tiny could, also, sing so softly and sweetly that nothing like her singing had ever before been heard.

One night, while she lay in her pretty bed, a large, ugly, wet toad crept through a broken pane of glass in the window, and leaped right upon the table where Tiny lay sleeping under her rose-leaf quilt. "What a pretty little wife this would make for my son," said the toad, and she took up the walnut-shell in which little Tiny lay asleep, and jumped through the window with it into the garden.

In the swampy margin of a broad stream in the garden lived the toad, with her son. He was uglier even than his mother, and when he saw the pretty little maiden in her elegant bed, he could only cry, "Croak, croak, croak."

"Don't speak so loud, or she will wake," said the toad, "and then she might run away, for she is as light as swan's down. We will place her on one of the water-lily leaves out in the stream; it will be like an island to her, she is so light and small, and then she cannot escape; and, while she is away, we will make haste and prepare the state-room under the marsh, in which you are to live when you are married."

Far out in the stream grew a number of water-lilies, with broad green leaves, which seemed to float on the top of the water. The largest of these leaves appeared farther off than the rest, and the old toad swam out to it with the walnut-shell, in which little Tiny lay still asleep. The tiny little creature woke very early in the morning, and began to cry bitterly when she found where she was, for she could see nothing but water on every side of the large green leaf, and no way of reaching the land. Meanwhile the old toad was very busy under the marsh, decking her room with rushes and wild yellow flowers, to make it look pretty for her new daughter-in-law. Then she swam out with her ugly son to the leaf on which she had placed poor little Tiny. She wanted to fetch the pretty bed, that she might put it in the bridal chamber to be ready for her. The old toad bowed low to her in the water, and said, "Here is my son, he will be your husband, and you will live happily in the marsh by the stream."

"Croak, croak, croak," was all her son could say for himself; so the toad took up the elegant little bed, and swam away with it, leaving Tiny all alone on the green leaf, where she sat and wept. She could not bear to think of living with the old toad, and having her ugly son for a husband. The little fishes, who swam about in the water beneath, had seen the toad, and heard what she said, so they lifted their heads above the water to look at the little maiden. As soon as they caught sight of her, they saw she was very pretty, and it made them very sorry to think that she must go and live with the ugly toads.

"No, it must never be!" so they assembled together in the water, round the green stalk which held the leaf on which the little maiden stood, and gnawed it away at the root with their teeth. Then the leaf floated down the stream, carrying Tiny far away out of reach of land. Tiny sailed past many towns, and the little birds in the bushes saw her, and sang, "What a lovely little creature;" so the leaf swam away with her farther and farther, till it brought her to other lands.

A graceful little white butterfly constantly fluttered round her, and at last alighted on the leaf. Tiny pleased him, and she was glad of it, for now the toad could not possibly reach her, and the country through which she sailed was beautiful, and the sun shone upon the water, till it glittered like liquid gold. She took off her girdle and tied one end of it round the butterfly, and the other end of the ribbon she fastened to the leaf, which now glided on much faster than ever, taking little Tiny with it as she stood. Presently a large cockchafer flew by; the moment he caught sight of her, he seized her round her delicate waist with his claws, and flew with her into a tree. The green leaf floated away on the brook, and the butterfly flew with it, for he was fastened to it, and could not get away.

Oh, how frightened little Tiny felt when the cockchafer flew with her to the tree! But especially was she sorry for the beautiful white butterfly which she had fastened to the leaf, for if he could not free himself he would die of hunger. But the cockchafer did not trouble himself at all about the matter. He seated himself by her side on a large green leaf, gave her some honey from the flowers to eat, and told her she was very pretty, though not in the least like a cockchafer. After a time, all the cockchafers turned up their feelers, and said, "She has only two legs! how ugly that looks."

THE LEAF NOW GLIDED ON MUCH FASTER

"She has no feelers," said another. "Her waist is quite slim. Pooh! she is like a human being."

"Oh! she is ugly," said all the lady cockchafers, although Tiny was very pretty. Then the cockchafer who had run away with her, believed all the others when they said she was ugly, and would have nothing more to say to her, and told her she might go where she liked. Then he flew down with her from the tree, and placed her on a daisy, and she wept at the thought that she was so ugly that even the cockchafers would have nothing to say to her. And all the while she was really the loveliest creature that one could imagine, and as tender and delicate as a beautiful rose-leaf.

During the whole summer poor little Tiny lived quite alone in the wide forest. She wove herself a bed with blades of grass, and hung it up under a broad leaf, to protect herself from the rain. She sucked the honey from the flowers for food, and drank the dew from their leaves every morning. So passed away the summer and the autumn, and then came the winter,— the long, cold winter. All the birds who had sung to her so sweetly were flown away, and the trees and the flowers had withered. The large clover leaf under the shelter of which she had lived, was now rolled together and shrivelled up, nothing remained but a yellow withered stalk. She felt dreadfully cold, for her clothes were torn, and she was herself so frail and delicate, that poor little Tiny was nearly frozen to death.

It began to snow too; and the snow-flakes, as they fell upon her, were like a whole shovelful falling upon one of us, for we are tall, but she was only an inch high. Then she wrapped herself up in a dry leaf, but it cracked in the middle and could not keep her warm, and she shivered with cold. Near the wood in which she had been living lay a corn-field, but the corn had been cut a long time; nothing remained but the bare dry stubble standing up out of the frozen ground. It was to her like struggling through a large wood. Oh! how she shivered with the cold. She came at last to the door of a field-mouse, who had a little den under the corn-stubble. There dwelt the field-mouse in warmth and comfort, with a whole roomful of corn, a kitchen, and a beautiful dining room. Poor little Tiny stood before the door just like a little beggar-girl, and begged for a small piece of barley-corn, for she had been without a morsel to eat for two days.

TINY STOOD AT THE DOOR AND BEGGED FOR A BIT OF BARLEYCORN. "YOU POOR LITTLE CREATURE," SAID THE FIELD-MOUSE

"You poor little creature," said the field-mouse, who was really a good old field-mouse, "come into my warm room and dine with me." She was very pleased with Tiny, so she said, "You are quite welcome to stay with me all the winter, if you like; but you must keep my rooms clean and neat, and tell me stories, for I shall like to hear them very much." And Tiny did all the field-mouse asked her, and found herself very comfortable.

"We shall have a visitor soon," said the field-mouse one day; "my neighbor pays me a visit once a week. He is better off than I am; he has large rooms, and wears a beautiful black velvet coat. If you could only have him for a husband, you would be well provided for indeed. But he is blind, so you must tell him some of your prettiest stories."

But Tiny did not feel at all interested about this neighbor, for he was a mole. However, he came and paid his visit dressed in his black velvet coat.

"He is very rich and learned, and his house is twenty times larger than mine," said the field-mouse.

He was rich and learned, no doubt, but he always spoke slightingly of the sun and the pretty flowers, because he had never seen them. Tiny was obliged to sing to him, "Lady-bird, lady-bird, fly away home," and many other pretty songs. And the mole fell in love with her because she had such a sweet voice; but he said nothing yet, for he was very cautious. A short time before, the mole had dug a long passage under the earth, which led from the dwelling of the field-mouse to his own, and here she had permission to walk with Tiny whenever she liked. But he warned them not to be alarmed at the sight of a dead bird which lay in the passage. It was a perfect bird, with a beak and feathers, and could not have been dead long, and was lying just where the mole had made his passage.

The mole took a piece of phosphorescent wood in his mouth, and it glittered like fire in the dark; then he went before them to light them through the long, dark passage. When they came to the spot where lay the dead bird, the mole pushed his broad nose through the ceiling, the earth gave way, so that there was a large hole, and the daylight shone into the passage. In the middle of the floor lay a dead swallow, his beautiful wings pulled close to his sides, his feet and his head drawn up under his feathers; the poor bird had evidently died of the cold. It made little Tiny very sad to see it, she did so love the little birds; all the summer they had sung and twittered for her so beautifully. But the mole pushed it aside with his crooked legs, and said, "He will sing no more now. How miserable it must be to be born a little bird! I am thankful that none of my children will ever be birds, for they can do nothing but cry, 'Tweet, tweet,' and always die of hunger in the winter."

"Yes, you may well say that, as a clever man!" exclaimed the field-mouse, "What is the use of his twittering, for when winter comes he must either starve or be frozen to death. Still birds are very high bred."

Tiny said nothing; but when the two others had turned their backs on the bird, she stooped down and stroked aside the soft feathers which covered the head, and kissed the closed eyelids. "Perhaps this was the one who sang to me so sweetly in the summer," she said; "and how much pleasure it gave me, you dear, pretty bird."

The mole now stopped up the hole through which the daylight shone, and then accompanied the lady home. But during the night Tiny could not sleep; so she got out of bed and wove a large, beautiful carpet of hay; then she carried it to the dead bird, and spread it over him; with some down from the flowers which she had found in the field-mouse's room. It was as soft as wool, and she spread some of it on each side of the bird, so that he might lie warmly in the cold earth.

"Farewell, you pretty little bird," said she, "farewell; thank you for your delightful singing during the summer, when all the trees were green, and the warm sun shone upon us." Then she laid her head on the bird's breast, but she was alarmed immediately, for it seemed as if something inside the bird went "thump, thump." It was the bird's heart; he was not really dead, only benumbed with the cold, and the warmth had restored him to life. In autumn, all the swallows fly away into warm countries, but if one happens to linger, the cold seizes it, it becomes frozen, and falls down as if dead; it remains where it fell, and the cold snow covers it. Tiny trembled very much; she was quite frightened, for the bird was large, a great deal larger than herself,—she was only an inch high. But she took courage, laid the wool more thickly over the poor swallow, and then took a leaf which she had used for her own counterpane, and laid it over the head of the poor bird. The next morning she again stole out to see him. He was alive but very weak; he could only open his eyes for a moment to look at Tiny, who stood by holding a piece of decayed wood in her hand, for she had no other lantern. "Thank you, pretty little maiden," said the sick swallow; "I have been so nicely warmed, that I shall soon regain my strength, and be able to fly about again in the warm sunshine."

"Oh," said she, "it is cold out of doors now; it snows and freezes. Stay in your warm bed; I will take care of you."

Then she brought the swallow some water in a flower-leaf, and after he had drank, he told her that he had wounded one of his wings in a thorn-bush, and could not fly as fast as the others, who were soon far away on their journey to warm countries. Then at last he had fallen to the earth, and could remember no more, nor how he came to be where she had found him. The whole winter the swallow remained underground, and Tiny nursed him with care and love. Neither the mole nor the field-mouse knew anything about it, for they did not like swallows. Very soon the spring time came, and the sun warmed the earth. Then the swallow bade farewell to Tiny, and she opened the hole in the ceiling which the mole had made. The sun shone in upon them so beautifully, that the swallow asked her if she would go with him; she could sit on his back, he said, and he would fly away with her into the green woods. But Tiny knew it would make the field-mouse very grieved if she left her in that manner, so she said, "No, I cannot."

"Farewell, then, farewell, you good, pretty little maiden," said the swallow; and he flew out into the sunshine.

Tiny looked after him, and the tears rose in her eyes. She was very fond of the poor swallow.

"Tweet, tweet," sang the bird, as he flew out into the green woods, and Tiny felt very sad. She was not allowed to go out into the warm sunshine. The corn which had been sown in the field over the house of the field-mouse had grown up high into the air, and formed a thick wood to Tiny, who was only an inch in height.

"You are going to be married, Tiny," said the field-mouse. "My neighbor has asked for you. What good fortune for a poor child like you. Now we will prepare your wedding clothes. They must be both woollen and linen. Nothing must be wanting when you are the mole's wife."

Tiny had to turn the spindle, and the field-mouse hired four spiders, who were to weave day and night. Every evening the mole visited her, and was continually speaking of the time when the summer would be over. Then he would keep his wedding-day with Tiny; but now the heat of the sun was so great that it burned the earth, and made it quite hard, like a stone. As soon, as the summer was over, the wedding should take place. But Tiny was not at all pleased; for she did not like the tiresome mole. Every morning when the sun rose, and every evening when it went down, she would creep out at the door, and as the wind blew aside the ears of corn, so that she could see the blue sky, she thought how beautiful and bright it seemed out there, and wished so much to see her dear swallow again. But he never returned; for by this time he had flown far away into the lovely green forest.

When autumn arrived, Tiny had her outfit quite ready; and the field-mouse said to her, "In four weeks the wedding must take place."

Then Tiny wept, and said she would not marry the disagreeable mole.

"Nonsense," replied the field-mouse. "Now don't be obstinate, or I shall bite you with my white teeth. He is a very handsome mole; the queen herself does not wear more beautiful velvets and furs. His kitchen and cellars are quite full. You ought to be very thankful for such good fortune."

So the wedding-day was fixed, on which the mole was to fetch Tiny away to live with him, deep under the earth, and never again to see the warm sun, because he did not like it. The poor child was very unhappy at the thought of saying farewell to the beautiful sun, and as the field-mouse had given her permission to stand at the door, she went to look at it once more.

"Farewell bright sun," she cried, stretching out her arm towards it; and then she walked a short distance from the house; for the corn had been cut, and only the dry stubble remained in the fields. "Farewell, farewell," she repeated, twining her arm round a little red flower that grew just by her side. "Greet the little swallow from me, if you should see him again."

"Tweet, tweet," sounded over her head suddenly. She looked up, and there was the swallow himself flying close by. As soon as he spied Tiny, he was delighted; and then she told him how unwilling she felt to marry the ugly mole, and to live always beneath the earth, and never to see the bright sun any more. And as she told him she wept.

"Cold winter is coming," said the swallow, "and I am going to fly away into warmer countries. Will you go with me? You can sit on my back, and fasten yourself on with your sash. Then we can fly away from the ugly mole and his gloomy rooms,—far away, over the mountains, into warmer countries, where the sun shines more brightly—than here; where it is always summer, and the flowers bloom in greater beauty. Fly now with me, dear little Tiny; you saved my life when I lay frozen in that dark passage."

"Yes, I will go with you," said Tiny; and she seated herself on the bird's back, with her feet on his outstretched wings, and tied her girdle to one of his strongest feathers.

Then the swallow rose in the air, and flew over forest and over sea, high above the highest mountains, covered with eternal snow. Tiny would have been frozen in the cold air, but she crept under the bird's warm feathers, keeping her little head uncovered, so that she might admire the beautiful lands over which they passed. At length they reached the warm countries, where the sun shines brightly, and the sky seems so much higher above the earth. Here, on the hedges, and by the wayside, grew purple, green, and white grapes;

lemons and oranges hung from trees in the woods; and the air was fragrant with myrtles and orange blossoms. Beautiful children ran along the country lanes, playing with large gay butterflies; and as the swallow flew farther and farther, every place appeared still more lovely.

At last they came to a blue lake, and by the side of it, shaded by trees of the deepest green, stood a palace of dazzling white marble, built in the olden times. Vines clustered round its lofty pillars, and at the top were many swallows' nests, and one of these was the home of the swallow who carried Tiny.

"This is my house," said the swallow; "but it would not do for you to live there—you would not be comfortable. You must choose for yourself one of those lovely flowers, and I will put you down upon it, and then you shall have everything that you can wish to make you happy."

"That will be delightful," she said, and clapped her little hands for joy.

A large marble pillar lay on the ground, which, in falling, had been broken into three pieces. Between these pieces grew the most beautiful large white flowers; so the swallow flew down with Tiny, and placed her on one of the broad leaves. But how surprised she was to see in the middle of the flower, a tiny little man, as white and transparent as if he had been made of crystal! He had a gold crown on his head, and delicate wings at his shoulders, and was not much larger than Tiny herself. He was the angel of the flower; for a tiny man and a tiny woman dwell in every flower; and this was the king of them all.

"Oh, how beautiful he is!" whispered Tiny to the swallow. The little prince was at first quite frightened at the bird, who was like a giant, compared to such a delicate little creature as himself; but when he saw Tiny, he was delighted, and thought her the prettiest little maiden he had ever seen. He took the gold crown from his head, and placed it on hers, and asked her name, and if she would be his wife, and queen over all the flowers.

This certainly was a very different sort of husband to the son of a toad, or the mole, with my black velvet and fur; so she said, "Yes," to the handsome prince. Then all the flowers opened, and out of each came a little lady or a tiny lord, all so pretty it was quite a pleasure to look at them. Each of them brought Tiny a present; but the best gift was a pair of beautiful wings, which had belonged to a large white fly and they fastened them to Tiny's shoulders, so that she might fly from flower to flower. Then there was much rejoicing, and the little swallow who sat above them, in his nest, was asked to sing a wedding song, which he did as well as he could; but in his heart he felt sad for he was very fond of Tiny, and would have liked never to part from her again.

"You must not be called Tiny any more," said the spirit of the flowers to her. "It is an ugly name, and you are so very pretty. We will call you Maia."

"Farewell, farewell," said the swallow, with a heavy heart as he left the warm countries to fly back into Denmark. There he had a nest over the window of a house in which dwelt the writer of fairy tales. The swallow sang, "Tweet, tweet," and from his song came the whole story.

XXVI

THE EMPEROR'S NEW CLOTHES

MANY years ago there was an emperor who was so fond of new clothes that he spent all his money on them. He did not give himself any concern about his army; he cared nothing about the theater or for driving about in the woods, except for the sake of showing himself off in new clothes. He had a costume for every hour in the day, and just as they say of a king or emperor, "He is in his council chamber," they said of him, "The emperor is in his dressing room."

Life was merry and gay in the town where the emperor lived, and numbers of strangers came to it every day. Among them there came one day two rascals, who gave themselves out as weavers and said that they knew how to weave the most exquisite stuff imaginable. Not only were the colors and patterns uncommonly beautiful, but the clothes that were made of the stuff had the peculiar property of becoming invisible to every person who was unfit for the office he held or who was exceptionally stupid.

"Those must be valuable clothes," thought the emperor. "By wearing them I should be able to discover which of the men in my empire are not fit for their posts. I should distinguish wise men from fools. Yes, I must order some of the stuff to be woven for me directly." And he paid the swindlers a handsome sum of money in advance, as they required.

As for them, they put up two looms and pretended to be weaving, though there was nothing whatever on their shuttles. They called for a quantity of the finest silks and of the purest gold thread, all of which went into their own bags, while they worked at their empty looms till late into the night.

"I should like to know how those weavers are getting on with the stuff," thought the emperor. But he felt a little queer when he reflected that those who were stupid or unfit for their office would not be able to see the material. He believed, indeed, that he had nothing to fear for himself, but still he thought it better to send some one else first, to see how the work was coming on. All the people in the town had heard of the peculiar property of the stuff, and every one was curious to see how stupid his neighbor might be.

"I will send my faithful old prime minister to the weavers," thought the emperor. "He will be best capable of judging of this stuff, for he is a man of sense and nobody is more fit for his office than he."

So the worthy old minister went into the room where the two swindlers sat working the empty looms. "Heaven save us!" thought the old man, opening his eyes wide. "Why, I can't see anything at all!" But he took care not to say so aloud.

Both the rogues begged him to step a little nearer and asked him if he did not think the patterns very pretty and the coloring fine. They pointed to the empty loom as they did so, and the poor old minister kept staring as hard as he could—but without being able to see anything on it, for of course there was nothing there to see.

"Heaven save us!" thought the old man. "Is it possible that I am a fool? I have never thought it, and nobody must know it. Is it true that I am not fit for my office? It will never do for me to say that I cannot see the stuffs."

"Well, sir, do you say nothing about the cloth?" asked the one who was pretending to go on with his work.

"Oh, it is most elegant, most beautiful!" said the dazed old man, as he peered again through his spectacles. "What a fine pattern, and what fine colors! I will certainly tell the emperor how pleased I am with the stuff."

"We are glad of that," said both the weavers; and then they named the colors and pointed out the special features of the pattern. To all of this the minister paid great attention, so that he might be able to repeat it to the emperor when he went back to him.

And now the cheats called for more money, more silk, and more gold thread, to be able to proceed with the weaving, but they put it all into their own pockets, and not a thread went into the stuff, though they went on as before, weaving at the empty looms.

After a little time the emperor sent another honest statesman to see how the weaving was progressing, and if the stuff would soon be ready. The same thing happened with him as with the minister. He gazed and gazed, but as there was nothing but empty looms, he could see nothing else.

"Is not this an exquisite piece of stuff?" asked the weavers, pointing to one of the looms and explaining the beautiful pattern and the colors which were not there to be seen.

"I am not stupid, I know I am not!" thought the man, "so it must be that I am not fit for my good office. It is very strange, but I must not let it be noticed." So he praised the cloth he did not see and assured the weavers of his delight in the lovely colors and the exquisite pattern. "It is perfectly charming," he reported to the emperor.

Everybody in the town was talking of the splendid cloth. The emperor thought he should like to see it himself while it was still on the loom. With a company of carefully selected men, among whom were the two worthy officials who had been there before, he went to visit the crafty impostors, who were working as hard as ever at the empty looms.

"Is it not magnificent?" said both the honest statesmen. "See, your Majesty, what splendid colors, and what a pattern!" And they pointed to the looms, for they believed that others, no doubt, could see what they did not.

"What!" thought the emperor. "I see nothing at all. This is terrible! Am I a fool? Am I not fit to be emperor? Why nothing more dreadful could happen to me!"

"Oh, it is very pretty! it has my highest approval," the emperor said aloud. He nodded with satisfaction as he gazed at the empty looms, for he would not betray that he could see nothing.

His whole suite gazed and gazed, each seeing no more than the others; but, like the emperor, they all exclaimed, "Oh, it is beautiful!" They even suggested to the emperor that he wear the splendid new clothes for the first time on the occasion of a great procession which was soon to take place.

"Splendid! Gorgeous! Magnificent!" went from mouth to mouth. All were equally delighted with the weavers' workmanship. The emperor gave each of the impostors an order of knighthood to be worn in their buttonholes, and the title Gentleman Weaver of the Imperial Court.

Before the day on which the procession was to take place, the weavers sat up the whole night, burning sixteen candles, so that people might see how anxious they were to get the emperor's new clothes ready. They pretended to take the stuff from the loom, they cut it out in the air with huge scissors, and they stitched away with needles which had no thread in them. At last they said, "Now the clothes are finished."

The emperor came to them himself with his grandest courtiers, and each of the rogues lifted his arm as if he held something, saying, "See! here are the trousers! here is the coat! here is the cloak," and so on. "It is as light as a spider's web. One would almost feel as if one had nothing on, but that is the beauty of it!"

"Yes," said all the courtiers, but they saw nothing, for there was nothing to see.

"Will your Majesty be graciously pleased to take off your clothes so that we may put on the new clothes here, before the great mirror?"

The emperor took off his clothes, and the rogues pretended to put on first one garment and then another of the new ones they had pretended to make. They pretended to fasten something round his waist and to tie on something. This they said was the train, and the emperor turned round and round before the mirror.

"How well his Majesty looks in the new clothes! How becoming they are!" cried all the courtiers in turn. "That is a splendid costume!"

"The canopy that is to be carried over your Majesty in the procession is waiting outside," said the master of ceremonies.

"Well, I am ready," replied the emperor. "Don't the clothes look well?" and he turned round and round again before the mirror, to appear as if he were admiring his new costume.

The chamberlains, who were to carry the train, stooped and put their hands near the floor as if they were lifting it; then they pretended to be holding something in the air. They would not let it be noticed that they could see and feel nothing.

So the emperor went along in the procession, under the splendid canopy, and every one in the streets said: "How beautiful the emperor's new clothes are! What a splendid train! And how well they fit!"

No one wanted to let it appear that he could see nothing, for that would prove him not fit for his post. None of the emperor's clothes had been so great a success before.

"But he has nothing on!" said a little child.

"Just listen to the innocent," said its father; and one person whispered to another what the child had said. "He has nothing on; a child says he has nothing on!"

"But he has nothing on," cried all the people. The emperor was startled by this, for he had a suspicion that they were right. But he thought, "I must face this out to the end and go on with the procession." So he held himself more stiffly than ever, and the chamberlains held up the train that was not there at all.

XXVII

THE DARNING-NEEDLE

There was once a darning-needle who thought herself so fine that she fancied she must be fit for embroidery. "Hold me tight," she would say to the fingers, when they took her up, "don't let me fall; if you do I shall never be found again, I am so very fine."

"That is your opinion, is it?" said the fingers, as they seized her round the body.

"See, I am coming with a train," said the darning-needle, drawing a long thread after her; but there was no knot in the thread.

The fingers then placed the point of the needle against the cook's slipper. There was a crack in the upper leather, which had to be sewn together.

"What coarse work!" said the darning-needle, "I shall never get through. I shall break!—I am breaking!" and sure enough she broke. "Did I not say so?" said the darning-needle, "I know I am too fine for such work as that."

"This needle is quite useless for sewing now," said the fingers; but they still held it fast, and the cook dropped some sealing-wax on the needle, and fastened her handkerchief with it in front.

"So now I am a breast-pin," said the darning-needle; "I knew very well I should come to honor some day: merit is sure to rise;" and she laughed, quietly to herself, for of course no one ever saw a darning-needle laugh. And there she sat as proudly as if she were in a state coach, and looked all around her. "May I be allowed to ask if you are made of gold?" she inquired of her neighbor, a pin; "you have a very pretty appearance, and a curious head, although you are rather small. You must take pains to grow, for it is not every one who has sealing-wax dropped upon him;" and as she spoke, the darning-needle drew herself up so proudly that she fell out of the handkerchief right into the sink, which the cook was cleaning. "Now I am going on a journey," said the needle, as she floated away with the dirty water, "I do hope I shall not be lost." But she really was lost in a gutter. "I am too fine for this world," said the darning-needle, as she lay in the gutter; "but I know who I am, and that is always some comfort." So the darning-needle kept up her proud behavior, and did not lose her good humor. Then there floated over her all sorts of things,—chips and straws, and pieces of old newspaper. "See how they sail," said the darning-needle; "they do not know what is under them. I am here, and here I shall stick. See, there goes a chip, thinking of nothing in the world but himself—only a chip. There's a straw going by now; how he turns and twists about! Don't be thinking too much of yourself, or you may chance to run against a stone. There swims a piece of newspaper; what is written upon it has been forgotten long ago, and yet it gives itself airs. I sit here patiently and quietly. I know who I am, so I shall not move."

One day something lying close to the darning-needle glittered so splendidly that she thought it was a diamond; yet it was only a piece of broken bottle. The darning-needle spoke to it, because it sparkled, and represented herself as a breast-pin. "I suppose you are really a diamond?" she said.

"Why yes, something of the kind," he replied; and so each believed the other to be very valuable, and then they began to talk about the world, and the conceited people in it.

"I have been in a lady's work-box," said the darning-needle, "and this lady was the cook. She had on each hand five fingers, and anything so conceited as these five fingers I have never seen; and yet they were only employed to take me out of the box and to put me back again."

"Were they not high-born?"

"High-born!" said the darning-needle, "no indeed, but so haughty. They were five brothers, all born fingers; they kept very proudly together, though they were of different lengths. The one who stood first in the rank was named the thumb, he was short and thick, and had only one joint in his back, and could therefore make but one bow; but he said that if he were cut off from a man's hand, that man would be unfit for a soldier. Sweet-tooth, his neighbor, dipped himself into sweet or sour, pointed to the sun and moon, and formed the letters when the fingers wrote. Longman, the middle finger, looked over the heads of all the others. Gold-band, the next finger, wore a golden circle round his waist. And little Playman did nothing at all, and seemed proud of it. They were boasters, and boasters they will remain; and therefore I left them."

"And now we sit here and glitter," said the piece of broken bottle.

At the same moment more water streamed into the gutter, so that it overflowed, and the piece of bottle was carried away.

"So he is promoted," said the darning-needle, "while I remain here; I am too fine, but that is my pride, and what do I care?" And so she sat there in her pride, and had many such thoughts as these,—"I could almost fancy that I came from a sunbeam, I am so fine. It seems as if the sunbeams were always looking for me under the water. Ah! I am so fine that even my mother cannot find me. Had I still my old eye, which was broken off, I believe I should weep; but no, I would not do that, it is not genteel to cry."

One day a couple of street boys were paddling in the gutter, for they sometimes found old nails, farthings, and other treasures. It was dirty work, but they took great pleasure in it. "Hallo!" cried one, as he pricked himself with the darning-needle, "here's a fellow for you."

"I am not a fellow, I am a young lady," said the darning-needle; but no one heard her.

The sealing-wax had come off, and she was quite black; but black makes a person look slender, so she thought herself even finer than before.

"Here comes an egg-shell sailing along," said one of the boys; so they stuck the darning-needle into the egg-shell.

"White walls, and I am black myself," said the darning-needle, "that looks well; now I can be seen, but I hope I shall not be sea-sick, or I shall break again." She was not sea-sick, and she did not break. "It is a good thing against sea-sickness to have a steel stomach, and not to forget one's own importance. Now my sea-sickness has past: delicate people can bear a great deal."

Crack went the egg-shell, as a waggon passed over it.

"Good heavens, how it crushes!" said the darning-needle. "I shall be sick now. I am breaking!" but she did not break, though the waggon went over her as she lay at full length; and there let her lie.

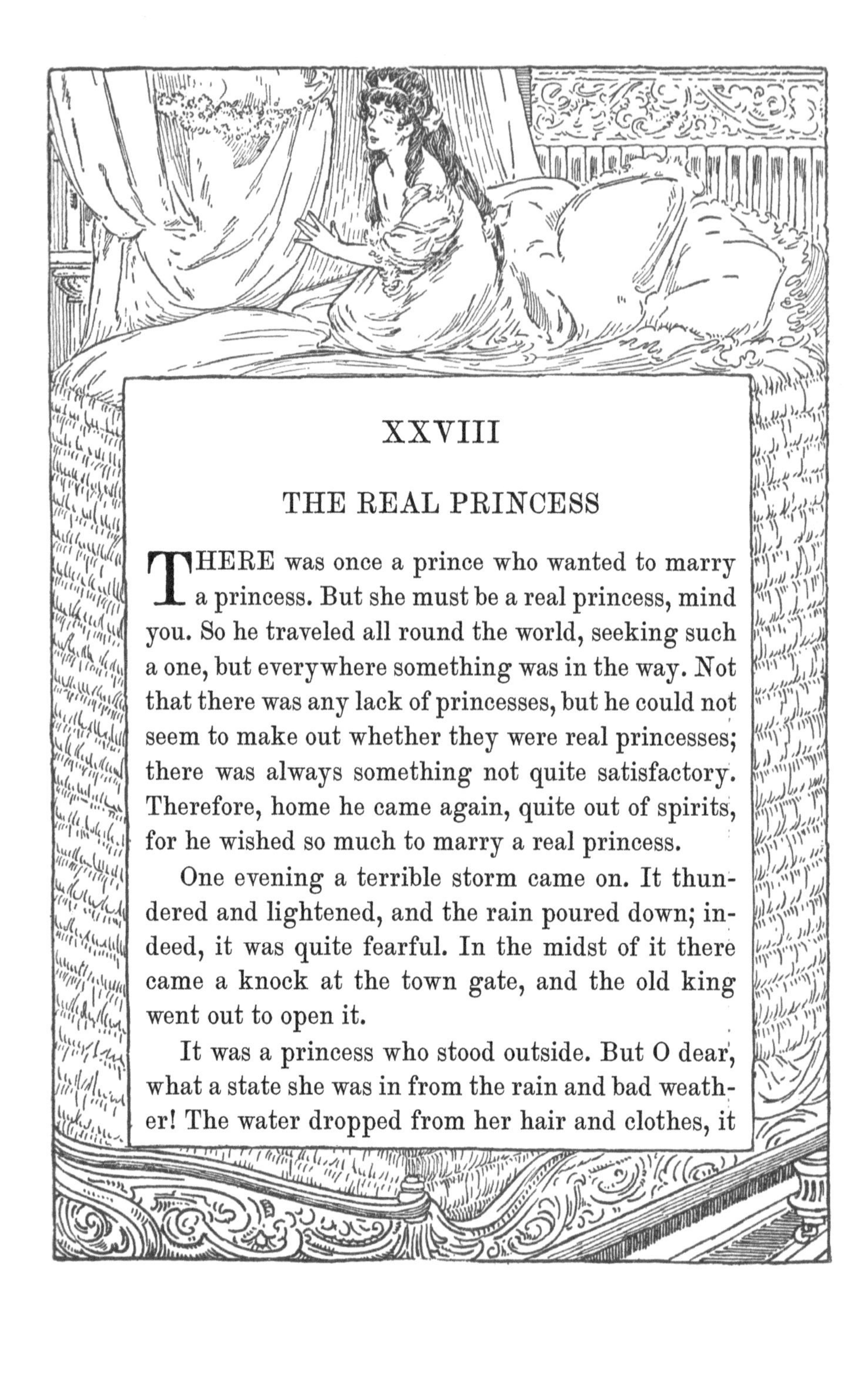

XXVIII

THE REAL PRINCESS

THERE was once a prince who wanted to marry a princess. But she must be a real princess, mind you. So he traveled all round the world, seeking such a one, but everywhere something was in the way. Not that there was any lack of princesses, but he could not seem to make out whether they were real princesses; there was always something not quite satisfactory. Therefore, home he came again, quite out of spirits, for he wished so much to marry a real princess.

One evening a terrible storm came on. It thundered and lightened, and the rain poured down; indeed, it was quite fearful. In the midst of it there came a knock at the town gate, and the old king went out to open it.

It was a princess who stood outside. But O dear, what a state she was in from the rain and bad weather! The water dropped from her hair and clothes, it ran in at the tips of her shoes and out at the heels; yet she insisted she was a real princess.

"Very well," thought the old queen; "that we shall presently see." She said nothing, but went into the bedchamber and took off all the bedding, then laid a pea on the sacking of the bedstead. Having done this, she took twenty mattresses and laid them upon the pea and placed twenty eider-down beds on top of the mattresses.

The princess lay upon this bed all the night. In the morning she was asked how she had slept.

"Oh, most miserably!" she said. "I scarcely closed my eyes the whole night through. I cannot think what there could have been in the bed. I lay upon something so hard that I am quite black and blue all over. It is dreadful!"

It was now quite evident that she was a real princess, since through twenty mattresses and twenty eider-down beds she had felt the pea. None but a real princess could have such delicate feeling.

So the prince took her for his wife, for he knew that in her he had found a true princess. And the pea was preserved in the cabinet of curiosities, where it is still to be seen unless some one has stolen it.

And this, mind you, is a real story.

XXIX

THE SHEPHERDESS AND THE CHIMNEY SWEEP

HAVE you ever seen an old wooden cabinet, quite worn black with age, and ornamented with all sorts of carved figures and flourishes?

Just such a one stood in a certain parlor. It was a legacy from the great-grandmother, and was covered from top to bottom with carved roses and tulips. The most curious flourishes were on it, too; and between them peered forth little stags' heads, with their zigzag antlers. On the door panel had been carved the entire figure of a man, a most ridiculous man to look at, for he grinned—you could not call it smiling or laughing—in the drollest way. Moreover, he had crooked legs, little horns upon his forehead, and a long beard.

The children used to call him the "crooked-legged field-marshal-major-general-corporal-sergeant," which was a long, hard name to pronounce. Very few there are, whether in wood or in stone, who could get such a title. Surely to have cut him out in wood was no trifling task. However, there he was. His eyes were always fixed upon the table below, and toward the mirror, for upon this table stood a charming little porcelain shepherdess, her mantle gathered gracefully about her and fastened with a red rose. Her shoes and hat were gilded, and her hand held a shepherd's crook; she was very lovely. Close by her stood a little chimney sweep, also of porcelain. He was as clean and neat as any other figure. Indeed, he might as well have been made a prince as a sweep, since he was only make-believe; for though everywhere else he was as black as a coal, his round, bright face was as fresh and rosy as a girl's. This was certainly a mistake—it ought to have been black.

There he stood so prettily, with his ladder in his hand, quite close to the shepherdess. From the first he had been placed there, and he always remained on the same spot; for they had promised to be true to each other. They suited each other exactly—they were both young, both of the same kind of porcelain, and both equally fragile.

Close to them stood another figure three times as large as themselves. It was an old Chinaman, a mandarin, who could nod his head. He was of porcelain, too, and he said he was the grandfather of the shepherdess; but this he could not prove. He insisted that he had authority over her, and so when the crooked-legged field-marshal-major-general-corporal-sergeant made proposals to the little shepherdess, he nodded his head, in token of his consent.

"You will have a husband," said the old mandarin to her, "a husband who, I verily believe, is of mahogany wood. You will be the wife of a field-marshal-major-general-corporal-sergeant, of a man who has a whole cabinet full of silver plate, besides a store of no one knows what in the secret drawers."

"I will never go into that dismal cabinet," declared the little shepherdess. "I have heard it said that there are eleven porcelain ladies already imprisoned there."

"Then," rejoined the mandarin, "you will be the twelfth, and you will be in good company. This very night, when the old cabinet creaks, we shall keep the wedding, as surely as I am a Chinese mandarin." And upon this he nodded his head and fell asleep.

But the little shepherdess wept, and turned to the beloved of her heart, the porcelain chimney sweep.

"I believe I must ask you," she said, "to go out with me into the wide world, for here it is not possible for us to stay."

"I will do in everything as you wish," replied the little chimney sweep. "Let us go at once. I am sure I can support you by my trade."

"If we were only down from the table," said she. "I shall not feel safe till we are far away out in the wide world and free."

The little chimney sweep comforted her, and showed her how to set her little foot on the carved edges, and on the gilded foliage

THE CHIMNEY-SWEEP SPOKE SENSIBLY TO HER

twining round the leg of the table, till at last they both reached the floor. But, turning for a last look at the old cabinet, they saw that everything was in commotion. All the carved stags stretched their heads farther out than before, raised their antlers, and moved their throats, while the crooked-legged field-marshal-major-general-corporal-sergeant sprang up and shouted to the old Chinese mandarin, "Look! they are eloping! they are eloping!"

They were not a little frightened at this, and jumped quickly into an open drawer in the window seat.

Here lay three or four packs of cards that were not quite complete, and a little doll's theater, which had been set up as nicely as could be. A play was going on, and all the queens sat in the front row, and fanned themselves with the flowers which they held in their hands, while behind them stood the knaves, each with two heads, one above and one below, as playing cards have. The play was about two persons who were not allowed to marry, and the shepherdess cried, for it seemed so like her own story.

"I cannot bear this!" she said. "Let us leave the drawer."

But when she had again reached the floor she looked up at the table and saw that the old Chinese mandarin was awake, and that he was rocking his whole body to and fro with rage.

"The old mandarin is coming!" cried she, and down she fell on her porcelain knees, so frightened was she.

"I have thought of a plan," said the chimney sweep. "Suppose we creep into the jar of perfumes, the potpourri vase which stands in the corner. There we can rest upon roses and lavender, and throw salt in his eyes if he comes near."

"That will not do at all," she said. "Besides, I know that the old mandarin and the potpourri vase were once betrothed; and no doubt some slight friendship still exists between them. No, there is no help for it; we must wander forth together into the wide world."

"Have you really the courage to go out into the wide world with me?" asked the chimney sweep. "Have you considered how large it is, and that if we go, we can never come back?"

"I have," replied she.

And the chimney sweep looked earnestly at her and said, "My way lies through the chimney. Have you really the courage to go with me through the stove, and creep through the flues and the tunnel? Well do I know the way! we shall come out by the chimney, and then I shall know how to manage. We shall mount so high that they can never reach us, and at the top there is an opening that leads out into the wide world."

And he led her to the door of the stove.

"Oh, how black it looks!" she said. Still she went on with him, through the stove, the flues, and the tunnel, where it was as dark as pitch.

"Now we are in the chimney," said he; "and see what a lovely star shines above us."

There actually was a star in the sky, that was shining right down upon them, as if to show them the way. Now they climbed and crept—a frightful way it was, so steep and high! But he went first to guide, and to smooth the way as much as he could. He showed her the best places on which to set her little china foot, till at last they came to the edge of the chimney and sat down to rest, for they were very tired, as may well be supposed.

The sky and all its stars were above them, and below lay all the roofs of the town. They saw all around them the great, wide world. It was not like what the poor little shepherdess had fancied it, and she leaned her little head upon her chimney sweep's shoulder and wept so bitterly that the gilding was washed from her golden sash.

"This is too much," said she; "it is more than I can bear. The world is too large! I wish I were safe back again upon the little table under the mirror. I shall never be happy till I am there once more. I have followed you out into the wide world. Surely, if you really love me, you will follow me back."

The chimney sweep tried to reason with her. He reminded her of the old mandarin, and the crooked-legged field-marshal-major-general-corporal-sergeant, but she wept so bitterly, and kissed her little chimney sweep so fondly, that he could not do otherwise than as she wished, foolish as it was.

So they climbed down the chimney, though with the greatest difficulty, crept through the flues, and into the stove, where they paused to listen behind the door, to discover what might be going on in the room.

All was quiet, and they peeped out. Alas! there on the floor lay the old mandarin. He had fallen from the table in his attempt to follow the runaways, and had broken into three pieces. His whole back had come off in a single piece, and his head had rolled into a corner. The crooked-legged field-marshal-major-general-corporal-sergeant stood where he had always stood, reflecting upon what had happened.

"This is shocking!" said the little shepherdess. "My old grandfather is broken in pieces, and we are the cause of it," and she wrung her little hands.

"He can be riveted," said the chimney sweep; "he can certainly be riveted. Do not grieve so! If they cement his back and put a rivet through his neck, he will be just as good as new, and will be able to say as many disagreeable things to us as ever."

"Do you really think so?" asked she. Then they climbed again up to the place where they had stood before.

"How far we have been," observed the chimney sweep, "and since we have got no farther than this, we might have saved ourselves all the trouble."

"I wish grandfather were mended," said the shepherdess; "I wonder if it will cost very much."

Mended he was. The family had his back cemented and his neck riveted, so that he was as good as new, only he could not nod.

"You have become proud since you were broken to shivers," observed the crooked-legged field-marshal-major-general-corporal-sergeant, "but I must say, for my part, I don't see much to be proud of. Am I to have her, or am I not? Just answer me that."

The chimney sweep and the shepherdess looked most piteously at the old mandarin. They were so afraid that he would nod his head. But he could not, and it would have been beneath his dignity to have confessed to having a rivet in his neck. So the young porcelain people always remained together, and they blessed the grandfather's rivet and loved each other till they were broken in pieces.

XXX

THE FLAX

The flax was in full bloom; it had pretty little blue flowers as delicate as the wings of a moth, or even more so. The sun shone, and the showers watered it; and this was just as good for the flax as it is for little children to be washed and then kissed by their mother. They look much prettier for it, and so did the flax.

"People say that I look exceedingly well," said the flax, "and that I am so fine and long that I shall make a beautiful piece of linen. How fortunate I am; it makes me so happy, it is such a pleasant thing to know that something can be made of me. How the sunshine cheers me, and how sweet and refreshing is the rain; my happiness overpowers me, no one in the world can feel happier than I am."

"Ah, yes, no doubt," said the fern, "but you do not know the world yet as well as I do, for my sticks are knotty;" and then it sung quite mournfully—

"Snip, snap, snurre,
Basse lurre:
The song is ended."

"No, it is not ended," said the flax. "To-morrow the sun will shine, or the rain descend. I feel that I am growing. I feel that I am in full blossom. I am the happiest of all creatures."

Well, one day some people came, who took hold of the flax, and pulled it up by the roots; this was painful; then it was laid in water as if they intended to drown it; and, after that, placed near a fire as if it were to be roasted; all this was very shocking.

"We cannot expect to be happy always," said the flax; "by experiencing evil as well as good, we become wise." And certainly there was plenty of evil in store for the flax. It was steeped, and roasted, and broken, and combed; indeed, it scarcely knew what was done to it. At last it was put on the spinning wheel. "Whirr, whirr," went the wheel so quickly that the flax could not collect its thoughts.

"Well, I have been very happy," he thought in the midst of his pain, "and must be contented with the past;" and contented he remained till he was put on the loom, and became a beautiful piece of white linen. All the flax, even to the last stalk, was used in making this one piece.

"Well, this is quite wonderful; I could not have believed that I should be so favored by fortune. The fern was not wrong with its song of

'Snip, snap, snurre,
Basse lurre.'

But the song is not ended yet, I am sure; it is only just beginning. How wonderful it is, that after all I have suffered, I am made something of at last; I am the luckiest person in the world—so strong and fine; and how white, and what a length! This is something different to being a mere plant and bearing flowers. Then I had no attention, nor any water unless it rained; now, I am watched and taken care of. Every morning the maid turns me over, and I have a shower-bath from the watering-pot every evening. Yes, and the clergyman's wife noticed me, and said I was the best piece of linen in the whole parish. I cannot be happier than I am now."

After some time, the linen was taken into the house, placed under the scissors, and cut and torn into pieces, and then pricked with needles. This certainly was not pleasant; but at last it was made into twelve garments of that kind which people do not like to name, and yet everybody should wear one.

"See, now, then," said the flax; "I have become something of importance. This was my destiny; it is quite a blessing. Now I shall be of some use in the world, as everyone ought to be; it is the only way to be happy. I am now divided into twelve pieces, and yet we are all one and the same in the whole dozen. It is most extraordinary good fortune."

Years passed away, and at last the linen was so worn it could scarcely hold together. "It must end very soon," said the pieces to each other; "we would gladly have held together a little longer, but it is useless to expect impossibilities." And at length they fell into rags and tatters, and thought it was all over with them, for they were torn to shreds, and steeped in water, and made into a pulp, and dried, and they knew not what besides, till all at once they found themselves beautiful white paper.

"Well, now, this is a surprise; a glorious surprise too," said the paper. "I am now finer than ever, and I shall be written upon, and who can tell what fine things I may have written upon me. This is wonderful luck!" And sure enough the most beautiful stories and poetry were written upon it, and only once was there a blot, which was very fortunate. Then people heard the stories and poetry read, and it made them wiser and better; for all that was written had a good and sensible meaning, and a great blessing was contained in the words on this paper.

"I never imagined anything like this," said the paper, "when I was only a little blue flower, growing in the fields. How could I fancy that I should ever be the means of bringing knowledge and joy to man? I cannot understand it myself, and yet it is really so. Heaven knows that I have done nothing myself, but what I was obliged to do with my weak powers for my own preservation; and yet I have been promoted from one joy and honor to another. Each time I think that the song is ended; and then something higher and better begins for me. I suppose now I shall be sent on my travels about the world, so that people may read me. It cannot be otherwise; indeed, it is more than probable; for I have more splendid thoughts written upon me, than I had pretty flowers in olden times. I am happier than ever."

But the paper did not go on its travels; it was sent to the printer, and all the words written upon it were set up in type, to make a book, or rather, many hundreds of books; for so many more persons could derive pleasure and profit from a printed book, than from the written paper; and if the paper had been sent around the world, it would have been worn out before it had got half through its journey.

"This is certainly the wisest plan," said the written paper; "I really did not think of that. I shall remain at home, and be held in honor, like some old grandfather, as I really am to all these new books. They will do some good. I could not have wandered about as they do. Yet he who wrote all this has looked at me, as every word flowed from his pen upon my surface. I am the most honored of all."

Then the paper was tied in a bundle with other papers, and thrown into a tub that stood in the washhouse.

"After work, it is well to rest," said the paper, "and a very good opportunity to collect one's thoughts. Now I am able, for the first time, to think of my real condition; and to know one's self is true progress. What will be done with me now, I wonder? No doubt I shall still go forward. I have always progressed hitherto, as I know quite well."

Now it happened one day that all the paper in the tub was taken out, and laid on the hearth to be burnt. People said it could not be sold at the shop, to wrap up butter and sugar, because it had been written upon. The children in the house stood round the stove; for they wanted to see the paper burn, because it flamed up so prettily, and afterwards, among the ashes, so many red sparks could be seen running one after the other, here and there, as quick as the wind. They called it seeing the children come out of school, and the last spark was the schoolmaster. They often thought the last spark had come; and one would cry, "There goes the schoolmaster;" but the next moment another spark would appear, shining so beautifully. How they would like to know where the sparks all went to! Perhaps we shall find out some day, but we don't know now.

The whole bundle of paper had been placed on the fire, and was soon alight. "Ugh," cried the paper, as it burst into a bright flame; "ugh." It was certainly not very pleasant to be burning; but when the whole was wrapped in flames, the flames mounted up into the air, higher than the flax had ever been able to raise its little blue flower, and they glistened as the white linen never could have glistened. All the written letters became quite red in a moment, and all the words and thoughts turned to fire.

"Now I am mounting straight up to the sun," said a voice in the flames; and it was as if a thousand voices echoed the words; and the flames darted up through the chimney, and went out at the top. Then a number of tiny beings, as many in number as the flowers on the flax had been, and invisible to mortal eyes, floated above them. They were even lighter and more delicate than the flowers from which they were born; and as the flames were extinguished, and nothing remained of the paper but black ashes, these little beings danced upon it; and whenever they touched it, bright red sparks appeared.

"The children are all out of school, and the schoolmaster was the last of all," said the children. It was good fun, and they sang over the dead ashes,—

"Snip, snap, snurre,
Basse lure:
The song is ended."

But the little invisible beings said, "The song is never ended; the most beautiful is yet to come."

But the children could neither hear nor understand this, nor should they; for children must not know everything.

XXXI

THE LEAP-FROG

A Flea, a Grasshopper, and a Leap-frog once wanted to see which could jump highest; and they invited the whole world, and everybody else besides who chose to come to see the festival. Three famous jumpers were they, as everyone would say, when they all met together in the room.

"I will give my daughter to him who jumps highest," exclaimed the King; "for it is not so amusing where there is no prize to jump for."

The Flea was the first to step forward. He had exquisite manners, and bowed to the company on all sides; for he had noble blood, and was, moreover, accustomed to the society of man alone; and that makes a great difference.

Then came the Grasshopper. He was considerably heavier, but he was well-mannered, and wore a green uniform, which he had by right of birth; he said, moreover, that he belonged to a very ancient Egyptian family, and that in the house where he then was, he was thought much of. The fact was, he had been just brought out of the fields, and put in a pasteboard house, three stories high, all made of court-cards, with the colored side inwards; and doors and windows cut out of the body of the Queen of Hearts. "I sing so well," said he, "that sixteen native grasshoppers who have chirped from infancy, and yet got no house built of cards to live in, grew thinner than they were before for sheer vexation when they heard me."

It was thus that the Flea and the Grasshopper gave an account of themselves, and thought they were quite good enough to marry a Princess.

The Leap-frog said nothing; but people gave it as their opinion, that he therefore thought the more; and when the housedog snuffed at him with his nose, he confessed the Leap-frog was of good family. The old councillor, who had had three orders given him to make him hold his tongue, asserted that the Leap-frog was a prophet; for that one could see on his back, if there would be a severe or mild winter, and that was what one could not see even on the back of the man who writes the almanac.

"I say nothing, it is true," exclaimed the King; "but I have my own opinion, notwithstanding."

Now the trial was to take place. The Flea jumped so high that nobody could see where he went to; so they all asserted he had not jumped at all; and that was dishonorable.

The Grasshopper jumped only half as high; but he leaped into the King's face, who said that was ill-mannered.

The Leap-frog stood still for a long time lost in thought; it was believed at last he would not jump at all.

"I only hope he is not unwell," said the house-dog; when, pop! he made a jump all on one side into the lap of the Princess, who was sitting on a little golden stool close by.

Hereupon the King said, "There is nothing above my daughter; therefore to bound up to her is the highest jump that can be made; but for this, one must possess understanding, and the Leap-frog has shown that he has understanding. He is brave and intellectual."

And so he won the Princess.

"It's all the same to me," said the Flea. "She may have the old Leap-frog, for all I care. I jumped the highest; but in this world merit seldom meets its reward. A fine exterior is what people look at now-a-days."

The Flea then went into foreign service, where, it is said, he was killed.

The Grasshopper sat without on a green bank, and reflected on worldly things; and he said too, "Yes, a fine exterior is everything—a fine exterior is what people care about." And then he began chirping his peculiar melancholy song, from which we have taken this history; and which may, very possibly, be all untrue, although it does stand here printed in black and white.

XXXII

BUCKWHEAT

IF YOU should chance, after a tempest, to cross a field where buckwheat is growing, you may observe that it looks black and singed, as if a flame of fire had passed over it. And should you ask the reason, a farmer will tell you, "The lightning did that."

But how is it that the lightning did it?

I will tell you what the sparrow told me, and the sparrow heard it from an aged willow which stood—and still stands for that matter—close to the field of buckwheat.

This willow is tall and venerable, though old and crippled. Its trunk is split clear through the middle, and grass and blackberry tendrils creep out through the cleft. The tree bends forward, and its branches droop like long, green hair.

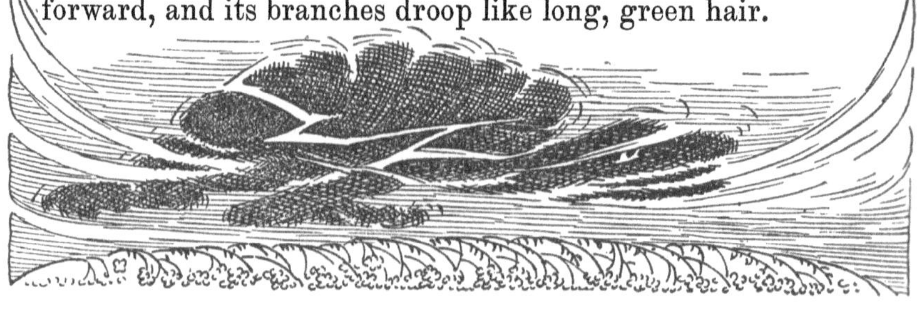

In the fields around the willow grew rye, wheat, and oats—beautiful oats that, when ripe, looked like little yellow canary birds sitting on a branch. The harvest had been blessed, and the fuller the ears of grain the lower they bowed their heads in reverent humility.

There was also a field of buckwheat lying just in front of the old willow. The buckwheat did not bow its head, like the rest of the grain, but stood erect in stiff-necked pride.

"I am quite as rich as the oats," it said; "and, moreover, I am much more sightly. My flowers are as pretty as apple blossoms. It is a treat to look at me and my companions. Old willow, do you know anything more beautiful than we?"

The willow nodded his head, as much as to say, "Indeed I do!" But the buckwheat was so puffed with pride that it only said: "The stupid tree! He is so old that grass is growing out of his body."

Now there came on a dreadful storm, and the flowers of the field folded their leaves or bent their heads as it passed over them. The buckwheat flower alone stood erect in all its pride.

"Bow your heads, as we do," called the flowers.

"There is no need for me to do that," answered the buckwheat.

"Bow your head as we do," said the grain. "The angel of storms comes flying hither. He has wings that reach from the clouds to the earth; he will smite you before you have time to beg for mercy."

"But I do not choose to bow down," said the buckwheat.

"Close your flowers and fold your leaves," said the old willow. "Do not look at the lightning when the cloud breaks. Even human beings dare not do that, for in the midst of the lightning one may look straight into God's heaven. The sight strikes human beings blind, so dazzling is it. What would not happen to us, mere plants of the field, who are so much humbler, if we should dare do so?"

"So much humbler! Indeed! If there is a chance, I shall look right into God's heaven." And in its pride and haughtiness it did so. The flashes of lightning were so awful that it seemed as if the whole world were in flames.

When the tempest was over, both the grain and the flowers, greatly refreshed by the rain, again stood erect in the pure, quiet air. But the buckwheat had been burned as black as a cinder by the lightning and stood in the field like a dead, useless weed.

The old willow waved his branches to and fro in the wind, and large drops of water fell from his green leaves, as if he were shedding tears. The sparrows asked: "Why are you weeping when all around seems blest? Do you not smell the sweet perfume of flowers and bushes? The sun shines, and the clouds have passed from the sky. Why do you weep, old tree?"

Then the willow told them of the buckwheat's stubborn pride and of the punishment which followed.

I, who tell this tale, heard it from the sparrows. They told it to me one evening when I had asked them for a story.

XXXIII

THE NIS AT THE GROCER'S

THERE was once a Student—a proper Student; he lived in an attic, and owned just nothing at all. There was also a Grocer—a proper Grocer; he lived in a comfortable room, and owned the whole house. So the Nis[1] clung to the Grocer, for the Grocer could give him, every Christmas eve, a bowl of groats, with such a great lump of butter in it! The Student could not afford him that; so the Nis dwelt in the shop, and was right comfortable there.

One evening the Student came by the back-door into the shop to buy candles and cheese; he had no servant to send so he came himself. They gave him what he wanted, he paid the money, and the Grocer and Madam, his wife—she was a woman! she had uncommon gifts of speech!—both nodded "Good evening" to him. The Student nodded in return, and was turning away when his eye fell upon something that was printed on the paper in which his cheese was wrapped, and he stood still to read it. It was a leaf torn out of an old book, a book that ought never to have been torn up, a book full of rare old poetry.

"Plenty more, if you like it," quoth the Grocer; "I gave an old woman some coffee-beans for it; you shall have the whole for eight skillings."[2]

[1] The Nis of Denmark and Norway is the same imaginary being that is called Brownie in Scotland and Kobold in Germany. He is represented as a dwarf, dressed in gray, with a pointed red cap.

[2] A skilling is a small Danish coin, in value a little less than a cent.

"Thank you," said the Student, "let me have it instead of the cheese; I can very well sup off bread and butter, and it would be a sin and a shame for such a book as this to be torn up into scraps. You are an excellent man, a practical man, but as for poetry, you have no more taste for it than that tub!"

Now this speech sounded somewhat rudely but it was spoken in jest; the Student laughed and the Grocer laughed, too. But the Nis felt extremely vexed that such a speech should be made to a Grocer who was a householder and sold the best butter.

So when night was come, the shop shut up, and all except the Student were gone to bed, the Nis stole away Madam's tongue—she did not want it while she slept. And now whatever object he put it upon not only received forthwith the faculty of speech, but was able to express its thoughts and feelings to the full as well as Madam herself. Fortunately the tongue could be in only one place at a time, otherwise there would have been a rare tumult and chattering in the shop, all speaking at once.

And the Nis put the tongue on the tub wherein all the old newspapers lay. "Is it really true," he asked, "that you do not know what poetry is?"

"Don't I know!" replied the Tub; "it is something that is put into the newspapers to fill them up. I should think I have more of it in me than the Student has, though I am only a Tub at the Grocer's!"

And the Nis put the tongue on the coffee-mill,—oh, how bravely it worked then!—and he put it on the money-box and on sundry other articles; and he asked them all the same question, and all gave much the same answer; all were of the same opinion, and the opinion of the multitude must be respected.

"Now for the Student!" and the Nis glided very softly up the back stairs leading to the Student's attic. There was light within, and the Nis peeped through the keyhole to see what the Student was about. He was reading in his new-found treasure, the torn old book. But oh, how glorious! A bright sunbeam, as it were, shot out from the book, expanding itself into a mighty, broad-stemmed tree, which raised itself on high and spread its branches over the student. Every leaf on the tree was fresh and green, every flower was like a graceful, girlish head—the faces of some lit up with eyes dark, thrilling, and passionate, and others animated by serene blue orbs, gentle as an angel's. And every fruit was like a glittering star, and such delicious melody was wafted around!

No, such glory and beauty as this never could the little Nis have imagined. And, mounted on tiptoe, he stood peeping and peeping, till at last the bright light within died away, till the Student blew out his lamp and went to bed. Nor even then could little Nis tear himself away, for soft, sweet music still floated around, lulling the Student to rest.

"This is beyond compare!" exclaimed the little Nis; "this could I never have anticipated! I believe I will stay with the Student henceforth." But he paused and reflected, and reasoned coolly with himself, and then he sighed, "The Student has no groats to give me." So down he went; yes, back he went to the Grocer's; and it was well that he did, for the Tub had, meantime, nearly worn out Madam's tongue by giving out through one ring all that was rumbling within it, and was just on the point of turning in order to give out the same through the other ring when the Nis came and took the tongue back to Madam. But from that time forward the whole shop, from the cash-box down to the pinewood fagots, formed their opinion from that of the Tub; and they all had such confidence in it, and treated it with so much respect, that when the Grocer read aloud in the evening art and the stage criticism from the Times, they all thought it was the Tub's doings.

But the little Nis was no longer content to stay quietly in the shop, listening to all the wit and wisdom to be gathered there; no, as soon as ever the lamp gleamed from the attic chamber he was gone; that slight thread of lamplight issuing from under the Student's door acted upon him as it were a strong anchor-rope drawing him upward; he must away to peep through the key-hole. And then he felt a tumult of pleasure within him, a feeling such as we all have known while gazing on the glorious sea when the Angel of the Storm is passing over it; and then he would burst out weeping, he knew not why, but they were happy, blessed tears. Oh, delightful beyond conception would it have been to sit with the Student under the tree; but that would be too much happiness, content was he and right glad of the keyhole. And there he would stand for hours in the draughty passage, with the bleak autumn wind blowing down from the trap-door in the roof full upon him; but the enthusiastic little spirit never heeded the cold, nor, indeed, felt it at all until the light in the attic had been extinguished and the sweet music had died away in the mournful night wind. Ugh! then he did shake and shiver, and crept back into his comfortable warm corner. And when Christmas eve came, and the great lump of butter in his groats—ah! then he felt that the Grocer was his master after all!

But one midnight the Nis was awaked by a terrible rat-tat upon the window-shutters; a crowd of people outside were shouting with all their might and main; the watchman was sounding his alarum; the whole street was lit up with a blaze of flame. Fire! where was it? at the Grocer's, or next door? The tumult was beyond description. Madam, in her bewilderment, took her gold ear-rings off her ears and put them in her pocket by way of saving something; the Grocer was in a state of excitement about his bonds, the maid wild for her silk mantilla. Every one would fain rescue whatsoever he deemed most precious; so would the little Nis. In two bounds he was up-stairs in the attic. The Student was standing at the open window, calmly admiring the fire, which was in the neighbor's house, not theirs; the marvelous book lay on the table, the little Nis seized it, put it into his red cap and held it aloft with both hands: the most precious thing the house possessed was saved! Away he darted with it, sprang upon the roof, and in a second was seated on the chimney-pot, the glorious raging flames like a halo around him, both hands grasping firmly the little red cap wherein lay his treasure. And now he knew where his heart was, felt that the Student was really his master; but when the fire was extinguished and he recovered his senses— what then? "I will divide my allegiance between them," quoth he; "I cannot quite give up the Grocer, because of my bowl of groats."

Now this was really quite human. The rest of us stick to the Grocer—for groats.

XXXIV

IT'S QUITE TRUE!

That is a terrible affair!" said a Hen; and she said it in a quarter of the town where the occurrence had not happened. "That is a terrible affair in the poultry -house. I cannot sleep alone to-night! It is quite fortunate that there are many of us on the roost together!" And she told a tale at which the feathers of the other birds stood on end, and the cock's comb fell down flat. It's quite true!

But we will begin at the beginning; and that was in a poultry-house in another part of the town. The sun went down, and the fowls jumped up on their perch to roost. There was a Hen, with white feathers and short legs, who laid her right number of eggs, and was a respectable hen in every way; as she flew up on to the roost she pecked herself with her beak, and a little feather fell out.

"There it goes!" said she; "the more I peck myself the handsomer I grow!" And she said it quite merrily, for she was a joker among the hens, though, as I have said, she was very respectable; and then she went to sleep.

It was dark all around; hen sat by hen, but the one that sat next to the merry Hen did not sleep: she heard and she didn't hear, as one should do in this world if one wishes to live in quiet; but she could not refrain from telling it to her next neighbour.

"Did you hear what was said here just now? I name no names; but here is a hen who wants to peck her feathers out to look well. If I were a cock I should despise her."

And just above the Hens sat the Owl, with her husband and her little owlets; the family had sharp ears, and they all heard every word that the neighboring Hen had spoken, and they rolled their eyes, and the Mother-Owl clapped her wings and said,

"Don't listen to it! But I suppose you heard what was said there? I heard it with my own ears, and one must hear much before one's ears fall off. There is one among the fowls who has so completely forgotten what is becoming conduct in a hen that she pulls out all her feathers, and then lets the cock see her."

"*Prenez garde aux enfants,*" said the Father-Owl."That's not fit for the children to hear."

"I'll tell it to the neighbor owl; she's a very proper owl to associate with." And she flew away.

"Hoo! hoo! to-whoo!" they both hooted in front of the neighbor's dovecot to the doves within. "Have you heard it ? Have you heard it? Hoo! hoo! there's a hen who has pulled out all her feathers for the sake of the cock. She'll die with cold, if she"s not dead already

"Coo! coo! Where, where?" cried the Pigeons.

"In the neighbor's poultry-yard. I've as good as seen it myself. It's hardly proper to repeat the story, but it"s quite true!"

"Believe it! believe every single word of it!" cooed the Pigeons, and they cooed down into their own poultry-yard. There"s a hen, and some say that there are two of them, that have plucked out all their feathers, that they may not look like the rest, and that they may attract the cock's attention. That's a bold game, for one may catch cold and die of a fever, and they are both dead.'

"Wake up! wake up!" crowed the Cock, and he flew up on to the fence; his eyes were still very heavy with sleep, but yet he crowed."Three hens have died of an unfortunate attachment to a cock. They have plucked out all their feathers. That's a terrible story. I won't keep it to myself; let it travel farther."

"Let it travel farther!" piped the Bats; and the fowls clucked and the cocks crowed,"Let it go farther! let it go farther!" And so the story travelled from poultry-yard to poultry-yard, and at last came back to the place from which it had gone forth.

"Five fowls," it was told, "have plucked out all their feathers to show which of them had become thinnest out of love to the cock;

and then they have pecked each other and fallen down dead, to the shame and disgrace of their families, and to the great loss of the proprietor."

And the Hen who had lost the little loose feather, of course did not know her own story again; and as she was a very respectable Hen, she said,

"I despise those fowls; but there are many of that sort. One ought not to hush up such a thing, and I shall do what I can that the story may get into the papers, and then it will be spread over all the country, and that will serve those fowls right, and their families too."

It was put into the newspaper: it was printed; and it's quite true—*that one little feather may swell till it becomes five fowls.*

XXXV

THE SUMMER GOWK[1]

DEEP lay the snow, for it was winter time, the air was cold, the wind sharp: but within doors all was snug and warm. And within doors lay the flower; in its bulb it lay, under earth and snow.

One day there fell rain; the drops trickled through the snow coverlet, down into the earth, and stirred against the flower-bulb, telling of the world of light above. And presently a sunbeam, pointed and slender, came piercing its way to the bulb, and tapped on it.

"Come in," said the Flower.

"That I can't," said the Sunbeam "I am not strong enough to lift the latch. I shall be strong in summer."

"When will it be summer?" asked the Flower; and it asked this again whenever a sunbeam pierced down to it. But summer was still far away: the ground was covered with snow, and every night there was ice on the water.

"How long it is! how long it is!" said the Flower. "I feel quite cribbed and cramped. I *must* stretch myself: I must raise myself: I must lift the latch and look out, and nod good-morrow to the summer; and that will be a merry time!"

And the Flower rose and strained from within, against the thin shell that had been softened by the rain, warmed by the earth and snow, and tapped upon by the sunbeam. It shot up from under the snow, with a pale-green bud on its tender stalk, and narrow thick leaves, that curled around it for a screen. The snow was cold, but glittering with light, and easy enough to push through; and here came the sunbeams with greater strength than before.

[1] *Sommergjoek* (meaning summer-dupe) is a Danish name for the snowdrop.

"Welcome! welcome!" sang every Sunbeam; and the Flower raised itself above the snow, up into the world of light. The sunbeams kissed and caressed it till it fully unfolded itself, white as snow, and decked with green stripes. It bowed its head in gladness and humility.

"Beautiful flower!" sang the Sunbeams. "How fresh thou art, and pure! Thou art the first one: thou art the only one! Thou art our darling! Thou art like a bell ringing up the summer, lovely summer, over towns and fields. All snow shall melt; the cold winds be chased away; we shall reign, and all things will grow green. Then thou wilt have fellowship, the lilacs and laburnums, and last of all the roses. But thou art the first, so tender and so pure!"

This was a deep delight to the Flower. It seemed as if the air it breathed was music, and as if its leaves and stem were full of thrilling sunbeams. There it stood, so fine and fragile, and yet so vigorous, in the beauty of youth—stood in its white kirtle with green bands—and praised the summer. But summer was not yet come; clouds began to hide the sun; sharp winds blew down upon the Flower.

"Thou art a little too soon," said Wind and Weather. "We still hold sway; this thou shalt feel to thy cost! Why not have kept indoors instead of running out here in thy finery? It is not time for that yet!"

It was biting cold. The days came and never brought a sunbeam. It was weather to freeze it to pieces, such a delicate little flower! But there was more strength in it than it knew of. It was strong in its glad faith in the summer, that must be near; for thus its own heart had foretold it, and the sunbeams had confirmed the tale. And so with patient hope it stood in its white dress, in the white snow, bowing its head when the flakes fell thick and heavy and when icy blasts came driving over it.

"Crouch, cringe!" they howled. "Wither and starve! What doest thou here in the cold? Thou hast been lured abroad; the sunbeam hath mocked thee. Now make the best of it, thou summer-gowk!"

"Summer-gowk!" echoed the keen airs of morning.

"A summer-gowk!" shouted children, who came down into the garden; "there it stands so pretty, so beautiful—the first, the only one!"

And the words did good to the Flower; they were like warm sunbeams. In its gladness it never once noticed that it was being plucked. It lay in a child's hand, was kissed by a child's mouth, brought into a warm room, gazed at by kind eyes, and set in water—so strengthening, so enlivening. The Flower thought it had passed into the middle of summer.

The daughter of the house was a pretty little lass, just confirmed, and she had a little sweetheart, also just confirmed, who was studying for his livelihood. "He shall be my summer-gowk," said she; and took the fine flower and laid it in a scented paper that was written all over with verses about the flower, beginning with summer-gowk, and ending with summer-gowk— "now, sweetheart, be my winter-fool!"—she had mocked him with the summer. Yes, that was the meaning of the verses. They were folded up as a letter, and the Flower was slipped inside, and there it lay all in the dark, as dark as when it lay in the bulb. It had to go on a journey, squeezed into the corner of a post-bag; this was not at all pleasant, but it came to an end at last.

The journey was over, the letter was opened and read by the young sweetheart. He was so delighted he kissed the Flower. It was locked up, with the verses around it, in a drawer where there were many charming letters, but without a single flower in them. Here again it was the first, the only one, as the sunbeams had called it, and that was something to think about.

It was left to think at leisure for a long time; and it went on thinking throughout the summer and throughout the winter till another summer came round; then it was drawn forth again. But this time the youth looked by no means delighted. He gripped hold of the papers and flung away the verses, so that the Flower dropped out on the floor. Flattened and withered as it was, still it might not to have been thrown down on the floor; yet, after all, it was better off there than in the fire, where the verses and letters were blazing. What could have happened? What happens so often. The flower had mocked him; that was a joke: the maiden had mocked him; that was no joke: she had chosen another sweetheart for this midsummer.

The next morning the sun shone in on the little flattened Summer-gowk, that looked as if it was painted on the floor. The servant-girl, who was sweeping, picked it up and placed it in one of the books on the table, for she fancied it must have fallen while she was routing about and putting things in order. And again the Flower lay between verses—printed verses, and those are grander than written ones; at all events, they cost more.

Years passed away, and the book stood still on its shelf. At length it was taken down, opened, and read. It was a good book: songs and poems by the Danish poet, Ambrosius Stub, who is well worth knowing. The man who was reading turned a page of the book. "So here is a flower!" said he; "a summer-gowk! Not without meaning does it lie here. Poor Ambrosius Stub; he, too, was a summer-gowk, a poet-gowk. He came before his time, and so he had to face sharp winds and sleet on his rounds among the gentlemen of Fünen. Set up for a show, like the flower in a glass; sent on for a jest, like the flower in a valentine. He was a summer-gowk, a winter-fool, all fun and foolery; and yet the first, the only Danish poet of the time; and still, in his youthful freshness, the first, the only one! Aye, lie as a mark in this book, little Summer-gowk; thou art laid here with some meaning."

And thus the Summer-gowk was put back again into the book, and felt honored and delighted with learning that it was a mark in a beautiful song-book; and that he who had first written and sung about the Flower had himself been a summer-gowk and played the fool in winter. Now the Flower understood this in its own way, just as we understand anything in our way.

This is the fairy tale of the Summer-gowk.

XXXVI

THE NAUGHTY BOY

A long time ago, there lived an old poet, a thoroughly kind old poet. As he was sitting one evening in his room, a dreadful storm arose without, and the rain streamed down from heaven; but the old poet sat warm and comfortable in his chimney-corner, where the fire blazed and the roasting apple hissed.

"Those who have not a roof over their heads will be wetted to the skin," said the good old poet.

"Oh let me in! Let me in! I am cold, and I'm so wet!" exclaimed suddenly a child that stood crying at the door and knocking for admittance, while the rain poured down, and the wind made all the windows rattle.

"Poor thing!" said the old poet, as he went to open the door. There stood a little boy, quite naked, and the water ran down from his long golden hair; he trembled with cold, and had he not come into a warm room he would most certainly have perished in the frightful tempest.

"Poor child!" said the old poet, as he took the boy by the hand. "Come in, come in, and I will soon restore thee! Thou shalt have wine and roasted apples, for thou art verily a charming child!" And the boy was so really. His eyes were like two bright stars; and although the water trickled down his hair, it waved in beautiful curls. He looked exactly like a little angel, but he was so pale, and his whole body trembled with cold. He had a nice little bow in his hand, but it was quite spoiled by the rain, and the tints of his many-colored arrows ran one into the other.

The old poet seated himself beside his hearth, and took the little fellow on his lap; he squeezed the water out of his dripping

THERE STOOD A LITTLE BOY

hair, warmed his hands between his own, and boiled for him some sweet wine. Then the boy recovered, his cheeks again grew rosy, he jumped down from the lap where he was sitting, and danced round the kind old poet.

"You are a merry fellow," said the old man. "What's your name?"

"My name is Cupid," answered the boy. "Don't you know me? There lies my bow; it shoots well, I can assure you! Look, the weather is now clearing up, and the moon is shining clear again through the window."

"Why, your bow is quite spoiled," said the old poet.

"That were sad indeed," said the boy, and he took the bow in his hand and examined it on every side. "Oh, it is dry again, and is not hurt at all; the string is quite tight. I will try it directly." And he bent his bow, took aim, and shot an arrow at the old poet, right into his heart. "You see now that my bow was not spoiled," said he laughing; and away he ran.

The naughty boy, to shoot the old poet in that way; he who had taken him into his warm room, who had treated him so kindly, and who had given him warm wine and the very best apples!

The poor poet lay on the earth and wept, for the arrow had really flown into his heart.

"Fie!" said he. "How naughty a boy Cupid is! I will tell all children about him, that they may take care and not play with him, for he will only cause them sorrow and many a heartache."

And all good children to whom he related this story, took great heed of this naughty Cupid; but he made fools of them still, for he is astonishingly cunning. When the university students come from the lectures, he runs beside them in a black coat, and with a book under his arm. It is quite impossible for them to know him, and they walk along with him arm in arm, as if he, too, were a student like themselves; and then, unperceived, he thrusts an arrow to their bosom. When the young maidens come from being examined by the clergyman, or go to church to be confirmed, there he is again close behind them. Yes, he is forever following people. At the play, he sits in the great chandelier and burns in bright flames, so that people think it is really a flame, but they soon discover it is something else. He roves about in the garden of the palace and upon the ramparts:

yes, once he even shot your father and mother right in the heart. Ask them only and you will hear what they'll tell you. Oh, he is a naughty boy, that Cupid; you must never have anything to do with him. He is forever running after everybody. Only think, he shot an arrow once at your old grandmother! But that is a long time ago, and it is all past now; however, a thing of that sort she never forgets. Fie, naughty Cupid! But now you know him, and you know, too, how ill-behaved he is!

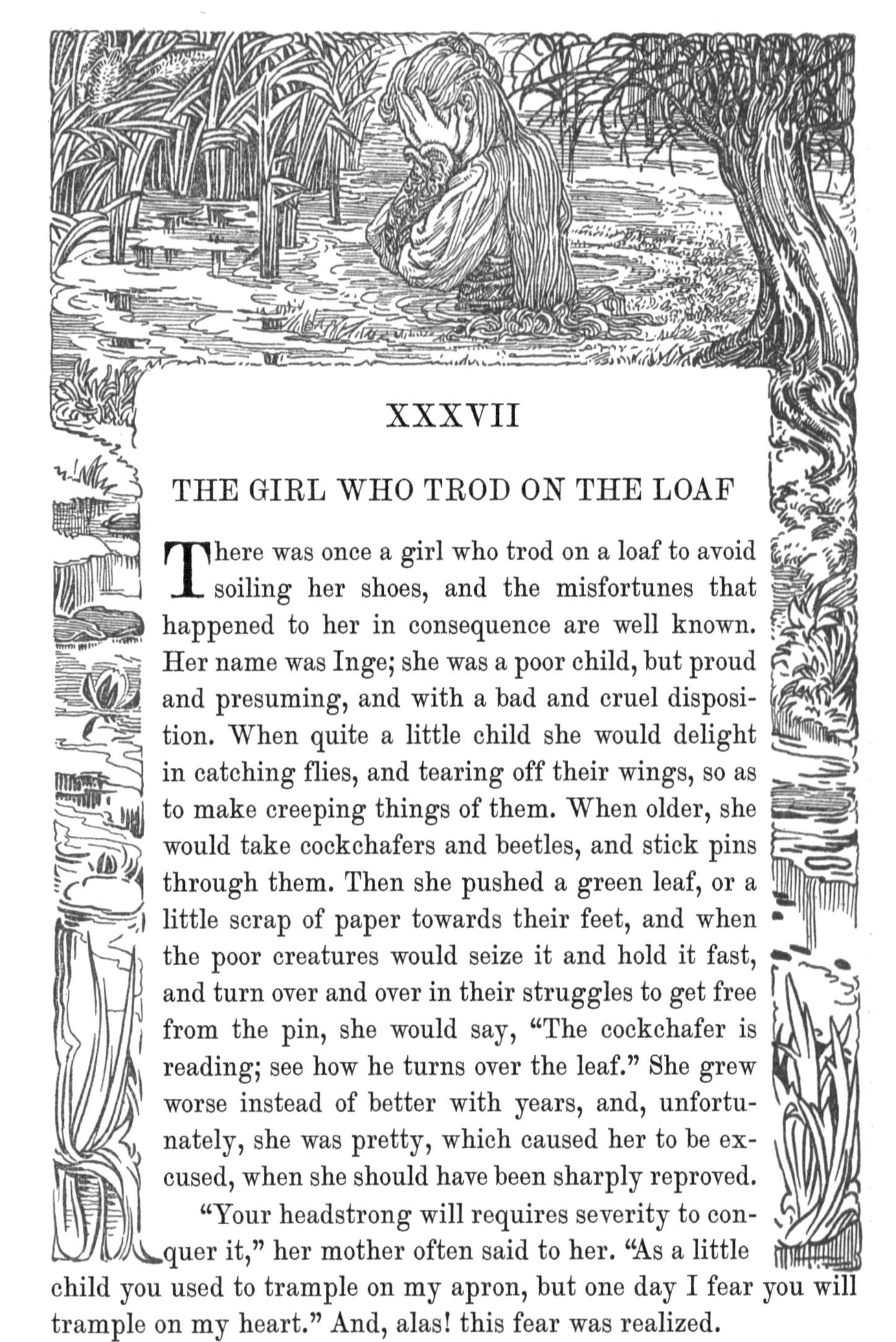

XXXVII

THE GIRL WHO TROD ON THE LOAF

There was once a girl who trod on a loaf to avoid soiling her shoes, and the misfortunes that happened to her in consequence are well known. Her name was Inge; she was a poor child, but proud and presuming, and with a bad and cruel disposition. When quite a little child she would delight in catching flies, and tearing off their wings, so as to make creeping things of them. When older, she would take cockchafers and beetles, and stick pins through them. Then she pushed a green leaf, or a little scrap of paper towards their feet, and when the poor creatures would seize it and hold it fast, and turn over and over in their struggles to get free from the pin, she would say, "The cockchafer is reading; see how he turns over the leaf." She grew worse instead of better with years, and, unfortunately, she was pretty, which caused her to be excused, when she should have been sharply reproved.

"Your headstrong will requires severity to conquer it," her mother often said to her. "As a little child you used to trample on my apron, but one day I fear you will trample on my heart." And, alas! this fear was realized.

Inge was taken to the house of some rich people, who lived at a distance, and who treated her as their own child, and dressed her so fine that her pride and arrogance increased.

When she had been there about a year, her patroness said to her, "You ought to go, for once, and see your parents, Inge."

So Inge started to go and visit her parents; but she only wanted to show herself in her native place, that the people might see how fine she was. She reached the entrance of the village, and saw the young laboring men and maidens standing together chatting, and her own mother amongst them. Inge's mother was sitting on a stone to rest, with a fagot of sticks lying before her, which she had picked up in the wood. Then Inge turned back; she who was so finely dressed she felt ashamed of her mother, a poorly clad woman, who picked up wood in the forest. She did not turn back out of pity for her mother's poverty, but from pride.

Another half-year went by, and her mistress said, "you ought to go home again, and visit your parents, Inge, and I will give you a large wheaten loaf to take to them, they will be glad to see you, I am sure."

So Inge put on her best clothes, and her new shoes, drew her dress up around her, and set out, stepping very carefully, that she might be clean and neat about the feet, and there was nothing wrong in doing so. But when she came to the place where the footpath led across the moor, she found small pools of water, and a great deal of mud, so she threw the loaf into the mud, and trod upon it, that she might pass without wetting her feet. But as she stood with one foot on the loaf and the other lifted up to step forward, the loaf began to sink under her, lower and lower, till she disappeared altogether, and only a few bubbles on the surface of the muddy pool remained to show where she had sunk. And this is the story.

But where did Inge go? She sank into the ground, and went down to the Marsh Woman, who is always brewing there.

The Marsh Woman is related to the elf maidens, who are well-known, for songs are sung and pictures painted about them. But of the Marsh Woman nothing is known, excepting that when a mist arises from the meadows, in summer time, it is because she is brewing beneath them. To the Marsh Woman's brewery Inge sunk down to a place which no one can endure for long. A heap of mud is a palace compared with the Marsh Woman's brewery; and as Inge fell she shuddered in every limb, and soon became cold and stiff as marble. Her foot was still fastened to the loaf, which bowed her down as a golden ear of corn bends the stem.

An evil spirit soon took possession of Inge, and carried her to a still worse place, in which she saw crowds of unhappy people, waiting in a state of agony for the gates of mercy to be opened to them, and in every heart was a miserable and eternal feeling of unrest. It would take too much time to describe the various tortures these people suffered, but Inge's punishment consisted in standing there as a statue, with her foot fastened to the loaf. She could move her eyes about, and see all the misery around her, but she could not turn her head; and when she saw the people looking at her she thought they were admiring her pretty face and fine clothes, for she was still vain and proud. But she had forgotten how soiled her clothes had become while in the Marsh Woman's brewery, and that they were covered with mud; a snake had also fastened itself in her hair, and hung down her back, while from each fold in her dress a great toad peeped out and croaked like an asthmatic poodle. Worse than all was the terrible hunger that tormented her, and she could not stoop to break off a piece of the loaf on which she stood. No; her back was too stiff, and her whole body like a pillar of stone. And then came creeping over her face and eyes flies without wings; she winked and blinked, but they could not fly away, for their wings had been pulled off; this, added to the hunger she felt, was horrible torture.

"If this lasts much longer," she said, "I shall not be able to bear it." But it did last, and she had to bear it, without being able to help herself.

A tear, followed by many scalding tears, fell upon her head, and rolled over her face and neck, down to the loaf on which she stood. Who could be weeping for Inge? She had a mother in the world still, and the tears of sorrow which a mother sheds for her child will always find their way to the child's heart, but they often increase the torment instead of being a relief. And Inge could hear all that was said about her in the world she had left, and every one seemed cruel to her. The sin she had committed in treading on the loaf was known on earth, for she had been seen by the cowherd from the hill, when she was crossing the marsh and had disappeared.

"THIS COMES OF WISHING TO HAVE CLEAN SHOES"

When her mother wept and exclaimed, "Ah, Inge! what grief thou hast caused thy mother" she would say, "Oh that I had never been born! My mother's tears are useless now."

And then the words of the kind people who had adopted her came to her ears, when they said, "Inge was a sinful girl, who did not value the gifts of God, but trampled them under her feet."

"Ah," thought Inge, "they should have punished me, and driven all my naughty tempers out of me."

A song was made about "The girl who trod on a loaf to keep her shoes from being soiled," and this song was sung everywhere. The story of her sin was also told to the little children, and they called her "wicked Inge," and said she was so naughty that she ought to be punished. Inge heard all this, and her heart became hardened and full of bitterness.

But one day, while hunger and grief were gnawing in her hollow frame, she heard a little, innocent child, while listening to the tale of the vain, haughty Inge, burst into tears and exclaim, "But will she never come up again?"

And she heard the reply, "No, she will never come up again."

"But if she were to say she was sorry, and ask pardon, and promise never to do so again?" asked the little one.

"Yes, then she might come; but she will not beg pardon," was the answer.

"Oh, I wish she would!" said the child, who was quite unhappy about it. "I should be so glad. I would give up my doll and all my playthings, if she could only come here again. Poor Inge! it is so dreadful for her."

These pitying words penetrated to Inge's inmost heart, and seemed to do her good. It was the first time any one had said, "Poor Inge!" without saying something about her faults. A little innocent child was weeping, and praying for mercy for her. It made her feel quite strange, and she would gladly have wept herself, and it added to her torment to find she could not do so. And while she thus suffered in a place where nothing changed, years passed away on earth, and she heard her name less frequently mentioned. But one day a sigh reached her ear, and the words, "Inge! Inge! what a grief thou hast been to me! I said it would be so." It was the last sigh of her dying mother.

After this, Inge heard her kind mistress say, "Ah, poor Inge! shall I ever see thee again? Perhaps I may, for we know not what may happen in the future." But Inge knew right well that her mistress would never come to that dreadful place.

Time-passed—a long bitter time—then Inge heard her name pronounced once more, and saw what seemed two bright stars shining above her. They were two gentle eyes closing on earth. Many years had passed since the little girl had lamented and wept about "poor Inge." That child was now an old woman, whom God was taking to Himself. In the last hour of existence the events of a whole life often appear before us; and this hour the old woman remembered how, when a child, she had shed tears over the story of Inge, and she prayed for her now.

As the eyes of the old woman closed to earth, the eyes of the soul opened upon the hidden things of eternity, and then she, in whose last thoughts Inge had been so vividly present, saw how deeply the poor girl had sunk. She burst into tears at the sight, and in heaven, as she had done when a little child on earth, she wept and prayed for poor Inge. Her tears and her prayers echoed through the dark void that surrounded the tormented captive soul, and the unexpected mercy was obtained for it through an angel's tears. As in thought Inge seemed to act over again every sin she had committed on earth, she trembled, and tears she had never yet been able to weep rushed to her eyes. It seemed impossible that the gates of mercy could ever be opened to her; but while she acknowledged this in deep penitence, a beam of radiant light shot suddenly into the depths upon her.

More powerful than the sunbeam that dissolves the man of snow which the children have raised, more quickly than the snowflake melts and becomes a drop of water on the warm lips of a child, was the stony form of Inge changed, and as a little bird she soared, with the speed of lightning, upward to the world of mortals. A bird that felt timid and shy to all things around it, that seemed to shrink with shame from meeting any living creature, and hurriedly sought to conceal itself in a dark corner of an old ruined wall; there it sat cowering and unable to utter a sound, for it was voiceless. Yet how quickly the little bird discovered the beauty of everything around it. The sweet, fresh air; the soft radiance of the moon, as its light spread over the earth; the fragrance which exhaled from bush and tree, made it feel happy as it sat there clothed in its fresh, bright plumage. All creation seemed to speak of beneficence and love. The bird wanted to give utterance to thoughts that stirred in his breast, as the cuckoo and the nightingale in the spring, but it could not. Yet in heaven can be heard the song of praise, even from a worm; and the notes trembling in the breast of the bird were as audible to Heaven even as the psalms of David before they had fashioned themselves into words and song.

Christmas-time drew near, and a peasant who dwelt close by the old wall stuck up a pole with some ears of corn fastened to the top, that the birds of heaven might have feast, and rejoice in the happy, blessed time. And on Christmas morning the sun arose and shone upon the ears of corn, which were quickly surrounded by a number of twittering birds. Then, from a hole in the wall, gushed forth in song the swelling thoughts of the bird as he issued from his hiding place to perform his first good deed on earth,—and in heaven it was well known who that bird was.

The winter was very hard; the ponds were covered with ice, and there was very little food for either the beasts of the field or the birds of the air. Our little bird flew away into the public roads, and found here and there, in the ruts of the sledges, a grain of corn, and at the halting places some crumbs. Of these he ate only a few, but he called around him the other birds and the hungry sparrows, that they too might have food. He flew into the towns, and looked about, and wherever a kind hand had strewed bread on the window-sill for the birds, he only ate a single crumb himself, and gave all the rest to the rest of the other birds. In the course of the winter the bird had in this way collected many crumbs and given them to other birds, till they equalled the weight of the loaf on which Inge had trod to keep her shoes clean; and when the last bread-crumb had been found and given, the gray wings of the bird became white, and spread themselves out for flight.

"See, yonder is a sea-gull!" cried the children, when they saw the white bird, as it dived into the sea, and rose again into the clear sunlight, white and glittering. But no one could tell whither it went then although some declared it flew straight to the sun.

XXXVIII

THE FARMYARD COCK AND THE WEATHERCOCK

THERE were once two cocks; one of them stood on a dunghill, the other on the roof. Both were conceited, but the question is, Which of the two was the more useful?

A wooden partition divided the poultry yard from another yard, in which lay a heap of manure sheltering a cucumber bed. In this bed grew a large cucumber, which was fully aware that it was a plant that should be reared in a hotbed.

"It is the privilege of birth," said the Cucumber to itself. "All cannot be born cucumbers; there must be other kinds as well. The fowls, the ducks, and the cattle in the next yard are all different creatures, and there is the yard cock—I can look up to him when he is on the wooden partition. He is certainly of much greater importance than the weathercock, who is so highly placed, and who can't even creak, much less crow—besides, he has neither hens nor chickens, and thinks only of himself, and perspires verdigris. But the yard cock is something like a cock. His gait is like a dance, and his crowing is music, and wherever he goes it is instantly known. What a trumpeter he is! If he would only come in here! Even if he were to eat me up, stalk and all, it would be a pleasant death." So said the Cucumber.

During the night the weather became very bad; hens, chickens, and even the cock himself sought shelter. The wind blew down with a crash the partition between the two yards, and the tiles came tumbling from the roof, but the weathercock stood firm. He did not even turn round; in fact, he could not, although he was fresh and newly cast. He had been born full grown and did not at all resemble the birds, such as the sparrows and swallows, that fly beneath the vault of heaven. He despised them and looked upon them as little twittering birds that were made only to sing. The pigeons, he admitted, were large and shone in the sun like mother-of-pearl. They somewhat resembled weathercocks, but were fat and stupid and thought only of stuffing themselves with food. "Besides," said the weathercock, "they are very tiresome things to converse with."

The birds of passage often paid a visit to the weathercock and told him tales of foreign lands, of large flocks passing through the air, and of encounters with robbers and birds of prey. These were very interesting when heard for the first time, but the weathercock knew the birds always repeated themselves, and that made it tedious to listen.

"They are tedious, and so is every one else," said he; "there is no one fit to associate with. One and all of them are wearisome and stupid. The whole world is worth nothing—it is made up of stupidity."

The weathercock was what is called "lofty," and that quality alone would have made him interesting in the eyes of the Cucumber, had she known it. But she had eyes only for the yard cock, who had actually made his appearance in her yard; for the violence of the storm had passed, but the wind had blown down the wooden palings.

"What do you think of that for crowing?" asked the yard cock of his hens and chickens. It was rather rough, and wanted elegance, but they did not say so, as they stepped upon the dunghill while the cock strutted about as if he had been a knight. "Garden plant," he cried to the Cucumber. She heard the words with deep feeling, for they showed that he understood who she was, and she forgot that he was pecking at her and eating her up—a happy death!

Then the hens came running up, and the chickens followed, for where one runs the rest run also. They clucked and chirped and looked at the cock and were proud that they belonged to him. "Cock-a-doodle-doo!" crowed he; "the chickens in the poultry yard will grow to be large fowls if I make my voice heard in the world."

And the hens and chickens clucked and chirped, and the cock told them a great piece of news. "A cock can lay an egg," he said. "And what do you think is in that egg? In that egg lies a basilisk. No one can endure the sight of a basilisk. Men know my power, and now you know what I am capable of, also, and what a renowned bird I am." And with this the yard cock flapped his wings, erected his comb, and crowed again, till all the hens and chickens trembled; but they were proud that one of their race should be of such renown in the world. They clucked and they chirped so that the weathercock heard it; he had heard it all, but had not stirred.

"It's all stupid stuff," said a voice within the weathercock. "The yard cock does not lay eggs any more than I do, and I am too lazy. I could lay a wind egg if I liked, but the world is not worth a wind egg. And now I don't intend to sit here any longer."

With that, the weathercock broke off and fell into the yard. He did not kill the yard cock, although the hens said he intended to do so.

And what does the moral say? "Better to crow than to be vainglorious and break down at last."

XXXIX

THE TOAD

The well was deep, and therefore the rope was long; the wheel went around with difficulty when the waterfilled bucket had to be pulled up over the side of the well. The sun could never mirror itself down in the water, no matter how brightly it shone; but as far down as its rays penetrated, green weeds were growing from between the stones.

There was a family of toads living down there. It was an immigrant family which, as a matter of fact, had come down there headlong in the person of the old toad mother, who was still living. The green frogs that swam in the water had made their homes there for a much longer time, but they acknowledged their cousins and called them "well guests." The latter, however, had no thoughts of ever leaving, they found it very comfortable here on the dry land, as they called the wet stones.

Mamma Frog had once traveled; she'd been in the bucket when it had gone up, but the light above had been too strong for her and given her a frightful pain in the eyes. Luckily she had managed to get out of the bucket. She'd fallen into the water with a tremendous splash and been laid up for three days with a backache. She didn't have much to tell about the world above, but she did know, and so did all the others, that the well wasn't the whole world. Mamma Toad, on the other hand, might have told them a few things about it, but she never answered when anyone inquired, so they stopped inquiring.

"Big and ugly, fat and loathsome, she is!" said the young green frogs. "And her brats are getting to be just like her!"

"Maybe so," said Mamma Toad, "but one of them has a jewel in its head, if I don't have it myself!"

And the green frogs listened and stared at her, and as they didn't like this news, they made faces at her and dived down to the bottom. But the young toads stretched out their hind legs proudly. Each of them thought it was the one which had the jewel, so they all kept their heads quite rigid, but at last they began to ask what it was they had to be proud of and just what a jewel was, anyway.

"It's something so glorious and precious," said Mamma Toad, "that I can't describe it. It's something you wear for your own pleasure and others become irritated over. But ask no more, for I won't answer."

"Well, I haven't got the jewel," said the smallest Toad, which was as ugly as it could be. "Why should I have anything so splendid? And if it irritates others, why, it wouldn't please me. No, all I want is to get up to the top of the well sometime and take one peep out! It must be wonderful up there!"

"Better stay where you are," said the old Toad. "You're at home here, and you know what it's like. Keep away from the bucket, or it may squash you! And even if you did get safely into it you might fall out. Not everyone can come down as luckily as I did and keep limbs and eggs all safe and sound."

"Croak!" said the little one; and that was the same as when we humans say, "Oh!"

It had such a great desire to get up to the top of the well and look out; it felt an intense longing for the green things up there. And next morning, when the bucket, filled with water, was being pulled up and happened to pause for an instant beside the stone where the Toad sat, the little creature quivered through and through and then jumped into the bucket. It sank to the bottom of the water, which soon was drawn up and emptied out.

"Phooie, what a nuisance!" said the man when he saw it. "That's the ugliest thing I've ever seen!" And then he kicked with his heavy wooden shoe at the Toad, which came close to being crippled, but managed to escape into the middle of some tall nettles. It saw stalk after stalk around it; it looked upward and saw the sun shining on the leaves, making them quite transparent.

For the Toad it was the same as it is for us when we come suddenly into a great forest, where the sun shines between leaves and branches.

"It's much prettier here than down in that well! You could stay here for your whole lifetime!" said the little Toad. It lay there for an hour; it lay there for two hours. "Now what could there be outside? Since I've come this far I might as well go farther." So it crept as fast as it could, until it came out into the road, where the sun shone on it; and then it was powdered with dust as it hopped across the road.

"Here one is really on dry land," said the Toad. "I'm getting almost too much of a good thing; it tickles right through me!"

Now it reached a ditch, where grew forget-me-nots and meadowsweet, while beyond it was a hedge of white thorn and elderbushes, with convolvulus creeping and hanging about it. What vivid colors there were to see here! And here flew a butterfly, too. The Toad thought it was a flower that had torn itself loose in order to get a better look at the world; that, of course, was very reasonable.

"If I could only move about like that!" said the Toad. "Croak! Oh! How glorious!"

For eight days and nights its remained by the ditch and felt no want of food. Then on the ninth day it thought, "Oh, forward." But was there anything more beautiful to be found anywhere? Perhaps a little toad or some green frogs; there had been a sound in the wind the night before which had seemed to indicate there were cousins in the neighborhood.

"It's wonderful to be alive! To come up out of that well and lie in the bed of nettles, to creep along and hop across the dusty road and rest in the wet ditch! But on, further forward! I must find frogs or a little toad; one can't do without companions, after all. Nature alone isn't enough for one!" And so it started its wanderings again.

In a field, it came to a large pond with rushes around it, and it went exploring in there.

"It's too wet for you in here, isn't it?" said the frog inside. "But you're quite welcome. Are you a he or a she? Not that it matters; you're equally welcome in either case."

INVITED TO A FAMILY CONCERT

And so it was invited to a concert that evening, a family concert, with a lot of gaiety and feeble voices; we all know that sort of affair. There were no refreshments, except free drinks - the whole pond, if they could drink it.

"Now I'll be traveling on," said the little Toad, which was always craving for something better.

It saw the stars twinkling, so large and so clear; it saw the new moon shine, and it saw the sun rise higher and higher.

"I think I'm still in a well, but a bigger well. I must get higher up! I feel a restlessness, a longing!" And when the moon was full and round, the poor creature thought, "I wonder if *that* is the bucket that's let down, and which I must hop into if I want to get higher? Or is the sun the big bucket? How large that is, and how bright! Why, it could hold all of us at once! I must watch for my chance! What a brightness there is in my head! I don't believe the jewel could shine more brightly. But I don't have the jewel, and I shall not cry for it. No; still higher in brightness and happiness! I feel confidence and yet fear. It's a hard step to take, but I must take it. On, further forward! Right on down the road!"

Then it moved along in leaps, as indeed such a creature can, until it reached the highway where humans lived. Here were both flower gardens and vegetable gardens. It stopped to rest by a cabbage garden.

"How many different beings there are that I've never known of! And how great and blessed the world is! But you must keep looking about you, instead of always sitting in the same place." And so it hopped into the cabbage garden. "How green it is here! How pretty it is here!"

"That I well know," said the Caterpillar on a cabbage leaf. "My leaf is the largest one here; it covers half the world, and the rest of the world I can do without!"

"Cluck! Cluck!" said somebody, and hens came hopping into the garden.

The first Hen was farsighted; she spied the worm on the curly leaf and pecked at it so that it fell to the ground, where it lay twisting and turning. The Hen looked at it first with one eye and then with the other, for she couldn't figure out what would become of that wriggling.

"It isn't doing that of its own accord," thought the Hen, and she raised her head to strike again. Whereupon the Toad became so frightened that it bumped right into the Hen.

"So that thing has auxiliary troops to fight for it!" she said. "Just look at that vermin!" Then the Hen turned away. "I don't care about that little green mouthful; it would only tickle my throat!" The other hens agreed with her, and so away they went.

"I got away from her with my wriggling," said the Caterpillar. "It's good to keep your presence of mind, but the hardest job is ahead - to get back up onto my cabbage leaf. Where is it?"

Then the little Toad came forward to sympathize. It was happy that its own ugliness had frightened away the Hen.

"What makes you think that?" asked the Caterpillar. "I wriggled away from her myself. You're indeed very unpleasant to look at! Let me get back to my own place. Now I can smell cabbage; I'm near my own leaf! There's nothing so beautiful as one's own. But I must get up higher."

"Yes, higher!" said the little Toad. "Higher up! It feels just as I do, but it isn't in a good humor today, because of its fright. We all want to get up higher!" And it looked up as high as it could.

A stork sat in his nest on the roof of the farmhouse; he clattered and the stork mother clattered.

"How high up they live!" thought the Toad. "If only I could get up there!"

In the farmhouse lived two young students; one was a poet, the other a naturalist. The one sang and wrote with gladness of all that God had created, as it was mirrored in his heart; he sang of it in short, clear, and rich, imposing verses. The other took hold of the creation itself, yes, and took it apart when it needed analyzing. He treated our Lord's work like a great piece of arithmetic; subtracted, multiplied, wanted to know it outside and inside, and to talk of it with intelligence, with complete understanding; and yet he talked of it with gladness and with wisdom. They were good, happy people, both of them.

"Why, there is a good specimen of a toad," said the Naturalist. "I must have it to preserve in alcohol!"

"You have two already," said the Poet. "Let it stay there in peace and enjoy itself."

"But it's so beautifully ugly!" said the other.

"If we could find the jewel in its head," said the Poet, "then I myself would give you a hand at splitting it open."

"The jewel!" said the other. "How well you know your natural history!"

"But isn't there something very splendid about the old folk legend that the toad, the ugliest of creatures, often has hidden in its head the most precious of jewels? Isn't it much the same with people? Wasn't there a jewel like that hidden in Aesop, and Socrates, too?"

The Toad didn't hear any more, and hadn't understood half of what it had heard. The two friends went on, and it escaped being preserved in alcohol.

"They were talking about that jewel, too," said the Toad. "It's good that I don't have it; otherwise I would have got into trouble."

Then there was a clattering on the farmer's roof. Father Stork was giving a lecture to his family, and they were all looking down askance at the two young men in the cabbage garden.

"A human being is the most conceited of creatures," said the Stork.

"Hear how they go on jabbering, and yet they can't even make as much noise as a rattle! They crow over their eloquence, their language! A fine language that is! It becomes more unintelligible even to them with each day's journey. We can speak our language the whole world over, in Denmark or in Egypt. As for flying, they can't do that at all. They crawl along by means of an invention they call a railway, but there they often get their necks broken. I get the shivers in my bill when I think of it! The world can exist without people. We could well do without them. May we only have frogs and earthworms!"

"My, that was a powerful speech!" thought the little Toad. "What a great man he is, and how high he sits up there! I never saw anyone that high before. And how well he can swim!" it exclaimed, for just then the Stork soared off into the air on outstretched wings.

And then Mother Stork talked in the nest. She told about the land of Egypt and the water of the Nile, and of all the wonderful mud there was to be found in foreign countries; it sounded entirely new and charming to the little Toad.

"I must get to Egypt!" it said. "If only the Stork would take me along, or if one of its youngsters would. I would do the little one some favor in turn, on his wedding day. Yes, I'll get to Egypt, because I'm lucky! All the longing and yearning I feel is surely better than having a jewel in one's head."

And still it had the true jewel! That eternal longing and desire to go upward, ever upward, was the jewel, and it shone within the little Toad, shone with gladness, shone brightly.

At that very moment the Stork came. He had seen the Toad in the grass, and now he swooped down and, not very gently, siezed the little creature. His bill pinched, and the wind whistled; this was anything but comfortable. But still the Toad was going upward, and off to Egypt, it knew; therefore its eyes brightened until it seemed as if a spark shot out from them.

"Croak! Oh!"

The body was dead; the little Toad had been killed. But the spark from its eyes - what became of *that*?

The sunbeam caught it up and bore away the jewel from the head of the Toad. Where?

You should not ask the Naturalist; rather ask the Poet. He'll tell it to you as a fairy tale; and the Caterpillar will be in it, and the Stork family will have a part in it. Just think - the Caterpillar will be changed into a beautiful butterfly. The Stork family will fly over mountains and seas to faraway Africa and yet find the shortest way home again to the land of Denmark, to the same village, to the same roof! Yes, it's all almost too much like a fairy tale, and still it is true! You may well ask the Naturalist about that; he'll have to admit *it*; and yet you know it yourself, for you've witnessed it.

But the jewel in the head of the Toad? Look for it in the sun; look at it if you can.

The brightness is too great. We have not yet eyes that can look directly at all the glories God has created, but someday we shall have them, and that will be the most beautiful fairy tale of all, for we ourselves shall have a part in it.

XL

THE HAPPY FAMILY

The largest green leaf in this country is certainly the burdock-leaf. If you hold it in front of you, it is large enough for an apron; and if you hold it over your head, it is almost as good as an umbrella, it is so wonderfully large. A burdock never grows alone; where it grows, there are many more, and it is a splendid sight; and all this splendor is good for snails. The great white snails, which grand people in olden times used to have made into fricassees; and when they had eaten them, they would say, "O, what a delicious dish!" for these people really thought them good; and these snails lived on burdock-leaves, and for them the burdock was planted.

There was once an old estate where no one now lived to require snails; indeed, the owners had all died out, but the burdock still flourished; it grew over all the beds and walks of the garden—its growth had no check—till it became at last quite a forest of burdocks. Here and there stood an apple or a plum-tree; but for this, nobody would have thought the place had ever been a garden. It was burdock from one end to the other; and here lived the last two surviving snails.

They knew not themselves how old they were; but they could remember the time when there were a great many more of them, and that they were descended from a family which came from foreign lands, and that the whole forest had been planted for them and theirs. They had never been away from the garden; but they knew that another place once existed in the world, called the Duke's

Palace Castle, in which some of their relations had been boiled till they became black, and were then laid on a silver dish; but what was done afterwards they did not know. Besides, they could not imagine exactly how it felt to be boiled and placed on a silver dish; but no doubt it was something very fine and highly genteel. Neither the cockchafer, nor the toad, nor the earth-worm, whom they questioned about it, would give them the least information; for none of their relations had ever been cooked or served on a silver dish. The old white snails were the most aristocratic race in the world,—they knew that. The forest had been planted for them, and the nobleman's castle had been built entirely that they might be cooked and laid on silver dishes.

They lived quite retired and very happily; and as they had no children of their own, they had adopted a little common snail, which they brought up as their own child. The little one would not grow, for he was only a common snail; but the old people, particularly the mother-snail, declared that she could easily see how he grew; and when the father said he could not perceive it, she begged him to feel the little snail's shell, and he did so, and found that the mother was right.

One day it rained very fast. "Listen, what a drumming there is on the burdock-leaves; turn, turn, turn; turn, turn, turn," said the father-snail.

"There come the drops," said the mother; "they are trickling down the stalks. We shall have it very wet here presently. I am very glad we have such good houses, and that the little one has one of his own. There has been really more done for us than for any other creature; it is quite plain that we are the most noble people in the world. We have houses from our birth, and the burdock forest has been planted for us. I should very much like to know how far it extends, and what lies beyond it."

"There can be nothing better than we have here," said the father-snail; "I wish for nothing more."

"Yes, but I do," said the mother; "I should like to be taken to the palace, and boiled, and laid upon a silver dish, as was done to all our ancestors; and you may be sure it must be something very uncommon."

"The nobleman's castle, perhaps, has fallen to decay," said the snail-father, "or the burdock wood may have grown out. You need not be in a hurry; you are always so impatient, and the youngster is getting just the same. He has been three days creeping to the top of that stalk. I feel quite giddy when I look at him."

"You must not scold him," said the mother-snail; "he creeps so very carefully. He will be the joy of our home; and we old folks have nothing else to live for. But have you ever thought where we are to get a wife for him? Do you think that farther out in the wood there may be others of our race?"

"There may be black snails, no doubt," said the old snail; "black snails without houses; but they are so vulgar and conceited too. But we can give the ants a commission; they run here and there, as if they all had so much business to get through. They, most likely, will know of a wife for our youngster."

"I certainly know a most beautiful bride," said one of the ants; "but I fear it would not do, for she is a queen."

"That does not matter," said the old snail; "has she a house?"

"She has a palace," replied the ant,—"a most beautiful ant-palace with seven hundred passages."

"Thank-you," said the mother-snail; "but our boy shall not go to live in an ant-hill. If you know of nothing better, we will give the commission to the white gnats; they fly about in rain and sunshine; they know the burdock wood from one end to the other."

"We have a wife for him," said the gnats; "a hundred man-steps from here there is a little snail with a house, sitting on a gooseberry-bush; she is quite alone, and old enough to be married. It is only a hundred man-steps from here."

"Then let her come to him," said the old people. "He has the whole burdock forest; she has only a bush."

So they brought the little lady-snail. She took eight days to perform the journey; but that was just as it ought to be; for it showed her to be one of the right breeding. And then they had a wedding. Six glow-worms gave as much light as they could; but in other respects it was all very quiet; for the old snails could not bear festivities or a crowd. But a beautiful speech was made by the mother-snail. The father could not speak; he was too much overcome. Then they gave the whole burdock forest to the young snails as an inheritance, and repeated what they had so often said, that it was the finest place in the world, and that if they led upright and honorable lives, and their family increased, they and their children might some day be taken to the nobleman's palace, to be boiled black, and laid on a silver dish. And when they had finished speaking, the old couple crept into their houses, and came out no more; for they slept.

The young snail pair now ruled in the forest, and had a numerous progeny. But as the young ones were never boiled or laid in silver dishes, they concluded that the castle had fallen into decay, and that all the people in the world were dead; and as nobody contradicted them, they thought they must be right. And the rain fell upon the burdock-leaves, to play the drum for them, and the sun shone to paint colors on the burdock forest for them, and they were very happy; the whole family were entirely and perfectly happy.

LXI

THE COURT CARDS

HOW many beautiful things may be cut out of and pasted on paper! Thus a castle was cut out and pasted, so large that it filled a whole table, and it was painted as if it were built of red stones. It had a shining copper roof, it had towers and a draw-bridge, water in the canals just like plate glass, for it was plate-glass, and in the highest tower stood a wooden watchman. He had a trumpet, but he did not blow it.

The whole belonged to a little boy, whose name was William. He raised the draw-bridge himself and let it down again, made his tin soldiers march over it, opened the castle gate and looked into the large and elegant drawing-room, where all the court cards of a pack—Hearts, Diamonds, Clubs, and Spades—hung in frames on the walls, like pictures in real drawing rooms. The kings held each a scepter, and wore crowns; the queens wore veils flowing down over their shoulders, and in their hands they held a flower or a fan; the knaves had halberds and nodding plumes.

One evening the little boy peeped through the open castle gate, to catch a glimpse of the court cards in the drawing room, and it seemed to him that the kings saluted him with their scepters, that the Queen of Spades swung the golden tulip which she held in her hand, that the Queen of Hearts lifted her fan, and that all four queens graciously recognized him. He drew a little nearer, in order to see better, and that made him hit his head against the castle so that it shook. Then all the four knaves of Hearts, Diamonds, Clubs, and Spades, raised their halberds, to warn him that he must not try to get in that way.

The little boy understood the hint, and gave a friendly nod; he nodded again, and then said: "Say something!" but the knaves did not say a word. However, the third time be nodded, the Knave of Hearts sprang out of the card, and placed himself in the middle of the floor.

"What is your name?" the knave asked the little boy. "You have clear eyes and good teeth, but your hands are dirty: you do not wash them often enough!"

Now this was rather coarse language, but, of course, not much politeness can be expected from a knave. He is only a common fellow.

"My name is William," said the little boy, "and the castle is mine, and you are my Knave of Hearts!"

"No, I am not. I am my king's and my queen's knave, not yours!" said the Knave of Hearts. "I am not obliged to stay here. I can get down off the card, and out of the frame too, and so can my gracious king and queen, even more easily than I. We can go out into the wide world, but that is such a wearisome march; we have grown tired of it; it is more convenient, more easy, more agreeable, to be sitting in the cards, and just to be ourselves!"

"Have all of you really been human beings once?" asked little William.

"Human beings!" repeated the Knave of Hearts. "Yes, we have; but not so good as we ought to have been! Please now light a little wax candle (I like a red one best, for that is the color of my king and queen); then I will tell the lord of the castle—I think you said you were the lord of the castle, did you not?—our whole history; but for goodness' sake, don't interrupt me, for if I speak, it must be done without any interruption whatever. I am in a great hurry! Do you see my king, I mean the King of Hearts ? He is the oldest of the four kings there, for he was born first,—born with a golden crown and a golden apple. He began to rule at once. His queen was born with a golden fan; that she still has. They both were very agreeably situated, even from infancy. They did not have to go to school, they could play the whole day, build castles, and knock them down, marshal tin soldiers for battle, and play with dolls. When they asked for buttered bread, then there was butter on both sides of the bread, and powdered brown sugar, too, nicely spread over it. It was the good old time, and was called the Golden Age; but they grew tired of it, and so did I. Then the King of Diamonds took the reins of government!"

The knave said nothing more. Little William waited to hear something further, but not a syllable was uttered; so presently he asked,—"Well, and then ?"

The Knave of Hearts did not answer; he stood up straight, silent, bold, and stiff, his eyes fixed upon the burning wax candle. Little William nodded; he nodded again, but no reply. Then he turned to the Knave of Diamonds; and when he had nodded to him three times, up he sprang out of the card, in the middle of the floor, and uttered only one single word,—

"Wax candle!"

Little William understood what he meant, and immediately lighted a red candle, and placed it before him. Then the Knave of Diamonds presented arms, for that is a token of respect, and said:— "Then the King of Diamonds succeeded to the throne! He was a king with a pane of glass on his breast; also the queen had a pane of glass on her breast, so that people could look right into her. For the rest, they were formed like other human beings, and were so agreeable and so handsome, that a monument was erected in honor of them, which stood for seven years without falling. Properly speaking, it should have stood forever, for so it was intended; but from some unknown reasons, it fell." Then the Knave of Diamonds presented arms, Out of respect for his king, and he looked fixedly on his red wax candle.

But now at once, without any nod or invitation from little William, the Knave of Clubs stepped out, grave and proud, like the stork that struts with such a dignified air over the green meadow. The black clover-leaf in the corner of the card flew like a bird beyond the knave, and then flew back again, and stuck itself where it had been sticking before.

And without waiting for his wax candle, the Knave of Clubs spoke:—

"Not all get butter on both sides of the bread, and brown powdered sugar on that. My king and queen did not get it. They had to go to school, and learn what they had not learnt before. They also had a pane of glass on their breasts, but nobody looked through it, except to see if there was not some. thing wrong with their works inside, in order to find, if possible, some reason for giving them a scolding! I know it; I have served my king and queen all my life-time; I know everything about them, and obey their commands. They bid me say nothing more to-night. 1 keep silent, therefore, and present arms!"

But little William was a kind-hearted boy, so he lighted a candle for this knave also, a shining white one, white like snow. No sooner was the candle lighted, than the Knave of Spades appeared in the middle of the drawing-room. He came hurriedly; yet he limped, as if he had a sore leg. Indeed, it had once been broken, and he had had, moreover, many ups and down in his life. He spoke as follows:—

"My brother knaves have each got a candle, and I shall also get one; I know that. But if we poor knaves have so much honor, our kings and queens must have thrice as much. Now, it is proper that my King of Spades and my Queen of Spades should have four candles to gladden them. An additional honor ought to be conferred upon them. Their history and trials are so doleful, that they have very good reason to wear mourning, and to have a grave-digger's spade on their coat of arms. My own fate, poor knave that I am, is deplorable enough. In one game at cards, I have got the nickname of 'Black Peter!'[1] But alas! I have got a still uglier name, which, indeed, it is hardly the thing to mention aloud," and then he whispered,—"In another game, I have been nicknamed 'Dirty Mads!'[2] I, who was once the King of Spades' Lord Chamberlain! Is not this a bitter fate? The history of my royal master and queen I will not relate; they don't wish me to do so! Little lord of the castle, as he calls himself, may guess it himself if he chooses, but it is very lamentable,—O, no doubt about that! Their circumstances have be-

[1] *Black Peter* is the name of a game in Denmark where it is called *Sorte Peer*, the word *sorte* denoting black. When the cards are dealt, he who happens to get the knave os spades is all the evening named Black Peter by his fellow-players, who paint his face black.

[2] *Dirty Mads* is another Danish game.

come very much reduced, and are not likely to change for the better, until we are all riding on the red horse higher than the skies, where there are no haps and mishaps!"

Little William now lighted, as the Knave of Spades had said was proper, three candles for each of the kings, and three for each of the queens; but for the King and Queen of Spades he lighted four candles apiece, and the whole drawing-room became as light and transparent as the palace of the richest emperor, and the illustrious kings and queens bowed to each other serenely and graciously. The Queen of Hearts made her golden fan bow; and the Queen of Spades swung her golden tulip in such a way, that a stream of fire issued from it. The royal couples alighted from the cards and frames, and moved in a slow and graceful minuet up and down the floor. They were dancing in the very midst of flames, and the knaves were dancing too.

But alas! the whole drawing-room was soon in a blaze; the devouring element roared up through the roof, and all was one crackling and hissing sheet of fire; and in a moment little William's castle itself was enveloped in flames and smoke. The boy became frightened, and ran off, crying to his father and mother,—"Fire, fire, fire! my castle is on fire!" He grew pale as ashes, and his little hands trembled like the aspen-leaf The fire continued sparkling and blazing, but in the midst of this destructive scene, the following words were uttered in a singing tone:—

"Now we are riding on the red horse, higher than the skies! This is the way for kings and queens to go, and this is the way for their knaves to go after them!"

Yes I that was the end of William's castle, and of the court cards. William did not perish in the flames; he is still alive, and he washed his small bands, and said: "I am innocent of the destruction of the castle." And, indeed, it was not his fault that the castle was burnt down.

XLII

THE BEETLE

There was once an Emperor who had a horse shod with gold. He had a golden shoe on each foot, and why was this? He was a beautiful creature, with slender legs, bright, intelligent eyes, and a mane that hung down over his neck like a veil. He had carried his master through fire and smoke in the battle-field, with the bullets whistling round him; he had kicked and bitten, and taken part in the fight, when the enemy advanced; and, with his master on his back, he had dashed over the fallen foe, and saved the golden crown and the Emperor's life, which was of more value than the brightest gold. This is the reason of the Emperor's horse wearing golden shoes.

A beetle came creeping forth from the stable, where the farrier had been shoeing the horse. "Great ones, first, of course," said he, "and then the little ones; but size is not always a proof of greatness." He stretched out his thin leg as he spoke.

"And pray what do you want?" asked the farrier.

"Golden shoes," replied the beetle.

"Why, you must be out of your senses," cried the farrier. "Golden shoes for you, indeed!"

"Yes, certainly; golden shoes," replied the beetle. "Am I not just as good as that great creature yonder, who is waited upon and brushed, and has food and drink placed before him? And don't I belong to the royal stables?"

"But why does the horse have golden shoes?" asked the farrier; "of course you understand the reason?"

"Understand! Well, I understand that it is a personal slight to me," cried the beetle. "It is done to annoy me, so I intend to go out into the world and seek my fortune."

"Go along with you," said the farrier.

"You're a rude fellow," cried the beetle, as he walked out of the stable; and then he flew for a short distance, till he found himself in a beautiful flower-garden, all fragrant with roses and lavender. The lady-birds, with red and black shells on their backs, and delicate wings, were flying about, and one of them said, "Is it not sweet and lovely here? Oh, how beautiful everything is."

"I am accustomed to better things," said the beetle. "Do you call this beautiful? Why, there is not even a dung-heap." Then he went on, and under the shadow of a large haystack he found a caterpillar crawling along. "How beautiful this world is!" said the caterpillar. "The sun is so warm, I quite enjoy it. And soon I shall go to sleep, and die as they call it, but I shall wake up with beautiful wings to fly with, like a butterfly."

"How conceited you are!" exclaimed the beetle. "Fly about as a butterfly, indeed! what of that. I have come out of the Emperor's stable, and no one there, not even the Emperor's horse, who, in fact, wears my cast-off golden shoes, has any idea of flying, excepting myself. To have wings and fly! why, I can do that already;" and so saying, he spread his wings and flew away. "I don't want to be disgusted," he said to himself, "and yet I can't help it." Soon after, he fell down upon an extensive lawn, and for a time pretended to sleep, but at last fell asleep in earnest. Suddenly a heavy shower of rain came falling from the clouds. The beetle woke up with the noise and would have been glad to creep into the earth for shelter, but he could not. He was tumbled over and over with the rain, sometimes swimming on his stomach and sometimes on his back; and as for flying, that was out of the question. He began to doubt whether he should escape with his life, so he remained, quietly lying where he was. After a while the weather cleared up a little, and the beetle was able to rub the water from his eyes, and look about him. He saw something gleaming, and he managed to make his way up to it. It was linen which had been laid to bleach on the grass. He crept into a fold of the damp linen, which certainly was not so comfortable a place to lie in as the warm stable, but there was nothing better, so he remained lying there for a whole day and night, and the rain kept on all the time. Towards morning he crept out of his hiding-place, feeling in a very bad temper with the climate. Two frogs were sitting on the linen, and their bright eyes actually glistened with pleasure.

"Wonderful weather this," cried one of them, "and so refreshing. This linen holds the water together so beautifully, that my hind legs quiver as if I were going to swim."

"I should like to know," said another, "If the swallow who flies so far in her many journeys to foreign lands, ever met with a better climate than this. What delicious moisture! It is as pleasant as lying in a wet ditch. I am sure any one who does not enjoy this has no love for his fatherland."

"Have you ever been in the Emperor's stable?" asked the beetle. "There the moisture is warm and refreshing; that's the climate for me, but I could not take it with me on my travels. Is there not even a dunghill here in this garden, where a person of rank, like myself, could take up his abode and feel at home?" But the frogs either did not or would not understand him.

"I never ask a question twice," said the beetle, after he had asked this one three times, and received no answer. Then he went on a little farther and stumbled against a piece of broken crockery-ware, which certainly ought not to have been lying there. But as it was there, it formed a good shelter against wind and weather to several families of earwigs who dwelt in it. Their requirements were not many, they were very sociable, and full of affection for their children, so much so that each mother considered her own child the most beautiful and clever of them all.

"Our dear son has engaged himself," said one mother, "dear innocent boy; his greatest ambition is that he may one day creep into a clergyman's ear. That is a very artless and loveable wish; and being engaged will keep him steady. What happiness for a mother!"

"Our son," said another, "had scarcely crept out of the egg, when he was off on his travels. He is all life and spirits, I expect he will wear out his horns with running. How charming this is for a mother, is it not Mr. Beetle?" for she knew the stranger by his horny coat.

"You are both quite right," said he; so they begged him to walk in, that is to come as far as he could under the broken piece of earthenware.

"Now you shall also see my little earwigs," said a third and a fourth mother, "they are lovely little things, and highly amusing. They are never ill-behaved, except when they are uncomfortable in their inside, which unfortunately often happens at their age."

Thus each mother spoke of her baby, and their babies talked after their own fashion, and made use of the little nippers they have in their tails to nip the beard of the beetle.

"They are always busy about something, the little rogues," said the mother, beaming with maternal pride; but the beetle felt it a bore, and he therefore inquired the way to the nearest dung-heap.

"That is quite out in the great world, on the other side of the ditch," answered an earwig, "I hope none of my children will ever go so far, it would be the death of me."

"But I shall try to get so far," said the beetle, and he walked off without taking any formal leave, which is considered a polite thing to do.

When he arrived at the ditch, he met several friends, all them beetles; "We live here," they said, "and we are very comfortable. May we ask you to step down into this rich mud, you must be fatigued after your journey."

"Certainly," said the beetle, "I shall be most happy; I have been exposed to the rain, and have had to lie upon linen, and cleanliness is a thing that greatly exhausts me; I have also pains in one of my wings from standing in the draught under a piece of broken crockery. It is really quite refreshing to be with one's own kindred again."

"Perhaps you came from a dung-heap," observed the oldest of them.

"No, indeed, I came from a much grander place," replied the beetle; "I came from the emperor's stable, where I was born, with golden shoes on my feet. I am travelling on a secret embassy, but you must not ask me any questions, for I cannot betray my secret."

Then the beetle stepped down into the rich mud, where sat three young-lady beetles, who tittered, because they did not know what to say.

BROUGHT THE BEETLE BACK

"None of them are engaged yet," said their mother, and the beetle maidens tittered again, this time quite in confusion.

"I have never seen greater beauties, even in the royal stables," exclaimed the beetle, who was now resting himself.

"Don't spoil my girls," said the mother; "and don't talk to them, pray, unless you have serious intentions."

But of course the beetle's intentions were serious, and after a while our friend was engaged. The mother gave them her blessing, and all the other beetles cried "hurrah."

Immediately after the betrothal came the marriage, for there was no reason to delay. The following day passed very pleasantly, and the next was tolerably comfortable; but on the third it became necessary for him to think of getting food for his wife, and, perhaps, for children.

"I have allowed myself to be taken in," said our beetle to himself, "and now there's nothing to be done but to take them in, in return."

No sooner said than done. Away he went, and stayed away all day and all night, and his wife remained behind a forsaken widow.

"Oh," said the other beetles, "this fellow that we have received into our family is nothing but a complete vagabond. He has gone away and left his wife a burden upon our hands."

"Well, she can be unmarried again, and remain here with my other daughters," said the mother. "Fie on the villain that forsook her!"

In the mean time the beetle, who had sailed across the ditch on a cabbage leaf, had been journeying on the other side. In the morning two persons came up to the ditch. When they saw him they took him up and turned him over and over, looking very learned all the time, especially one, who was a boy. "Allah sees the black beetle in the black stone, and the black rock. Is not that written in the Koran?" he asked.

Then he translated the beetle's name into Latin, and said a great deal upon the creature's nature and history. The second person, who was older and a scholar, proposed to carry the beetle home, as they wanted just such good specimens as this. Our beetle considered this speech a great insult, so he flew suddenly out of the speaker's hand. His wings were dry now, so they carried him to a great distance, till at last he reached a hothouse, where a sash of the glass roof was partly open, so he quietly slipped in and buried himself in the warm earth.

"It is very comfortable here," he said to himself, and soon after fell asleep. Then he dreamed that the emperor's horse was dying, and had left him his golden shoes, and also promised that he should have two more. All this was very delightful, and when the beetle woke up he crept forth and looked around him. What a splendid place the hothouse was! At the back, large palm-trees were growing; and the sunlight made the leaves—look quite glossy; and beneath them what a profusion of luxuriant green, and of flowers red like flame, yellow as amber, or white as new-fallen snow!

"What a wonderful quantity of plants," cried the beetle; "how good they will taste when they are decayed! This is a capital storeroom. There must certainly be some relations of mine living here; I will just see if I can find any one with whom I can associate. I'm proud, certainly; but I'm also proud of being so."

Then he prowled about in the earth, and thought what a pleasant dream that was about the dying horse, and the golden shoes he had inherited. Suddenly a hand seized the beetle, and squeezed him, and turned him round and round. The gardener's little son and his playfellow had come into the hothouse, and, seeing the beetle, wanted to have some fun with him. First, he was wrapped, in a vine-leaf, and put into a warm trousers' pocket. He twisted and turned about with all his might, but he got a good squeeze from the boy's hand, as a hint for him to keep quiet. Then the boy went quickly towards a lake that lay at the end of the garden. Here the beetle was put into an old broken wooden shoe, in which a little stick had been fastened upright for a mast, and to this mast the beetle was bound with a piece of worsted. Now he was a sailor, and had to sail away.

The lake was not very large, but to the beetle it seemed an ocean, and he was so astonished at its size that he fell over on his back, and kicked out his legs. Then the little ship sailed away; sometimes the current of the water seized it, but whenever it went too far from the shore one of the boys turned up his trousers, and went in after it, and brought it back to land. But at last, just as it went merrily out again, the two boys were called, and so angrily, that they hastened to obey, and ran away as fast as they could from the pond, so that the little ship was left to its fate. It was carried away farther and farther from the shore, till it reached the open sea. This was a terrible prospect for the beetle, for he could not escape in consequence of being bound to the mast. Then a fly came and paid him a visit. "What beautiful weather," said the fly; "I shall rest here and sun myself. You must have a pleasant time of it."

"You speak without knowing the facts," replied the beetle; "don't you see that I am a prisoner?"

"Ah, but I'm not a prisoner," remarked the fly, and away he flew.

"Well, now I know the world," said the beetle to himself; "it's an abominable world; I'm the only respectable person in it. First, they refuse me my golden shoes; then I have to lie on damp linen, and to stand in a draught; and to crown all, they fasten a wife upon me. Then, when I have made a step forward in the world, and found out a comfortable position, just as I could wish it to be, one of these human boys comes and ties me up, and leaves me to the mercy of the wild waves, while the emperor's favorite horse goes prancing about proudly on his golden shoes. This vexes me more than anything. But it is useless to look for sympathy in this world. My career has been very interesting, but what's the use of that if nobody knows anything about it? The world does not deserve to be made acquainted with my adventures, for it ought to have given me golden shoes when the emperor's horse was shod, and I stretched out my feet to be shod, too. If I had received golden shoes I should have been an ornament to the stable; now I am lost to the stable and to the world. It is all over with me."

But all was not yet over. A boat, in which were a few young girls, came rowing up.

"Look, yonder is an old wooden shoe sailing along," said one of the younger girls.

"And there's a poor little creature bound fast in it," said another.

The boat now came close to our beetle's ship, and the young girls fished it out of the water. One of them drew a small pair of scissors from her pocket, and cut the worsted without hurting the beetle, and when she stepped on shore she placed him on the grass. "There," she said, "creep away, or fly, if thou canst. It is a splendid thing to have thy liberty." Away flew the beetle, straight through the open window of a large building; there he sank down, tired and exhausted, exactly on the mane of the emperor's favorite horse, who was standing in his stable; and the beetle found himself at home again. For some time he clung to the mane, that he might recover himself.

"Well," he said, "here I am, seated on the emperor's favorite horse,—sitting upon him as if I were the emperor himself. But what was it the farrier asked me? Ah, I remember now,—that's a good thought,—he asked me why the golden shoes were given to the horse. The answer is quite clear to me, now. They were given to the horse on my account."

And this reflection put the beetle into a good temper. The sun's rays also came streaming into the stable, and shone upon him, and made the place lively and bright.

"Travelling expands the mind very much," said the beetle. "The world is not so bad after all, if you know how to take things as they come."

XLIII

WHAT HAPPENED TO THE THISTLE

AROUND a lordly old mansion was a beautiful, well-kept garden, full of all kinds of rare trees and flowers. Guests always expressed their delight and admiration at the sight of its wonders. The people from far and near used to come on Sundays and holidays and ask permission to see it. Even whole schools made excursions for the sole purpose of seeing its beauties.

Near the fence that separated the garden from the meadow stood an immense thistle. It was an uncommonly large and fine thistle, with several branches spreading out just above the root, and altogether was so strong and full as to make it well worthy of the name "thistle bush."

No one ever noticed it, save the old donkey that pulled the milk cart for the dairymaids. He stood grazing in the meadow hard by and stretched his old neck to reach the thistle, saying: "You are beautiful! I should like to eat you!" But the tether was too short to allow him to reach the thistle, so he did not eat it.

There were guests at the Hall, fine, aristocratic relatives from town, and among them a young lady who had come from a long distance—all the way from Scotland. She was of old and noble family and rich in gold and lands—a bride well worth the winning, thought more than one young man to himself; yes, and their mothers thought so, too!

The young people amused themselves on the lawn, playing croquet and flitting about among the flowers, each young girl gathering a flower to put in the buttonhole of some one of the gentlemen.

The young Scotch lady looked about for a flower, but none of them seemed to please her, until, happening to glance over the fence, she espied the fine, large thistle bush, full of bluish-red, sturdy-looking flowers. She smiled as she saw it, and begged the son of the house to get one of them for her.

"That is Scotland's flower," she said; "it grows and blossoms in our coat of arms. Get that one yonder for me, please."

And he gathered the finest of the thistle flowers, though he pricked his fingers as much in doing so as if it had been growing on a wild rosebush.

She took the flower and put it in his buttonhole, which made him feel greatly honored. Each of the other young men would gladly have given up his graceful garden flower if he might have worn the one given by the delicate hands of the Scotch girl. As keenly as the son of the house felt the honor conferred upon him, the thistle felt even more highly honored. It seemed to feel dew and sunshine going through it.

"It seems I am of more consequence than I thought," it said to itself. "I ought by rights to stand inside and not outside the fence. One gets strangely placed in this world, but now I have at least one of my flowers over the fence—and not only there, but in a buttonhole!"

To each one of its buds as it opened, the thistle bush told this great event. And not many days had passed before it heard—not from the people who passed, nor yet from the twittering of little birds, but from the air, which gives out, far and wide, the sounds that it has treasured up from the shadiest walks of the beautiful garden and from the most secluded rooms at the Hall, where doors and windows are left open—that the young man who received the thistle flower from the hands of the Scottish maiden had received her heart and hand as well.

"That is *my* doing!" said the thistle, thinking of the flower she had given to the buttonhole. And every new flower that came was told of this wonderful event.

"Surely I shall now be taken and planted in the garden," thought the thistle. "Perhaps I shall be put into a flowerpot, for that is by far the most honorable position." It thought of this so long that it ended by saying to itself with the firm conviction of truth, "I shall be planted in a flowerpot!"

It promised every little bud that came that it also should be placed in a pot and perhaps have a place in a buttonhole—that being the highest position one could aspire to. But none of them got into a flowerpot, and still less into a gentleman's buttonhole.

They lived on light and air, and drank sunshine in the day and dew at night. They received visits from bee and hornet, who came to look for the honey in the flower, and who took the honey and left the flower.

"The good-for-nothing fellows," said the thistle bush. "I would pierce them if I could!"

The flowers drooped and faded, but new ones always came.

"You come as if you had been sent," said the thistle bush to them. "I am expecting every moment to be taken over the fence."

A couple of harmless daisies and a huge, thin plant of canary grass listened to this with the deepest respect, believing all they heard. The old donkey, that had to pull the milk cart, cast longing looks toward the blooming thistle and tried to reach it, but his tether was too short. And the thistle bush thought and thought, so much and so long, of the Scotch thistle—to whom it believed itself related—that at last it fancied it had come from Scotland and that its parents had grown into the Scottish arms.

It was a great thought, but a great thistle may well have great thoughts.

"Sometimes one is of noble race even if one does not know it," said the nettle growing close by—it had a kind of presentiment that it might be turned into muslin, if properly treated.

The summer passed, and the autumn passed; the leaves fell from the trees; the flowers came with stronger colors and less perfume; the gardener's lad sang on the other side of the fence:

> "Up the hill and down the hill,
> That's the way of the world still."

The young pine trees in the wood began to feel a longing for Christmas, though Christmas was still a long way off.

"Here I am still," said the thistle. "It seems that I am quite forgotten, and yet it was I who made the match. They were engaged, and now they are married—the wedding was a week ago. I do not make a single step forward, for I cannot."

Some weeks passed. The thistle had its last, solitary flower, which was large and full and growing down near the root. The wind blew coldly over it, the color faded, and all its glory disappeared, leaving only the cup of the flower, now grown to be as large as the flower of an artichoke and glistening like a silvered sunflower.

The young couple, who were now man and wife, came along the garden path, and as they passed near the fence, the bride, glancing over it, said, "Why, there stands the large thistle! it has no flowers now."

"Yes, there is still the ghost of the last one," said her husband, pointing to the silvery remains of the last flower—a flower in itself.

"How beautiful it is!" she said. "We must have one carved in the frame of our picture."

And once more the young man had to get over the fence, to break off the silvery cup of the thistle flower. It pricked his fingers for his pains, because he had called it a *ghost*. And then it was brought into the garden, and to the Hall, and into the drawing room. There stood a large picture—the portraits of the two, and in the bridegroom's buttonhole was painted a thistle. They talked of it and of the flower cup they had brought in with them—the last silver-shimmering thistle flower, that was to be reproduced in the carving of the frame.

The air took all their words and scattered them about, far and wide.

"What strange things happen to one!" said the thistle bush. "My first-born went to live in a buttonhole, my last-born in a frame! I wonder what is to become of me."

The old donkey, standing by the roadside, cast loving glances at the thistle and said, "Come to me, my sweetheart, for I cannot go to you; my tether is too short!"

But the thistle bush made no answer. It grew more and more thoughtful, and it thought as far ahead as Christmas, till its budding thoughts opened into flower.

"When one's children are safely housed, a mother is quite content to stay beyond the fence."

"That is true," said the sunshine; "and you will be well placed, never fear."

"In a flowerpot or in a frame?" asked the thistle.

"In a story," answered the sunshine. And here is the story!

THE END

Made in United States
Troutdale, OR
06/19/2024